Lost Souls Café

Susie Newman

12/28/22

To Reno
Turn on your heartlight

Susie Newman

BLACK ROSE writing

ISBN: 978-1-61296-911-4
PUBLISHED BY BLACK ROSE WRITING
www.blackrosewriting.com

Printed in the United States of America
Suggested Retail Price (SRP) $19.95

Lost Souls Café is printed in Cambria

This book is dedicated to my husband John, who had me at first laugh and to my children Shea, Trevor, Nicholas and Ellie –
You are worthy of your dreams.

Acknowledgments

I am deeply thankful for the following; Black Rose Writing, and Reagan Rothe who believed in my story and gave me this wonderful opportunity. My longtime friend and comrade, Michelle Dranichak, who always has my back. My sister, Kristin Clark, for being my best friend and counselor. I am grateful for your never-ending encouragement, undying support and enthusiasm, three gifts that helped me have the confidence to write this book. My mother, Barbara Boley, I feel more love and appreciation than I can express. You have read my writings from the time I began turning words into sentences. It is because of your loving confirmation, brilliant guidance, smart editing and genes that I write. With my deepest love and affection, I thank John, my beloved husband, soul mate and life partner. Your support, encouragement, feedback and editing have made all the difference. Thank you for loving me completely, believing in me whole-heartedly and sharing the journey. Finally, Mozart's Bakery and Piano Café (Columbus, Ohio). It was here where my inspirations brewed, my story developed and I came to experience the splendor of tea leaves and the power of espresso.

Lost Souls Café

From K.O.A. to A- okay

December 1, 1999 – Dear Diary, As I sit staring out this long, wooden windowpane, I watch a bright orange sun emerge from behind snow-capped mountains. It is a show of fire and ice and I feel so damn content. More comfortable than maybe I have ever felt and that's why it seems so foreign. So this is what "at ease" is. Only, how can I be at ease when my life is so unsettled. It must be these mountains that bring me comfort. My home is among the trees and the breeze. Maybe I will name the wind, Gladden. He blows in from the west and across my front door. He lifts my hair when I walk outside and in the evening I can hear him sing. Maybe, Gladden will be my new love. At least I know he will never leave me.

This journal has become my best friend. It is whom I talk to when the rest of my house is quiet, which is only early mornings or late at night. Funny to think that it was Beau who bought me my first journal. It was after Henry was born and Roman was a toddler just learning to string sentences together. I told Beau I needed to write down all the cute things that Roman was saying. So, he bought me a journal. Really it is quite a corny looking thing with kittens in baskets on the front cover, not at all my taste, but still thoughtful. In the six years that followed, I wrote nearly nothing in my kitten journal, although life was full and abundant with so much to say. I think I was too happy to write, or maybe I was just comfortable. Whatever the reason I didn't feel the need to write about life, I just lived it. Then Beau left us and one sad day I picked up the journal, which I had titled, *Cute Things my Kids Say*. In six months time, I had filled its pages with my heartache and survival. In my abandonment, the need to write felt primal. Jotting down my days helped me walk through them. The kitten journal became my therapist and I unleashed and vented all my sadness, anger, fear and hope until every page wept with my heartache and laughed at my jokes.

The beautiful, leather bound journal I write in today was a gift from Mama Jaspers. I have told myself I should fill its pages with poetry and inspirations – light things as not to weigh down the pretty, manila pages with inked tears. I now find journals sacred. I honestly believe my ugly kitten journal saved my life. I have written purposefully since Beau's desertion; putting pen to paper in order to survive my long days and lonely nights and in doing so I have discovered that being left isn't the worst thing that can happen to a person. In fact, with Beau's leaving I have slowly found myself. In recording my days and hours I have logged evidence of change and effect - a sort of evolution. The first paragraphs written in my kitten journal were words soaked in sadness and sentences drenched in sorrow. But as the days moved forward and I continued to write I noticed a natural drying out, like clothes on the line. By the time six months had passed the pages had become white sheets flapping in the wind.

What I have learned through this self-discovery is that there is a colossal change that happens to a woman that has been cheated on and then left. Although the change is massive it is a slow gradual process that happens as the days move on. Like a metamorphosis, you begin to develop into something new. At first the days are filled with sadness so thick it is hard to rise from your bed and carry yourself through. I had no idea it was nearly impossible to carry a heavy heart, until one filled my chest. Eventually, the heaviness subsides and you are able to come out of your shell of sadness and get back to living. The point is, you have come out an entirely different thing from when you went in and the changes continue to progress. I am not the same person I was six months ago or three weeks ago or even yesterday, because every day I grow a little happier. One day I hope to find myself as this ecstatic old woman who claims to have lived a life of bliss. As for now, watching a December morning rise out of the mountains is my bliss. Soon this orange glow on sparkling white will be daylight and my house will wake with a baby's cry, a shout from young boys, running feet on wooden floorboards and another day begins.

Looking back, I can see how these ordinary days string together to create an extraordinary year. It's hard to believe that it's December already and that this crazy year of 1999, is coming to an end. This year seems to have moved so fast and yet so slow. In fact, I feel as if I have lost minutes or rather misplaced them. Maybe, I crammed them so full of heartache, happiness, work, errands and frustration that they burst apart and created change. Time is a peculiar thing and knowing that it is the simple, hectic, sad, happy, busy, boring days after days that have brought about my new existence stuns me.

A year ago I was a married woman living in Florida. We were a lucky little family that had just welcomed a newborn. Six months ago I was a hard working abandoned woman living in a trailer with two young boys and a baby. I am now a single mom, starting a new business, living in West Virginia and my youngest is a toddler. I have traded in a young, handsome husband for a stout elderly woman who is my best friend, roommate, and business partner and soon our new life will begin just in time for a new millennium.

In my previous life or rather the chapter right before this one, I was happily married to Beau Jaspers. At least one of us was happy, more than one; because I believe our three children were happy too. We lived an unusual yet carefree way of life, running and managing a KOA campground in Florida. Our job and life was an uncommon experience and I feel a little special to have lived it. Not everyone can say that they excel at living an unconventional lifestyle, but Beau and I did.

When you manage a campground there is always something to do. During the busy season, you are overwhelmed with vacationers and the turning of sights. Booking spots, maintaining the grounds, store orders, supply orders, family activities and itineraries make the days go on forever, and you walk briskly through them. During the slow season, you are just as busy with repairs and maintenance, trying to get everything ready for another busy season. Beau and I lived in a trailer on the campgrounds and not a double wide, but a rather small mobile home with our three kids, Roman, Henry and Sabrina. We sat on each other's laps, ate off each other's plates and often found ourselves in the same bed, a sweaty lump of bodies pressed together. We were crowded, but we were happy and although our living quarters were tight our space was gracious. We drank our coffee and ate our meals outside; we fished in our pond, went on long walks and bike rides and had nightly bonfires. It was within those 80 acres of KOA that we lived, worked, played, fought and loved. That was until the day Judy Mathers pulled in with her Deluxe Winnebago and big fake tits and began having an affair with my husband. Judy showed up just in time for Sabrina's birth and my postpartum depression, perfect timing on her part. Before Sabrina could even walk, Beau had climbed into Judy's Winnebago and off they went, leaving the kids and me to live and fight alone.

We did ok. The kids and I managed daily life by simply trudging through it. However, I went nearly crazy trying to run 80 acres of campground and mothering three young children. Roman is eight years old and has been very angry since his father left. Henry is six and he is much sadder than mad, but that's just because he has a different temperament and personality than his older brother. Sabrina now fifteen months old, was nine months when Beau walked away. Abandoned in a campground, I suppose it makes for good fiction, but it was our life story and it was scary. However, along with the abandonment I learned that most people are good and the friendships I built saved us. In the campground a community that loved us, surrounded us. Without these friends, I surely would have crumbled or at the least been turned in to children services for neglect. I call these people my earth angels. When I left Florida and the campground to move back home into a house that my dad had bought for me, one of my saviors came with me.

Hazel is my best friend, my earthly mother, and my inspiration. A widow with a heart of gold who began to nanny my children at the campground after Beau left. Without Hazel, I could not have done my job. I was truly on the verge of a nervous breakdown and she saved my life. I don't know if Hazel knows this. In fact, if you ask her, she will say that I was the one that saved her life and that the reason she rises everyday is because of the kids and me.

After Beau left, bits and pieces of my life began to fall apart. It's funny how one ordeal will spiral into another, and another, and another. Your husband leaves, so your car breaks down, your car breaks down so your kids get sick, your kids get sick so you bounce some checks, you bounce some checks and you can't fix your car. It's as if your life journey has become a path of torment and the best advise others have to offer is that, *"when it rains it pours."*

It was Hazel who showed up at my door one morning, umbrella in hand, wanting to give me shelter from my storm. She told me that I would be doing her a favor if I let her watch my kids all day for free. Can you imagine? I do believe if anyone else would have made me this proposition I would have called the Florida State Police and told them that there was a pedophile in the KOA Campground. Hazel explained to me that since her husband, Harry, had died she had been waiting for death to take her, maybe even wishing for it. Living out your days can be a long and torturous endeavor when your loved one has died.

Harry and Hazel never got the chance to raise children and not for lack of trying. Hazel spent many married years suffering miscarriage after miscarriage and three times Hazel actually carried a pregnancy to the point of delivery. Both of her daughters were very premature tiny, tiny girls. Her daughter Hope lived for a few days after birth and her second girl Grace lived a week. Angelo her son was stillborn. After Angelo, Hazel and Harry embraced a childless life. They stopped putting themselves through the grief and pain of losing babies and completed their life and marriage by wholeheartedly loving each other. When Harry died, Hazel felt completely alone, all of her losses rushing to her in waves of heartache. Hazel told me that her grief was so immense that every night she dreamed of following Harry to his grave. She would lay still and envision his coffin, a large shiny steel tomb sitting in a deep dark hole. She would see herself climbing down into the grave and lifting the heavy lid. Harry would be in a comfortable death sleep, his hands folded across his dark blue suit, his head resting on a pillow of gray silk. Hazel would lie down beside him and fling her large leg across his thighs just as they had always slept. In the morning when she awoke, she would be alone, hugging tightly the bulk of Harry's pillow. Hazel continued to mourn out the months of spring and summer alone at home in Indiana, like any other ordinary widow. But come late autumn just as she and Harry had always done, Hazel went through the annual motions of packing up their RV and driving it down to Florida to stay for the winter. She placed it in its usual spot at the KOA campground and then she just sat, through a winter that eventually turned to spring which grew into summer, and still Hazel sat.

Sitting quietly in a large lawn chair in front of an RV every day at a crowded campground, you notice a lot of things. What Hazel noticed most was me. She watched my abandonment in the form of gossip and voyeurism. With Harry's death, Hazel's life changed completely and became this quiet, still empty space to have to exist in. My abandonment looked nothing like that. In fact, my life had become a tornado and I existed in its core of pandemonium and disorder. I had no peace, no quiet, and no space in which to think or try to reassemble myself. Hazel noticed that our lives were polar opposites. Yet, we had two things in common, the loss of a husband and a terrible sadness. It was that revelation and the desperation of knowing she must go on that caused Hazel to get up out of her lawn chair, walk over to my trailer, and offer me a hand and her a new life.

Hazel asked me to give her "A Purpose." That is what she called it. She indicated that helping me out was something that she needed as much as I did. I suppose it is the same as those who gain sheer gratification from volunteering. Maybe the kids and I were Hazel's chosen charity, but I was not in a place where I could have been too proud or rather too stupid to turn her offer down. With Hazel's help, life in the campground became bearable again. I could actually do my job. My baby no longer spent her days strapped to my body in a snuggle sack being carried through frenzied and hectic hours of chaos. My boys were no longer running the grounds unsupervised and I could relax. As for Hazel, she began living again. How could she not with those three forces of life surrounding her, the boys circling her legs calling out for attention and the baby climbing on her lap, leaving wet kisses and comfortable hugs. It was with my babies that Hazel gave herself permission to be happy again and she was finally mothering children, well grandmothering children. Since my own mother died when I was young, a grandma is just what my children needed – just what I needed. Hazel was the missing piece to our puzzling life. I don't know what I would do without her. She helps carry me through each and every day. She is there for me as I try like hell to make my unsettled life stable. She is there to pamper and hold my daughter and laugh with my boys, to watch over them, calm their fears, make them healthy snacks and read them stories. She was there to help me move and move with me, company on the road and another adult for the trailer load of children and pets. She is here with me now as we start this adventure, our new life, settling in to this farmhouse and starting a business. Hazel and I are trying to create something that neither of us could offer alone. She is my business partner, my inspiration, my earth mother and I am so glad God planted Hazel into our lives. Together Hazel and I have gone from KOA to *a-okay.*

The Kitchen House

December 3, 1999 – Dear Diary, I've heard a home is what you make it - and Charlie and my daddy have surely made me a beautiful home. I'm feeling blessed.

Coming back home to Grace, West Virginia was a decision that I wrestled with. Sure I was struggling in Florida, but that battle was unseen by my family, Beau's family and the town that raised us. When you grow up in a small town it's like growing up in a reality TV show and everybody is watching you. Although they don't mean to, they surely love it when you fail. I believe it's because when people watch others fall apart they feel more together. Another man's fiasco gives you a chance to rationalize your own mess and conclude, it's not so bad after all. Sure my husband is a jerk, but at least he hasn't run off with some big tit redneck that drives a Deluxe Winnebago. How embarrassing for me!

It was my daddy who convinced me to come back home. My dad, Skip Cooper, is a schemer for sure. A man with a plan who's not worried about what anyone else thinks. Months before he even knew Beau and I were having troubles he had bought a house. A haunted house I might add that he had decided to fix up and use as rental property. This is not unusual, my daddy buys and resells things all the time, from riding mowers to tractors, boats, cars, motorcycles, and sometimes houses. It's his favorite hobby. As for making a living, he and my brother Charlie have a renovation business. They are Two Handy Dandy Men, which is actually the name of my daddy and brother's business, as well as a description. Daddy finds the work, the houses and has all the ideas, but it's Charlie who works wonders. He could literally turn a shack into a small palace. They mostly work on renovations for others, building a deck, patching a barn, that kind of thing. Sometimes they flip houses by buying cheap foreclosures. They update the inside, add a fresh coat of paint and sell the house for twice as much or rent it out. They had decided this house would be excellent rental property. It is the known haunted house of our town, a large white clapboard structure that is located in the center of our little city, across the street from our modest library and next to the post office. My daddy purchased the house in early spring and planned to have it ready to rent by late summer. However, in the midst of renovating the house, Daddy found out that Beau had left me. I talked to Daddy on the phone last summer more than we had ever talked before. I thought I was trying to comfort his worry. What I was actually doing was asking him to comfort my worries. During our weekly phone calls, I would tell him all about Hazel, how wonderful she is with the kids, how wonderful she is to me, and how each little thing that she touches becomes embedded with charm. It is the simple things that she does that are laced with this homemade magic, from baking cookies to making coffee, everything just tastes, smells and feels a little bit better. It was then that my daddy got the idea or rather what he called "An Epiphany" of a coffee house.

He envisioned this broken down, haunted, clapboard house, in the center of town, as a delightful and appealing coffee shop. A dwelling where country folks could come to share a cup of Hazel's delicious coffee and talk about the day. He saw women gathered in circles of gossip around kitchen tables. He thought of the farmers who had no inclination of going into a bar, but still needed a place away from their wives where they could relax and enjoy some refreshment. In my daddy's mind, a swank little coffee house is just what the town of Grace needs and who better to run the coffee house than me, Sissy, a girl with no man, no plan and no dreams of her own.

Before I had even agreed to come back to West Virginia, my daddy and Charlie, had already turned their rental property renovation into the design and creation of a coffee shop where the kids, Hazel and I would live. Live where you work. It's all I've ever known, first a campground, now a coffee house. At first, I was reluctant to mention my father's crazy idea to Hazel. It seemed a little presumptuous to me that Hazel would want to move to West Virginia and start up a business in an old haunted house. However, when I finally pitched my daddy's business idea, Hazel was excited. I believe she needed a change as much as I did. Hazel had become a nanny to my kids at the campground in order to pull herself out of a long, deep depression and she had succeeded. Maybe now she was ready for something more. I believe she thought running a coffee shop sounded so much cooler and adventurous than babysitting all day. So we packed her RV up to the brim and headed home to West Virginia.

Renovations on the house have taken a little bit longer than expected and I still have not officially opened. Daddy and Charlie began their coffee house construction five short months ago and the house has literally been given a facelift. They worked on the outside first, wanting to finish before winter flew down from the mountains and stayed awhile. The work they have done so far has both inspired and humbled me. The house is delightful and charismatic and it no longer looks haunted, even though the entire town of Grace knows it is. It also has stopped looking like an old farmhouse and now carries the charm of a Bed and Breakfast.

The once dingy white exterior has been painted light purple. Darker purple shutters have been hung beside the many long skinny windows. If you were to ask Charlie, he would tell you the home is the color of lilacs trimmed in wisteria. If Charlie weren't such a ladies' man I would swear he was gay. Charlie and Daddy extended the L shaped front porch so it now wraps nearly all the way around the house in the shape of a C and into the coffee house entrance, which is actually the back kitchen door. We will dress our linen white wraparound porch come spring when the snow no longer blows across its floorboards. How quaint the house will look come April with its several porch swings, rocking chairs and small café tables.

The kitchen is now huge from knocking down the walls that went from the mudroom into the kitchen and the wall that went from the kitchen into the dining room. This means that more than half of my downstairs is kitchen. My dad and Charlie have installed wooden beams from an old barn to serve as my support wall. The beams give the large spacious room a warm and rustic feel. Using wood from the same old barn, Charlie built a large vintage counter, or rather a coffee bar. The bar is gray in color with large knots and saw marks and it stretches nearly 10 feet across one side of the room. Seven wooden bar stools line the front of the coffee bar. Behind the counter is my new double-sided stainless steel sink and new black appliances. I now own a large black dishwasher (my first dishwasher ever); an enormous refrigerator, a double oven electric range and a turbo chef. I have become Betty Crocker or rather Sissy Crock-Pot. The entire room has been painted a light cappuccino except the wall behind my coffee bar. That wall has been coated black using chalkboard paint and it is where Hazel and I have scripted our menu and prices. In the coffee house there are five round tables with wooden chairs. The hardwood floors have been restored to their original shine and several large oriental rugs that Charlie found at flea markets have been placed about. In one corner of the room sits a firm, burnt orange couch, two comfy brown chairs and a coffee table that Charlie scrounged up somewhere. In another corner sits a desk and a computer. There is also a long bookcase, built by my daddy, that matches the coffee bar, and it runs down one wall. So far, I have filled this bookcase with my children's books, puzzles and toys with just a few adult fictions. The kid's collection of stories is a lot larger than mine and this makes for a good play area. In The Kitchen House there stands a playpen. This is because Sabrina is only a year and a half old. Even though we all seem to live together in just one room, there are times when Sabrina needs to be confined down to an even smaller space – a pen filled with toys. My favorite renovation piece is the large chandelier that Charlie found, cleaned, restored and then hung in the center of my coffee house. The chandelier makes my house the best swank little coffee shop for miles and miles. Often I close my eyes and dream about the days to come. In my mind's eye, I can already see a college student sitting at my desk, drinking an espresso or several housewives relaxing on the couch and chairs, drinking coffee and gossiping. As the house comes together I am starting to share my daddy's vision. I am hoping both visions come true. As for the rest of the house, it is coming along nicely. The walls have been painted the colors you might find in a wildflower garden and Hazel has furnished the rooms.

Once Hazel and I arrived back in West Virginia, we took a few days to rest and then we left the kids with Beau's parents and off we went to Indiana to check on Hazel's home and the things she had left behind. Hazel had decided that while she was on this little adventure with me she would rent out her home in Indiana. Hazel and I met and talked to Mr. Davey, Hazel's neighbor of forty years and he agreed to be her rental property manager. He is to watch over her property, rent it out to the appropriate tenant, collect the rent, pay himself and send her the rest. Mr. Davey seemed excited about his new job. Hazel described Mr. Davey as a retired busybody that watches everybody's house anyways. This is the perfect job for him. After making arrangements with Mr. Davey, Hazel and I took a few days to pack up her beautiful belongings to bring them to West Virginia, as I had no furniture. When leaving Florida, I only packed up our personal items, clothing and toys. The large furniture stayed behind in the mobile home and now belongs to the new manager of the KOA Campground. Hazel has furnished most all of our living space. Unfortunately we do not have room in The Kitchen House for Hazel's dining room table, hutch and buffet. She was forced to leave her formal dining set in Indiana, along with a piece of her heart. However, Hazel is great at rationalizing. She wiped her tears on the back of her hand, took one more look around her spaciously gardened yard and then told Mr. Davey to give her dining room furniture to his grandson Benny, who had just gotten married.

"It's so refreshing to be able to give where it's needed," she said, brushing away her own sentiments.

After four full emotional days of packing Hazel's home we returned to West Virginia. Hazel happily and graciously spent the following week beautifying our home. It is our space that I believe Hazel loves the most, the part of the house that holds the children, the large puppy and displays her crafty and pretty things.

There is an interior door from the coffee house that leads you into our living room. The space is quaint and appealing with maybe the feel of a ghost or two. On one wall stands a small white brick fireplace and on the other wall is a small cushioned built-in window seat in front of a long window. Hazel's television sits in her antique white finished armoire that stands tall next to the window seat and Hazel's floral couch lines the wall across from the window. Her soft blue rocker recliner is angled in the corner. I cringe every time my boy's jump up onto the sofa's well kept upholstery with their dirty feet. There is a true cottage feel that was born with the delivery of Hazel's things.

The walls in the living room are lilac and carry the same shade as the exterior of the house. The parlor sits directly off the living room and its walls are the color of honeydew. There is a pocket door that closes the parlor off from the living room allowing some privacy. Because of this as well as its size, the parlor has been converted into Hazel's bedroom and oh, has she made it a pretty room. This is the room that I try to keep the kids and puppy out of. But Hazel mostly keeps her door open and invites them all in, making me a nervous wreck. I often feel the urge to hang a red velvet rope across her threshold along with the words "Keep Out." Hazel owns an abundance of beautiful things and my children are capable of destroying it all in mere minutes.

Hazel and Harry must have been antique collectors or at least appreciators. Hazel has an antique treadle sewing machine and a padded cushion chair. She has an iron bed; made with a thick, white bedspread and skirt and its many colorful throw pillows. She has a painted vintage dresser that is very shabby chic and a fold down secretary desk in mahogany. She also has a beautiful floral chair (it matches the couch) and a long floor lamp. It is in this spot that Hazel reads every night before bed. Along the wall in Hazel's room, my daddy built a long closet with sliding doors and many shelves. Hazel has managed to fill this closet with her knick-knacks, clothes and crafts. There is a small bathroom off the parlor with just a sink and toilet, but at least Hazel doesn't have to climb the stairs at night to pee.

Up the stairs that lead from our foyer is where the kids and I sleep. The boys share a sky blue bedroom that has bunk beds and is decorated in toys. Sabrina's room is dusty rose with pine color baby furniture and a rocker that my daddy bought me. My room is coral. Hazel gave me a day bed from her guest room and a white dresser. My room is the plainest room in our house and I believe it is where our ghosts hang out, so I do not. Believe it or not, my favorite room is the bathroom. It is huge with a large claw tub and a warm wall furnace. The room is so big that this is where Hazel placed her massive vanity and bench seat. The walls of the bathroom are butter yellow, my favorite color, and this is where I retreat to relax. The house is charming to say the least with its odd shaped ceilings and many gables. My daddy and Charlie have outdone themselves with the remodeling of this charismatic home. And I am still in shock that I live here and that I am going to run a café.

So far my business has made no money and although he has not said, I'm sure my daddy has spent plenty. The positive is that Charlie and Daddy are not short on materials or ideas. Daddy is a hoarder of materials with several outbuildings and barns that are full of wood, drywall, paint, tools, and so much more. Charlie is known for scrapping junk and turning it into something beautiful. However, neither of them knows a thing about coffee other than brewing it in a Mr. Coffee maker.

Conversely, I have become a coffee connoisseur. I admit I was not much of a coffee enthusiast three months ago. But after educating myself on the coffee bean, which is actually quite fascinating, and meeting with hordes of coffee suppliers who had me taste nearly a billion different types of roast, Hazel and I have become coffee experts. I've learned that the difference between coffee and espresso is not the bean, but the roast, grind and brewing process. The beans for espresso are roasted until they're dark brown and have an oily shine. Those dark oily beans must be ground very fine, a much finer grind than drip coffee, so that the consistency is almost like powdered sugar. The finely ground beans are then packed into a puck and tampered down tightly. The puck is tightened onto the espresso machine. Espresso is made by pressure and force and it should only take about 15 seconds for boiling hot water to run through the tightly packed grounds and produce the perfect shot. There are three beautiful and distinct parts to a shot of espresso; the dark bottom is known as the heart, the lighter shade in the middle is called the body and the crema is the frothy top layer. I have learned much of what I know from the coffee salesmen I have met with over the last month. Since Hazel and I are not going to roast our own coffee beans we needed to find a coffee supplier that would give us the best tasting espresso. We began our search for coffee companies last month and in that time we have literally tasted a thousand cups of coffee. Each supplier claims to be a roast master and each coffee salesman is a pushy know it all, much like other salesmen. It truly was one of the hardest decisions to make, but both Hazel and I decided to go with The Velvet Cup. Their espresso is smooth, their salesman young and they are the newest roasters I've found, having just been in business for two years and already serving five states. The Velvet Cup is going to supply our espresso beans and black tea. We could also purchase our house coffee through The Velvet Cup or just use the same espresso bean with a different grind to create a full flavor dark roast drip coffee. Instead we are going with the standard Maxwell House. It is what West Virginians love and it will sell. We buy our Maxwell House in large economy size cans from the Wal-Mart.

Now that we have a coffee and a café, we have had to buy the things that will make me a barista. Like a jockey with his horse, I have become the proud owner of a restaurant style espresso machine with milk steamer and an industrial style coffee maker as well as an espresso grinder, small white espresso cups, 100 ceramic black coffee mugs, pastry plates, silver tea spoons, several glass sugar pourers, and the list goes on. Even though I have been frugal and thrifty, if this endeavor does not succeed I am afraid that I have placed not only myself, but also my father and brother into a large deep pit of debt. Just one more thing to keep a single mom awake at night.

So with all the hours in which I do not sleep, I have been studying up on espresso drinks. The computer is a wonderful thing. I have found you can do almost anything with espresso. Add hot water to an espresso and it's called an Americano. Add steamed milk and you have a Latte. Add foam to your Latte and you have a Cappuccino. Making foam is a bit tricky and somewhat of an art. I pour whole milk into a metal pitcher and use a steam wand to heat it. When making foam you insert the tip of the steam wand just under the surface of the cold milk. The effect is like blowing bubbles through a straw. It should take just a few seconds to have a significant amount of foam. Then you move your wand further down into the milk and continue to steam until the metal pitcher is nearly too hot to touch, but not so hot that you've burned the milk. Next you add your steamy milk and foam to your full-bodied shot of espresso. When pouring the steamed milk into the espresso, catch the foam with a spoon and add it to the top so it piles and spreads out evenly. Honestly, it has taken some time for me to perfect my Cappuccino, but I believe I have finally gotten it right. I don't feel vain at all when I say, "they are so damn pretty." It's true, I've even been teaching myself Latte Art. As for now, I can add a pretty leaf or heart to the top of your steaming cup of java. It's actually very fun and I have truly enjoyed trying out each and every mug. Maybe another reason sleep will not come is that I'm all jacked up on coffee drinks.

For the farmers who don't want anything funny done to their coffee, and this town is full of them, we have our boring Maxwell House. I know it will probably be our biggest seller, even though they all have a can in their own damn kitchen. However, the restaurant will also feature a House Coffee, known as Hazel's House Blend. This is the coffee that inspired the idea of a café. It is made from the Maxwell House with an added pinch of special. Hazel likes to sprinkle cinnamon into the grounds of coffee and put a splash of vanilla at the bottom of the pot. Its added extra creates our special recipe and the result is comforting, delicious and soothes you like a best friend. Besides Hazel's House Blend, I have been trying to come up with a coffee menu. Of course there will be the usual Espresso, Latte, Cappuccino and Mocha, but the menu is much longer than that with coffees that can come cold or hot.

The secret for a good iced coffee is to allow the coffee to cool. Don't pour hot coffee over ice because the ice melts and waters down the coffee and the taste or effect is not the same. You must allow the coffee to cool and then place the cooled coffee in a jug that goes in the refrigerator. You make your iced coffee with the cold coffee and cold whole milk. I plan on serving my iced coffee in mason jars. The coffees look as charming as they taste. I believe the iced drinks will be a hit with the younger generation.

I have chosen to give my coffee ghostly names to go with my haunted coffee house theme. I figure if I have to live and work in a haunted environment, I might as well embrace it. The Casper is coffee with added Nutella and marshmallow cream. The Poltergeist is simply a white chocolate mocha; while the Shadow is a dark chocolate Mocha with added raspberry. The Spirit is a chocolate mint coffee. The Spook may be my favorite; it is made with butterscotch chips. The Vision is a caramel coffee. The Zombie is what I call a shot of espresso in your coffee and it will keep you up for days. This coffee should be popular with the truck drivers that pass through.

While I have been working out coffee drinks, Hazel has busied herself with what food to offer that pairs well with coffee.

"We can't just sell coffee," she said. "Nobody would come just for some Maxwell House." Yet, neither of us wants to run a full restaurant with all its orders, work and food. We won't be able to keep up. Putting our heads together we came up with the idea of biscuits. We can make the biscuit dough in advance and place them in the freezer. It should be easy enough and now we have a gimmick, biscuits and coffee. Hazel has come up with several different biscuit ideas that she has been working out in our new double ovens. So far our menu consists of a buttermilk biscuit, sweet potato biscuit, blueberry biscuit, apple walnut biscuit, herb and cheese biscuit and a black pepper biscuit. To go with the biscuits we will have butter, honey and jams. We will also offer tuna salad and chicken salad that can be placed on your choice of biscuit. For kids we have hotdogs rolled up in a buttermilk biscuit. We call it The Mummy Dog. They're super cute and my kids love them. Besides coffee, we are going to offer ice tea and different flavors of hot teas. Of course, just like the coffee, we will have to offer the standard black Lipton. The people in this town are just plain funny about keeping things standard.

With all the work we have done we are almost ready to open, just waiting on the construction of a new bathroom. We can't very well open a restaurant without a bathroom for its patrons and I will be damned if I let them walk through the rest of my house and upstairs to the potty. We have decided just to add one bathroom with a one seater; it's all we have the money for. However it's coming along beautifully. My pedestal sink goes in tomorrow and the entire project should be complete by next week. I hope to have "The Kitchen House" open before Christmas day.

The Kitchen House is the name of my coffee house. Besides it being a perfect name for a large kitchen café, there is really no other name to choose. In reality, this house has been called The Kitchen House since the 1940's. That is when the Kitchen family resided in this home and that is who haunts this home today. The Kitchens were a well-known and liked family that lived in this house from 1942 until 1955. The house is over a hundred years old and I don't know who lived in it before the Kitchens. The Kitchens are its signature family. It was in 1955 that the Kitchen family all died, one by one, at the residence. First to die was William Kitchen, he was twelve years old and was chopped up in a horrible farming accident. A few months after William died, seven-year-old Sarah Kitchen, became ill with scarlet fever that weakened her heart and eventually caused her death. William and Sarah were the only children of Owen and Emma Kitchen. What a terrible fate, to bury both of your children, sometimes life is just cruel. Of course, Owen and Emma were beyond grief stricken and they could not bear their pain. Two days after burying young Sarah, they shared in the most romantic suicide I've ever heard told. Owen and Emma shared a bottle of poisoned wine along with some sleeping pills and then they lay upon their bed in a lover embrace to never wake again. They were found wrapped in each other's arms by someone who had come over bearing food and sympathy. Since 1955 the house has had many different owners, but none of them have stayed long, and none of them have been originally from the town of Grace. Everyone in Grace knows the story of the Kitchen Family and they would never be foolish enough to buy a house haunted by a family of ghosts. That is everyone except, Skip Cooper.

Bless this House

As soon as next week, our café will be open for business. There now hangs a large, beautiful, white wooden sign that swings in my front yard. It is scripted with italic, purple letters and reads *THE KITCHEN HOUSE*. Charlie completed the bathroom renovations yesterday. His finishing touch was bathroom art. Somehow, he came across a calendar of outhouses. I believe it is supposed to be artistic. Each month a photograph of some obscure or appealing outhouse is featured. Charlie ripped out six of his favorite months and framed them in dark oak frames and hung them on the sage green walls. It is spectacular and I love it. He also put a tall, wooden newspaper stand in the bathroom. I'm gonna get the daily paper along with a couple prints and magazines and keep them in there for the customers. I think it's as practical as it is funny, setting the newspaper stand beside the toilet, and not at the front door.

My daddy, Charlie, Hazel and I have also talked over the business figures and I am feeling a mixture of relief and fear. Hazel and I will be paying Daddy and Charlie for the house and renovation and then it is our business. It's not as bad as I thought it would be, because they got the house really cheap as a foreclosure and they are not charging us labor on the renovations. They are also taking payments as we can make them and not charging us a bunch of interest. It is a land contract deal that I can live with and so can they. I have worked out a monthly budget that would have the house and all paid off in just over five years. Now we just have to hope that this café actually brings in some business and money to live on.

I'm not as worried about Hazel as I am about the kids and myself.

Hazel had a life before this one. She still has Harry's pension and a home in Indiana. If this life fails her, she has something to go back too. On the other hand, I have nothing else and three small children to support. We must succeed.

The Kitchen House will have its Grand Opening on Friday evening December 17th. We are opening our doors with a tree lighting ceremony and Christmas carols. We will have sugar cookies and hot cocoa as well as coffee and biscuits. We will also have a craft table where little ones can make a Christmas card or ornament. The kids and I created a flyer with art work and Charlie had 300 of them printed out. I took the flyers up to school and left them in the office. They are to be handed out by the teachers to each pupil. We also hung a flyer up at the post office and at the library. I figure that should drum up some business. In reality, just pure curiosity is what is going to bring in the crowd at first. Everyone is talking about Sissy's return home, without Beau, and how crazy Skip bought her that haunted house and how they are going to turn it into some hoity-toity coffee shop. People are constantly driving by and just gawking at all the changes. I have caught the town residents peeking in my windows and a few have knocked on my front door asking for a sneak preview. I told them they have to wait like everybody else. This town really is so nosy and for once in my life it just might work in my favor.

In preparation for our Grand Opening and just because I felt the need, I spent this week having the house blessed. My first call was to the Catholic Church. I asked to speak to the priest. I told him that my three children, a friend, and I had just moved into the old farmhouse next to the post office. I then explained that we are starting up a business and would like to have the house blessed. I neglected to tell him that I was not Catholic nor have I ever been to his church. He said he knew the farmhouse and had heard of our plan and that he would be happy to come bless the house. On Tuesday morning when Hazel opened the door, I was shocked to see how very young and handsome Father McIntire is. I had no idea a priest could be such a pretty boy. I was expecting an old, wise, arthritic man with brandy breath. What arrived was a Greek God smelling of sport scent. He walked through each of our rooms with a golden ball of holy water swinging from its chain, baptizing and sanctifying our space. He spoke softly. His whispered voice of prayer was like listening to poetry. His tone was deep, yet almost silent as if it were springing from his soul. He gently swung his hand back and forth as he walked causing holy water droplets to rain like sacred tears. Sabrina was taking a morning nap in her room. In a whisper, Father McIntire asked me her name and then standing above her crib he prayed an almost silent blessing for my child. I felt a quiver run up my spine and I fell in love with Father McIntire.

After the house blessing, Father McIntire, Hazel and I sat at one of our kitchen tables. He prayed for our business venture and then he sampled our coffee and biscuits. He told us a little about himself (very little) and mostly asked how we were doing. He said he was impressed with the changes to our house and that he was excited for the both of us. He felt our house was a place of peace and that we were going to be fine. The entire time Father McIntire talked, I was mesmerized. He has the softest tone and the words he chooses to speak, each one precise, as if they have been molded to perfection by thought. After he left I felt completely perverse.

"Oh God," I told Hazel. "I was crushing on him so hard." A man of the cloth is standing in my home, blessing my child, and I only want to kiss his full praying lips. I was sure that my lustful thoughts had probably jinxed my house blessing.

"What is wrong with me? Damn it, I screw everything up!" Hazel begged me not to be so sensitive. She said it is harmless to crush on a priest, especially one that is so young and attractive. She was sure the house was fine. But, I couldn't let it go, I felt foolish and my shame was immense. The first sexual attraction I have had since Beau left and it happens to be a priest. I needed to fix my jinx. I went to the computer and typed in the words House Blessings on Google. I came away with the name Pixie Moon-Dust, a psychic medium that lives two towns over. I told Hazel that Pixie Moon-Dust was coming over on Wednesday.

"You do know that is a made-up name?" Hazel said.

"Yes," I responded. "I'm not stupid."

"Well if she has a made up name she is probably a made up psychic. If she were a real psychic she would use her real name." I understood Hazel's logic, but I still felt the need to have the house blessed one more time, and what harm could a pixie do?

Pixie arrived five minutes early on Wednesday afternoon and her appearance was as made-up as her name. For starters, her hair is blue, bright blue, I suppose the color she believes moon dust is, and she has a full back tattoo. I didn't notice the blue hair and tattoos at first, because Pixie was wearing a knit hat and a black Carhartt coat. But after being in the house for five minutes, walking in circles trying to measure its vibrations, Pixie peeled off her knit cap revealing two bright blue ponytails. She then hung her heavy coat on the back of a chair. Underneath the manly coat, Pixie was dressed feminine and maybe a little sleazy, wearing a slinky, low back shirt with no bra. The shirt made it easy to see the tattoo that covered her back. On one shoulder was an inked sun of yellow and orange and on the other shoulder sat a blue and purple moon, in-between her shoulder blades, was a galaxy of stars and flying pixies. The entirety of the tattoo was a celestial sky full of cosmic fairies. Unlike Father McIntire, Pixie did not have holy water. Instead she walked from room to room with a lit sage stick that she fanned forward using a large leaf of some exotic plant. The sage smelled an awful lot like pot and kind of made me want to smoke a joint, which I have not done in about 10 years and have never craved before. But just like my impure thoughts for the young, sexy priest, Pixie Moon-Dust had me hankering for a toke. Pixie's voice was not as soft as Father McIntire's and her words were not as poetic. She spoke to my ghosts as if she knew them and she assured me that they were here, but that they meant no harm and in fact they liked my kids. In truth, Pixie kind of freaked me out, yet I shared a cup of coffee with her too.

On Thursday morning the Mormons came, two very polite gentlemen in pressed white shirts and neckties. They told me my house was beautiful and had a peaceful presence. They did not walk through my home or concern themselves with ghost talk. Instead they asked to be seated at a table. They turned down my offer for coffee and instead drank water with lemon. Then they talked to Hazel and me for a full hour about The Church of Latter Day Saints. As soon as the two men left Hazel abandoned her cheerful disposition.

"Who else do you have scheduled to come out and bless this house?"

"The Jehovah Witnesses are coming around 4:00pm."

"Oh no they're not!" she said. "The Jehovah Witnesses want to bless this house as much as those Mormons did. They don't believe in all your talk about ghosts and house blessings. They are coming, because they see you as an open mind to hear about their church and they will try and convert you. Unless you want another lecture about God today I suggest you call off the Jehovah Witnesses. We are going to bless this house ourselves. Tomorrow evening, you the kids and I are doing our own house blessing. Hell, we are just as capable as that crazy Pixie."

I had never seen Hazel so exasperated before and as soon as she was done expressing her opinion she left the room in a huff. Although I tried to call off the Jehovah Witnesses they showed up anyways and Hazel was right. The two ladies were very sweet and loved the coffee. However, I did sit through another hour of talk as I leafed through a Watchtower pamphlet. Hazel on the other hand took the kids up to their room to play.

On Friday after school, Hazel suggested that we all go over to the General Store. In the store, Hazel led us down the aisle of candles and asked each one of us to pick our favorite color or scent. Hazel then chose a blue candle, smelling of ocean breeze for herself. Roman grabbed a very large dark red pillar candle that smelled of cranberries. Henry's candle was white and long like a sword with no scent and we had to buy a candleholder to fit it in. Henry then chose for Sabrina a small pink candle that smelled of rose petals. My candle was pale yellow wax in a glass jar that smelled of honeysuckle. After candle shopping we picked up a pizza and headed back to the house. At home, Hazel laid our candles out on the table and with the tiniest point of an exacto knife she engraved our first initial into the wax (H-H-S-S-R. Hazel, Henry, Sissy, Sabrina, Roman). She picked up the white candle with its etched H in its slender side.

"Henry this candle represents you, because the light of God lives inside of you and the light of God surrounds you. Do you understand that Henry?" Hazel asked.

"I think so," my doe eyed boy responded. His slow hesitation was a clear indication that he didn't understand at all.

"Well, there is this light," Hazel tried to explain. "The light lives inside of you. It is your center or maybe your soul. Everybody has it. It's actually called the light of God and it shines the brightest when you are kind or doing something you love. That's when you can feel the light of God and that's when others can see it." Henry's face was perplexed as he puzzled over the idea of a light shining inside his body. But Roman seemed to grasp at something bigger and he blurted out excitedly.

"Like E.T.?"

"Yes!" Hazel shouted pointing at Roman. "Exactly like E.T. It's your heart light! Good job Roman." Roman beamed having made such a fascinating discovery and it excited Hazel to the point where she began to sing.

"*Turn on your heart light, Let it shine wherever you go. Make a happy glow for all the world to see.*" Hazel loves Neil Diamond and I think she liked singing that song as much as she did lighting the candles, so of course I felt propelled to sing with her.

"*Turn on your heart light,*" we both bellowed as my children looked on in wonderment.

"Ok Henry," Hazel said after we finished our song and regained our composure. "It's just like Roman said. This candle represents your heart light; which is really God's light. It lives in your center, but shines out and wraps around you like a blanket and keeps you safe. You were born with this light and it will always be with you."

"Cool!" my boys replied and with satisfaction to their response, Hazel picked up the red candle.

"Roman this candle represents your heart light, because the light of God lives in you and the light of God surrounds you." She lit the candles and said her sentence until all five wicks were burning. We then held hands around the table and Hazel prayed out loud for our house.

"Dear God," she said. "We thank you so much for the blessings you have already bestowed on this house and on this family. You have blessed us with each other, good health and an inspiration. We are so grateful for all that lies ahead and we ask that you continue to bless us and keep us safe. In Jesus name we pray."

Then she began praying *The Lord's Prayer* and I joined in. Both Roman and Henry tried to mock our words, their voices trailing behind ours sounding like the sweetest of echoes and Sabrina, bless her heart, stayed silent through the whole ordeal. Hazel then addressed the Kitchen Family. She thanked them for their presence and the good luck that they are bound to give us. She said their name alone was a godsend since it is a perfect name for this coffee house. She talked as if all this was predestined. That this house was supposed to have belonged to them and carry a history and then belong to the kids and me and that we are meant to live happily in this house with a family of ghosts as our guardian angels. She put a spin on it that made it not so scary and quite comforting and I was happy she did this not only for me, but also for the boys who have been sleeping in my bed with the lights on.

After Hazel's beautiful blessing we all ate pizza around candlelight. When dinner ended we carried the candles into the living room and watched a movie in the dark. I rocked Sabrina to sleep and the boys eventually fell into unconsciousness. I stayed with a baby sleeping on my chest and left the boys tangled on the couch for a long time into the night, letting the candles burn way down. I eventually grew weary and had to blow them out, but I did so with a thank you to God that I had learned from Hazel.

December 10, 1999 -Dear Diary, After a full week of House Blessings and the entertaining of so many different minds of theology I have been quite confused. But then Hazel simplified all that for me, as only Hazel can do, with words and actions that I can actually grasp. Through Hazel's beautiful, yet simple, attempt at the illumination of faith, it became clear to me that I am going to be fine. It's easy, I carry the light of God inside of me and the light of God surrounds me. How beautiful is that?

Our Grand, Grand Opening

The Grand Opening of The Kitchen House was a total success. I admit it was a little frenzied as I tried to make espresso drinks for everyone who wanted to try them. As to be expected there were those who made fun of my espresso drinks and wanted plain, black coffee the way God had intended. Those old, boring farts got their wish and a dark roast espresso bean that seemed to hold a bit of power enlightened the others. Hazel and I had made six dozen Christmas cutout cookies that we sold individually for a dollar. We also sold baskets of warm biscuits and Hazel had made a large pot of bean soup. Many people purchased a bowl and then raved about it until someone else would purchase a bowl. I believe everyone would agree that Hazel is gifted in the kitchen. It truly is most amazing. Hazel is an artist to food as Charlie is an artist to refurbished material. Both of them have the ability to take something simple and ordinary, add another element of simple and ordinary and create something exotic. This coffee house's charm and appeal can be accredited back to those two. They create and I make good espresso.

In The Kitchen House, we had a craft table set up with foam balls, popsicle sticks, green and red squares of felt, markers, crayons, glue, scissors, thick white card stock, construction paper, ribbons, string, shiny foil and cotton balls. The kids made ornaments with their parents help. Earlier in the day, Daddy had brought over a huge live pine tree that he had set up in the corner of the coffee house and strung with lights. It was a night of festivities and it helped me get decorated for Christmas.

I believe most people came out to our grand opening simply out of curiosity. They wondered what all Skip and Charlie Cooper had done to that old haunted house and wanted to snoop around on the inside. I'm sure those people were quite impressed. The others came out for support. They care about the kids and me and are happy that we are home again. Beau's family came, his parents Pops and Mama Jaspers, along with several of his sisters and their children. The Jaspers were a great help to me that night keeping Roman, Henry and Sabrina occupied and watched. In fact, Sabrina spent most of the evening clinging to her paternal grandparents, which I assume made them feel very good. They are enjoying getting to know the grandchildren that have been living so far away and are grateful that they can help. I believe it helps ease the pain and disappointment caused by Beau. I know Mama Jaspers and Pops want me to do well. They care about me, love the children and suffer from the shame of Beau leaving us. I believe they may be more saddened by my absent husband than I am. They wear their humiliation in their weary eyes and they don't know what to tell their friends. It must be terrible to face a small, nosy community and admit that your son is a selfish dickhead that left his wife and kids in a campground and went off with another woman. I don't blame them for their son's behavior and for their sake and mine I hope the gossip of Beau dies down soon. People did their best to behave at my grand opening. I only heard a few whispers, which is the best I can hope for in this small town.

The best thing about my Grand Opening was the old friends from school that showed up, especially my best friend Rayland. I had not seen Rayland since my wedding day, so hard to believe since at one time we were inseparable. I had never known the indescribable, heart-melting feeling of seeing a long, lost friend until Rayland showed his beaming face. Seeing him again sent every significant, adolescent memory I have flooding back at me in full force. It was Rayland who stood beside me at my mother's funeral. The other kids were afraid to talk to me after my mama died; maybe they thought it was contagious. But Rayland's mama took him out of school that day and brought him to my mommy's funeral. Before the service started, when all the adults were hugging on my daddy and looking at family photos, Rayland grabbed my hand and pulled me outside. It was late April and the side yard of the funeral parlor was dotted in fresh, yellow dandelions. Rayland and I picked handfuls of those pesky, beautiful, vibrant, little weeds until we each had a large bouquet of dandelion sunshine. Then back into the funeral parlor we crept and up to my mama's casket where we threw our bouquets over the side and they landed in a spray of yellow flowers upon her chest, stomach and folded hands. The whole rest of that terrible day and week is a blur; the dandelion memory is the one I chose to keep.

As teens, Rayland and I used to spend our slow summer afternoons taking long walks through these mountains and woods. Often we would stop along the stream, sit on the bank, dangle our bare feet into the cold, clear water and watch the fish jump. Rayland would reveal to me all of his secrets even the disturbing ones. Later, at night, I would write his secrets down on paper as a process of releasing them and then burn the paper in an old can with a match destroying all evidence. I did the same with my own secrets. When Rayland saw me, he came towards me like a dream, a dream I have had a hundred times in the last nine years. He held my hands, kissed my cheek, and gave me the biggest of hugs. I introduced him to Hazel and he sampled every flavor of biscuit, moaning with each bite. I could tell Hazel liked him.

"Why didn't you marry him instead of that rat Beau?" she asked when he walked away.

"Because Rayland is the only flaming gay man in Grace, West Virginia," I told her.

I was not as happy to see some of my old schoolmates. Nearly every one of the girls in my senior class and the grade directly below wanted Beau for her man. Truth is Beau Jaspers is ruggedly handsome and I am no raving beauty. Perhaps it's Beau's light blond hair that darkened to a golden hue as he aged and not the shade of dirt that makes him so handsome. However, it could just as easily be his alluring eyes, the same color blue as a mountain stream. Then there is his strong and tempting body with firm muscles and a skin tone that has been forever kissed by the sun. My children have those same blue eyes. They have that same wispy blond hair and sun kissed skin. I look different and not as good. I don't think I'm ugly nor am I beautiful. I suppose I'm just simply the girl next door type. My hair is long, straight and auburn, which is perhaps my best feature. My eyes are small and green. My lips are thin and so is the rest of my physique, flat in every way. I used to have boobs, but by the time I had stopped nursing the third baby they were gone. I also have fair skin that gets burned by the sun and not kissed. I often think that people didn't understand what good-lookin Beau Jaspers saw in me, plain ole' Sissy Cooper. But it was plain ole' Sissy Cooper that Beau Jaspers got pregnant and then married, in that order. Everybody was shocked when it happened and then saddened because the blond, blue-eyed heartthrob, Beau Jaspers, had been taken out of the dating game and claimed by me. Shortly thereafter we ran off together to be free spirits in love or that's what we thought when we went to work and live in the campground. However that life and our children kept us pretty grounded, so much so that Beau felt the need to recapture his free spirit and fly away, leaving me to come home with a failed marriage and three handsome kids that look just like him. I believe some of those girls were gloating at the fact that my husband had abandoned me. I say let them gloat. At least I left these hills and actually did something and not only that I've come back an entrepreneur.

The two young and handsomely dressed men from the Mormon church and the two sweet, elderly ladies from the Jehovah Witness church showed up to the grand opening. Each mingled with people and passed out their tracts, which amused me, but unnerved Hazel something fierce. All four individuals are very nice and polite, yet they are opportunists and saw my grand opening as a way to reach the masses. Ironically, at one point the two Mormon gentlemen approached the two Jehovah ladies and they soon realized that there was a pretty hefty competition going on. The quest to save souls became even more awkward. Soon the ladies left. I think it had more to do with the tree lighting ceremony and Christmas theme and less to do with the Mormons. They probably felt they should leave before they were expected to glue pom-poms on a cardboard circle and hang it on the tree. Before leaving, they bought sugar cookies for the road, gave me a big hug, and congratulated me on the success of my opening. The young gentlemen stayed. They put away their pamphlets and like schoolboys, sat at a table and crafted two of the prettiest ornaments made that night. The impressive Mormon ornaments hang on the lower left hand side of my magnificent Christmas tree.

Pixie Moon-Dust also made an appearance at The Kitchen House that night and she brought us a very large basket of pinecones that she had picked up from the trees behind her house. I set them on the counter and they look rustic and beautiful. Hazel wants to add white lights to the basket to make it more festive. I admit that would be pretty, but I told her we should just leave them alone and admire them for what they are, a basket of pinecones collected by a pixie and given to us as a haunted housewarming gift. Hazel agreed that some things are better left untouched.

Father McIntire showed for our grand opening and he too brought a gift, a stunning crucifix that my father has hung above the door in The Kitchen House that leads into my living room. Like Rayland, Father McIntire also sampled biscuits and moaned with each bite and it was a complete turn on. He also ordered one of my fancy espresso drinks and said he loved it.

Daddy, Charlie, Hazel and I had worked so very hard for this grand opening; each one of us had a small piece of ourselves at stake, an exposed vulnerability awaiting criticism. Fortunately we received none, which allowed each of us to exhale slowly and relish the moment.

The children and parents hung their newly made ornaments and at 8 o'clock we lit the tree and sang Christmas Carols. We started with *Oh Christmas Tree* and went on from there. Patrons would shout out song titles and then all of us would join together in voice. *Joy to the World* someone would bellow and then *Joy to the World* we would all sing. Everybody seemed to be having a great time and it felt so good to be back in my mountains, back in my home.

December 18 - Dear Diary (about the Grand Opening) As the voices sang out I looked around The Kitchen House and tried to take it all in - my senses were on overload. The smell of fresh brewed coffee and sugar cookies, the feel of warmth from the ovens and many people, the sounds of song and laughter, the taste of honey on my tongue; it was enough to make me feel whole again. It was a surreal feeling that came over me as I stood among the family and friends that had been missing in my life since my marriage and move away. I suppose this is a time when I'm supposed to feel sad. It is nearly Christmas and my marriage is ending, my husband is bedding another woman, my children are fatherless, my finances insecure, my future unsure. Yet, when I looked around and saw all the smiling faces, my father and brother, my soon to be ex in-laws, my children, Hazel, old friends, new friends, a handsome priest and a blue-haired pixie, I felt doubly blessed.

After the Grand Opening ended, Charlie, my dad, Rayland and Pops helped me clean the mess while Hazel and Mama Jaspers put the kids to bed. As I was sweeping up the loose remnants scattered under the craft table I caught a vision out of the corner of my eye. I could have sworn I had perceived the shadowy figure of a thin lady wiping down the coffee bar. When I jerked my head up she was gone, yet the feel of her presence was still strong. I knew in my heart I had just spied Emma Kitchen. I also knew that she had enjoyed the grand opening, what a relief. The next day I was up before sunrise, flipping my closed sign over to open by 7:00am. Those are our hours 7:00am to 7:00pm closed on Sundays. Sundays are family day and will be a needed day off. Besides, I think I'm going to start going to mass.

This Christmas Sucks

I do believe that this has been the hardest Christmas I've endured since my mother died. What I remember most about that Christmas is the obscene amount of gifts Charlie and I received. We had far more gifts than if my mother had been living. She never would have been able to afford all those presents and my father would have never attempted to spoil us so. I'm sure he felt embarrassed by the amount of loot Charlie and I were given. But what was he to do? The teachers had taken up a collection and we were the adopted family of donations. It is by far so much easier to give than it is to receive. I'm sure our misfortune made it simpler for others to meet their Christmas aspirations. Like Grinch, their hearts grew two sizes bigger with every present wrapped for the lonely motherless children. Opening those gifts was like unwrapping the wounds we had been trying so hard to cover.

This year my children were the recipients of a charitable Christmas. It was not nearly as bad for me as it had been for my father, because our charity came from family and not strangers that pity you. Pops and Mama Jaspers did their best to spoil the kids rotten this year. They brought everything over to my house a week before Christmas. They showed up late one night after the kids were already in bed. They had a sack full of presents that were wrapped and tagged. They told me to call them the minute the kids woke on Christmas day so they could come over and watch them open their gifts. I was very touched at this gesture. My kids are not their only grandchildren. They have many others. The Jaspers family is huge. Beau is the youngest of their nine children and the only boy. Having eight older sisters that behaved like little mommies helped to make him the self-centered, spoiled brat he became. The Jaspers are a hard working modest family. They're large in number and in heart, but money is always tight. I'm sure Beau's sisters helped Ma and Pops by buying a gift for my children as they struggled to shop for their own. The whole Jaspers family took a role in playing Santa to my kids trying to compensate for the deadbeat dad that they had raised. Pops and Mama Jaspers were very excited, giddy and happy when dropping the presents off. However, Christmas morning they were different. They showed up early, just as they said they would, but their enthusiasm was not with them. They sat silently on the couch; sipping coffee and watching the kids open the presents they had bought them, or rather the Santa Claus gifts. They did so with a smile glued across their face yet their eyes held back tears of a sentimental sadness and I knew something was up.

As it turns out, that something was Beau. He had come home for Christmas. Beau and his girlfriend Judy had arrived Christmas Eve at the Jaspers' house pulling up in Judy's Deluxe Winnebago during *It's a Wonderful Life*. Ma and Pops broke the news to me as gently as they could and away from the children. Of course, Beau wanted to see the kids. The kids he walked away from six months ago and other than a few phone calls there has been nothing. I honestly did not know how to handle the situation or what to tell my babies. I thought of the emotions that would stir inside my young children, the anger that would soon be expressed by Roman. Anger is his method for dealing with pain. Henry my sensitive, teary-eyed boy will be brokenhearted. However, I don't think I'm allowed to deny Beau from seeing his kids. I wonder how this is in the best interest of my children. The legality of divorce and separation sucks. Mama Jaspers and Pops left with an invite for the kids to come to Christmas dinner.

I let the kids play with their new toys all morning and afternoon. They scooted around on my polished floor in PJ bottoms until after 4:00pm as I sat on the couch sullenly watching. My daddy stopped by around noon with an armful of gifts and Charlie showed up around 12:30 bringing more, including a coat tree he had made for the restaurant.

The coat tree was actually made from a real tree. A smooth, solid round trunk approximately eight inches in diameter, with the bottom carved into four legs for it to stand upon. It is so beautiful and well crafted and my emotions were so raw and exposed that when Charlie gave it to me, I set it by the door, hung a hat on it and then cried like a baby, startling everyone.

I felt very depressed. It didn't help that everyone was so lavish with their gift giving and my presents were lacking. I did try though. I made sure that I filled my children's stockings with precious tidbits of simple things. I also bought each child a book, as I do every year. The kids were to receive so much from others that I stopped there with mixed emotions of relief and sadness. I made something for my daddy, Charlie, Mama Jaspers, Pops and Hazel. I am not the artist that Charlie is or that my mother was, but I try. For each one of them I painted a watercolor on large sheets of white paper. For Charlie, I painted a pine forest and for Hazel a sunset. I swirled watercolors into wild flowers to give to Ma and Pops Jaspers and for Daddy I painted the mountains. On top of the watercolor paintings, in my finest calligraphy, I scripted a poem of love and family. I framed my watercolor poems in 11x14 frames with 8x10 mats. The paintings all looked so insignificant sitting among the store-bought presents that littered The Kitchen House, but I kept my head up, because at least I had made them. Then Charlie had to bring in that stunningly crafted coat tree and I felt even more like a failure. Stupid I guess, but with Beau's homecoming, girlfriend in tow, and my measly gifts, I was stuck in a dark mood and a gloom surrounded me.

Hazel tried to be the bright spirit and happy one. She talked and laughed with my daddy and brother, played with the boys, took care of Sabrina and tried to feed us. She made healthy dishes of fruits and veggies, a plate of cheese wedges beside rolled salami and many sugary goodies. I on the other hand, had ceased functioning. Daddy and Charlie stayed only a couple of hours. I think I made them feel uncomfortable. They're a great pair of guys that would do anything for me. However, a female's emotional state is not something that either one of them can deal with and at the first chance, without looking rude, they slipped away.

At 4:30 pm I called the boys to me and they leaned against my drab robe and touched my unbrushed hair as I spoke to them. I told them that their daddy had come to town, because he had missed them so much and he wanted to see them. I confessed that he was at Mama Jaspers and Pops house right now waiting to have a big Christmas dinner with them. I saw the rollercoaster of emotions reflect in their blue eyes. They were happy and confused. Children are forgiving souls. My boys love their daddy and their love is pure and unconditional. What happens to the heart and soul when someone you love walks away and doesn't see you for a very long time? It's a torturous thing and just as you begin to learn how to live without that person, they have the nerve to pop back in and want to say hi. How freaking cruel is that? It's a selfish son-of-a-bitch that does such a horrible thing.

I dressed the kids in their new Christmas outfits bought by the Jaspers. Hazel took the kids to their grandparent's house and stayed with them. I believe she mostly hung out with Mama Jaspers. The two probably spent the evening in her kitchen having a heart to heart talk and commiserating about life. Mama Jaspers has to deal with Beau and his girlfriend and Hazel has to deal with me and my emotional shutdown. Hazel and Mama Jaspers have become pretty close friends in the short time we've been home. They are around the same age and they share my children as their grandchildren. Mama Jaspers is touched by all that Hazel does for me and the kids. She knows that while we were in Florida, Hazel was my lifesaver; my rock and that my children love her.

While Hazel and the kids were gone I retreated to my bathroom. I filled our claw tub with steaming hot water, lit the remnants of our personalized candles, just a bit of wax and wick left and soaked in a hot tub, filling it with my tears. I then put on a clean pair of pajamas and sat in the dark. My ghosts kept me company until my family came home. I could hear the phantom footsteps above my head and the rocking chair that sits in Sabrina's room. I usually hear the rocking chair around 7:30pm each night and I have told myself it is Emma Kitchen rocking young Sarah. I hollered out into the dark "Merry Christmas" to my ghosts, but I heard nothing back.

The kids were exhausted when they came home from Pops and Mama Jaspers' house. It had been a long day and one full of emotion. I believe they were as emotionally wiped out as they were physically drained and nobody was up for words so we didn't talk much. I peeled off their Christmas clothes in silence and put them in warm comfy PJ's. I gathered them all into my bed where we all fell into an exhausted, hard sleep. It wasn't until the next day that I heard Roman had called Judy a daddy thief and Beau an asshole. My sentiments exactly, but maybe Roman needs some counseling.

Christmas Day 1999 - Dear Diary, once again my heart is broken. After spending the last six long months, piecing jagged edges back together, I dropped it. It shattered into a million pieces and is lying on the floor around my feet. Yet, I have made a promise to be positive as I write upon your lovely manila pages. So tonight I try to think of all the things I am grateful for. First, my children and their health, I do not know the suffering of Emma and Owen Kitchen and with the grace of God, I never will. Second, my father and brother and the beautiful house they have created for me. Because of them I get to live in an enchanted purple house that is warm and smells of coffee. Of course, I am grateful for Hazel, my earth mother, who sets my days with charm and optimism. Although Beau is a rat, his family is good and good to me. I appreciate the Christmas they gave to my kids, even though like long ago each present opened was a scab being peeled away. I am grateful for these mountains, they are my home, and I am so grateful to be home. Sometimes pain is so intense that you feel nothing else. I refuse to have that Christmas again. I use these feelings of gratitude to block and absorb the pain so that it cannot touch my soul. I am sad, but I am also happy.

He's Just a Ho-Beau

December 28, 1999 - Dear Diary, what a relief it was that Christmas fell on a Saturday so I could be closed the next day with reasons other than a devastated heart and upset stomach. Sunday gave me time to recoup and be with the kids. I had to address the remarks that Roman had made, although I agreed with him completely. However, I so badly want to erase the feeling of abandonment from my child's heart. I know this feeling intimately and there is no pain more severe. I tried to reassure Roman that Beau still loves him. What do you say to the crying eyes of a child about divorce and in our case desertion? I explained that Beau left, because he fell out of love with mommy and in love with Judy, although the love for his children is still strong. I also said that I know what it feels like when someone you love goes away. I told Roman that when I was his age my mommy died and I was very sad and very angry. But, as time went on Charlie, Grandpa and I built a life of our own. We became a family of three and slowly we began to have fun. Even though my mommy wasn't with us, her spirit was always there, because she lives in my heart-light.

I told him these things, because I know Beau will not stick around long. My husband has blown into town for a few days only to leave again and I will be left to console our children. I guess hindsight is 20/20, because it is clear to me now that Beau is a tramp. I mean honestly, who chooses life in a campground for their family? A vagabond that's who, someone who wants a home on wheels and every evening spent under the stars. In fact, his name should be Hobo instead of just Beau.

In the six, long emotional months since Beau's leaving I have felt shock, anger, guilt and depression. It is just recently, like within the last twenty-four hours, that I have reached acceptance. This place of hope does not only make my future look optimistic, it makes the past understood. Maybe it is not Beau's fault he left me. Perhaps it was written in the stars. It's quite possible that it was meant to be. I do believe that bad things sometimes happen to make room for good things.

If I am being honest with myself, then I know that it was not smart to get pregnant by a young nomad before he has had time to travel. Some would say that I tried to hold him back and that's a terrible thing to do to a dreamer.

Ever since Beau and I were children, he did nothing but talk about leaving home and seeing the world. I suppose I only half-heartedly listened to Beau, because I love West Virginia with its lush mountains and transparent streams. I see our hometown as America's hidden gem. Sure we have a bad rep of being ignorant and poor, but the ones that live here know true beauty. West Virginia is a romantic state with star-studded skies, long winding roads, folklore and stories of hardship as well as affection. Yet, Beau took for granted this land's beauty and in his dreams there were other mountains to climb, rivers to cross and valleys to see.

I became pregnant with Roman six months after high school graduation and right before Beau had the chance to escape this small town. I suppose Beau tried to do the right thing. He married the young girl who he had not planned on marrying before and he still tried to be true to his nomadic soul. To his credit, by the time that we were both twenty Beau had figured out how he could have it all, a family and a life under the stars. He secured a job in a KOA campground that came with a home, a paycheck and a life spent outdoors. I believe in our bliss we got pregnant again, this time for Henry. With a new baby and a toddler, the reality of a job, kids and responsibility came crashing down on us.

Still, Beau tried to find happiness when all he really wanted to do was wander off. Instead, he put in for a transfer. It was a noble attempt at keeping us whole, and we moved our little gypsy family to a new state and a new campground. The move created a happiness of passion that stirred in Beau long enough for me to become pregnant a third time. We would now have three kids and manage an even larger campground than before. We had successfully increased our family, our workload, our responsibilities and Beau's misery.

Then Judy showed up with her big fake tits, long oiled legs and a house on wheels. I'm sure Beau saw this as a divine intervention; God had sent him a whore. Judy was able to entice Beau with her sex appeal and a home that moved while I changed dirty diapers and breastfed. I admit that there were days I was so worn out from kids and campground that I would fall into bed too tired to even brush my teeth. Judy's teeth shone like pearls and she flashed them constantly at my husband. I like to believe that Beau tried to be strong and it took her more than a minute to lure him into her bed. I do know that it wasn't the sex that stole my husband it was that damn Winnebago. He saw the reality of a dream coming true. With Judy and the Winnebago, Beau could travel state to state, see the world, wander off and get lost which is all he has ever wanted to do; an innate desire, that he could not quash.

I am angry with Beau for wanting to fly away, but I also know that I was the one who had clipped his wings. It's really not my fault. We do this to wild creatures all the time. We see their splendor, they enthrall us, and we find ourselves mesmerized by their untamed spirit. So we capture them, trying to hold onto their beauty. We put them in pens and then with fascination we watch them pace. I see now that Beau stayed with me as long as his spirit could hold out. He put in nine years trying to be happy and change who he was, which is really nothing more than a rambling man. He was bound to leave. My lesson from this is not to fall for another rambler no matter how romantic I think they might be.

The news of Beau and Judy's homecoming has traveled through the phone lines of Grace, West Virginia, zipping from pole to pole and satellite to satellite, in a game called telephone, where some of the information is misconstrued. However, gossip is what keeps this small town lit up. Gossip, in fact, is our theatre - our show and it is usually spectacular at keeping us entertained. Who's to say we're not cultured people. Our gossip is skilled and goes further than talk. We actually spy on one another. You can bet the residents of Grace have driven by the Jaspers' house and have seen Judy's Deluxe Winnebago obscenely sprawling across the driveway like the slut mobile that it is. Quite frankly, this drama has been good for business. It is a week in the year, between two holidays when nobody has any money and I thought I would see no business. Yet my gawkers come through the front door just to see how I'm holding up. Their friend, Curiosity, brings them into The Kitchen House and then leads them to their enemy, Guilt, who persuades them to buy a coffee.

What I've learned about Judy this week is much more than I knew before. I don't know who's talking, but Judy is under somebody's radar and they are spreading the word. No doubt, one of Beau's sisters has figured out how to get the inside scoop. They are relentless and very protective of their baby brother. I knew that Judy is older than Beau by fifteen years, which makes him her little boy toy. What I didn't know was that before Beau, Judy was a trophy herself. Married to a very rich man, twice her age. When he died, less than a year into their marriage from heart complications, his grown children made it their mission that Judy would not get their mother's home or their inheritance. His kids were able to secure the estate and receive most of the funds. However, Judy didn't come away empty handed. She was given a large amount of money, the Winnebago and a request to live out her life somewhere else. Am I to believe that it was destiny that brought her to our campground? I mean why did it have to be a Deluxe Winnebago? If she had been given a tent, I would still have my husband. The universe doesn't always play fair.

It won't be long now until those two vagabonds climb back into their home on wheels and head through the mountains, leaving a mystifying cloud of gossip and confusion behind them. It will be me who is left again to console the children by trying to quiet their anger and wipe away salty tears. I will act like I'm fine in front of everyone during the day and keep my sadness for myself, like a blanket that I wrap myself in at night. I will explain to the kids again that Daddy is a rolling stone. However, I am a boulder that you cannot budge. I am solid and loyal and will be here every morning when they wake and every night I will put them to bed. I think it is important for them to know that not everybody leaves and that we four are a family that is inseparable. We are in this together, a collective bunch of personality and love, and as for Beau, happy trails.

Honestly, what baffles me most is how could Beau leave these kids? I accept that I can be replaced. I know I am not the prettiest woman, greatest lover, or best wife. However, he never complained when we were together. But then again, maybe men don't complain. It's women who are the complainers. Men just move on. My question is, how does one move on and away from their young children? I have guilt if they spend a day at the babysitters. I couldn't possibly walk away and expect someone else to raise my kids. I would miss them too much. Since their birth, they have become my life and that is something I cannot change.

Besides, I like hanging out with my kids. Each of them is unique with a different personality and specific talents.

I love Roman's independent disposition, stubborn streak and soft center. He is a little man-child, beautiful and strong. He looks the most like Beau with golden blond hair and beige skin. Very soon he will be a heartthrob. He's athletic, outdoorsy and artistic. He's also argumentative and headstrong. All these distinct characteristics will eventually serve him well.

Henry is different from his big brother. He's smaller in stature. His blond hair is tinted with natural red highlights. His little nose and cheeks are speckled with freckles. He has a contagious laugh and a quick wit. He's very funny for a boy of seven. Not only can he get a joke, he can tell one. Henry is compassionate and an animal lover. He adores all creatures big and small. If he could own a zoo of pets he would. Since he lives his childhood in a café we try to keep his pets manageable and hidden from the customers. Henry has a border collie and lab mix, named Dr. Seuss that hangs out in our living room or on the front porch. All other pets live in a cage in Henry's room. He has a small aquarium with several fish and a larger tank that's home to a box turtle. He has a hamster cage that twists with tunnels and two dwarf hamsters living inside. As if that's not enough, Henry begs to have a bird.

Sabrina is just a baby, tiny for her age. She walks on her tiptoes, gives wet sloppy kisses, speaks in words that start with "B" ball, book, bye-bye, baby, bottle. She loves music and loves to climb. She's an active toddler, running after her brothers and getting into things. But when she's tired she will mold herself into your body and sleep soundly on your chest.

I watch my children grow, discover, learn and change and I wonder where their talents will take them. I see these three individuals as fascinating beings. Their existence is so much bigger than me. I am the vessel that brought them into being. Now I am blessed with watching them grow into who they're supposed to be. As their mommy, I am part of a gigantic plan and a miraculous design. Now tell me, how does somebody walk away from life's blueprint?

New Year, New Beginning

January 8, 2000 – Dear Diary, it is a New Year and I am living a new kind of life, nestled in a purple house against snow-covered mountains. The Christmas gifts have been put up and the tree is down, its pine needles swept away. The kids are back in school to face the second half of the year. The Kitchen House has officially been open for one month and business is slow. Beau and Judy drove off in their gypsy mobile two days ago after Beau signed dissolution papers, giving me full custody of our kids. As far as support goes, I will get little. He is supposed to send me $300.00 a month, not very much money to raise three kids, but he currently has no employment. He is officially a kept man whether he knows this or not. As far as I'm concerned Judy can keep him.

If you had asked me ten years ago, in June of 1990, the year Beau and I graduated high school, what my life would be like in the year 2000, I would have never said single mom, three kids, living in a coffee house. Six months after high school graduation, New Year's Eve 1991, the very night Roman was conceived, you could not have convinced me that this is how Beau and I would end up, yet here I am and there he goes.

I really wasn't in the mood to do much this New Year's Eve. I just wanted to spend some time relaxing with my kids and Hazel. But Rayland insisted that we bring in the millennium together, and not just us, but with a party.

"Girl with the year that you've had, you need a party," he said. Which I thought was the last thing I needed.

"We need to celebrate your changes. Say goodbye to your old life and leave it behind in the 1999 and welcome in a new life and new millennium."

Rayland went on and on until he finally convinced me that a party was a good idea. I let Rayland and Hazel plan it, since I wasn't in a festive mood. Together, they came up with an assortment of little party platters and tasty dips. Rayland invited a couple of his neighbors to the party and the ladies from his clog dancing class and their families.

Rayland is a dance instructor and he has a dance studio in Charleston, West Virginia, where he lives. Charleston is about a forty-five minute drive through the mountains from Grace. Rayland thought it was a great idea to bring people from the city into The Kitchen House to see my hidden gem. Daddy agreed that it was great idea and he came to my party to hear their comments and offer a hand if I needed it. Charlie came too and brought a date. Rayland insisted that I invite someone to the party. I told him my only friends would already be there, him and Hazel.

"Sissy, although flattered by your comment I'm also saddened. You now own a business; you must think like a businesswoman. You need to be friends with your whole community. Folks need to come to your little café, because it is inviting with fresh brewed coffee and friendship. Girl, you gonna have to be the toast of this town, whether you like it or not. Everybody's gonna have to love you."

I thought about this and Rayland was right. I do need to be everybody's best friend. I just feel too worn out to do it. I'll start small I thought and with people I actually enjoy, so I called Pixie Moon-Dust and Father Timothy McIntire. Rayland laughed at my invites. He said I was the only person he knew that would invite a priest and a psychic to a party.

Although I had not wanted to extend invitations to our New Year's Eve party, I was so happy when both Pixie and the priest arrived. They showed up around the same time. Again, Pixie brought Hazel and I a gift. She is such a sweet and mannerly girl for someone who looks so outrageous. This time she presented us with a glass vase that held an arrangement of bare tree branches. Oddly enough the stark bending sticks looked beautiful, like a winter bouquet. I placed the vase on our coffee table in front of the couch. The basket of pinecones still sits on my vintage counter. I love the look of both gifts. They each hold a raw and

49

visible beauty. I mostly love the fact that they are gifts from the woods, gathered by a pixie and delivered to me.

"She's not a real pixie," Hazel smirked when I expressed this.

"Oh, but I kind of think she is."

Father McIntire had no gift but he extended his hand with the warmest of shakes, his hot skin sent shivers up my spine and when he took off his coat, I nearly gasped.

"Father!" I blurted. "Where is your collar?"

"I'm not wearing my collar," he began to explain. "I feel the need to relax. I do that best without my collar. Plus, I want others to feel at ease in my presence. Collars sometimes make people nervous."

"Oh," I said nervously. "Well, you look nice."

Nice being a complete understatement, the man was beautiful in crisp blue jeans and a gray wool sweater. It's crazy that I have only been attracted to two men in my whole life, Father McIntire, a Catholic Priest and Beau Jaspers, a Hobo. As I meditate on this, I realize that I must desire men that are emotionally unavailable and poor, or rather absent of possessions. Neither Beau nor Father McIntire own a pot to piss in, how sad.

I admit now that the party was good, especially for my boys who have been a sensitive mess since their father's coming and going. Rejection sucks, and of course, they feel rejected. The week prior to New Year's had been a long one full of sensitivity and emotion. On New Year's Eve all of their heightened feelings lay still for the evening as the boys laughed, played and danced the night away. It was so nice just to watch them have fun being little boys, without a concern in the world. The party was also good for business. Rayland was right. Charleston needs to know of my little gem and New Year's Eve was a good start. Every guest that he invited adored The Kitchen House. I made my specialty coffees with their ghostly names for my guests and they were loved. I hope to have impressed the Charleston folks and I hope they return to our coffee house and bring friends.

Rayland and his partner Cody, meaning business partner as well as lover, brought music to the party and a portable little dance floor, a handy little stage. We moved the tables up against the walls and made room for some entertainment. The cloggers from his class were awesome. Rayland is obviously a great dance instructor and loves what he does. It's really amazing how wonderful those ladies dance and their boundless energy is fantastic. Each one of them is of middle age and a bit heavy set with a style of their own, but similar to one another. These ladies come from Lee Press On Nails, Mary Kay make-up and Aqua Net. Some of them not only wear Mary Kay, they sell it. In fact, there was a gorgeous pink Cadillac parked right outside my back door. How's that for success? These gals are funny too, the loudest people in the room, and so quick witted. They have the ability to crack jokes, one after the other, and leave you in stitches; and boy, can they dance. Rayland is just wonderful with them, kind of like a modern day Richard Simmons. You can see the fun his dancers are having, their energy bouncing all over the room. Rayland dances with them. He positions himself out front and center stage, leading the group and making them sparkle. Cody is also an awesome dancer and he did a couple of numbers, but mostly Cody took charge of the music and let Rayland shine: I believe he is just generous, in that sort of way. I loved watching the little show that Rayland and his ladies put on. The happiness that radiated off each dancer was contagious and caused you to tap your feet. The dance number to *1999* by the artist formally known as Prince, was awesome. I suppose they have been perfecting this dance since 1998 and it was flawless. After the chorus "I'm going to party like it's 1999," each clog dancer with bowed head jumps forward then simultaneously they snap their necks up and in a come-hither voice they each breathe out 2000. It was sexy cool and the room exploded in applause. As much as I liked the performance, I also enjoyed watching the spectators watch the show. As those plump, older ladies danced about, their husbands watched them with adoring eyes. You could tell that those old truck drivers or coal miners, with their straight, black boring coffee, love their wives and I felt a tinge of jealousy that I tried to conceal.

After a show of several songs, Rayland invited everyone to dance. He taught dance steps to anyone interested and the music kept playing. Hazel tried some dance steps. Rayland took her through a few moves, but she easily winded and decided to sit down and just watch. Roman and Henry did some clogging. I think Henry may be a natural. Those little feet can stomp to a rhythm. Roman is good also, but I see him as more of a hip-hop or breakdancing kind of guy. I wish I had the money and time to put the boys in a dance class. But it is time and money that are my antagonists and they keep me away from so many things I truly want.

As for me, I did not dance, I watched. I watched Charlie and his date dance slowly with their bodies pressed tightly together even though the songs were quick and upbeat. I watched Sabrina run around on her tiptoes, imitating dance steps while she pulled her dress up over her head. Pixie Moon-Dust was another one that danced to her own rhythm. Pixie kind of just swayed around the room in a Stevie Nicks style, looking a little high, her blue hair whipping back and forth to the beat of her own heart. My daddy danced some, he's always good for a party, but mostly he mingled and I think he made a few contacts for some new work. Then I noticed sitting in the opposite corner, alone, just like me was Father McIntire, he too was watching. His foot tapped absently under the table and he seemed to be studying his surroundings. I decided I should sit with him. If there are two lonely people at a party, it just makes sense that they should sit together. I told Father McIntire that I could tell he wanted to dance by his foot tapping. He just smiled at me and said he liked watching people have fun. He also said I could call him Tim. I continued to call him Father McIntire.

While music played and folks danced, ate, talked and laughed, the door opened and in stepped a lady about my age. I could tell she was bewildered the minute she entered. She looked a little dazed and confused as she glanced around. My first thought was, she must be one of Rayland's friends arriving late. She was wearing black frame glasses that she pushed up her thin nose as she scanned the room. A large designer handbag hung heavily on her shoulder. She set the bag on the floor, tucked her brown bob haircut behind her ears and continued to look about in puzzlement, not recognizing anyone. That's when I realized this classic looking stranger was clearly lost. So, I approached her and asked if I could help.

"Yes, do you have a room for the night?" she asked tucking, her already tucked, brown hair behind her ears again, obviously a nervous habit.

"I'm not a hotel," I informed her.

"Oh, you're not? How embarrassing," she said in a deflated voice. "I thought that you must be a Bed and Breakfast and I'm so tired, much too tired to drive any further through these winding roads. I was praying for a hotel when your place came into view and I assumed my prayers were answered."

"I'm sorry, but Charleston is just about forty-five more minutes down the road and they have plenty of hotels."

"Ok," came her flattened response. She then put her hands over her face and began to sob. I really was unsure how to respond to this suffering woman. Her tears were unsettling and caused my energy to rev up to the emotion of worry. I hate worry. It is a horrid emotion that sits in your stomach as an unmoving boulder while your blood races quickly around it.

"Come sit," I said as I led her to a table. "Actually, my place is a coffee house," I tried to explain. "I'm sorry it confused you, let me get you something to drink."

The lady took off her glasses, wiped her crying eyes and quickly composed herself.

"Just water," she said. "And can I use your bathroom before I leave?" I showed her the bathroom and then went over to my daddy for some advice.

"She'll make it to Charleston," he said. "Don't worry." But when she came out of the bathroom twenty minutes later with a swollen red nose from crying, he looked at me and mouthed, "Let her stay." As the woman pulled on her long white coat and headed towards the door I stopped her.

"Hey, I'm Sissy," I said properly introducing myself. "Welcome to The Kitchen House. Tonight we are having a New Year's Eve party and you are more than welcome to stay."

"Oh no. I couldn't do that," she said as she grabbed the door handle and headed back out into the wind. "Thanks but no." I followed her out onto the porch.

"I'm sorry... but, honestly, I'm just not comfortable allowing you to leave. I don't mean to be nosy, but you can't possibly drive through these mountains crying at night, on icy roads with blustery winds. Gladden seems a little angry tonight."

"Gladden?"

"Oh that's just what I call the wind," I said shooing away my remark. I had managed to spook the lady even more by naming the wind.

"Just please come back in, it's freezing out here." She allowed me to lead her back inside. "This is not a Bed and Breakfast," I told her. "And it won't be fancy, but it will be a free nights stay. We can put up an air mattress for you in the kitchen and in the morning, after you try my coffee, you can head into Charleston." I don't believe the woman knew how to respond. She must have felt unsure and overwhelmed and you could see that she was so tired. Fatigue slumped her shoulders forward and she barely held up her head. I sat her next to Father Tim McIntire.

"Let me get you a snack," I said heading towards a party platter.

"My name is Lenore," she said tucking her hair once again.

"Nice to meet you Lenore," I responded handing her some cheese and crackers.

Lenore sat with Father McIntire nibbling on crackers and sipping her water. She was silent at first and Father McIntire did the talking. I'm sure he was just conversing to calm her fears. After building up a bit of strength and energy from a wedge of cheese, it was Lenore who talked and Father McIntire who listened. I heard bits of their conversation as I checked on my kids, informed Hazel of our houseguest and mingled with people. I heard Lenore tell him the story of her horrid journey through this damn Appalachian state. How many times that day she felt she might die, sliding around mountain curves and getting lost on a holler road. Holler roads do not make good detours as this lady found out. In fact, you end up driving down and around into places too obscure to be placed on a map. Lenore finally pulled into a driveway to turn around and was greeted by about 10 barking dogs that surrounded her car and a one-legged man who hopped out of his trailer with a shotgun pointed at her windshield. Lenore frantically trying to back up could barely move her car because of the dogs, which the one-legged man shooed away and then gave Lenore garbled directions that she could not understand. Lenore eventually made it out of the holler and back onto the main stretch of highway, but thought for sure she was going to die on these dark, icy mountain roads. She felt lost, scared, out of control, near panicky. She began praying for a place to stay.

"Dear God anywhere, just give me safe shelter now." As soon as she had finished that sentence of prayer, she slid around the bend and our little town and my purple house stood in her view. The Kitchen House sign was swinging hard against the winter wind. There were cars in its parking lot and she believed that God had placed this purple Bed and Breakfast right in her midst. The thing I found amusing was that Lenore did not realize she was giving her confession to a priest. Father McIntire assured her that God had surely answered her prayers.

Around 11:00pm or so, the music was turned off and the television was turned on. Folks had decided it wouldn't be New Year's without watching Dick Clark and the ball drop on Times Square. Hazel and Rayland refilled each and every party platter. My round tables were full of guests. A couple card games began at some of the tables. People were having fun and as I scanned the room I noticed that Hazel was doing the same thing. We caught each other's eye and we both could not help but smile big.

Sabrina was finally worn out, although the boys were still going strong. I held my baby to my chest and swayed her back and forth as I watched guests enjoying themselves. Pixie was involved in a game of cards with some of the husbands, and as she shuffled the deck, I heard her give a big, burly guy some spiritual news.

"Your sister whose name begins with an L has crossed over into the light, she wants you to know that she is ok, and that she loves you." The big man was visibly shaken.

"Thank you. Thank you so much," he said with tear rimmed eyes. Later his wife told me that his sister Lynette died two months ago from cancer. Well I'll be damned and I had thought Pixie Moon-Dust was a fake.

At midnight the strangest thing happened. We were all excitedly counting down the minutes with Dick Clark when directly after the stroke of midnight the lights went out. For several seconds we all stood in complete darkness, everyone too shocked to speak. The eerie silence was broken when Pixie shouted out.

"Happy New Year Kitchen Family!" With that the lights popped back on.

My home erupted in laughter and gasps, each of us full of an excitement that was tinged with disbelief. Sabrina woke from my chest and looked around and the boys began to chant.

"We got ghosts! We got ghosts!" Hazel and I both looked at each other and giggled.

Soon after midnight, people began leaving and they did so with a story of how awesome tonight was. I thought of suggesting to Lenore that she follow Rayland into town and he could help her locate a hotel, but then I thought against it. The girl looked so emotionally drained that it's probably best she just start fresh tomorrow. My daddy inflated the air mattress and placed it where Rayland's stage had sat moments before. I looked at Lenore in her soft, black, cashmere turtleneck and stiff dark jeans and doubted she had ever slept on an air mattress before. I handed the kids off to Hazel and she was putting them to bed while I retrieved blankets and a pillow for Lenore. As Lenore settled down for the night she asked,

"Is this house really haunted?"

"It is," I responded. "But, no worries they're friendly ghosts." I then opened the door that led into my living room. "Good night," I said and as I locked the door from the other side I could hear Lenore once again begin to cry.

When I awoke on New Year's Day I thought I would find our houseguest up and eager to be gone from The Kitchen House. How surprised I was to see that Lenore was still unconscious, sprawled across the air mattress in a dead sleep. She slept sound till after ten o'clock. Not even the noise of children that fills a house on a subtle morning caused her to stir.

"That girl must be plumb worn out," Hazel said as she stood over the inflatable bed with her hands on her hips. When Lenore finally did wake up it was as if she was coming out of a coma. Her confusion spilled forth and flooded my home, her darting eyes swam in search of something recognizable to grasp. I watched a torrent of remembrance rush across her transparent face, recollection like a life boat leading her into the shallows of comprehension until she dredged up the memory of, yes I did sleep on the floor of a haunted coffee house last night. I fixed Lenore coffee and biscuits and Hazel scrambled her a couple of eggs.

"Where are you heading?" I casually asked Lenore as she sat humbled and embarrassed eating her breakfast.

"Where am I?" she asked, surprising me with her response. How can a person not know where they are?

"Grace West Virginia," I told her. She seemed amused by the name.

"Really, the name of this town is Grace?"

"It is."

"Well, truthfully I don't have anywhere in particular I was heading to, just kind of looking for a new place, you know, to start fresh."

"Like a do over?" I asked.

"Exactly, like a do over."

"Well, I'll be honest with you, there are no jobs in Grace, West Virginia. There are a few rental homes though. In fact, my dad and brother have a couple properties if you're interested."

"Could you call them?"

It was a Tea, "to a T"

January 12, 2000 - Dear Diary, Lenore is settled into the yellow house that sits next to the train tracks, another one of Daddy's treasured gems. The house is very small with a large deep yard and although the trains can be loud and offensive at times the home is tranquil, the color of sunshine, with peaceful little window boxes and a still front porch. Lenore comes into the coffee house daily, drinks Hazel's House Blend and gets on our computer desperately searching for work. She told me she has her own laptop, but has not been successful getting on the internet. Truth is the internet is so sketchy in these mountains. It's a wonder that I stay connected, must be the help of my ghosts.

Lenore is not our only regular. We have a couple. But it has grown so cold outside that mostly folks just stay home. It is the ones that have to be out that like to swing into The Kitchen House. Jean, the school bus driver, comes twice every day. She has even switched up her route and now begins each day at my house. She grabs a black coffee, an apple walnut biscuit and my two boys. In the afternoon, she ends her route here as well, but usually just comes in to use the bathroom. The boys hate that they now have the longest school bus ride. They think it is ridiculous since my house is really closer to the school than so many of the other kids. Since Jean starts her morning with our House Blend the boys end up riding up and over hills, picking up kids, for over an hour before they reach their destination, which is just three miles down the road from their home. They want me to start driving them. Jean says they're fine and that most often the boys fall asleep on the way to school and get a little catnap.

I told the boys they need to stop all their whining. It only makes sense that Jean gets them first as she gets her coffee and biscuits, she is our first real regular and we depend on her.

Joe, the mailman, is another one that is out and about and comes in every day, whether I have mail or not. He also uses our bathroom as his rest stop; which makes no sense since the post office is right next door. I'm sure they have a toilet for their employees. I think Joe just likes our bathroom better; maybe it's the reading material. Anyways he always buys a cookie. Hazel has been making cookies. She fixes up a batch of peanut butter or chocolate chip every couple of days. She puts the cookies on a cake platter and covers them with a glass lid. The ones that are not eaten up by my children sell for a dollar a piece.

Besides Jean and Joe there are about three to five factory guys that come in most mornings. They are all just coming off third shift and stop at The Kitchen House to wind down. They sit at a round table drinking black coffee, eating biscuits and just talking before heading home. They are usually here a couple of hours and fill the house with needed noise. After they leave it's quiet here until Joe swings in with a piece of mail or Jean drops the kids off. I spend the rest of my afternoon playing on the floor with Sabrina. I am so worried about money that my mood is often down. I know Hazel feels my stress and tries to be my anchor.

"Stop all that worrying, Sissy. It's not good for your health. You don't need to think about money all the time. I promise you I have enough money that we can float awhile until this business takes shape."

I don't want to float on Hazel's money. How could I possibly face myself in the mirror every day knowing that I was living off the pension of Hazel's dead husband and her social security? I believe that would be ten times worse than just collecting welfare and I can't do that either. Although I'm sure I would qualify. Somehow I have to figure out how to make a café a profitable business in an Appalachian town where most folks would rather stay home and drink their own damn coffee. Maybe a business in Grace, West Virginia is the craziest idea ever. I'm sure it is, since it bloomed out of the head of Skip Cooper, a man who kind of figures anything is possible and doesn't bother himself with worry. Talking to my daddy about money problems is like talking to a wall.

"It will work out Sissy," is all he ever says. "You'll make it happen."

I suppose I should appreciate the fact that he believes in me, but instead I'm too worried about disappointing him. I can't talk to Hazel about money either, not without her opening up her purse strings and throwing more pity my way. So, I have been complaining to Rayland.

I feel terrible venting to Rayland. He is such a sweet and sensitive man with the gift (or maybe curse) of taking another's misery and feeling it way down into his own soul. Rayland is an empathetic man. If I were to tell him I was having a bad period he would double over with cramps. Seriously, Rayland cannot watch someone cry without producing his own set of tears. He hurts when you hurt and it is real. I should not bother him with my problems. Besides, Rayland has more stress than I do. To be honest, Rayland's life is more stressful than anyone I know. He is also trying to keep a business alive. I believe his financial situation is much better than mine simply because he is established. However, his home life is somewhat horrendous, and unpredictable. Rayland has been given the role of caretaker much too early. His Mama, Lucinda, has grown old far too soon. Lucinda is a woman I have known my whole life and have loved from the beginning.

Not long ago Lucinda was the picture of style. She has always been trendy for a mountain woman with a collection of magazines that could inspire an ape. Lucinda didn't just have a Sears and Roebuck Catalog delivered to her home, she also received Cosmopolitan, Vogue, People, Better Homes and Gardens, Southern Living and Star. One of Rayland's and my favorite pastimes was to lie on Lucinda's thick shag carpet and flip through her stockpile of magazines. Sometimes Lucinda would let Rayland and I cut up a magazine and we would glue our favorite photos and words in a hodgepodge of overlap onto thick construction paper and call it a personality collage. Lucinda stayed abreast with all the new looks, styles, dramas, fashions, and trends. Her mountain home had the feel of Green Acres with French provincial furniture and heavy, crushed red velvet curtains that hung royally in her small country windows.

Lucinda was the only woman I had never seen without makeup. She woke every morning and had her hair, face and skin glowing with perfection before most of us had even taken the time to wipe the crust off our eyes. I saw Lucinda as the representation of the perfect lady, a living Barbie doll that awed me. Lucinda always wore heels on her tiny, narrow feet. Her fingernails were always manicured and painted red. Her eyebrows stayed plucked into a thin line sketched faintly across her forehead. Her bleached hair held wings and a style that could summon envy from the Mandrell Sisters. Lucinda loved tight clothes that hugged her slim figure and she is the first lady I've known to buy herself a pair of tits. Fact is, in buying tits Lucinda committed a mortal sin that is still talked about today.

West Virginians work hard for their money and quite frankly there is a shortage of it. Men risk their lives and blacken their lungs daily in this state just to put food on their table. Farmers and factory workers have long ago abandoned the idea of sleep and live on prayers. So for Lucinda to secretly stash away hard earned cash and then spend it on tits was a selfish sin of immense caliber. Talk of that sin floated down from the mountains and into the hollers for years. Lucinda's tits stirred the emotions of Appalachia creating lust in men and boys, rage and envy in the women and admiration in the hearts of the girls. Any little girl would have loved to have Lucinda as a mother.

Lucinda did not mother girls - instead she had sons. Rhett and Rodrick, Rayland's two older brothers, are macho, aggressive, rugged and selfish; qualities possessed by many males. So, when Rayland was born with delicate features and more estrogen than a boy should have, Lucinda embraced his feminine side. She gladly let him be himself and if a dance class is what Rayland desired then a dance class is what he received. Although Lucinda desperately loved Rayland, his childhood was difficult. It's not easy growing up gay in a redneck town. In fact, I'm sure it's equivalent to one of the nine levels of hell. Rayland survived his childhood. He escaped the sneers and punches thrown at him by the homophobic that live up and down this mountain range and created a life that has been interrupted by the burden of disease and the stress of caretaking.

As for now, Lucinda is the prisoner of a chaotic mind. At sixty-three years young, she has been stricken with early onset Alzheimer's Disease. Her beauty is still very much present, but it is like viewing it through a smoke screen. It is an unfaltering attractiveness that stares back through the haze that covers her eyes. Rayland and Cody have become Lucinda's full-time caretakers. Rayland's father died five years ago. It is Rayland and Cody who decipher Lucinda's word salad and try to make sense of her thoughts. They make sure she is properly dressed in the morning and that her bra is worn under her clothes and not neatly fastened on top of her sweater. They help her with her cosmetics. Makeup has been

Lucinda's morning ritual since she was a pre-teen. Less than a year ago, before Rayland and Cody intervened with Lucinda's care, she would walk lost around our small town, looking like a clown with lipstick on her eyelids and blue shadow on her cheeks. Now Rayland and Cody even cart her off to work with them to sit among the dance moms at the studio. I know that this is most trying, because Lucinda can be stubborn, confused and unpredictable. Her personality has changed so with the Alzheimer's. Lucinda has lost her inhibitions and tactfulness. She has been known to swear like a sailor in a pre-ballerina class, unnerving the mothers of three year olds. Several times she has taken off her shirt in the middle of the studio and she wanders off. Rayland and Cody approach each situation with humor and laugh through their tears. Rhett and Rodrick help by taking turns with Lucinda on holidays and some weekends. They do not know how to deal with their confused mother in her dementia state, so their help is limited.

How inconsiderate of me to mention money problems to Rayland when he's busy trying to quiet the frantic mind of his beloved mother. Yet, Rayland seemed happy to talk to me about business figures. He loves the creativity and passion it takes to birth a dream.

"I have some ideas Sissy," he said. "Let's have a true heart to heart, tomorrow around noon. Dance classes don't begin until after 4:00pm that day so I'm free to create. I will bring Lucinda and we can have a real life tea party for her. Oh, she would just love to wear a big ugly hat and sip tea in your haunted home."

"A tea party?" I asked.

"Yes, a tea party. Sissy, are you a girl or not? Now do it up pretty for Lucinda. Maybe Sabrina would like to invite a couple of her teddy bears. Wouldn't that be cute?"

"I suppose." I could tell Rayland was getting frustrated with me.

"Well, don't sound so enthused," he said. "Listen girl, you create a tea party and I'll bring you business ideas. Don't you see I'm already giving you one?"

"A tea party," I slowly said again before hanging up. I immediately went to Hazel and asked for her ideas for a tea party. Hazel delighted in the idea of hosting a tea party for an Alzheimer's lady and her gay son. It sounded completely lovely to Hazel and she began making little tea cookies that night. Her little lemon cookies were baked to crispness and then generously sprinkled with powdered sugar, tasting a little bit like sunshine on a snowy day. The next morning Hazel and I made tiny sandwiches. We had egg salad, tuna salad, cucumber dill, grilled cheese and peanut butter with honey. We cut our sandwiches into triangles, squares, ovals and stars and arranged them on a silver platter. They were precious. Hazel also made a nice, thick tomato soup that clung to your spoon and slid down your throat like velvet; and we had a basket of warm biscuits served with marmalade and jam. We set the table with items from a box of old china that Charlie had purchased at an auction for $25.00 a couple months ago. I had already taken the four flowered teapots out of the box and they sat behind my vintage counter in a decorative fashion, never thinking I would put them to use. The rest of the box was filled with teacups, small plates, saucers, as well as goofy stuff like gravy boats and candy dishes. It was really just a collection of ornaments. On our table sat a white teacup with pink flowers and a pink teacup with blue flowers and so on. The saucers underneath also alternated in colors and patterns. No two items matched. The only correlation the tea pieces shared was charm. On two of the chairs I sat teddy bears. The effect was most delightful and everything was perfect tea party motif including the large ugly hat that sat upon Lucinda's small head and the red smear of lipstick that circled her mouth. The six of us, Hazel, Sabrina, Rayland, Cody, Lucinda and I stuffed our mouths for over an hour with delicate pieces of food. As we ate, Rayland spoke of his business idea with enough expression and excitement to make me believe it just might work.

He suggested that his clogging class begin performing at The Kitchen House every Saturday night. He knows his ladies will love the idea of getting a chance to perform weekly. He will bring his portable stage and his dancers will clog from 7:00 to 9:00 with small breaks in-between. The entertainment will be free. Both Rayland and Cody agree that it will bring housebound people out into the coffee shop. This winter has been so long and getting out to watch some free entertainment may be the distraction that everyone needs.

When we had finished the dainty yet satisfying meal and I had begun to clear the table, Lucinda spoke out in a loud and suggestive tone.

"Let's all smoke," she said.

Since we were the only ones in the restaurant I didn't mind obliging Lucinda's request. So, we smoked, everyone that is except Hazel and

Sabrina. As Hazel and Sabrina departed to take a nap, the rest of us began puffing away on long, thin, white cigarettes that Lucinda had nestled in her bra. Although I've never been a smoker, I wasn't too bothered by the stale, light taste of the skinny cigarette. It was like smoking an old cloud and it fit nicely into our game of tea party play. Lucinda sucked on her cigarette in the most sensual way, as if she were making love to it. The look on Rayland's face held a tinge of embarrassment as his mother moaned and puffed beside him.

"I usually don't allow her to actually smoke," he said. "I mean she always has a pack of cigarettes in her bra, but we don't actually light them and there are no matches or lighters in our home, God forbid! We just let her pretend to smoke, but even that sometimes gets so obscene."

I personally found Lucinda's smoking to be great and maybe even inspiring. I guess I viewed it as hopeful. What I mean is that, the aging process is such a dreadful thing. I see it as the cruelest stage of living and in Lucinda's case it came on far too early. The idea of slowly losing one's mind, independence, dignity and identity scares the shit out of me. Seeing Lucinda diminish from a radiant beauty into a helpless woman is torturous. Watching her smoke with such profound gratification softens the blow. It's proof that pleasure can be found until the end.

As the four of us sat kicked back, puffing away, a large smoky cloud hovering around our table, Father McIntire walked in. I was the only one to jump to my feet and stamp out my cigarette, the three others stayed relaxed and in character as I switched gears and stumbled across my words.

"Father McIntire, what brings you in today?" Father McIntire surveyed the scene, and a smile broke across his face.

"We're having a tea party for Lucinda," I tried to explain.

"It looks lovely Sissy, what a great idea. I just came in to buy a basket of your warm buttermilk biscuits to take to Esther Connell. She's been under the weather lately and I was going to check in on her."

"Oh that's so nice. Let me get you a basket ready. Will you want some honey too? I could put some in a little jar for you."

"Great idea, honey too."

I warmed up the biscuits as Father McIntire talked with Rayland, Cody and Lucinda. This priest never fails to surprise me. He has such an easy way with others, and I believe he is truly non-judging, a modern day Jesus.

I listened to him laugh with Rayland and Cody, the only two openly gay men in these parts and maybe even flirt a bit with Lucinda as she puffed on her long cigarette and blew the smoke in his face. The entire scene was surreal. I gave Father McIntire his biscuits wrapping them in a towel to keep them warm before putting them in a sack with a jar of honey. He paid for the biscuits and honey, stuck a dollar in our tip jar and was then off to run his errand of goodwill and kindness.

Rayland took Lucinda to the restroom before heading home. It was then that Cody commented on how lovely the tea party actually was. He thought the entire setup was delightful and charming and he suggested that I have tea party reservations for anyone who would be interested. He seems to think that I could host a birthday tea party for little girls or a garden tea party when it gets warmer outside or simply a tea for two. He thinks it's an idea that would take off. He was super excited when he spoke and he told me that he would think up a clever way we could advertise our tea parties. I love the way both Rayland and Cody's ideas and visions rain down like confetti. They are the most inspiring men. As the two wrestled with Lucinda putting her coat on, she turned to me.

"Thank you dear, you have a lovely whore house."

"Thank you Lucinda," I giggled.

"Mother, this is not a whore house," Rayland corrected. "You're in a charming haunted café."

"Are you sure?" she said as they led her to the car.

65

Mountain Mama

January 25, 2000 - Dear Diary, on Sunday I woke to a day that was bright and crisp. The sun rose through my bedroom window in an orange light and I tried to let its happy glow fill me up, wanting desperately to absorb every bit of winter rays that this day was gifting. The night before had been a success. The temperature was mild for a January evening and folks actually came out of their homes and into the coffee house to watch Rayland and his cloggers and just hang out with each other. People laughed, danced, talked, drank coffee and tea and ate a bit. Hazel had made several apple pies and we actually sold out of them. At $2.50 a slice we did pretty good. Most everybody who came were related to the cloggers, but there were a few locals, and I've lived in Grace long enough to know that as the word spreads more will come, many more. The dancing and music filled my home in a happy kind of way. It caused you to tap your feet and involuntarily smile. It was a feeling of good that entered your dancing toes and traveled through the body until you were snapping your fingers and shaking your head. By the end of the night, I felt a delirious kind of happiness. When I put my boys to bed, long after their bedtime I promised them, like a drunk mommy that is full of kisses and hugs, that in the morning we would have a special day, just the three of us. Sunday's forecast was sunny and cold, but not so cold that I could not make our special day happen.

I have been taking the boys to church mass at eleven. Hazel does not go. She says her church is a morning of quiet and solitude. Instead, she stays home and keeps Sabrina, who I don't think gives her much quiet or solitude, but she says she's happy to do it. This particular Sunday, I told Hazel that the boys and I would not be home directly after church for our usual soup and sandwiches. Instead, we were going to take a winter hike through the pine forest that stretches up the hills behind the church. I made sure to pack extra clothes to keep us warm, thermal underwear to go under our jeans and sweaters, thick socks, insulated boots, hats, gloves and our warmest coats. We added our layers of clothes and insulation in the bathroom after mass and walked out five pounds heavier than when we went in. I retrieved a backpack from the car that I flung on my shoulders and off we headed on foot into the lush pines. I had filled the pack with water and snacks, food to be scattered for cold, hungry deer and rabbits and food that we would eat on our hike. I also had my camera. I was excited to get some winter pictures of the boys. Nearly every photo I have of my children has been taken while living in Florida. The boys were so excited to take a winter hike. As simple as that sounds, we have neglected this activity all winter. Both of my boys love nature, hikes and exploring the outdoors. Although Roman can spend an obscene amount of time in front of the television passionately playing games, I can tell that the forest and mountains fill him with a glory that only nature can produce; towering trees, the smell of fresh pine and the way the needles blanket the ground on winter days in bits of gold.

Roman likes nature in its hugeness and peril. He likes jagged rocks and cliffs that fall straight to the bottom. He likes rushing streams that churn and splash and carry off leaf boats and fallen branches. He likes waterfalls that cascade in a rush of force and power and explode when they hit bottom creating a rainbow of mist and showers. Roman likes caves, deep, dark and mysterious and crevices in the side of the earth where he tries to squeeze his small body, only to shout, "Take my picture." Every giant tree that Roman passes, he envisions as a tree fort. Roman likes the trees with massive trunks and thick twisting branches that reach out like crooked arms. He likes the trees that humble you and can hold your weight and the weight of a fort built from thick plywood. Roman likes the risks that come with a hike. He likes the twists, turns and bumps in the road and during the times your hike should be taken with cautious steps, Roman likes to run.

Henry is different, his love for nature is much more intricate and subtle. It is not just the immense and obvious, such as whitecaps and waterfalls that he finds beautiful. Henry is pulled to the elusive. As Roman keeps watch on the hawk that circles and swoops above us, Henry notices the tiny field mouse that is to be his prey. Henry is a lover of creatures. They must all know of this love and speak out to him in voices that only he can hear, because Henry is aware of their presence when the rest of us are totally oblivious. Henry instinctively knows which rocks the snake curls under. He can spot silent owls, obscured and hidden waiting for moonlight. He often stops to check out a spider web and the spider living in it. Henry is in awe over the silky strings that stretch from branch to branch, spun silver, woven in a delicate pattern of lace and beauty and then Roman will poke the web with a stick and Henry will cry. His tears usually last for a minute and I believe he is given comfort by the whisper of a spider that assures him she will just spin another beautiful, delicate web to rest upon.

The boys get their love for nature honestly. Both Beau and I love the outdoors, hence living out our marriage in a campground. I personally find the woods and mountains to be a place of comfort and my home. I am a mountain girl and these woods are where I played as a child. Charlie and I spent endless days getting lost among the trees and streams, games of hide and seek and tag as we followed the squirrels from limb to limb. In these woods I have witnessed both death and life. I have seen the vulnerable and meek rabbits and chipmunks be squeezed to death by the impressive hawk and I have watched baby birds miraculously poke and push themselves out of tinged blue shells cradled in a nest. It is in the stillness among the trees that I feel most alive. After months of living out long days in a coffee house, I needed the awakening that the woods provide. A trek among the trees is by far my favorite pastime and a winter hike is most invigorating. The snow is just one more layer of astonishing beauty in a place of wonderment.

The boys loved the blanket of snow beneath our feet and they made sure to touch the crystals as much as possible, knocking drifts off tree branches and scooping up fistfuls to throw or eat. We looked for footprints in the snow and tried to name the animals. Henry was most gifted at this game.

"Hey look, raccoon tracks!" he would often shout out.

We ate our sandwiches as we walked. We scattered sunflower seeds and nuts near the base of trees for the birds. I had brought apples and a knife. I would cut a slice and give it to the boys. They ate what they wanted and then stuck the rest of the slice on the pointy end of tree branches to share with the deer. We saw many deer in clusters of three and once a lone buck standing strong and silent among the bare branches and snow. After one of us spotted a deer, we would alert the others in a whispered hush. Crunching down to make ourselves smaller, we would become three silent voyeurs awestruck with the magnificence of the creature before us. The deer would stare us down, large brown eyes searching into our souls, cautious and frightened unsure of our intentions. "Please don't shoot," their eyes begged. These were hunted deer, fearful of man and rightly so. Venison is a staple in an Appalachian household. The deer would engage us for several minutes in silent communication and for a short moment in time we would be connected. Once they had their fill, they would swiftly run off, jumping over snowdrifts and fallen logs with grace and ease. Then the boys and I would break our silence in an exhilaration of whoops and cheers that traveled on the wind and filled our massive space. We three are fans of these mountains and they fill us up with grandeur. As we headed back down, crunching through the snow towards the church, Henry veered off our path.

"Hey what's over here?" he shouted, springing over logs and snow like a deer. Roman followed in hot pursuit. I tried to run after them, but the cold wind filled my lungs and the snow kept my feet grounded. They were way ahead of me, and I was left behind hopelessly praying they were not running towards danger. When I reached the boys, I found them standing in a small clearing between the forest pines and in front of an impressive and spellbinding man-made shelter. Someone had primitively and expertly constructed a magnificent gazebo. There were no sides to this structure, just four massive bare tree trunks attached onto a square of wooden floor planks and a roof made of branches with shagbark for shingles. Under the roof stood a crudely built desk crafted from a walnut tree. The trunk of the tree had been sawed in half creating a smooth surface desktop that had been varnished to a shine. The desktop rested upon four massive walnut branches at each corner. The top had been bolted onto its four strong legs and stood sturdy. Beside the desk sat a chair, fashioned from the trunk of an ash tree. It was really just a tall stump with a high back. On the stump sat a round, dark blue pillow, comfort on top of raw beauty.

The boys were under the gazebo and all over the desk oohing and ahhing at the contents that sat on the tabletop. The person that created this structure was a gifted woodworker, carving bits of splendor from fallen trees. Most of the carvings were of animals. There were figures of deer, rabbit, fox and bear, the creatures that inhabit this mountain and live off its soul. As I was admiring the craftsmanship of each little figurine, I noticed the stunning crucifix resting to my left and I knew. It was the same beautiful crucifix that hung in my kitchen above the door to my living room. This gazebo was the sanctuary of Father McIntire and we were trespassers.

"Come on boys, we should go," I said trying to unglue their impressed minds from the artifacts and surroundings that lay before them. It was all just too captivating and I had a hard time getting their attention.

"Hey," I said. "This is someone's secret hideout and it's very cool. But it's like walking into someone's home not invited. It is rude of us to stay here."

"But Mom," argued Roman, who always argues. "This guy don't own this mountain, we can be here too."

"Roman, what if you had a secret fort and someone found it and went inside and snooped all around. Would you like that?" Roman thought for a minute, wanting to argue back, but instead he envisioned one of his own fantasy tree houses.

"Let's go Henry," said Roman. All three of us were reluctant when leaving the gazebo, we had found glory and she was restricted from us. We walked silently away carrying deep inside the wonder we had discovered mixed with a streak of disappointment.

As we came out of the clearing and back onto the path we ran right into Father McIntire.

"Well, hello gang," Father McIntire said. "Good day for a hike."

"Hi Father Tim," the boys sang out confused to see him tromping through the woods in a pair of old heavy boots.

"What are you doing out here?" they asked in unison. The boys had begun to call Father McIntire, Father Tim, because that is what all the children at the parish called him, as well as most of the adults, and half of the community. After all, the man's name is Timothy McIntire. He had told me his full name and asked me to call him Father Tim at the Grand

Opening, but because of my involuntary and inappropriate crush on him I feel the need to keep it more formal.

"Well," the priest responded coolly to my boys. "I was thinking about making a snowman, but I'm not very good at it, would you mind helping me?"

"Yeah! We're great snowman builders," Roman informed the priest.

"I have no doubt," responded Father McIntire.

"First you gotta roll out three balls of snow," my sons explained to the humble priest who smiled down on them. The boys had become snow experts this year, having lived out most of their lives under the Florida sun, the snow was a glorious thing and they had been discovering it in all its magical wonder. They flew to the windows each morning to greet the snow. It was a dazzling blanket of white drifts that sparkled like diamonds against the ray of the sun, snow that was so light and bright it caused your eyes to blink and tear. The blinding crystals of perfected ice had captured the hearts of my children. My boys had fallen in love with winter and they could not feel its cold, only its glory.

The boys and priest had been working hard when I decided to join them. They had already rolled out a ball of snow nearly as big as Henry.

"This snowman is going to be ginormous," said Roman.

Father McIntire began rolling out the middle ball as I went in search of branches to be used as arms. The second ball of snow turned out to be almost as large as the first and it took all four of us to lift it up onto the large bottom ball. We lost some of it as its weight crushed against us, but we were able do some patch work around the middle on all four sides and the body of our snowman was turning out to be mighty tall and fat. Roman made a large round head that we placed on top and I handed a branch to each boy. They gleefully inserted the arms into the sides of the snowman. Conversation began about our snowman's features. Henry found a pinecone that soon became a fine nose. My backpack still held a Tupperware container of grapes, which we used to make eyes, a mouth and buttons. Father McIntire took off his scarf and wrapped it around the snowman's neck. The boys climbed under a pine and brought me fistfuls of tiny branches of pine needles, which I delicately poked into the top of our snowman's head, creating the most horrendous hairstyle.

"I like it!" shouted Henry.

"So do I," said Father McIntire as he stepped back to admire our work.

"Thank you so much boys. I couldn't have made this guy without you."

"What ya gonna name him?" Henry asked.

"Well, that's a good question, haven't thought that far ahead. Do you boys have any suggestions?"

"Our mom named the wind Gladden," said Roman thoughtfully. "It's a good name."

"You named the wind?" The priest smiled and turned to me.

"I did," I shyly admitted. Just then, as if on cue, a gentle breeze kicked up blowing snow off branches and lightly smacking our faces causing us all to giggle nervously.

"Gladden the wind," the priest shouted out to the breeze. "I would like you to meet Gladden the snowman."

"Yeah Gladden!" the boys cheered. Roman took a stick and etched the letters G-L-A-D-D-E-N in front of the snowman. I took a few photos of the boys making goofy poses in front of their new snow friend. I made the priest get in one photo and like a good sport he made a silly face. Then during that moment when silence falls abruptly into a space that was just active, I spoke.

"We should go now boys, I'm cold." Without argument, proof that they too had grown cold, they started to head down the mountain.

"Goodbye Father Tim. Goodbye Gladden."

"Goodbye boys."

I opened my mouth to bid farewell to our friendly priest and instead surprised myself by extending an invitation.

"Do you want to come with us? I'm sure that Hazel has a pot of hot cocoa simmering on the stove as we speak and the whipped cream at The Kitchen House is Hazel made and ten times better than Cool Whip."

"A cup of hot chocolate does sound good," said Father McIntire and I could tell that he was completely sincere.

"You can just ride over with us and I will drive you back when you're ready to leave."

"I don't want to put you to any trouble."

"Are you kidding," I joked. "This may be my easiest task of the day."

I was slightly embarrassed when I had to remove the trash from the front seat so Father McIntire could sit down, but my embarrassment rose to full fledge when I turned the ignition and *AC/DC, She shook me all night long* came booming from my speakers.

"Music wakes me up," I explained as I quickly switched the knob to off.

"Well, I do like the congregation to be wide awake," he smartly responded. Just when I thought the rest of the ride would be smooth sailing, the boys began to speak.

"Guess what Father McIntire," Henry said. "Our house has ghosts."

"I heard."

"Do you believe in ghosts?" Roman asked. Before Father McIntire could answer Henry spoke again.

"You don't have to be scared. Our mom says there is nothing to be afraid of, because our ghosts are a nice family that used to live in our house. They loved it so much that after they died they decided they still wanted to live there. So, instead of just going up to heaven they stayed. Our ghosts sometimes turn off the lights and they make Dr. Seuss bark."

"Dr. Seuss is our dog," I tried to explain.

"I got that," smiled the handsome priest.

"Yeah and our ghost rocks the chair in Sabrina's room too," Roman chimed in. "And they make plastic bags float around in the wind and land in our yard. My mom has to go outside and pick up plastic bags all the time cause the wind just carries them all over to our house to float around and then land in the bushes."

The priest listened inquisitively to the boys and I was so nervous about his insight and thoughts on the subject, but he kept quiet and offered no theological opinions, which is good cause the last thing I need is an exorcism. Just when I thought the boys couldn't get any more shocking Roman farted and little boy laughter and funk filled my car.

"I just let go of a bomb," snarled Roman. "A big, fat stink bomb!" He wasn't lying. Roman's fart did smell terrible and caused me to crack the car window in the dead of winter.

"Roman! That's rude, you need to apologize." I tried to get Roman to express regret, but instead he made fart noises out of the side of his mouth. Henry laughed hysterically and started singing.

"Roman's a stink bomb fart butt."

Father McIntire tried to ignore my children's ruckus although I could see he was smiling to himself. My face held no smile, my eye ticked and my teeth clenched. I eventually lost it and shouted out at the top of my lungs.

"Boys stop it now!" My command echoed loud enough to cause silence and embarrass myself more. However, the quiet and shock only lasted a few minutes and was then disrupted by Henry.

"Our dad doesn't live with us anymore cause he got a girlfriend."

"Shut up Henry," Roman said as he punched him in the leg.

"Ouch," Henry cried. "Mom, Roman hit me!"

"Roman, don't hit! Please boys, let's just be quiet for a minute." I was clearly exasperated and wondering why in the hell did I invite this holy man into my car - into my life. I'm sure he was wondering the same thing as he smiled back at the boys while Roman defiantly kicked the back of my seat and Henry cried.

"Well, that was the longest car ride I've ever taken," I said to the priest pulling into my driveway. The boys bolted out the back seat and went flying up to the door.

"No worries," said Father McIntire. He patted my knee, opened up the car door and headed up to the house with a happy sigh.

"Hmmm hot chocolate."

I took my time gaining composure before joining everyone inside. The woods and car ride had been surreal and I needed a minute to wrap my head around it all. I leaned on the steering wheel and took several cleansing breaths, which may have helped me relax if I had not honked the horn using my own forehead. Sabrina was a crying mess when I walked in the door to join everybody.

"What's wrong little monkey?" I scooped up my baby girl and sat her on my hip.

"She was looking for you," Hazel explained.

"Silly girl, I'm right here." I instinctively wiped my bare hand across my daughter's face, mopping up tears, snot and drool that I then rubbed on my jeans. Father McIntire looked down into his hot chocolate and I went to retrieve a tissue. Sabrina now sat quiet on my hip except for a few long sighs. She laid her head on my shoulder, popped her thumb in her mouth and tangled her fingers into my long straight hair and I rocked her back and forth like mothers always do.

"It smells so good in here," I said to Hazel.

"It's the pot roast."

"Ready for dinner," I asked the priest.

"Oh Sissy, it was not my intent to crash your family dinner."

"You're not crashing, you've been invited. Besides, I'm not taking you home until everybody eats and this baby finally lets me put her down."

I think Father McIntire felt a little uncomfortable, but soon the boys were talking over each other telling Hazel about our walk in the woods, the snowman, and feeding deer. Hazel listened and laughed as she busied herself preparing the rest of our meal and I rocked a baby on my chest. I think Father McIntire was enjoying watching the workings of a family and maybe he didn't feel so lonely. I often get a sense when I'm with this man that he is a lonely soul.

"And we found a secret hideout fort," Henry said.

"It was so cool," informed Roman. "It was made out of tall trees and had a roof and inside there was a table and wood chips."

"Yeah," said Henry. "And all these little carved animals."

I wasn't sure how to stop the boys from revealing that we had invaded the priest's sanctuary, so I didn't. I simply laid my head back on my chair, closed my eyes and prayed while my boys ran off at the mouth with zest and excitement. When I looked forward, the priest was staring at me, a slight smile on his face.

"Mom, said the fort is a secret and it belongs to someone and we shouldn't go back there or tell anyone about it," said Henry looking at me. "But, it's alright to tell Hazel cause she can keep a secret huh?"

"Yes you can tell Hazel," I said to Henry as I smiled at Father McIntire. I decided to join in the boys' conversation and reveal to the priest how impressed I was. I explained to Hazel that it wasn't a fort, but rather a gazebo. A beautiful shelter made from trees where you could sit during rain, sleet or snow and watch the woods around you. In all honesty, I was taken in with the gazebo as much as the boys and I wanted to talk about it too. Standing in those woods under that shelter felt sacred and consecrated. You could actually feel the holiness and it caused you to step silently.

"A gazebo," said Hazel, truly interested. "I would love to see it sometime."

"Can we take her Mom? Can we?" the boys shouted together.

"Not in this snow," I said stalling for time. "Now let's eat. Hazel, what can we do to help you?"

"Roman carry over this bowl of potatoes and carrots. Be careful it's hot," Hazel instructed. "Henry you come get plates to set the table."

"I'll slice the pot roast," Father McIntire said getting up from his chair. "Hazel this roast is so tender it can be cut with a fork."

"Of course it can," responded Hazel.

As always supper was scrumptious, the boys, priest and I ate ferociously and quietly. We were hungry from our hike in the woods and a little speechless after the gazebo confession.

"Oh Sissy," said Hazel quickly remembering something. "Pixie Fairy-dust called for you."

"Fairy-dust?" I said cracking up, "Hazel, you mean Moon-Dust."

"Huh?"

"Pixie Moon-Dust not Fairy-dust."

"Oh," say's Hazel. "Did I say Fairy-dust?"

Hazel then began giggling at her own mistake. Hazel is an emotional soul and once she gets started laughing or crying it's hard for her to stop. Hazel's giggle soon became a full-fledged belly laugh with tears. This caused my boys to laugh and then Sabrina and finally Father McIntire joined in. We must have laughed for five minutes at Hazel who once again had taken something nice, like dinner, and made it delightful, like dinner in a comedy club.

After eating, I scooped up Sabrina who was covered in applesauce and asked Father McIntire if he could excuse me for a few minutes while I bathed the baby and then I would take him home. The boys followed me into the main part of the house where they greeted Dr. Seuss with a stolen piece of roast. Then they jumped onto the couch with Dr. Seuss at their feet.

"Don't let that dog on Hazel's couch," I warned the boys as I started up the stairs. Roman flipped on the television and the three settled in. When I returned to the kitchen with a sweet smelling baby in tote, Father McIntire and Hazel had already cleaned up dinner. Working side by side on the dishes they talked like old friends and I almost hated interrupting them. The priest turned towards me drying his hands on a dishcloth and leaning on the sink. He looked so damn ordinary and not like a priest at all. I set Sabrina down and she ran over to the bookshelf and grabbed a picture book off the shelf and then she stumbled towards Hazel.

"Must be story time," Hazel said retrieving baby and book.

"Thank you so much for dinner Hazel. Everything was just wonderful."

"You're welcome Padre, anytime."

"Be back in a minute," I said to Hazel as I grabbed my coat.

"Bye boys," the priest hollered into the living room.

"Bye," came their tired, unison response.

"Hazel is just wonderful," the priest said on our drive home. "And she sure does love you."

"Well, the love is mutual. I am so lucky to have Hazel; I suggest every single mom get one. Having a Hazel is one hundred times better than having a husband. Well, except for missing sex."

And as soon as those final words had left my mouth I remembered that I was talking to a priest and not just a good friend. Humiliation quickly flowed through me like a stream of disgrace that started first in my brain, with a surge of realization as to what I had said and then began a downward wave of shame until even my toes gushed embarrassment. The priest too had become mute and an uncomfortable quiet filled the car.

"I understand that frustration," Father McIntire said, breaking the silence. More awkward stillness followed until I had safely delivered the priest to the door of the rectory.

Homework Help Center,
Tips Are Sincerely Appreciated

February 12, 2000- Dear Diary, things seem to be constantly evolving at The Kitchen House. Lenore has set up a homework help center at one of my round tables and is here Monday through Friday from the hours of 4:00pm to 6:00pm. Families are able to stop by The Kitchen House every weekday after school. While Mom or Dad enjoy a cup of coffee, Lenore helps the kids with their homework. Her services are free except for the large tip jar that sits in the center of the table. I encourage everyone to tip if they can. The Homework Help Center, as we call it, was accidental and happened purely by chance or through divine intervention, as I believe.

Since the second half of the school year and Beau's coming and going, Roman has had trouble getting back on track. I have met with his teacher once in person and have received numerous notes from the desk of Mrs. Decker. Often Roman is irritable, argumentative, disruptive or lost in space, as she puts it. I have tried to be considerate of Roman and his feelings. Of course, I believe that Beau is to blame for it all. Yet, no matter how tolerant I try to be with Roman, homework is a freaking nightmare. I usually start off fine with the intention of being patient and empathetic; I give Roman a few minutes to settle in after school. I let him get a snack, go to the bathroom, pet the dog and stall, stall, stall. Eventually I grow tired of this game and insist he sit down and get his work done. I try to help Roman with his spelling words or math problems as he scribbles, breaks pencils, cuts paper, looks out the window and tips his chair. Eventually I lose it, hollering at my child as I pour steamed milk into a cup of espresso. Our loyal patrons witness this scene on a daily basis. Lenore is usually there. It is the time of day when she has come in to search our internet in hopes of finding employment. She also grabs the newspaper from the bathroom and circles the want ads, scheduling out her tomorrow. This time as Roman and I argued back and forth, me completely overwhelmed and Roman feeling defeated, Lenore stepped in.

"Hey Roman, can I look at that?" she said pointing to the ditto of problems that lay before him. "Yeah, math stinks sometimes. But, I know some secrets? Sissy, do you mind if I help Roman with his work? I know a few tricks that might make it easier."

"What do you say Roman, can Lenore help?" I asked.

"Whatever," replied my sad boy.

Lenore sat with Roman at a round table that was already strewn with paper, pencils and candy wrappers. I busied myself with Henry, who also had homework, but it was just a coloring page, not really sure why they are given so much busy work. Henry colored, Sabrina played, I washed the daily dishes, Hazel started dinner, and Roman and Lenore sat quietly at the table merrily working out math problems. It was the biggest stress reliever I have had since the time Hazel first knocked on my door and offered to babysit. I had to pull back the urge to run over to Lenore and hug her around the neck. Roman responded great and within twenty minutes, accurate time for third grade homework, his math paper was complete. The next day, before Roman and I had a chance to start fighting, Lenore offered more help.

"Hey kid, let's see your homework," she said casually. I was amazed at how positive Roman responded to Lenore and she actually seemed to be teaching him. Lenore and Roman worked together every day after school that week and I was having an inner struggle trying to figure out how I was going to pay Lenore for her services. Lenore had asked for nothing, but I knew that she was desperately seeking work and somehow she had fallen into tutoring my son. It was obvious I was going to have to come up with some kind of compensation. Then on Friday evening of that week, Beau's sister, Misty Dawn, came in to the Kitchen House to get a cup of coffee. She is addicted to Hazel's House Blend. Noticing Lenore and Roman she asks me how I can afford a tutor.

"Sissy, you got a homework helper for Roman, isn't that expensive?"

"Well, actually she's just a friend that is doing me a favor. I haven't really figured out what I owe her yet and she hasn't said."

"Well, ask her if she can tutor Jackson too. I can't pay much, but I would gladly give a little something for some help. He's doing algebra now and me and his daddy can no longer help him."

"I'll ask," I said thoughtfully, a notion forming in my head. I approached Lenore with my idea after she and Roman had finished working and he was off to play video games. Thirty minutes of video games is his reward for thirty minutes of schoolwork.

"Hey Lenore, I so appreciate all the help you have given Roman this week. You have made a huge difference; really it's just incredible. I can't pay much but I want to give you something." I said handing her twenty-five dollars.

"Oh, Sissy I don't want your money. I helped Roman this week cause of all the help you have given me. "

"How so?"

"For starters, you let me crash your party and stay here for a night. Then you fed me breakfast in the morning and told me it was free. You helped me find a home and you let me sit on your computer every day. I figure I owe you nearly five times that much."

"No Lenore, I was just doing the right thing. That's really nothing."

"Well, I think it's something and I've enjoyed working with Roman. I think he has that math concept down and he pretty much knows his spelling words for next week already. Let me know when he needs any further help."

"Actually Lenore, I was hoping that you continued to work with Roman and not just Roman, but maybe some other kids that need help too. You just seem to be so natural at it. I was thinking that you could come to The Kitchen House every day after school like you've been doing and we can have a little area set up for you. Maybe make a sign that says homework help and kids are free to come up and ask questions and you can have a little tip jar." Lenore tilted her head turning my concept over and causing it to move through her brain. I could tell my idea was sketching a picture, so I continued.

"You'd kind of be like Lucy from *The Peanuts*," I joked. "You know, psychiatry 5 cents. Only I hope you would get more than 5 cents." She broke a small smile.

"The truth is Lenore, the people in these parts are nowhere near rich. Money is tight and nobody can afford private tutoring for their child. But I guarantee that each one of these folks would pull a little something from their pockets if you helped their child with schoolwork and took some stress off their plate. The people of Grace are proud, Lenore. Pride just happens to be a trait that each one of us is born with and everyone here wants their child to do well in school and get a good education. It is the dream of all truck drivers, mill workers, tree loggers, coal miners and farmers that they have a child that goes off to college. Yet, as bad as we want our children to succeed, we are not all equipped to help them get there. The kids have to do it on their own. If you offered your services you could make a huge difference in these children's lives, just like you made one in Roman's. Just think, in return you could have a little spending money, not to mention corn up to your eyeballs and free car repairs for as long as you live in Grace. We are very good at the barter system and the scratching of each other's backs."

"I don't know Sissy." Lenore seemed much more unsure than I thought she would be. After all, I thought my idea was brilliant.

"I'll have to think about it."

"Well, Lenore I'm not suggesting that you try and make a living out of tutoring kids. I know that will never work. I just thought it was something you could do while you look for a job. Even after you find something, it may still be something you can offer. We can always tweak the hours and days."

"Sissy, I'm just going to have to get back to you," responded Lenore. I had clearly shaken her by something I said and she left the twenty-five dollars on the table when she headed out The Kitchen House door. I told Hazel I had somehow offended Lenore and was worried she wouldn't be back. However around 8:30pm after we had closed up shop and I had just laid the kids down to bed, I heard a knock on the back Kitchen House door from the front room. The soft tapping actually caused me to swear out loud thinking some other wandering stranger was looking for a place to stay.

"Damn it!" I said. "Can't they tell I'm closed?" When I opened the door, there stood Lenore, shaking like a leaf, a scarf wrapped around her head and mouth, protection from the wind.

"Sissy can I talk to you for a minute?" she asked through the thick purple knitted yarn that wrapped around her face.

"Of course you can, get in here." I responded by opening the door wider and summoning her in out of the cold.

As Lenore slowly removed her layers of outerwear I could tell she was building up the courage to tell me a story, so I put on a pot of chamomile tea.

Lenore and I sat at the table for two hours that night just talking and getting to know each other. She started slowly, frightened to tell her story. The fear of judgment had formed like a dark cloud and was looming over her head. I felt sorry for her as she unleashed a truth that she was running from, unsure what I might do with it. Would she need to run from Grace as well?

Lenore confessed that she used to be a high school math and science teacher in Connecticut. Lenore is obviously brilliant. She graduated high school a year earlier than the rest of her class and went off to college on a full scholarship. She had earned her master's degree by twenty-three years of age and began teaching. By twenty-four she was married and working full-time in a school she loved.

Lenore's husband was ten years older than her. A police officer who was sweet and gentle during the short six months they dated and then controlling and oppressive after the wedding vows. Lenore stated that she became sad and depressed during her marriage. She went from being madly in love with a feeling of bliss to hating the man who was so needy and paranoid. Lenore's husband was jealous of everyone. He shut down her communications with her friends and family, because they took up too much of her time. He kept tabs on her, checking in with her constantly, running by the school with his patrol car during the day. Everyone thought he was so nice. Little did they know that she had married Dr. Jekyll-Mr. Hyde. Lenore became more and more unhappy. She had always been in such control of her life and now she felt she had no control. In fact, she was being controlled. Not knowing how to cope, she threw herself into work as she often did when things bothered her. She found joy in her students and in teaching. She found happiness during the day, working out problems and formulas. She was teaching through a passion and inspiring young minds. She was a good teacher. She met the students on their level and coaxed them through. She believed that their success as a pupil was proof of her success as a teacher. If they were failing she made sure to try and reach out and help them bring up their grade. If there was a lesson that was too complicated and the students didn't quite grasp it, she went over it again with a different approach. She figured out what it took to reach them. If they were a behavior problem, she did not judge too harshly, but rather offered up a friendship. When Lenore spoke of teaching, her posture changed and a smile hinted at the corners of her mouth and I knew Lenore loved teaching. Then Lenore began to speak to me of a particular student and again her posture changed and her smile faded.

Christopher was a gothic teen with black hair that fell sideways across his forehead and covered one icy blue eye that was lined in black. Lenore was sure that Christopher was a genius. He barely looked up during class and instead doodled inside his chemistry book, sketching and writing poetry on scraps of paper. Yet, he would ace every test she gave and because of this she did not demand his attention, but rather became fascinated with Christopher. She noticed that Christopher walked the halls alone in his torn jeans and black boots, always a sketchpad cradled under his arm. He seemed to operate the same in each of his classes. Christopher always took a seat at the back of the room. He barely focused on teacher or lesson. Instead he scripted and sketched away. Even so, he carried an A average in all of his classes. Oddly, nobody seemed to notice this boy genius that knew more than his teachers. Through observation Lenore felt that Christopher came to school only because he had to. He showed up physically and went through the motions every day, but mentally he was always somewhere else. Christopher kept quiet and withdrawn. He did not participate in class, nor socialize with other students. He seemed to not want to be bothered with school life and yet he could not be stumped. Christopher knew all the answers, despite his lack of trying. School and teachers were just something Christopher was going to have to endure until the time he could graduate from this institution and become his authentic self. Lenore asked the other teachers about Christopher and none of them seemed impressed by this student. They all just stated that he was quiet, not a behavior problem and they felt they were teaching him well, because he knew the material. At times teachers can be such pompous creatures giving themselves credit for things that they had nothing to do with.

One day as Christopher was leaving Lenore's classroom, a sheet of paper fell from the pages of his notebook onto the floor. Lenore did not tell Christopher he had dropped something. Instead she waited for all her students to leave before she picked up the folded piece of paper and read what this mysterious kid had been secretly writing. To Lenore's shock, she had just retrieved a suicide note. It was written in slanted, dark scroll and read like sinister poetry. Although dark, there was a beauty that lay between the painful lines and confessions. It had a very Edgar Allan Poe feel. Christopher used words like throe and wretchedness to describe his misery. His suicide note was dramatic, to say the least, as probably all suicide notes must be. It was rich in words and imageries of melancholy and ethereal wonder. Along the margin of the paper were black and white pencil sketches of sorrowful things. Not just doodles, works of art. Christopher had drawn a ship with torn flags crashing against the waves of a violent ocean and an iron gate weaved with roses. There were many pencil sketches of nudes in different broken positions. Depictions of nude men curled up in a fetal position, crouched in a corner, or on their knees in prayer. These haunting sketches were dark images of life interrupted by madness. As Lenore studied the words and sketches of murky gloom, she discovered a light that was deeply entrenched into this written and drawn art. She thought about turning the note into the guidance counselor (which is what she should have done). However, she surmised that it would fall into numb hands and an even duller mind. Christopher was too bright and beautiful to be helped by that soon-to-be-retired counselor. So instead, Lenore placed the suicidal poetry into her purse and decided that she could help fix Christopher.

Lenore waited by Christopher's locker after school and when he didn't appear she looked up his address in his school file and waited in her car near his home. She finally made contact with the boy as she watched him walk slowly down his street and up to his attractive house made of brick.

"Hey!" Lenore shouted out as Christopher approached his front lawn. Christopher did a good job of hiding his surprise regarding Lenore's visit.

"Yeah," he stated. "You need something?"

"Well, yes. Umm...actually you dropped something in class and I wanted to return it to you," stammered Lenore as she held out the note.

"Thanks," Christopher said as he grabbed the paper and shoved it into his pocket.

"Want to talk about it?" Lenore asked.

"No," was his quick response.

"You're actually a beautiful writer and to tell you the truth I was quite impressed," Lenore said not knowing really where she was going with this conversation. "It's just the subject matter that has me worried."

"You liked the poem?"

"Well yes and no. No, because I think it may be a suicide note and yes, I think you're a beautiful poet."

"It's not a suicide note," Christopher informed her. "It's a poem. Actually, it's a poem in the form of a suicide note that is fictional."

"Fictional?"

"Yes, fictional. I write them all the time. Poems that is, in the form of something I call, artistic freedoms. They usually tell a story. In this case the story happens to be of suicide."

"Well, if that's the case Christopher, I would like to read more of them and see more of your sketches."

"I'm really not into sharing my work with others. You know, it's kind of private."

"Well that sounds like something a person says about a diary or the writings of truth. I thought yours were fictional."

"They are, but they can still be private."

"You're right, but if you throw me something every once in a while I will know not to worry nor share my concern with others."

Lenore believed that by threatening Christopher of exposure she could convince him to surrender some and let his guard down, if only to her. Christopher needed to trust in someone to be reached and she was offering herself up. Lenore thought if she could study Christopher's poetry and art she would find out what was really going on in that brilliant mind. Fictional or not, Christopher needed a friend.

The next day, as Christopher left Lenore's classroom, he placed an envelope on her desk. It contained a note that Lenore did not open until that evening when she sat down to grade papers. Christopher really was a clever boy and just as dramatic as the suicide note had been, Christopher had created a fictional letter addressed to Dear CrAbby, with a headline *Advice Needed For The Empathetic*. The prose that followed the title described empathy like a disease, where traces of God could be found. It was cancer with a spiritual side and it was painful and terminal with intermittent twinkles of divine light. Lenore had to read the column twice to get its full meaning. Often, Christopher wrote over one's head and used words in which you needed a dictionary. She found he was a wordsmith. He signed the fictional letter *Too Sensitive - In Connecticut*. Below the signature, Christopher had written a response from Dear CrAbby.

Too Sensitive,

Drugs and alcohol work wonders at numbing the mind and soul. Consider these forms of medication to get through your exhausting days.

Lenore made a copy of the letter that she kept and the original she returned to Christopher. On the bottom of the page she had written, "Beautiful use of language, bad advice. I hope you are finding other ways to deal with pain than drugs and alcohol. Exercise is a great stress reliever as is art."

Two days later she received a sketch from Christopher. He had titled his sketch *Exercise Beats Empathy*. The drawing was of a jogger running through a stately park. Along the left corner of the page he had sketched a trash can overflowing with bags. Christopher had drawn the image of a homeless, legless man sitting among the trash, tin can in his hand, his wheelchair skewed and parked off to the side. The jogger was running with his nose in the air, unaware of the homeless man's presence. The sketch felt like a slap in her face, but she saw his point and felt the grief of empathy, as a tear absently rolled down her cheek, while she focused her gaze solely on the homeless man.

Christopher's gifts came sporadically at first. They were always very smart writings streaked with heartache; a dark limerick, a poignant haiku, and lots of free verse. Once he wrote her fourteen lines of a beautiful Shakespearean style poem that he titled *A Sonnet of Tears*. Lenore loved his writings and kept each one in a file folder in her desk. She began writing back to Christopher, but not in poetry; simply letters of encouragement trying to reach this sad, young man. Through their writings a friendship grew. Soon they were talking after school in her classroom. They had developed a friendship that she did not hide. In fact, she felt it positive that she was reaching out to a student in need.

During this time, Lenore's husband, Bill, switched to second shift and sometimes he didn't come home until after 1:00am. He also had a new female partner. He was still controlling of Lenore, but had loosened up some, almost to the point of not caring, which caused Lenore to think he was having an affair. Instead of feeling jealous or suspicious, Lenore took her newly found freedom as a reprieve. She enjoyed her evenings alone reading or watching old classic movies, or talking on the phone with Christopher.

In December, Lenore took Christopher out to dinner for his eighteenth birthday. She gave him a sketchpad and a set of charcoals and they talked over their burgers and fries like best friends. It was two weeks after Christopher's birthday that they kissed for the first time and although it was a surprise, Lenore had felt it coming. Over Christmas break they began making love. Christopher still wrote his poetry for Lenore, but his darkness had turned to passion and his pain into love. Lenore knew she was in over her head, but she had never met anyone like Christopher. She found him to be so beautiful and smart and she could not push him away. She was bothered more by their relationship student versus teacher than she was by their age difference. Lenore was twenty-six and Christopher just eighteen. Sure, eight years seems like a lot, but Christopher was an old soul, brilliant and mature beyond his years.

Lenore and Christopher were honestly raw with each other, a trait that Christopher brought to the table. They confessed secrets to one another while tangled in each other's arms, whispering in each other's ears and in writings that they both kept sacred and hidden. Christopher learned all about Lenore's mentally abusive marriage and her desire to flee. Lenore learned that Christopher was the only child of two brilliant parents. His father is a highly recognized psychiatrist, who sleeps with his lovely, lonely patients and not his wife. His mother is a mentally disturbed artist who barely leaves the confines of her art studio and when she does it is to spend hoards of money and binge drink.

Lenore and Christopher devised a plan to run off together. Lenore had her childhood savings account that still held every bit of birthday money and babysitting tips she had ever been given. Lenore's early love for math had helped her create a fat and secret savings account. She loved watching numbers add up. As a child, Lenore very happily took her pennies to the bank, just to have the bank teller stamp her book. A new ink blotted line of numbers that increased as time passed. As a young teen, she would much rather put her earnings into a savings account than into a wardrobe. After years of hoarding her money with a decent amount of interest, Lenore had built a nice nest egg. In the beginning of her marriage, Lenore did not reveal this account, because she did not think of it. Bill and Lenore's relationship had moved so fast it just didn't occur to her. After a few months of marriage she kept quiet about this account in case she ever needed it.

Lenore and Christopher could leave after graduation. Christopher began applying to schools out west. He had the grades and test scores, which probably could have gotten him into any college in the east, but both Christopher and Lenore felt the need to move far away. Lenore began applying for jobs close to UC Berkeley where Christopher was accepted due to his outstandingly high SAT score.

It was two days after spring break and three weeks away from graduation when Lenore was arrested while teaching her fourth period chemistry class. She was handcuffed in front of her students including Christopher and led down the halls in front of the gaping mouths of nearly half the school. The principal did not want it to go down like this, but he had no control over Bill who had plotted and planned the arrest. Bill had known for awhile of Lenore's love affair and he had played it cool and callous. He had secretly been investigating his own wife for quite some time. The problem was that Bill believed that Lenore and Christopher began their sexual relationship at the beginning of the year, which was not the case. Lenore was charged with statutory rape and corruption of a minor. Bill made sure her bail was set high and she was considered a flight risk. Lenore told her frugal and uptight father not to post her bond; she would rather sit in jail, waiting for trial. The truth was that Lenore did not want the media on the lawn of her parent's home. She did not want reporters loitering in the neighborhood that held her childhood memories. She would rather sit quietly in jail than to face anyone. Lenore figured charges would be dropped soon. Both Lenore and Christopher had the same story and although they were both interrogated several times and they were always consistent Lenore still faced trial. Bill had convinced everyone, which wasn't hard to do, that Lenore had seduced a young and introverted teen and made him her boy toy.

Lenore spent a total of four months in jail before she was acquitted at trial. The jury decided that Lenore and Christopher's relationship was indeed mutual. Christopher was not the innocent, introvert described by the prosecution and he was of the age of sexual consent even if the affair began before his eighteenth birthday. That decision did not erase the months of humiliation and shame felt by Lenore and Christopher's family or the months Lenore spent behind bars. It did not soften the depression that over took Christopher while he watched Lenore's life come undone. Of course, Lenore was fired from her job and forced to give up her teaching license. Bill was given his divorce and their home, which he now shares with his partner.

After the trial, Lenore kept her distance from Christopher. He was scheduled to leave for college. Lenore had ruined enough of his life dragging him through police interrogation, the media and public shame. Further, she had no teaching license or means of support. Her career, reputation and dreams had been destroyed. Lenore was no good for anyone. Christopher kept at her with his letters that he sent to her sister's apartment, the place she was hiding out until she figured out where to go and what to do. She left the letters unopened piling up on her sister's table. She hoped that Christopher could find peace in Berkeley as well as some nice, smart college girl that would brighten his days.

It was in November that Christopher's father phoned Lenore to tell her of Christopher's death. He told her that it was an accident and that he was not alone. Christopher had ingested pills with alcohol at a party. However, Lenore knew that it was no accident. Christopher had committed suicide. The party had just been the means to make suicide not so scary. Lenore knew that Christopher feared dying alone so much more than actually dying and she had the poetic suicide note to prove it. Lenore attended Christopher's funeral, coming in late and sitting in the back. At the burial sight she stayed long after everyone left, pacing the frozen ground and screaming out to the night.

When she could no longer stand the look of her own face in the mirror she withdrew all her money from her kiddy account, packed up her vehicle and began driving, holding it together until she reached Grace, where she broke down in my bathroom.

At the end of Lenore's story, I was spent and so was she. This poor creature had just emptied her soul onto my kitchen table and left it there damaged and I had no words, so what came out was probably lame.

"Well Lenore, as far as I see it, Christopher lived longer than he had planned. I agree that first poem was a suicide note and your beautiful friend was just counting hours. You saved him, at least for a while. You brought him out of the dark and into the light. You showed him love and taught him about passion before he died. Your story is safe with me and I only hope that while living in Grace you learn to forgive yourself." Lenore was crying hard by this time, sobs that shook her whole being.

"Lenore, I have not changed my mind. I would still like for you to tutor these kids that need help with their homework. It's just a small thing, but it would help these families so much and maybe it could help you. You might as well think about it. Nobody here is going to ask for your teaching license just to have some help with Algebra homework."

Lenore wearily pulled herself up from my kitchen table.

"Thank you Sissy," was all she had the strength to say before hugging me goodbye and walking out into the wind.

I believe Lenore showed up at my door and told me her story, because she needed to tell someone. Sometimes a secret can keep you from breathing right. Secrets are heavy things and when you got such a big one sitting on your chest it's hard to exhale. Just by telling one person you can kind of lighten the load and breathe just a bit easier. I plan to keep my promise to Lenore about secrecy. I have not even told Hazel.

Everyone loves the Homework Help Center. It is a welcome addition to the town of Grace and I'm selling more afternoon coffees.

Psychic Readings & Pinewood Derby

Well, I have finally connected with Pixie Moon-Dust. I had tried to return her call a couple of times but I kept missing her. I do believe that girl keeps odd hours. After a few missed calls and a couple of goofy messages left by me, Pixie decided a face to face would be better. She showed up on a snowy, sunny morning with her blue hair piled high up on her head and gloves with finger holes. Pixie sat at the coffee bar, ordered a couple of apple walnut biscuits and a shot of espresso. She asked if Hazel and I had a few minutes to listen to her grand idea. What Pixie pitched to us next was a bit unconventional, an out of the ordinary request from an unusual girl.

Pixie asked us if she could have psychic readings at The Kitchen House. She said most of the readings would be done after hours unless her client is set on a daytime appointment and then they can sit off in the corner. Pixie had already worked out the details in her head and what she pitched to us was a business proposition. Basically, she just wants to use our space. Pixie said she would let us know of her appointments in advance. If it is an evening appointment we will leave The Kitchen House door open for Pixie who will arrive thirty minutes before her client, ample time she claims to purify the space and do some light meditation. Pixie charges $90.00 for a reading, which lasts an hour. Out of that $90.00 she would pay $25.00 for use of The Kitchen House. Rental space is what she called it.

Hazel responded a bit apprehensively to Pixie's request and had some legitimate concerns, while I was in total shock that you could make $90.00 an hour.

"I don't know?" said Hazel. "What does a psychic reading entail?"

"Typically, people want to know about their future, things like work and romance. I try to give them that information, but mostly what I do is speak to their loved ones that have passed over. I relay any messages back to the living. I am more of a medium than a psychic," Pixie explained to us.

"You saying you talk to dead people?" Hazel asked.

"Yes Ma'am."

"Well how can you promise us that nothing dark or evil will show up to talk to you and then decide to hang around?"

"Well, first of all I don't dabble in darkness Hazel. I take my gift seriously and I do believe it is a gift from God. I am a communicator that is connecting two worlds. I spend plenty of time praying to God and thanking him for my gift and before every reading I light a candle and ask God to surround me in light."

Now she was talking Hazel's language and Hazel smiled at the blue haired girl whose eyes had become fiery.

"Besides Hazel," said Pixie. "Nothing dark wants to be here."

"What do you mean?"

"This home is a place of peace," Pixie responded. "I'm serious, y'all are living on sacred ground, hallowed and blessed. That is why I am asking to do my readings here, where there is a serenity that is pure and reverent. In truth, this house is the perfect place for connecting with the other side in a positive light. I believe the tranquility of this home and land is a product of Owen and Emma Kitchen. It seems once they were reunited with their children, after death, they all just decided to stay at the house. They could have transcended into the heavens if they wanted to, but they were blissful in their home, so they just brought a piece of heaven down. By doing so, they hallowed this here piece of land. In their construction of heaven on earth, they created a place where spirits like to pass through and rest, kind of like a retreat."

"Retreat?" I interrupted. "Are you suggesting my house is a vacation home for ghosts?"

"Not really a vacation home, more like a gathering place."

"A gathering place?" Hazel and I both asked at the same time.

"Well yes," said Pixie calmly. "It seems spirits like it here and the Kitchens are a welcoming family, real social butterflies to say the least. They surely have been enjoying all the activity that has been coming around. Really, Sissy at times you got quite a jubilee going on."

Both Hazel and I stood astonished behind the coffee counter. It was quite the shocker to find out that our home wasn't just haunted by a family of ghosts, but rather a hot spot for vacationing spirits.

"How many readings do you do a week?" Hazel asked.

"There have been some good weeks where I have had two or three. Some weeks I have no readings at all. It's a hard business. I'm hoping that by advertising on the internet with a photo of The Kitchen House and a description which will read, *Psychic Readings done in a charming and haunted café,* that business will pick up."

Once Pixie said that, I knew that my dad would love the idea of internet advertising and psychic readings. Hell, he might even want to add a couple of extra bedrooms and turn this place into an Inn where folks could actually spend the night and get the real haunted experience.

"Well Pixie, you've given Hazel and I much to discuss. But, we're going to need time to talk this over and then get back to you."

"I understand, and if you want I can stay here and run the café for a few minutes. You and Hazel can go into the house and talk in private."

"Oh," I said not having thought about that. Pixie sure seemed to be in a hurry for an answer, which led me to believe that she had already scheduled a reading in my coffee shop. Hazel and I agreed to go talk a bit, mostly because we were both busting at the seams to discuss it all. As soon as we were on the other side of the door I asked Hazel what she thought.

"I think that girl may be a little more enlightened than I thought she was. However, I have some reservation about letting her have access into The Kitchen House so she can talk to dead people."

"Well, when you put it like that Hazel, it does seem a little uncomfortable. But I don't know, I kind of like the idea of our place being a happy gathering place for friendly spirits. I mean, I never thought I'd like the idea of living in a haunted house, but our home doesn't feel haunted; it feels blessed."

"I agree, I think it's pretty neat and I hope Harry is here enjoying himself."

"I bet he is," I said as I gave Hazel a pat and a smile.

"I do know your daddy would love to talk to Pixie Moon-Dust about advertising The Kitchen House on the internet and doing psychic readings. He surely would believe this could be a money maker."

"Daddy is a fan of the obscure that's for sure. He loves anything that will get people talking."

"Hell Sissy, let's do it. I don't think it's going to interfere with what we do and twenty-five dollars for nothing plus some free advertising sounds like a smart business move."

I hugged Hazel around the neck, because she had just confirmed my own thoughts and made me not feel so crazy.

When we returned to the kitchen, Father McIntire was sitting at the coffee bar and Pixie Moon-Dust was steaming some milk.

"I just came by for some of Hazel's hot chocolate," said the handsome priest when he saw Hazel and I.

"Well, I figured out how to steam the milk, but I will leave the rest to Hazel," said Pixie stepping away.

Hazel added her own mixture of cocoa powder and sugar to the steamed milk. Then she placed a dollop of her whipped cream and a pinch of chocolate shavings to the top. It was such a pretty and inviting drink. Father McIntire smiled like a child when she set the steaming mug in front of him.

"Well?" asked Pixie right in front of the priest.

"We've agreed it will be fine," I said exciting the medium and confusing the padre.

"Awesome!" said Pixie giving us both big hugs. "This is going to be great. You won't regret it, you'll see. This is going to change all of our lives." As she headed out the door she added, "I should know - I'm psychic!"

Father McIntire sat quietly at the coffee bar drinking his cocoa and I gave him no explanation as to what he had just witnessed. Instead, I excused myself from the coffee bar by telling Hazel and the priest I had to go check on Sabrina who was taking her morning nap, which I did after I called Rayland. I was so excited to tell someone about Pixie's visit and Rayland is my confidant. It was good that I made that call, because Rayland, my business advisor, was quick to remind me that Pixie cannot schedule any readings for Friday or Saturday night.

Rayland and his clogging dancers take precedence on Saturday nights, which has actually brought in a ton of business. Due to Saturday night's success, Rayland and Cody suggested we host local entertainment on Friday nights. There are enough guitar players and fiddle pickers in this area to fill a year of Fridays and all of them are looking for an audience to play for. So far, Rayland has been able to book the next three Friday nights in a row.

After Rayland and I hung up, I called Pixie right away to let her know about Friday and Saturday nights. I'll be damned if that girl didn't tell me that she was glad I called, because she had just confirmed an appointment for 7:30pm that night. I knew she had already booked The Kitchen House before Hazel and I had told her yes. I decided not to get angry, instead I looked forward to the twenty-five dollars I was given at the end of the night. It actually worked out well for a first time reading, because Hazel, the kids and I were not at home. It was the night of the pinewood derby race and we went to the school for a Cub Scout banquet.

At 4:00pm that day, my boys came tearing into the house wired and excited, jumping all over the place.

"They've been in hyper-mode since I picked them up," said Jean, the bus driver, as she exited my bathroom, drying her hands on a paper towel. The boys had been waiting for this day for weeks, ever since they brought home a block of wood from cub scouts and were told it had to be transformed into a racecar.

"Sissy, the pinewood derby races are a big thing for a little fellow," Jean reminisced. "I remember my little Leo's pinewood derby car. It was bright orange like the General Lee from *The Dukes of Hazard*. Let's see your cars boys."

Both boys went tearing off through the house to retrieve their car. Henry's car was sleek with back wings and was painted a sort of metallic blue. Roman's car had a curved front like a corvette and it was candy-apple red with a black stripe.

"Them sure are some handsome cars," Jean said inspecting both sets of wheels. She rested the cars on the palms of her hands and then raised her hands up and down in the air a few times as if she were the scale of justice.

"They're a good weight too," she said. "Yep, these two cars are gonna be the ones to beat." The boys snagged their cars out of Jean's hands and went off tearing through the house again.

Anyone who has ever built a pinewood derby car knows about the weight and all the derby rules. For starters, the length of the car cannot exceed seven inches. The width of the car shall not exceed two and three/fourth inches and the weight of the car cannot exceed 5.0 ounces. I mean to tell you, the boy scouts are anal about their rules. There are even rules about the wheels, which they provide. There is an inspection committee and an official race scale. Weighing the car seems to be most crucial. Once the car passes inspection and is entered into the race, nobody can touch it except a committee member. If by some chance your car does not qualify, it is impounded. It all seems a bit excessive to me and the men involved seem just as ridiculous as their rulebook.

The pinewood derby race actually turned out to be fun, but it was more of a competition between my brother and dad than it was between Roman and Henry, which is just as well. However, my dad and brother had been driving me nuts with their competitive car building. When the boys brought home their blocks of wood I suggested they call Grandpa. Soon after that phone call was made Charlie was involved and both men kind of just took over. It was actually a huge relief to me. At least I didn't have to try and whittle a car out of a block of wood and the boys were having some manly one on one attention. Charlie would pick up Roman and they would work on his car together while my dad would take Henry. It was good for all four of them.

An hour before the derby races, the boys ran around the house like heathens and Sabrina cried to be picked up. Hazel and I had to ignore them all and busy ourselves with closing up The Kitchen House. We packed up nearly four dozen mummy dogs and pizza biscuits; which was our contribution to the potluck. Then we hung a sign on The Kitchen House door that said *Closed - Went to Pinewood Derby Races.* The people in our town surely understand that.

As we walked into the school gymnasium that night, I couldn't help but be overwhelmed by all the dirty-blond heads and blue uniforms running around in chaos. The volume of the gym alone was about five octaves higher than normal and it wasn't just the young boys that expelled wildly hyper energy. The fathers themselves had a bit of nervous, testosterone vigor bouncing about. I spotted my dad and brother over at the cookie table and I headed over with Sabrina to get a little snack. Roman and Henry waited in the long line for car inspection.

Once the cars had been weighed in they were laid on a long table beside a number making it easy to check out the competition. All of the derby cars held a bit of personality and flare that reflected nicely upon the child who claimed it. Some of the cars were elaborate in color and sleek in design and you could tell that this was the work of the father and not the son. There were a couple of cars that you could tell had only touched the child's hands. The cars of absent fathers and stressed out mothers stood out with their messy paint job, wobbly wheels and bulky design. Those were the cars that I wanted to win. I let out a silent prayer for the fatherless cars and thanked God for my dad and brother.

"Look at that one," Henry said pointing to a car that had been crafted into the shape of a sleek rocket. This was definitely a physics game and these mountain men had suddenly become scientific engineers. Most of the fathers walked around the room in a rooster strut, cocky and uncouth. Some of them had even brought power tools; sand paper and graphite for last minute touch ups right before weigh in. The men working the pit crew were serious and a bit dickish about the check in process. They didn't mind the hurt feelings of a young boy if his car didn't pass inspection. An impounded vehicle was simply a hard lesson learned for both child and parent not to mess with the derby rules. The impound lot was a card table roped off by caution tape. Gathered around it, were crying cub scouts and fighting parents. I watched one woman punch her husband square in the arm and shout, "I told you not to razor the wheels you dumbass!"

The racetrack was a long, wooden, straight track with four lanes for cars. The start of the track was a steep, inclined plane that then leveled out at the bottom into a long straight path with a timer at the finish. The race began with the Tiger Cubs. Henry squealed as his car zipped down the track, clearly one of the fastest. I must admit it was exhilarating. The entire gym had become a madhouse and I didn't dare put Sabrina down. Instead, we huddled in as close as we could to the track and watched the races with enthusiasm, However, at times I became distracted as I watched the people watch the races. Some of the cars had incredible speed and smoked past the cars of lesser design. One car lost its wheels during a race, they just fell off and the father began to cry. "It's ok dad," his young son said patting him on the back. It was a very touching scene and it brought tears to my eyes. Another car stopped mid-track, just stopped as if a teeny tiny rabbit had run in front of it. Roman and Henry's cars were in the winner's circle, holding their own. One particular car clearly stood out as being fast and I believe the car belonged to Avery Banks, because he shouted and applauded from his wheelchair every time that car zipped down the track.

When there were just a few cars left in the running, Henry's car was put on the track backwards.

"Turn it around," both Henry and Roman shouted, but the gatekeeper ignored the boys and raced the car backwards. Henry's car flew past the rest, surprisingly quicker backwards than when raced forward.

"Well, would you look at that?" my dad expressed. "Henry we got to get that car to race backwards every time."

After a couple more heats, Roman's car was out of the race and he took his defeat like a trooper. Charlie on the other hand, showed a bit of disappointment. I gave Roman a hug, Charlie a pat and then gripped the shoulder of Henry who was still in the race. Henry's car had been raced backwards twice now and each time its speed was incredible. It was in the start of the final heat when they turned Henry's car around to race it as it had been intended.

"Turn the damn thing around," shouted both my dad, and Hazel who had been in hysterics through the whole race. I had no idea that Hazel was so competitive. Yet, the gate went up and the cars sped down and Henry's car came in second place, a mere fraction of a second, behind the car of Avery Banks. As I consoled Henry and my father, Avery Banks cheered from his wheelchair.

"Did you see that Father Tim! Did you see that? We won!" I looked over to see Father McIntire standing with Avery's mother celebrating with her young son.

It wasn't long before Father McIntire headed our way. He congratulated Henry on his second place win, admired both Roman and Henry's cars and talked to my dad and brother for a few minutes about the race and the backwards speed of Henry's car.

"Well, hell," my dad said. "At least I know what to do next year."

When the priest came up to greet me, I could only smile.

"Did you help Avery Banks build that car?' I asked.

"Well, his mother called me to see if I knew any men in the church that could help and I suppose I liked the request so much that I volunteered myself."

"That's nice," I said.

"Honestly, I think the experience was more a blessing to me than it was to Avery and his mother." The priest and I talked for a few more minutes and then he humbly left before the awards ceremony began. Hard-ass Christy Banks, Avery's mom, cried when her little boy wheeled himself up to the front of the room to receive his trophy, which made others cry too.

February 19, 2000 - Dear Diary, Henry received a second-place medal for his pinewood derby car that he wears like a necklace. Every day he hangs his medal around his neck like a cross on a Christian. Roman tries hard to conceal his jealousy. However, he does let us all know that Henry only won second place cause his car was raced backwards. Henry pays no mind to Roman's remarks; he's too busy beaming. Since Pixie has done a few psychic readings, The Kitchen House has taken on a different feel. It's as if the atmosphere has become sacred. I know I must sound crazy, but walking into my quiet kitchen has the same sense I get when walking into a quiet cathedral. It is that feeling I had standing in the winter woods under Father McIntire's gazebo. It is holy and the best part is that after every reading twenty-five dollars sits neatly on a table and the smell of cinnamon and sage lingers in the air.

Nights Made of Espresso & Dreams

March 1, 2000 - Dear Diary, if it wasn't for Rayland and Cody, The Kitchen House would be desolate. Friday and Saturday nights at The Kitchen House are slammed. This town and the towns around it have taken to our entertainment nights as the thing to do. Not only that, on Saturday afternoon I hosted my first birthday "Tea Party" for a little girl in Cody's pre-ballerina class, that just turned six. It was adorable with little girls in princess dresses and tiny tea sandwiches. I could tell that it planted a seed in the minds of the other mothers. I'm sure that there will be more tea parties to follow. I'm feeling very blessed. Since Beau left me, I feel that God has surrounded me with people I need. My friends fit nicely into my life and improve my existence. Rayland and Cody were both born with dancer's feet and a business head; Hazel is a culinary artist, crafter and caretaker; Lenore is blessed with brains and the love of teaching; my daddy is gifted with ingenuity and skill; Charlie is a natural artisan; Pixie a mystic and Father McIntire is sainted with divinity. And as for me, well my life has been beatified by these people who are in it.

Weekdays at The Kitchen House run so slow with just the occasional regular stopping in for coffee. The morning hours creep by until about 3:30pm when the after-school crew bombards us. This consists of teenagers struggling with algebra or geometry. The teens like my fancy coffees with added whipped cream and they all love Lenore. They see her as old enough to be smart and sophisticated and young enough to still be cool. The young children who come in for homework help are given enough crumbled dollars to buy a cookie, a glass of milk and a tip for Lenore's glass vase. Moms of some of the younger kids follow them into The Kitchen House, buy a house blend coffee, and then sit to gossip with other moms. Others just drop and go. They have other children to look after, dinner to cook, and jobs to do and I can respect that. Lenore isn't making much money, but I believe she is enjoying herself. There is a glimmer of happiness that shines in her sad eyes when she teaches.

I am grateful for our Friday and Saturday night entertainment. I love the country singers that come through here and the dancing feet and contagious smiles of Rayland's clogging class. On these nights my home is filled with dancing, music, laughter and fun. These are the nights made of espresso and dreams. It is exhilarating and it is exhausting. On Sundays, I can barely get out of bed and we have been skipping mass. Hazel and I looked over figures and had a long talk. We have decided to ask Lenore if she would like to work at The Kitchen House on Friday and Saturday nights as well as help with hosting any of our scheduled tea parties. We seem to make enough money on those events that we could pay her out of the register and under the table. We also have made slight changes with our days and hours. We will remain closed Sundays and on Mondays we will not open until 3:30pm, for homework help. Since the day is so slow we will not lose much money. Besides, the needed rest is worth the cost.

If I was truly honest with myself, I would know that it is not the music and people that wear me out and cause my fatigue. It is actually the after hour wind down I spend with Rayland and Cody. On both nights the music stops by nine and our patrons head home. The folk singer packs up his guitar and collects his tips. The cloggers with their flushed faces and happy smiles head off with their husbands. Hazel puts the kids to bed. Lucinda sits comfortable on the couch in The Kitchen House; she snuggles into the cushion and usually falls asleep. Rayland, Cody and I close up shop. Then we sit at a table until late in the night telling our secrets. I have told them all about the last year at the campground. Beau's affair that went on just three trailers down from our home, while I breastfed an infant and the boys ran through the campgrounds unsupervised. I confessed that my life was hell and when Beau left, it got worse, until the day God sent me Hazel.

They tell me about the last couple years with Lucinda and the year before the diagnosis. At first it was simple things that Lucinda did, that we all do, like forgetting what you are about to say or mixing up your words. She became forgetful and odd. Rayland began checking on her more and when he did he would find strange things like the keys left in the door and the newspaper in the refrigerator. Her home became more and more messy. She left things out, scattered all over the table, piles on the floor. She told Rayland she didn't want to put things away, because she forgot where they went. When he suggested she find a new place to put her things, she told him she had already tried that, and has forgotten where that was. It was easier for Lucinda to leave her essential things scattered before her. That way when she needed something, she could find it. Rayland became frantic at the things he saw. His always-beautiful mom with her elegant home now resembled a hoarder with smeared lipstick. He called his brothers and told them he thought their mother had a brain tumor or something. When they received the actual diagnosis, early onset Alzheimer's disease, it was worse than his worst nightmare.

Lucinda took her fate bravely. She continued to live on her own. She devised her lifestyle and days so that she could function. For relaxation, she drove, winding through the mountains, lost for hours. Rayland would become a nervous wreck when Lucinda was missing, frantically pacing until her return. Lucinda told Rayland not to worry, sometimes she felt she needed to get lost, and find her way back home. When Rayland could no longer sleep at night and Lucinda began putting her clothes on backwards they made her move in with them and she's still pissed.

Since Lucinda's move into Rayland and Cody's small place, she has rapidly declined. Rayland blames himself for taking her out of her home, but it just wasn't safe. He and Cody may have to leave their apartment that sits above the dance studio in Charleston and move into Lucinda's pretty home that sits on Vine Street in Grace. Now that spring is coming the commute won't be so bad and maybe Lucinda will gain back her spark and have less confusion. For now, Rayland and Cody try to find humor in the chaos and light in the dark. Lucinda finds her happiness coming into The Kitchen House. The music fills her up and makes her smile. She even flirted a little with the middle-aged, longhaired folk singer and I had to laugh when she seductively stroked his guitar and told him he had a nice pickle.

Watching Avery Banks

Dear Diary, it's March 13ᵗʰ and here in Grace, a fresh new green earth shows through the patches of snow. The mirrored lakes have thawed and broken chunks of ice float like raft boats, rapidly down the river bend. Gladden, the wind, is still fiercely blowing, yet we merge outside in our flannel shirts, without our coats, and breathe in the cool air. In the springtime all is awakened in the mountains, including the people. We emerge from our caves of hibernation like bears, feeling refreshed and energetic after our long winter of slumber; and though each person I see is budding with life, no one is more lively than my father. My dad is in the process of designing and building a gigantic playground for my children that may end up covering half of my back yard. My boys are very excited, as he rolls out his plans on the table and asks for their opinions. However, if the kids think this playground is solely for them, a gift from their grandfather, they are surely mistaken. The playground is actually his latest business idea. If my yard resembles a park where all the children want to play, certainly their parents will have to come in and buy a coffee.

A playground at The Kitchen House is actually a great idea. Since I run a business out of my home all day, the kids are stuck with me at work. A playground should help a lot, especially now, since I've started watching Avery Banks.

Christy, Avery's mom, called me in a panic two weeks ago. She said her babysitter quit with no warning and she had to be at work the next morning by 7:00am. Christy admitted to me that I was the last person she

104

was going to call before calling off work. She had gone through the school directory and phoned all the other moms she knew and also liked, which wasn't many, but they all declined. Christy figured I would say no and when I didn't she was quite surprised.

"Sure, we would love to have Avery," I told her. "The boys will be so happy." It worked out so well that I volunteered to watch Avery every week.

It may seem crazy to offer babysitting while you're trying to run a business. I hadn't intended to become a babysitter, but Roman and Henry were so happy when Avery was here. My boys haven't been truly happy since their daddy left and it breaks my heart. I was overwhelmed by smiles that first Saturday as I watched the kids play and interact. I realized that day that they all had something in common. They are three little fatherless boys with hard working mamas. The three giggled and played all day, building multiple Lego structures and having gunfights.

"It would be great if you could watch me all the time Miss. Sissy," Avery said. His sweet enthusiasm caused my heart to swell and me to offer babysitting services to Avery and Christy Banks.

It's really not so bad, Christy works twelve hour shifts three days a week at the hospital. On Tuesdays, Thursdays and Saturdays we are gifted with the presence of Avery Banks, a remarkable little boy with twisted legs, a crooked smile and a zest for life.

Selfishly, I like the feeling I get from helping Christy and Avery Banks. They are people with too much on their plate. Some people get all the shit. Christy is certainly one of those people. Christy and I went to school together. We knew each other well, but didn't hang out. Christy ran around with a large rowdy crowd and I ran around with Rayland, a sensitive, gay teen. However, just about the time I became pregnant by Beau Jaspers, Christy became pregnant by Billy Dean. Roman was born in September, a year after we graduated. He was a perfect baby with pale blue eyes and blond ringlets of curls. Avery was born in October with unworkable legs that were crudely twisted about his tiny body. Beau and I took our perfect baby to the campground to work. It was a position that he had described to everybody as his dream job and we looked like a happy little hippie family, one that caused people to smile. Christy and Billy took their crippled baby to Dean's Holler to live and they looked pathetic, which caused people to frown with pity and shake their head.

Really, life can be so unfair and sometimes people are given more than they know how to deal with, which pretty much sums up Billy Dean's life.

Billy Dean was a handsome guy. He was rough and not much of a student in school, but he had been raised tough in a poor family and he did the best he could. He had a soft layer under a rough exterior, which can be doubly hard, and he was in love with Christy Banks, probably much more than Beau Jaspers ever loved me.

On a cold and icy night in February 1992, Avery Banks screamed for food. Christy added water to a near empty gallon of milk and bottle-fed her tiny, twisted baby the cloudy liquid between his sobs. It was more than Billy Dean could stand. He had to do something. Instead of asking someone for help, he jumped into his beat up truck and drove twenty-five country miles on the icy roads to a shabby and disgusting store that sits directly up against the mountains and is appropriately named The Butt Whole. The dirty, little store is actually a headshop that specializes in selling cigarettes, bags of tobacco, pipes, rolling papers, paraphernalia, and stuff like that. The store's equally disgusting owner believed himself to be a comic genius when he named his hole in the wall cigarette shop, The Butt Whole. Billy Dean entered the nasty shop with a ski mask pulled over his face and an empty gun in his hand. He robbed the owner of three hundred dollars and on his way out he was shot in the back; whereas Billy Dean's gun contained no bullets, the asinine owner of The Butt Whole, was fully loaded. Billy Dean died, face down in the snow, at the entrance of a head shop, in a drastic attempt to feed his child. The state authorities justified the store owner's action. Like an ignorant, badass hillbilly, he ran his mouth until one of the Dean brothers waited for him outside his shop and knocked the shit out of him.

Even though Billy Dean was the perpetrator and what he did was completely wrong, I always felt sorry for him and not for the shop owner. I believe Billy Dean could have tried to rob any store that night, but he didn't. Instead, he chose to drive past the respectable businesses with kind, honorable owners to a disreputable shop with an asshole owner, if only to justify his desperate action. After the police delivered the news of Billy's death to Christy they went out and bought her baby formula and diapers. I hate The Butt Whole, the dirty little shop that sits up against my beautiful Allegheny Mountains like foul graffiti and I hate its gross owner, the butthole who shot Avery's daddy.

Surprisingly, Christy and Avery have done well and Billy would be proud. Christy got a clerk job at the hospital in the pediatric unit where Avery had spent so much time. They eventually moved out of the holler and away from Billy Dean's dysfunctional family. Christy bought her and Avery a cute little ranch house in town not far from mine and they seem to be happy.

Avery looks just like his daddy, and he is also tough and strong. I had thought I might have to help Avery get along and it would be a lot to watch him. I figured he would remain in his wheelchair until I lifted him out and that I would have to help him with the bathroom. I could not have been more wrong. Avery compensates for his crooked legs with his strong arms and even stronger will. That child is the most independent cuss I have ever seen. He's much more self-sufficient than my boys and I cannot get over his agility and strength. He climbs in and out of his chair with ease and I believe he would just as soon be out of it. He doesn't mind scooting around and in fact, he prefers it. Actually, Avery's favorite mode of transportation is his skateboard, which he sits on and maneuvers accurately with his arms and hands. His precision and speed is that of a racecar driver and now Roman wants a skateboard.

In truth, Avery is a joy to have around the house and Hazel has fallen in love with him. On Saturdays, the three boys help Hazel make the biscuit dough that is used throughout the week. They measure, pour, and stir together each concoction, with the guidance of Hazel and then they roll the dough into perfect biscuit shapes and stick them in freezer bags. They also spend time baking cookies, brownies or whatever else Hazel decides to whip up. When Hazel is not cooking with the boys, allowing them to stick their hands in gooey bowls with cracked eggs, she is coloring with them. Hazel loves to color and will sit for an hour with a coloring book and crayons like a contented child. All three boys, Roman, Henry and Avery are pretty good artists and Hazel has many crafty ideas that keep them busy on windy and cold afternoons.

Saturdays at The Kitchen House move swiftly and Avery adds joy to the hours. It's so nice to see Roman happy at play and the television off. It's a sweet change from the angry child with a remote that we've been living with for the past year. All three are happy and Henry's giggles fill The Kitchen House as he interacts with the older boys. Both Henry and Avery are little comedians and try to out do each other with foolishness.

Saturdays are spent laughing, which has been a complete transformation, because not too long ago it was a day of outbursts and tears. Maybe, we're getting better and I deeply believe that this house and Avery Banks are our healers.

On Saturdays, Rayland and Cody arrive at 5:00pm to move tables and set up their portable platform. They work like a handsome stage crew in their fresh black t-shirts and crisp blue jeans. They may be the only two men from these parts that have traded in their brown Timberline boots for a pair of tap shoes and they wear them well. Lucinda looks attractive too. She has taken to wearing silky outfits in royal shades. She has gold, silk pants with a gold silk button up top, and the same outfit in burgundy, ruby red and royal blue. On her tiny feet she wears black ballerina slippers. Three gold chains in different lengths, hang around her neck. I believe Rayland and Cody have been shopping for Lucinda in the lingerie department and she is wearing silk pajamas. However, with her hair and makeup done and wearing jewelry, Lucinda actually looks like she's dressed up and not at all ready for bed. Rayland and Cody are fashion geniuses and they have created a style that is so perfect for Lucinda and one that she can manage. The pants are easy for Lucinda to pull up with no confusing snaps or hooks, the shirts are easily pulled over her head without unbuttoning and she seems so comfortable. There is ease in the way she plops down on the sofa at The Kitchen House and snuggles into the cushion looking content.

Lenore shows up to work right before our regulars begin to arrive. Lenore has been in Grace for over two months now and I can see that she is slowly becoming more comfortable. Between the Homework Help Center and serving coffee she has met a lot of people and they all seem to like her, even though she is much more quiet than the rest of us. Lenore is friendly, but a bit reserved. She is mannerly and polite, a good listener who knows when to laugh. But in truth, a Connecticut Scholar is very different from a West Virginia Redneck. I hope we don't scare her.

Beau's family, the Jaspers, always come out to The Kitchen House on Friday and Saturday nights and it's good to see them. They watch over the kids while Hazel, Lenore and I work like crazy women. I pretty much stay behind the counter, make coffee drinks and fill glasses of water for Lenore to run around. We decided to create specials for our entertainment nights that don't require too much work. On Friday afternoon, I assist

Hazel, as she prepares a large pot of something good. On Saturday, if needed, we add to it, and we serve the same thing both nights. The patrons who come both Friday and Saturday night don't seem to mind eating the same thing twice. It's always delicious, hearty and five dollars a bowl. So far, we've served chili with a black pepper biscuit, vegetable beef stew with a cheddar biscuit, and bean soup with corn bread. We also sell a lot of Mummy dogs on those nights. Even though the menu is easy, I feel that by the end of the night we have worked hard. Thank God it's so enjoyable and that on Sunday we are closed.

On Saturday evenings when Christy Banks comes to pick up Avery, she stays. She purchases her five dollar bowl of dinner, sits back and watches Avery bounce all over the place. Believe it or not, Avery is a wonderful dancer. His head and shoulders keep time and rhythm and when he brings his skateboard up on two wheels and spins in a circle, I can't help but clap.

The energy in The Kitchen House on Saturday nights is unreal and if you were to ask Pixie Moon-Dust, who can be found sitting off in the corner, just how unreal it is, she would tell you things that you couldn't possibly believe. In order to understand you must stop, become silent, focus and observe the things that Pixie is observing. Then you will see that it is quite possible that a relaxed, contented and smiling Lucinda is snuggled up against her dead husband and that a laughing, spinning Avery is really dancing with his daddy. Pixie told me that a beautiful, dark haired young man that is surrounded by white light follows Lenore. She believes him to be her angel. She also said that Harry, Hazel's deceased, is ornery rotten and keeps sampling bites of Hazel's soup. It was no surprise to me when she said that my mama, with her black wild hair and equally wild personality, takes center stage among the dancers on Saturday nights and she looks just like a rock star.

A Pixie's Story

March 21, 2000 – Dear Diary, I am learning that people come into our life for all kinds of reasons and that somehow through life's twists and turns and ups and downs we find the ones we are supposed to meet, and soon after, they begin making a difference.

People surprise you. It's been said that you don't really know someone until you've walked in his or her shoes. Well, I'd like to walk in the shoes (she actually wears moccasins) of Pixie Moon-Dust. That girl is full of surprises. Rayland called me last week and asked me if I knew that Pixie was a home health aide.

"No," I told him." I just thought she was a medium."

I guess being a medium in a small Appalachian town doesn't pay the bills, so Pixie supplements her income by being a home health aide. She has several elderly clients that she provides with care. She takes them to their doctor's appointments or grocery store, helps them with their housework, prepares their meals, dispenses their meds and mostly just keeps them company. Just recently Pixie Moon-Dust added Lucinda to her list of clients.

Lucinda wasn't happy at Rayland and Cody's apartment and her unhappiness caused restless nights, grumpy moods, a confused state and outbursts of profanity. Rayland and Cody reluctantly decided that Lucinda would do better if they took her home, and it worked. Lucinda finds peace living among her own things. She sleeps better in her own bed made up with pink satin pillows and relaxes on her couch of red leather. For Lucinda, life has become more suitable. For Rayland and Cody, life just got even more inconvenient. Because they feel that Lucinda requires full-time care, they have had to move out of their apartment over the dance studio and into Lucinda's house nearly an hour away from work. Now, Lucinda doesn't want to leave her house to accompany them to the dance studio and it seems cruel to make her. Rayland and Cody decided that with the lapses of time that Lucinda would be on her own, they needed the help of a home health aide. Lucinda's doctor gave Rayland a list of home health aide companies in the area and surprisingly Pixie Moon- Dust's name was on it. Rayland knew there couldn't be more than one Pixie Moon-Dust so he called her. Rayland told me that Pixie picked up the phone on the first ring.

"Oh Rayland is that you?" Pixie asked, before he had a chance to say anything.

"I had a feeling you would call and yes, I would love to help with Lucinda." Rayland was completely freaked out at first, but now he feels at ease and a schedule of care has been worked out for Lucinda.

I personally like having Rayland so close. It feels like old times with him right down the road and I see Lucinda all the time. Pixie Moon-Dust may be the only person in this town who truly appreciates espresso and when she comes in for a coffee fix she brings Lucinda with her. I've actually gotten to know Pixie quite well, with her daily shots of espresso and evening psychic readings. She is by far the most interesting person I have ever met.

Last week curiosity got the best of me. I needed to know what kept Pixie another hour after her psychic readings and what made my house smell and feel so good. I watched for Pixie's appointment to leave after their session. Staring from my bedroom window I witnessed the dark figure in a long coat make his exit. He walked fast down my sidewalk and into his car. Like a perched hawk, I kept watch until his headlights pulled away from my house and down my long drive and then I went downstairs and entered The Kitchen House. Pixie was focused on the inner door, anticipating my arrival, which startled me at first.

"You can stay," Pixie said. "Your mood is happy, your vibrations good. It may even help."

I had no idea what she was talking about, so I sat quietly down in a chair trying to be as small as possible. I wanted to be a fly on the wall and not a huge presence. There was a gigantic candle burning on the center table. I could tell Pixie made this candle herself. It was a huge, unsophisticated ball of wax molded around cinnamon sticks. The bottom of the candle was flat so it sat nicely and the smell was intense. First, Pixie opened up all the windows and the door including the screens. She stuck her head out and breathed in a nice long breath of cold fresh air.

"Opening the windows allows the spirits to leave and the air to circulate," Pixie explained. I nodded in agreement.

"Come with me," she said. "I could use a hand." I got up and followed Pixie out the door. We walked to her car and she popped open the trunk. The space held the contents of a janitor's closet. Pixie handed me a large bucket full of supplies and a mop. She grabbed a broom and a small vacuum cleaner and we headed back in.

"It's important to purify the house after each reading. It's needed to get rid of any negative energy lingering in the walls or floors."

'You mean like ghosts?" I asked a little frightened.

"Not necessarily, we are all full of energy. Where do you think the energy goes when you shout, scream, cry, or holler?" I shook my head not knowing the answer.

"Into the woodwork that's where. The objects in the house absorb it. In truth, somebody else's crappy mood can really funk up your house." I followed Pixie back into the house and then I took my seat in the corner. I didn't want to get in the way of purifying or mess anything up.

First, Pixie pulled a spray bottle full of rose water and a rag from her bucket. There was an abundance of red petal floating in the clear liquid and I knew that Pixie had created this mixture herself. Pixie began by spraying the walls as far up as she could reach. She started in the corner of one wall, and sprayed and wiped, sprayed and wiped moving down as she worked. Very Soon Pixie had wiped down all four walls and was spraying my coffee bar.

"Roses are the flowers of love," Pixie informed me. She continued to spray her concoction of love on the tables and chairs humming a sweet melody as she worked. Next, Pixie grabbed her broom. Again, you could tell Pixie had made this. The handle is long and rustic, fashioned from ash I believe. At the top of the handle a hole was drilled and three little golden bells are tied onto its end. The bristles are held tight with a cord. I have seen other homemade brooms at art fairs and flea markets; Pixie's was quite impressive.

"What are the bristles?" I asked inquisitively.

"Broomcorn," Pixie informed me. "I grow it myself, in the field. It looks a lot like sweet corn, except there are no cobs."

Pixie first swept the corners of my ceilings.

"It's important to knock down any cobwebs," Pixie said over the jingling of bells. Next, Pixie began sweeping at the far end of The Kitchen House and worked her way to my front door. She moved her arms in a rhythmic way and the golden bells sang out a little tune.

"Bells fill a room with crystal clear energy," she informed me. Pixie swept straight out my front door and out onto the porch, sweeping and jingling until every crumb of energy had been pushed away from my house and down the front steps.

From the bucket, Pixie pulled a container of spices, which she then began to sprinkle, like carpet fresh, onto my oriental rugs.

"Cinnamon and allspice," she explained. "Allspice is known to inspire conversation, and creates a cozy and welcoming atmosphere. Cinnamon produces a feeling of propriety and cheerfulness, and there is nothing wrong with good manners and fun. In fact, it's better for business. I made that cinnamon candle especially for The Kitchen House. "

"Thank you." I was touched that she cared about my business. Pixie allowed the spices to sit on the rugs for a few minutes before she vacuumed them up. Still working my floors, Pixie sprayed her bottle of rose water onto my hardwood and then dry mopped over it. The mop also had a bell tied to its end. Just one large silver bell with a clang much deeper than the three little golden bells dangling from the broom. Again, Pixie went to her bucket, and this time she pulled out a large baggie of rock salt. Pixie placed salt in each corner of the room.

"Leave the salt there," she instructed. "Salt may be the most important element in purifying, it absorbs negative energy." Pixie and her bucket began to remind me of Mary Poppins. Next, Pixie pulled out a handmade ceramic bowl, no doubt made by her own hands. She sat it on my table and then withdrew a bottle of olive oil and a head of garlic. She poured just a little of the oil into the bowl.

"Oil or water can be made holy," Pixie stated. She then broke the garlic and placed a clove in the center of the bowl. "Garlic rids away evil spirits."

I felt a little uncomfortable at first, but then Pixie began to pray. Her prayer was silent, but intense. I heard the whispered word God pass through her lips several times, and it made me feel good. Pixie picked up the ceramic bowl of oil and garlic and walked over to the open window. She dipped two fingertips into the oil and ran them across my window frame, as she did this, she quietly sang out a mantra.

"Bless this house with love and light," she repeated as she rubbed all four sides of the window frame. I too began repeating Pixie's mantra in my head, trying hard to bless my house, and in doing so; I could truly feel its atmosphere of sanctity. Pixie went to every window in The Kitchen House, dipped her fingers in the oil, rubbed them on the frame and repeated her mantra. Last, Pixie did the two doors. In the center of each door, with the oil, Pixie made a cross.

Finished with the cleansing, Pixie began putting all of the items back in the bucket. Last, she picked up the cinnamon candle, blew out its light and then she wafted the smoke around in a circular motion while speaking another silent prayer.

"If you want, "Pixie said holding out the candle, "You can keep this to burn during the day when customers are here. I can make another."

"Thank you," my words were hesitant. I was calm but curious. "Why do you do such an intense house cleansing, when you said nothing bad wants to be here?"

"Nothing bad is here," Pixie responded. "And nothing bad is invited to come." I suddenly understood Pixie's rituals and message. Everything I had just witnessed and had explained to me was so beautiful with a deep sense of holiness, yet so different from what others practice.

"It's not so different," Pixie said obviously reading my mind. "It's the same as your church. Do you know why your church has a feeling of blessedness and purity?"

"Because it's a church?" I stupidly answered.

"That's true," Pixie confirmed making me feel better. "A church is built with a sacred purpose and its intentions are good. But, more importantly the people purify it. Churches are full of prayer and hymns. Bells chime, an organ plays, candles and incense burn and water is made holy."

Pixie's analogy made sense to me. I knew the feeling she was talking about, that hallowed sense I get when walking into an empty cathedral. I had that feeling in the woods under the gazebo built by Father McIntire and now in my own home, thanks to Pixie Moon-Dust.

"Would you like a cup of tea?" I offered. "If you don't have to hurry off, we can just sit and talk awhile." Pixie accepted my invitation and over a cup of chamomile lemon, Pixie told me her story.

As a child, Pixie heard voices she couldn't explain. She noticed things out of the corner of her eye, but when she turned, they weren't there. She always felt followed and scared. Pixie had vibrant dreams that made no sense, but they would eventually unfold truths. In school, she was timid and shy, often lost in her own thoughts. She suffered lots of headaches and almost always had an upset stomach. Pixie confessed that her given name is Priscilla, but it was her father who began to call her Pixie because of her size and the way she owned the woods. She did not tell me her real last name and I did not ask. She did tell me that she has an older sister named Cecilia. Pixie and Cecilia were raised deep in the mountains. She said her father is a bootlegger and her mother is a mystery.

Pixie said even her earliest memories are of her mother leaving. For some reason, Pixie's mother could not stand to be contained within the walls that made up their home, so she walked. At any random moment during the day, without a word, Pixie's mother would walk out the front door into the deep woods and be gone for hours. She walked in winter, summer, snow or rain. At times, she walked in her nightgown, or barefoot. She would leave on frigid days and forget her coat. She walked with unbrushed hair and whatever she was wearing the moment she decided to leave. She walked on Christmas, birthdays and the first day of school. What Pixie remembers about her mother is she walked. When Pixie was ten years old, her mother walked out the door in her usual fashion and never came back. Pixie's father had always been the nurturer. Life wasn't so different without her mother, except for the worry they all felt, the mystery and unrest of it all and the sadness in her father's eyes. Hearing this part of her story made me realize why I feel such a connection to Pixie. She too was left by a wild mother and raised with one sibling by an unconventional father. It's funny how unusual things can be so common.

After Pixie's mother left, the voices Pixie heard became louder, the shadowy figures bolder. The dreams turned to nightmares and Pixie lived frightened every day. Pixie knew that Cecilia heard the voices too, but when Pixie tried to talk to her about them, Cecilia would deny hearing them and punch Pixie in the arm. The two girls saw and heard the same eerie things, yet they had very different reactions. Pixie was constantly scared and Cecilia was always angry. Brave, thirteen-year-old Cecilia would shout into the darkness, demanding her nightmares to "go away!" She fought her bad dreams viciously; leaving the bed covers a tangled mess. She told the voices to shut up and the shadowy figures to leave. Cecilia did not spend a childhood scared like her little sister. She spent it angry.

Pixie loves her daddy, the one warm and gentle person in her life. After a nightmare, Pixie would run from her room through the dark shadows to her daddy asleep in the front room recliner. Pixie would climb up onto his lap. He would rock the small ten-year-old like a baby, usually falling back to sleep first, his hot moonshine breath, a comfort on her head. Pixie began to follow her daddy into the woods when he went to check on his stills. She had to be very quiet, because this was forbidden, his one and only strict rule. No matter how quietly she crept he always knew she was there. Halfway through his walk he would turn and go to the tree that Pixie was crouched behind and tell her to wait there for him. On one particular very hot afternoon he gave her different directions.

"Hey Pix," he said. "I'm going to be gone for a couple of hours. If you go over this hill there is a stream where you can play. If you decide to follow the stream around the side of the mountain, there is a cabin. A woman lives in the cabin, you can eat her fruit, she won't mind."

Apprehensively, Pixie followed the stream and just as her father had said, near the water's edge sat a rustic log cabin with a large front porch. The cabin was old, but inviting with its many flower pots and garden beds. Along the perimeter of the cabin grew herbs and wildflowers in abundance. Behind the cabin was a large vegetable garden and a small orchard. Both of them sat in the confines of a split rail fence covered in wire mesh, a desperate attempt to keep the animals out.

As Pixie sat on the bank of the river, her feet dangling in the cool water, the woman came out on her front porch. Pixie knew she was an older woman, but her face looked kind of young and her hair was bright red and tied upon her head in a messy kind of way.

"Is that my Priscilla?" she said. "Come child up on the porch, I'll give you something cold to drink." Pixie wanted a coke so bad she could taste it, but the woman gave her chilled cucumber water. To her surprise, Pixie enjoyed the refreshment as much as coke and gulped it down quickly. Next, the woman handed Pixie a burlap sack.

"Come with me," she said. Pixie followed her around the yard. In the garden, she picked some beans and she made Pixie help. From the orchard, she gave her three pears and three plums. Next she went to her herbs, describing the plants and flowers to Pixie as they went. She stopped at mint and picked a handful of leaves and tied the bunch with a piece of twine from her pocket.

"This is mint," she said. "It helps soothe an upset stomach. Put a sprig in your tea." Down from the mint, little yellow and white flowers grew like small daisies in a cluster. The woman picked a small bouquet. "Feverfew," she said tying the spray.

"Chew the petals of this flower when your head hurts. It will not harm you."

Pixie's head was swirling. She had a million questions, but said nothing; instead, she followed the woman inside her home. The cabin walls were lined with wooden shelves. From the bottom of the shelves hung dried flowers and herbs. On top of the shelves were bottles upon bottles of oils; stones and crystals of all shapes, sizes and colors; baskets of twine and sticks; candles and incense; leaves, bark and every earthly thing that could be brought indoors. From the shelf, the woman brought down a wreath of garlic.

"Do not eat this," she instructed. "Hang it from your bedroom window." Pixie placed it in the sack and was then handed two sachets of lavender and a small bottle of lavender oil.

"Place the sachets under your pillow and put two drops of the oil on top of your pillow before laying down." The last gift to go in the sack was the most beautiful stone Pixie had ever seen. It was oddly shaped, fairly large and slightly heavy. Its color was grayish brown and it was translucent.

"Smokey quartz," the woman said. "This stone will give you protection. Put it in your room."

"How do you know all this?" Pixie asked. "How do you know me?"

"I just know," said the woman. "The same as you just know, we are different from others. If you like I will teach you to take control of the things you know and not be frightened. Come back soon and as often as you like. As for now, you've been here too long, your father is waiting, it's time for you to go."

Pixie hefted the now heavy sack over her back and turned to leave, then stopped.

"What do I call you?" she asked. The woman smiled.

"You may call me Yama."

When Pixie arrived back to the spot where her father had left her, he was sitting on the bank waiting, just as the woman had predicted. Pixie handed him the sack to carry and they started their walk home.

"Who is she?" Pixie asked.

"Who did she say she was?"

"She didn't, she just told me to call her Yama."

"Yama," her father smiled. "Pixie, she is your grandmother. Your mother never wanted you to meet her mom. She thought she was doing the right thing to keep you separate. She believed it best for you and Cecilia. Folks call your Yama a witch. They call your mommy one too. Your mama tried to deny it all and in rejecting the truth she went crazy and ran away. Don't deny any gifts you have Pixie. Go to Yama if you need and take Cecilia with you."

Pixie began to visit Yama every day and over the years Yama taught her how to develop her craft and not be afraid. Cecilia would occasionally visit Yama with Pixie and she collected just enough knowledge to survive the nights.

Two years ago Yama died. She left the cabin to Pixie who lives in it today, not far from her father, who is still a bootlegger. Pixie said her dad is also in the business of spirits, he just happens to bottle his. He has successfully grown his corn whiskey operation to include his homemade beers and wines. He has five different types of craft and the best elderberry wine ever tasted, often compared to a fine red.

Cecilia threw herself into school and art, and as soon as she could, she fled the mountains. She left West Virginia just weeks after graduation and went to Chicago. She found a job, a small apartment and went to school for fine arts and photography. She now rents a little gallery in a swanky part of the city and hosts local artists. She hangs around with an eccentric crowd. For her insomnia, she drinks red wine and for panic attacks she takes Xanax. As far as the voices go, Cecilia has told them to shut up so many times that Pixie believes they remain quiet out of respect, or maybe they don't. Pixie says she understands why Cecilia had to leave the mountains.

"Cecilia and my mama didn't want to be bothered by spirits, so they tried running away from their ghosts. Who can blame them? Conveying the messages of spirits is an odd and upsetting responsibility. If you don't understand them properly they can surely frighten the hell out of you. Besides that, people find you evil and call you a witch. Others believe you to be a scam artist or nut case. Being a medium is not an easy path to take, but it was the only one I saw before me."

I told Pixie, that I am glad she chose to embrace her gifts and follow her course and I for one feel personally blessed to have made her acquaintance. How many others can say that they have a friend who is a psychic medium witch that works as a home health aide? Pixie has not seen her mama since the day she left. However, she believes that she is still alive, her reasoning, "If she died, she surely would visit."

A Playground for Patrons

April 17, 2000 – Dear Diary, it seems the playground my daddy is building has turned into a project for everybody. The whole town has come by to peek at his creation and give him their advice. In truth, I can't blame them. It is so very exciting watching and helping it all come together. I'm very proud of my father. He has worked on the playground most every evening for over a month now, showing up after he's already worked a full day. Sometimes he's here after dark, a big spotlight tightened to one of the wooden rails, allowing him to see. But that's my daddy, a tireless constructor who doesn't stop. On the weekends he gives the playground a full day, arriving early for his coffee and not stopping until our entertainment starts. The boys have helped him every step of the way. They fly out the door as soon as his truck pulls in. They have learned how to measure; carry; pile and sort lumber; saw; use a drill; hammer; properly steer a wheelbarrow; mix cement and dig. They have spent the last month dirty and exhausted. At the end of each day their anticipation covers them like a blanket and they sleep so good at night, unaware of our active ghosts. The boys are so excited about the playground and they have already claimed parts of it as their own. Sabrina has helped too. She has learned tools and can hand my father a hammer and a nail. She knows the level by its size and color. When my dad shouts down from his ladder, "Brina, go get the yellow level," she picks up the tool that is over half her own length and clumsily toddles it over. I have happily been videotaping the entire process in pieces and I hope to compose a treasured video for my father.

My daddy's idea for a park in my yard bloomed this winter when the kids were stuck in the house all day and I wasn't able to just close up shop and take everyone out to play. It was then he decided to build a park right outside my back door. His first thought was a couple of swings and a fort with a slide, but when he began looking up the plethora of playground designs, inspiration bloomed. He has taken every idea that he has seen, added a few of his own and created a recreational area that takes up half of my full two acres of back yard.

My daddy's plan consists of two very tall and large towers at each end of the playground and a swinging bridge that connects them. The towers look like a combination between royal and rustic, a castle made from wood with high peak rooftops, shingled in green. In each tower are two small windows that open and shut. Drilled into the walls are several round peek holes. The holes are the perfect width for the muzzle of a squirt gun. You can reach the towers by a series of inclines and platforms and every level holds its own unique characteristics. From bumpy slides to sensory walls, my daddy has thought of it all; including the children who will play here. He has designed the playground to be completely wheelchair accessible with ramps that run in every direction. This particular feature made Christy Banks cry humble tears of joy.

From one tower you can take a yellow tube slide down to the bottom and from the other my dad created a zip line. Upon completion, the playground will include several swings hanging in different corners, a tire swing, a wooden rope swing, a plastic and chain swing, a baby swing, and one very expensive handicapped swing that my father had to special order. There is also the making of a sand stream, bordered in stones and river rock, and a climbing wall. Already this playground has pulled people together and brought patrons into The Kitchen House before its completion.

The crowd began to form on the first day when my daddy surveyed the yard and mapped out his idea with wooden stakes and twine. Nosy neighbors came over to ask what Daddy was building now and after their quick interrogation, guilt made them buy a coffee. Now they come with drills in their hands and an empty thermos that I fill. Like schoolboys, they are so excited to help build the big wooden jungle gym.

For my father there has been much support and only one hindrance, the weather. My father started building just weeks before the start of spring and he has dealt with cold, snow, sleet, wind, rain and mud. The day my dad chose to dig the holes to set the posts was a beautiful day with a mild temperature of sixty degrees and a bright blue sky. My daddy, brother and children worked for hours, digging hole after hole and piling the pulled earth into one corner of my yard. They finished in eight hours time, sore, dirty, tired and ecstatic. That night while they slept, Gladden blew in large black clouds to hover over our town and it rained a ferocious downpour. I did not think about the rain the next morning when Roman, Henry and Avery went out to play. That was until one of the neighbors called The Kitchen House to tell me to look outside as Christy Banks was surely going to kick my ass. I will confess the fear of an ass beating did sweep over me when I saw Avery's wheelchair covered in mud and carelessly parked askew in a puddle. I didn't see the boys at first and panic began rising as I scanned the yard. I then heard the shouts and laughter and looked over to the far back corner of my yard to where the dirt had been piled. Sure enough there they were. Henry and Roman were crouched down on either side of the large pile of pulled earth; flinging mud balls back and forth at each other. Avery had pulled himself up to the top of the pile and sat like king of the hill. In his hand was a wooden stake that he wielded like a sword while shouting out fictional commands. I spewed out a list of swear words as I watched the boys play. Hazel on the other hand, looked out the window and began to laugh, as if it were the most amusing thing she had witnessed all year.

"They sure found some fun," she said.

"And how in the hell are we supposed to clean them up?" I asked.

All three boys were covered in mud from head to toe. They had played in every last mud puddle on their way to the pile of dirt and left the wheelchair stuck in a rut. I couldn't take these wet and mud dripping children into the restaurant or through my front door and it was too cold to spray them down with a hose. As I dragged the baby pool out of the shed, Hazel began preparing buckets of warm soapy water. Mr. Baxter, the nosy neighbor who had called to warn me of an ass beating was now standing on my back porch drinking Hazel's House Blend coffee, while I single-handedly carried approximately ten buckets of water outside to fill the pool.

I called over all three boys and stripped them down to their underwear. Avery's pants were difficult to get off his twisted legs. He helped me, as I had no idea what I was doing. I plopped all three boys into the pool of bubbles and let them splash away. When the spring wind hit their naked, wet bodies, they shivered and giggled with blue lips and dancing eyes. Hazel made up more buckets of warm water and I dumped those on the boys' heads. When I was certain that nearly all of the mud was out of their hair and their bodies looked mostly clean I wrapped them in towels and carried them one by one into The Kitchen House. Hazel had set out clean clothes for all three boys and as they got themselves dressed, I went outside to retrieve the wheelchair. It took me a bit of a struggle to get the chair upright and out of the mud and Mr. Baxter offered no help. I sprayed the chair down with the hose and wiped it with a towel. I rinsed out the clothes in the pool of mud and bubbles and hung them on the line. Just as I was dumping the baby pool of water, my daddy showed up. He examined each posthole expecting to find them full of water. He was delighted to see that the boys had scooped it all out using plastic cups and flung it at each other in their game of war.

"Hey, them boys did a great job! Thanks to those rascals, we're gonna be able to set the posts and do the framing today just like I'd hoped." He then invited the boys to come out and help and they got muddy and cold all over again.

That day Daddy's crew consisted of my brother Charlie, Pop Jaspers, Avery Banks, Roman and Henry. The men and children worked until dusk two days in a row and by the end of the weekend they had completed the framing of the largest backyard swing set that's ever been built. Since that day, Daddy's crew has grown. The first to offer a helping hand was Father Tim McIntire. This did not surprise me, as every aspect of the playground appeals to his nature. For starters, he is a woodworker and carpenter and like my dad and brother, he has a desire to create. He also seems to have a soft spot for the children. I think he likes them better than the adults. Also, this playground has come to represent community; something a priest values. Since volunteering, Father McIntire has been here nearly as much as daddy and more than Charlie.

Interestingly enough, Lenore helps fairly often. Daddy is usually just arriving as Homework Help Center ends and Lenore seems rather eager to head outside and pound some nails. She has even begun wearing old jeans and a ball cap to do homework, something she never did before. Daddy, who is an exceptional builder, has even asked for her advice in terms of measuring and physics in regards to the zip line. I think the playground gives Lenore one more thing to keep her mind and time occupied. She still has not found a job and I believe she struggles both financially and mentally. She often seems depressed. She is a woman who needs to keep busy to keep from crying.

Rayland and Cody lend a helping hand two days a week. I know they would like to be here more, but Lucinda has developed a terrible cough and cold this spring. Often, she seems so tired. When they do come, they place Lucinda on the couch with a blanket on her lap. She snuggles into the spirit of her dead husband while the men work outside. Both Rayland and Cody are excited about the completion of the playground and have told me they will be here all day when it comes time to stain the wood. They love to paint.

Pixie Moon-Dust does not help. Nevertheless, she is here as much as anybody and is our biggest spectator, with the exception of Mr. Baxter. Pixie has two other clients, in addition to Lucinda, that she watches on different days throughout the week. Pixie enjoys bringing them out of their homes for exercise and over to The Kitchen House to watch the construction. Old Man Reardon, one of Pixie's clients, truly loves this activity. When I was a child, Mr. Reardon was a giant of a man. He stood a lean and strong six foot seven and was clearly the tallest man in Grace, West Virginia. He is now frail, thin and crooked, resembling a bent rail. Hunched over his walker, he takes painfully slow and feeble steps. Nonetheless, when Pixie sits him down in front of the playground construction, a foreman comes to life. He begins bossing people around while shaking a weak fist.

Pixie has told me that the ghost children at The Kitchen House are already enjoying the playground and she likes to watch them play. Oddly enough, my dad cannot keep track of his tools, which he says has never been a problem before. He blames the boys when he finds his drill under the large oak or his tape measure on the porch, but I wonder if it's not our happy, little, ghost children prancing about.

Just as my dad wanted The Kitchen House renovation complete by Christmas, he is now trying to finish the playground before Easter, which is six days from now on April 23rd. On Saturday the 22nd The Kitchen House is hosting an Easter egg hunt. These are things I feel I must do to draw in business, So on top of everything else; I've been shoving pieces of candy into plastic eggs for over a week now. Hazel, bless her heart, has sewn a bunny costume and it's adorable. The costume has gigantic feet, a purple satin vest and a bow tie. I'm proud to say that I made the bunny head. I crafted the giant thing from paper mache. I worked on it at night after the kids were in bed and Pixie had finished her psychic readings. Although I'm tired, it felt therapeutic. I used to love doing paper mache in high school. I would create and paint elaborate masks and hang them on the walls of my teenage bedroom. The bunny head turned out great. I painted rosy cheeks, big buckteeth and long ears with pink insides. Hazel laughed hysterically when she saw it. She said it is the cutest thing I've ever done. Lenore has agreed to wear the costume and be our bunny from the hours of 2:00 to 4:00pm. The Easter festivities will end when the clogging begins. I hope families stay to watch the dancers and buy something to eat.

The Kitchen House is still stressed financially. It seems we dump more money into the business than we make. It's possible we will never make much. I mean, how many cups of coffee can you sell in a small town? Yet, I look at what The Kitchen House has done and I know this business was the right decision and that I must believe in this dream. Besides coffee, The Kitchen House has given the town of Grace entertainment on Friday and Saturday nights (something much needed). In doing so, we have placed a spotlight on those who love to shine. We've provided the children a place to play, help with their homework and brought a close community even closer together. All that is worth more than coffee sales.

Seeing is Believing

April 24, 2000 – Dear Diary, I could very easily start a newspaper and call it The Kitchen House Gazette. Since becoming the town's coffee bartender people have been revealing to me their personal drama. It must be the warmth of the cappuccino colored walls, the charisma of The Kitchen House or the taste of cinnamon, vanilla coffee that causes people to relax, let down their guard and tell their story. Whatever it is, they come sit at my coffee bar, spill forth their truths, and my ghosts and I get an earful. Just as Rayland suggested, I have become the town's best friend, as well as counselor and keeper of secrets. I have been told many things I probably shouldn't know. But, people need to talk, and if you stand quiet long enough they will begin to talk to you.

I know that Joe the mailman had a colonoscopy last week and it revealed polyps. I know that Jean the bus driver has a son in jail and a daughter that is a born-again Christian. She's not sure which child she finds more frustrating. I know that Lydia, the librarian, and her husband, Hank, have not had sex in eight years. A fact she has told me twice, so I know it really bothers her. I know that Christy Banks smokes pot every evening after Avery falls asleep, because it helps her relax. I know that Mrs. Baxter's sister has gone crazy and lives with twelve cats. I know that Ezra Landis has a crush on Hazel. Hazel would know this too if she wasn't oblivious of her own charm. I know the secrets of Lenore and the story of a Pixie.

The person I know nothing about, despite his frequent visits to my coffee house is Father Timothy McIntire. He is a man of anonymity. Hazel says that is the way of a priest. They are taught that it would be considered vain to talk about themselves. She says a priest is to listen to others, offer advice, and pray, anything beyond that is too intimate. Hazel may be right, but I believe there is something more to Father McIntire than a white collar and good manners. He's sociable, kind, and selfless, but there is a distance in his interactions that is not just formal and shyness in his demeanor. He laughs easily; carries a smile on his face, but his eyes are sad and often teary. Another thing, I don't know how comfortable he is within the confines of the church. Sure, on Sunday mornings he plays the role and seems perfect in his sacred setting, but as soon as the bells clang and the people aren't looking, he escapes into the mountain woods. If it's not the mountains that are calling him away from the cathedral it's nearly anything else; hot chocolate, a folk singer, cloggers, errands, and a variety of good deeds, which included, the building of a playground.

Father McIntire's passion and hard work matched my daddy's when it came to the wooden recreational area outside my back door. Often the two men worked late into the night by clamping a large light onto a wooden beam in order to see. Strangely enough, my father and the priest worked well together despite the distinct differences in their personalities. Daddy tackles work with a cigarette dangling from his lips and a collection of swear words sitting on the tip of his tongue. Father Tim hums a sweet melody while carefully focused on the task before him. The two men managed to complete construction on Good Friday and on Saturday the children of Grace initiated our backyard park with an Easter egg hunt.

On Easter night, I heard a presence in my back yard. I looked out the window, anticipating my daddy's truck, assuming he had come over in the middle of the night to tighten screws or add something new. To my surprise, the person climbing around on the gigantic wooden structure was Father McIntire. I watched him for several minutes; not sure how long he had been there or what he was doing. Curiosity soon got the best of me and I threw shoes on my feet and went outside onto the porch.

"Father Tim?" I called out into the darkness startling the priest.

"Oh Sissy, I'm sorry. I didn't mean to scare you. I'm just," he hesitated.

"Just what?"

"I'm just creating a surprise for the boys." I walked out into the yard.

"What is it?" I asked.

I could see the woodburning tool in his hand and when I got closer I could smell the effects of it on the hard lumber. Father McIntire seemed embarrassed to have been caught. He led me up the series of wooden ramps to the high fort with the zip line. From the pocket of his jacket he pulled out a flashlight and shined it on the fortress. I stood amazed. Above the door in a high arch were the words ROMAN'S TOWER. Each letter meticulously scripted. This was the fort that Roman had claimed for himself since the beginning. The sentiment was so sweet that tears welled in my eyes.

"Oh Father Tim, he'll love it."

"Come," he said. We turned from the fort and walked out onto the long swinging bridge. On the railing, in lettering just as beautiful as the tower, burned the words HENRY'S BRIDGE. Father McIntire knew, just as Roman had claimed the tower, Henry had claimed the bridge. I could not help but giggle out loud.

"Oh my gosh, you got it so right. This is absolutely perfect." I could tell that Father McIntire was relieved and excited that I was happy. He was now energized.

"I have something else to show you," he said grabbing my hand. We ran together like school children down the wooden ramps to the bottom. Directly behind the playset my daddy had made the sand stream. I noticed the discarded soup can and paintbrush first and then Father Tim shined his light on the rocks that border the river of sand. On the outer side, near the middle, on each flat stone, he had painted a letter so that the length of the sand bed read SABRINA'S STREAM. The effects of his surprise made me giddy and happy. I jumped into his arms and hugged him tightly.

"It's so awesome," I said releasing my embrace.

"I'm glad you like it," he said. "I asked your dad's permission yesterday at the egg hunt. He thought it was a fine idea. I just think it's important for your children to have some ownership of their playground. Especially when a community acts like they own it."

"Yes, I agree. The sharing of the playground has bothered me all along. Not that we can't share. I didn't mean it that way. Of course my children share, they were raised most of their lives in a campground where everything was community property and now their home is a business. My kids were not born with the option of selfishness. It's just so nice to see their names on the backyard park that their granddaddy created. I mean after all, they helped build it."

My excitement had caused me to ramble and talk too fast. The priest was smiling, clearly amused by my emotions. I took a breath and tried again.

"By burning the kids' names into the wood you gave them the gift of possession or maybe the rights of possession. I don't know what I'm trying to say. I just thank you, thank you, thank you."

Once I stopped speaking, I realized that I was still holding onto his hands.

"You're welcome," he said, giving me a little grip. I let go of his hands and asked him to come inside.

"We can drink herbal tea and talk," I suggested. He looked at the light on his watch and since it was nearly midnight he said he needed to go. I helped him collect his stuff, the woodburning kit, paint, paintbrush, and soup can. We placed it all into a black bag. I gave Father McIntire one last hug and thank you and he gave me one last smile. Then he turned for home. I stood in my yard and watched him walk to the car he had parked down the street. The night air felt good. I am so glad that spring has finally arrived and Gladden is being kind.

I was still pumped up from Father McIntire's surprise, so I decided to sit on my porch awhile and just rock. I love my porch. In fact, I think I love my porch more than I love my bathroom. Since the warmer weather has started settling in, this wrap around porch has become an extension of The Kitchen House. The long veranda is set with several small marble café tables and wrought iron chairs. There are also three white wooden rockers and two porch swings, one at the front of the house and one at the back. In the evenings, I like to sit in a rocking chair and look at the star-studded sky beyond the mountains. Some nights there seems to be a billion points of light in the sky before me. On other nights, there is a hazy fog and a misty moon. I find both types of night enchanting.

Looking at the moon, I thought I heard a giggle. My eyes quickly focused down onto the playset. It took a minute before I saw him; the pale shadowy figure of a young boy. I froze and focused on the child, yet I did not feel scared. It was more of an alarming feeling. Like being caught off guard. I could see that he had thick curly hair and was wearing bib overalls and snow boots. He began to run down the ramps and I heard the giggle again. When he reached the bottom he ran behind the playground as if he was going to circle it and take another turn, but he disappeared. It was then I felt scared or maybe just uneasy. I left the porch and quickly went inside. I checked my kids, although I'm not really sure why, and then I tried to sleep.

At daybreak I went outside into the orange glow to check the playground. I climbed up to the high fort and read the words *Roman's Tower*. I crossed *Henry's Bridge* and then I took the same course the ghost child had taken. When I turned the corner at the bottom ramp I noticed something on the ground. It was a rabbit's foot, dyed purple and hanging on a key chain. I remember having one of these, I thought. I had a yellow one and Charlie had a black rabbit's foot. Mine sat for years on my bedroom dresser, but Charlie fastened his to the belt loop of his jeans. The rabbit's foot looked old and worn, a bit of its color and hair had been rubbed off in some spots. I knew this piece of nostalgia had to belong to the ghost boy. I could feel the hair on the back of my neck raise as I put the foot in my pocket. I spoke an out loud, "thank you," to the child, because I believe he had dropped it on purpose.

I went to the porch and sat watching the orange glow turn to yellow light, and meditated on what had just happened. I know my ghosts are real, I hear them all the time and now I have seen them twice; Emma Kitchen wiping down the counter and the little boy playing. Most of the time I do a great job of accepting the paranormal without fear. However, seeing them causes me to feel crazy, excited, scared and uneasy all rolled into one. I want so badly to accept the spirits in a matter of fact way, like Pixie does. When you think about it, I have been given proof that we all contain a soul, that there is everlasting life and that God exists. Knowing this should make me feel good. Why doesn't it?

I eventually pulled myself out of the rocker. The boys needed to be up. They had just finished a long, holiday weekend and now school was waiting for them. I had decided to let the boys discover their names just as the priest had intended. It didn't take them long. Before the bus had pulled up to the house, the boys had found their names on the wooden play gym and excited shouts woke up any sleeping neighbors.

"Thank Father Tim," I told them. "He did it."

It's Been One Hell of a Week

On Tuesday mornings we have been having story time at The Kitchen House; another idea from Rayland and Cody. They came up with this one morning as they sat sipping coffee in The Kitchen House and watching me read to Sabrina. Sabrina loves books. So, when I read to her I use lots of emotion and expression in my voice. I try to give the characters a personality, which is fun, because Sabrina giggles all the way through the stories.

"You should host a story time," Rayland said during my rendition of *Green Eggs and Ham*. "Moms can drink coffee while their preschoolers have playtime and listen to stories." I agreed to this idea reluctantly. I love reading to Sabrina. It's our own personal time together and I didn't want it crashed by a bunch of other kids. However, I have found that when you're a business owner you do what you must do. Besides, Rayland and Cody wouldn't let up. They even went to the library and checked out a bunch of picture books. They also gave me a cd with songs like The *Wheels On The Bus* and *Five Monkeys Jumping On The Bed*. Needless to say, Story Time Tuesdays at 10:00am was created. On the first Tuesday, only one other child showed up so that was really awkward. I read to the two toddlers while his mom read a *People* magazine and then the kids played with blocks and puzzles for an hour. The following Tuesday three more guests were added. The Tuesday after that five babies danced to *The Itsy Bitsy Spider* while three moms drank coffee. The Story Time Tuesdays have continued to increase slowly and I have begun enjoying them; with the exception of this Tuesday.

This week was insane when twenty-three women brought their babies into The Kitchen House and Hazel and I counted twenty-nine toddlers running about. Turns out that a mom here the prior week belongs to a big Baptist church three towns over. There are more Baptists in these parts then I can shake a stick at. This particular Baptist church has a large mom's group with over thirty members. These ladies decided that The Kitchen House Story Time would be a nice field trip for the group and they invaded us. Hazel and I were completely blindsided and overwhelmed as each lady wanted a specialty coffee and the babies ran about pulling books from the shelf and dumping puzzles onto the floor. I was near tears and Sabrina was in a full-blown outburst when I put in an emergency call to Lenore. She came quickly and saved the day. Lenore gathered the babies onto a rug, put in the cd and danced with them while I made coffee drinks. She then read two stories and I read three. After stories, we suggested the moms take them outside to play. They ran through Sabrina's stream kicking sand up everywhere and fought over the slides and the baby swing. They were here nearly three hours before heading home. I think they had a great time at The Kitchen House, but I hope like hell they never come back, at least not in a group.

Later that day, I ran over to the Wal-Mart to pick up my pictures. I had taken a slew of photographs at the egg hunt of little boys and girls with baskets full of colored eggs and chocolate grins. I had also snapped a series of pictures of the playground construction and not a single damn one of them turned out. Every single photograph developed looked as if it was being viewed through a haze of bubbles. I knew the photographs were mystic and I showed them to Pixie that night when she came in to do a reading.

"Wow, Sissy," she said. "These are the best photographs of orbs I have ever seen."

Pixie confirmed my suspicions. I had heard of orbs before. I had even seen them in photographs usually appearing as a small circular ball of light floating above someone's shoulder. Some say they are proof of guardian angels while others blame them on dust particles and rain droplets. If my photos are of orbs they are orbs in abundance. On each photo were layers upon layers of translucent circles covering the subject. Some of the orbs are colorful with a hue of violet or a tint of blue. Some of them are streaked with a bright tail and appear to be moving. Looking at the photographs it's hard to focus on the happy children through the rings of light. You only see the light.

"Can I take these?" Pixie asked. " I want to scan them and put'em up on my web page. These are beautiful. I knew you had a lot of spirits show up for your gathering, but even I'm shocked. Sissy, there must be a thousand people here."

My photos overjoyed Pixie, but I felt slightly sick at the thought of a thousand ghosts.

"You can have them," I said. "But, only post the ones of my children on the internet and not the other kids."

"Sure."

I knew she wouldn't mind. The majority of the photographs were of my children anyway. Before handing them over to Pixie, I looked at them once again. There was one photograph in particular that struck me. It was of Avery Banks underneath a veil of luminous globes, his cute face with a large laughing smile. On either side of him, positioned on the handles of his wheelchair rested vibrant balls of blue light. I couldn't help but think that the sapphire spheres were the hands of Billy Dean, pushing his son through my yard. I plucked the photo out of the pile.

"'I'm keeping this one," I said. I wanted to give it to Christy Banks and tell her that Avery's daddy is watching over him. I gave Pixie the rest of the stack and then went into the house so Pixie could perform a psychic reading in my café'. As absurd as the day was, the rest of the week got even crazier.

On Wednesday, we had a pretty big dinner crowd, which is crazy, because neither Hazel nor I opened The Kitchen House with the intent of owning a restaurant. The Kitchen House is meant to be a small charming café with a few food items. Once again, when you own a business you must make life work around it. Since The Kitchen House is the only kitchen in our house the kids have been having dinner very late, after it closes, or just eating biscuits and hotdogs. Hazel strongly believes that the kids should eat a balanced meal and do so at 6:00pm, which is when they start showing signs of hunger and acting out. This would mean that my family would be sitting down for dinner an hour before the cafe closes. Hazel came up with the idea that at 5:00pm she would ask the patrons in the restaurant who would like to eat dinner? She tells them what we're having and she charges them seven dollars for The Blue Plate Special. We even bought blue plates. She takes the orders and makes a little more for anyone who comes in the next hour. We usually have about two or three dinner guests at the most. Most of our patrons have dinner at home or if they do eat out they head on over to Janelle's Family Diner on State Route 356.

However, on Wednesday night, Pixie came in with her crew of elderly friends. Pixie had six senior citizens with her, Lucinda being one of them. They were all excited and happy to be out. They said Pixie was treating them for dinner before their private party and they all wanted to come to The Kitchen House. I had no idea what they meant by "private party" and I did not ask thinking maybe they were just confused. Although Pixie helped to slam us with a dinner rush, it was nice seeing her take such good care of the elderly. These are the people that nobody else has the time or patience for, the ones with dementia, whose minds and bodies have failed them. Pixie tries to nurture their jumbled minds and feeble bodies. I noticed she had tied a sachet around Lucinda's neck. It had a strong odor and when I asked Pixie what it was she said eucalyptus. I assumed it was for Lucinda's nasty cough and wheezing. In addition to Pixie and her six friends, we also had Ezra Landis for dinner. Ezra has become our one and only dinner regular who eats with us every night. I believe this is because Ezra is sweet on Hazel.

Ezra Landis arrives at The Kitchen House every day at 5:00pm. He sits at the far end of the coffee bar and watches Hazel. Ezra is a widower. His wife, Rosie, was a fiery redhead who henpecked the hell out of Ezra when she was living. Together, they had four wild boys, which Rosie tried to tame with her temper, while Ezra remained the quiet, gentle farmer. Two of those boys now help Ezra with the farm while the other two have taken off for greener pastures. Hazel is good about fixing Ezra a nice plate of dinner with big servings. She believes he misses home-cooked meals since his wife died and she feels a little sorry for him. Ezra tries to chat with Hazel through dinner. He asks her about her day, tells her stories and bad jokes and always invites her to go fishing with him when he leaves. Hazel listens to his stories, laughs at his bad jokes, but rejects his offer to go fishing. She uses the kids for an excuse or says she's tired.

Besides Pixie's party of seven and Ezra, a van of eight traveling college students just happened to stop at The Kitchen House to get carryout coffee and use the bathroom. The last one out of the bathroom and out the door heard Hazel's dinner announcement and I'll be damned if he didn't go out to the van and convince his friends to come back in for dinner. Again, I was forced to call in Lenore for some help. We also needed her to stop at Johnson's Meats for two more pounds of sirloin. Hazel had told everybody the dinner special was meatloaf, mashed potatoes and buttered corn. Hazel, Lenore and I managed to feed and serve all nineteen, counting my children. Afterwards, we were exhausted and people didn't start leaving until thirty minutes past closing time. It took another hour to clean up the mess. Hazel and I have decided that we will no longer offer dinner at 6:00. Instead, we will have a soup of the day. I don't think the kids will mind eating soup every day as long as we keep it creative. I hope Ezra doesn't mind. As I did dishes and Hazel put away food, I tried to talk to her about Ezra Landis. I told her that a fishing trip sounded like a nice time and she told me she couldn't do it because of Harry.

"It just doesn't feel right," she said. "Harry is always with me. I feel his presence all the time and I smell his Old Spice. Going fishing with Ezra would feel like cheating."

"Hazel, you have to do more than fish to cheat. Besides, Harry would want you to go have fun." Hazel shook her head, so I tried to expound. "It's kind of like my mom, she's here too. Just as you smell Old Spice, I smell Wild Musk. It is a constant scent that lingers around this house, but that doesn't stop me from wanting you to grandmother my kids. My children are blessed to have a Grandma Hazel and I believe my mom is happy too. Harry would not care if you had a friend. In fact, he would be happy. Don't stop living because Harry died."

I didn't mean to hurt Hazel's feelings, but when we finished cleaning up The Kitchen House she went to her room and shut the door. That night I dreamed of Harry. I was walking by a stream when I ran into him. He was wearing a fishing hat and a Hoosier's sweatshirt. I asked how he was doing and he said, "just fine." Then he told me to ask Hazel to take him fishing. I said, I would and then I woke up. The dream felt so real and Harry looked just like I remembered. He was that same ornery man who used to pull his mobile dream home into the campground every November and stay until spring.

Thursday morning started out crazy. I told Hazel about my dream and she said she dreamed of Harry too. They sat together on the edge of her bed talking and holding hands. He told her to go fishing and then he gave her some advice before she woke.

"Life is a river, let the current take you." Hazel said she had never heard Harry try to be poetic before and she didn't know if he was joking or not.

Pixie Moon-Dust had come in that morning, looking a little tired. She sat down at the bar and ordered a double shot espresso, as if she were a coffee lush. Hazel and I immediately began to talk to her about our dreams.

"Bottom line is, Harry does not feel threatened by Ezra Landis," Pixie said. "Harry is having a grand ole time on the other side and he wants you to enjoy the rest of the life you have. Soon enough Hazel, you will join him and then you two will spend the rest of eternity in each other's company. Fishing with Ezra Landis is not going to change that."

Just about the time Pixie finished her little monologue, Rayland came through the front and he was mad as hell.

"Pixie Moon-Dust!" he said. "Did you devise some freaky party at my house last night with a bunch of old people?"

"Well kind of," Pixie answered. "Your mama wanted a get together with some of her friends, so I hosted something at the house while you and Cody were at your spring dance recital."

"Those are not her friends, Pixie. My mama has never hung out with that bunch of old coots before. Those are your friends and that little get-together was a séance. A Goddamn, crazy séance."

Hazel and I stood motionless. I had never seen Rayland so angry, but Pixie remained cool and composed.

"There is nothing damned or crazy about my séances."

"Listen here you voodoo queen, you can't just come into a person's house and start conjuring up spirits with their sick mama!"

"Rayland calm down," I said, trying to intervene. "I'm sure Pixie has a good explanation."

"Sissy, did you know about this?" Rayland had now turned on me, which was unusual.

"No but, I'm sure it's fine."

"Fine for you maybe. You like living in a haunted home. I don't!" Rayland looked away from me and turned his focus on Pixie.

"I mean really Pixie, the nerve! At first I thought mama was just being

136

crazy when she was talking about seeing my daddy and then she said her favorite Aunt Nellie had come over last night. She also said that it was so nice to see Marcy, Mr. Reardon's wife. That woman has been dead for at least twelve years. I let her go on and on thinking she was having an incoherent moment and then I got a call from Esther Williams' daughter. She said her mama was talking the same sort of nonsense and told her that she went to a séance party at Lucinda's house."

Hazel and I were shocked. So that was the private party the old people kept talking about last night. Pixie seemed unfazed by Rayland's hysterics and she did her best to explain.

"A séance is nothing more than a reading. People come to me all the time to connect with those on the other side. A séance is just that."

"Well, don't you think you should get the family's permission if you're going to host a séance with their elderly?" Rayland asked.

"No!" Pixie said through a laugh. "They're your parents not your children. They don't need your permission. These are grown people. Wise people I might add. For them, the other side is not too far off, if they want to learn more about it, why the hell not. Would you keep your mother from learning about Italy if she was about to move to Rome?" Pixie had stumped Rayland and for a moment he hesitated.

"Did you play light as feather stiff as board?" he finally asked.

"Oh, that was just in good fun after the séance," Pixie said waving her hand in the air as if she was batting pesky questions out of her face.

"Good fun! My mama claims that y'all levitated Old Man Reardon."

"Mr. Reardon weighs barely a hundred pounds. I could levitate him myself if he wasn't so damn long."

"Pixie I don't think you understand how upset I am."

"I understand."

"Then you know, I may not want you to watch my mama any longer."

"That would be a mistake Rayland."

"Well, it's my mistake to make." Rayland turned to leave, but stopped when he reached the door. "And another thing, stop tying that damn sack of moth balls around Lucinda's neck."

"It's eucalyptus you asshole! And it's helping her to breathe. Her damn doctors are wrong Rayland."

Rayland stopped suddenly. He became less mad and more concerned.

"What do you mean they're wrong?"

137

"They've been treating her with antibiotics and inhalers. She doesn't have asthma, bronchitis or even pneumonia. She needs an MRI or chest x-ray and she needs it now."

The house fell into an awkward silence. Pixie had won and Rayland stood defeated.

"How bad is it?" he asked.

"Bad. Bad enough to want to connect with the other side."

On Friday, Rayland called me with the news. Lucinda has lung cancer. It seems she won't die from Alzheimer's because cancer will take her first. On Saturday, my dad set up the stage and the dancing went on without Rayland. On Sunday, we all went to church and prayed.

April 30, 2000 – Dear Diary, I am so tired from this long week and overwhelmed with deep sadness. You would think that Alzheimer's would be enough suffering to afflict on one woman, one family. To add a cancer diagnosis just seems additionally cruel. Then I think again, maybe cancer is the escape from Alzheimer's. It seems to be the more traditional way to go and in Lucinda's case it won't take as long.

The Confessions of a Priest

May 8, 2000 – Dear Diary, all week people have stopped by The Kitchen House to hear how Rayland and his mama are doing. It seems nobody can comprehend the misfortune of our beautiful Lucinda. It was not that long ago that Lucinda was this town's representation of style. A beautiful, intriguing woman who charmed everyone she met. Any bad things ever said about Lucinda were done out of spite. In truth, this striking woman was an object to envy. Nobody is jealous now.

Lucinda is in the hospital. Rayland, Cody and Pixie are by her side. It seems as soon as the word cancer was spoken out loud, Lucinda gave herself permission to decline rapidly. Rayland was told his mama's cancer is stage four. They have decided not to treat the cancer because of the Alzheimer's and to just keep her comfortable. Rayland is beating himself up. He said he should have known. He is no longer upset with Pixie and in fact, she has become his closest friend and counselor. The doctors say that Lucinda's left lung is already gone, eaten up by cancer, and that the right lung has just a small opening that carries her breath. It's as if Lucinda is breathing through a straw and has been for some time. I wish they would bring her home from the hospital and over to The Kitchen House, let her sit on my couch and snuggle up to her dead husband and rest. When I expressed this to Pixie she said that Lucinda's husband is with her at the hospital.

Father McIntire started the week by coming to The Kitchen House every day. He asks if I'd like to pray and I tell him I have been praying on my own. I have actually been meditating on Hazel's prayer, wrapping

Lucinda in the white light of God and asking for protection. On Friday night after our folk singer had ended his repertoire of James Taylor hits and the crowd had left, I stood at the register counting money. Father McIntire approached. I believe he was going to offer up another prayer, but stopped abruptly when he saw the purple rabbit's foot sitting in the cash drawer.

"Where did you get that?" he asked.

"You wouldn't believe me if I told you."

"Tell me anyways."

I wasn't sure how to explain a ghost child to a priest, but I gave it my best shot.

"I found it Easter night, after I caught you burning the kids' names in the playground. You left and I sat on my porch soaking in moonbeams. Then I heard him."

"Him?" the priest interrupted me.

"A little boy," I said. "He was there playing on the wooden gym."

"A little boy was playing in the middle of the night?" Father McIntire seemed clearly confused and a little uneasy.

"Not an actual little boy, but a spirit child. Maybe he was even an angel. I don't know, but he was there. He had curly hair and snow boots on his feet. I heard his laugh first, a happy giggle. When I looked to the playground he was running down the ramps. He must have dropped it, because when he disappeared the rabbit's foot was there."

"I have to go," Father McIntire said backing up quickly and accidently knocking over a barstool.

"I'm sorry Sissy," he said. And as he uprighted the stool I saw tears in his eyes.

I didn't see Father McIntire on Saturday. I thought he would stop by, but he didn't. The boys played outside all day on the playground and I couldn't stop thinking of the ghost child and rabbit's foot. On Sunday, Hazel and I took the kids to church to light another candle for Lucinda. After church, Hazel and the kids had plans to go to Mama Jaspers' house. It was spring cleanup and planting time. All of their cousins would be there. I did not go. Instead I headed to the hospital to check on Lucinda. I ran into Rayland's brothers in the parking lot. They were leaving as I was coming. Rhett, Lucinda's first born named for her favorite leading man, gave me a big hug. I enjoy Rhett, like his fictional namesake, he is tall, dark, handsome and arrogant enough to be charming. Rodrick, Lucinda's middle son, is a family man. Once a star quarterback at Grace High, he is now the father of five young'uns, two of them being twins. Rayland says Roderick's house looks like Sesame Street with little kids and shaggy monsters running everywhere. Besides five children Roderick has sheep, a sheep dog, two border collies and a Shetland pony. No wonder he couldn't help Rayland more. I talked with both men and told them I was sorry about their mama. They thanked me for being so good to Lucinda and it caused me to start crying before I even made it inside the hospital.

Walking into Lucinda's room knocked the wind out of me. It took a moment to catch my breath. In all the years I've known Lucinda, I've never seen her so sick. She looked extremely fatigued, as if it took everything just to breathe. She had oxygen that hung around her neck like a cheap paper necklace, but I'm not sure how much it helped. Her skin and lips were pale with no red shimmer to brighten them. Rayland and Cody were on either side of her bed and Pixie was at the end rubbing thick creamy oil onto Lucinda's feet. Lucinda smiled at me when I entered the room and motioned me towards her bed. I leaned over and gave her a hug and when my tears fell on her shoulder and seeped through her thin gown she began to rub my hair. Her gesture made me feel guilty and realize a mother is a mother until the end. I was there to comfort her not the other way around. I stayed for over an hour in Lucinda's room visiting and in truth it was hard. I feel bad saying I wanted to leave immediately. It was a feeling of helplessness that made me want to run and I had to force myself to sit awhile.

After I left the hospital, I needed time to clear my head. I drove to the church, sat in my car and cried. I then took a hike up the mountain behind the church, in the same spot where I had hiked with my boys. I walked through the woods praying and took notice of an abundance of spring blossoms and the approach of summer. Life was blooming in the mountains and Lucinda was dying in the spring. I trekked through the trees around bending streams and waterfalls, my subconscious leading the way. The earth was soft and my tennis shoes became caked with mud, however, I did not veer from my route and I ended up at the gazebo.

Father McIntire was there, sitting on his tree chair whittling a hiking stick. Next to him a second tree chair had been built. He looked up and smiled.

"Come sit," he said. "Rest your feet."

"When did you build a second chair?" I asked.

"It's been awhile. I thought if you ever needed a place to go you'd be welcome here and now you even have your own chair." I stepped up into the gazebo and sat on the red cushion of my tree chair.

"Thanks," I said. "You're very nice."

Father McIntire and I sat in silence for a few minutes. He kept with his whittling and I kept my eyes on the forest. It was beautiful to view the trees from the gazebo. The mountain looks much different in the spring than in the winter with its own distinctive beauty and wonder, but still sacred and holy.

"How's Lucinda?" he asked.

"Not good. Her mind has been wrecked with Alzheimer's and her body destroyed by cancer. It's truly a terrible ending for a beautiful princess."

"I'm sorry."

"Can we talk about the rabbit's foot?" I finally asked.

"I don't know if I can," he said. I didn't push and he didn't give. We sat quiet for a long time and listened to the songs of birds, the chattering of squirrels and the crunch of dried leaves under the feet of small creatures. Then gradually, as if his weighty words and heavy thoughts were being pulled from the depths by a chain, Father McIntire dredged up enough strength to tell me his story.

"It belongs to Thomas," he said.

"Thomas?"

"My little brother. He died young. He bought that purple rabbit's foot at a gas station on a family trip, loved it, kept it in his pocket, and believed in its luck."

Father Tim McIntire talked soft and slowly as he spoke of his childhood. He told me that he is from Wisconsin. He did not say that his family was rich, but I got the idea they were. He did say that they lived on a house with a lake and that he was a hockey player. Timothy McIntire said he loved hockey and he was good at it. He never tired of skating. He was always on a rink dragging his parents from game to game. During the long winter season of Wisconsin he practiced on the family lake skating until after dusk, just as one might practice basketball on the driveway. Father McIntire told his story gently, he paused often to cry and he tiptoed on each word as if it were fragile enough to be broken.

"I was fourteen years old and Thomas was seven. Our parents were going out with friends and I was left in charge. It was late February. Although it was a cold night we had a warm spell a couple days before. My mother told me not to go out on the ice, but I disobeyed her. I told Thomas to stay inside and watch television, but he wanted to be with me. He always wanted to be with me. Tommy idolized me. I helped him get bundled up in his heavy coat and snow boots. I grabbed my stick and puck and out we went. I had told Thomas to stay near the side of the lake as I skated fast circles on the ice. I was so sure of myself, convinced I knew the ice and the secrets of our lake. I knew where I could skate, the spots I could trust, and the spots to avoid when a thaw started. Thomas walked out further than he should have.

I was in my own zone, skating fast and hard, when I heard the breaking and I knew the lake had opened up and betrayed me. The slick sheet of glass shattered beneath his feet so quickly, not at all like I would expect. By the time I turned he was already submerged into the black hole. I screamed and skated to the hole. Thomas was shouting my name, calling out for my help. He was fighting to stay afloat and ice was breaking all around us. I held my hockey stick out and his little hands grabbed it for a minute. "Come on buddy. You can do it," I cried. But his coat and boots were so heavy and the icy water so cold. Before I could pull him in, he lost his grip and slipped under. I screamed. I tried to break more ice. I jumped into the water, but I could not find him. I climbed out quickly because I was afraid to die. It was a neighbor that heard my shouts and screams. He came quickly and called 911. He wrapped me in a blanket, but I threw it off and shouted into the black water. I was begging God one moment and cursing him the next. "Goddamn you! Tommy, please don't die!" Police reached my parents at their dinner party and brought them home. Thomas was in the water four hours before divers pulled him from the frozen lake. My mother was distraught and our family was devastated. My parents never forgave me and I never forgave myself. I had traumatized my family and killed my brother."

Father Timothy was painfully solemn when he finished his story. His face wet with tears.

"You didn't kill him," I said crying along with the priest. "It was an accident."

"No Sissy, it was my fault. I was supposed to take care of him and instead I led him out onto thin ice and let him drown."

The priest began to cry uncontrollably, his body trembling with sobs. I got up from my tree chair and went to him. I stood by his side and he leaned into my stomach and wept like no man I had ever seen. It was nearly ten minutes before he stopped shaking then he began to speak.

"My family never recovered from the death of Thomas. We moved away from the lake that swallowed my brother. We spent our days in sorrow ignoring one another. My parents worked long days. Afterwards my mother would retreat to her room with a book and my father to his office with a brandy. I stayed in my bedroom. I never played hockey again, or anything else for that matter. After high school graduation, I left the house and my parents left each other. I didn't know what to do with myself. I did not believe I deserved a life, a career, a love, or a future. So I went to the monastery. There it was okay to not have visitors, to be silent, to live in your own thoughts and work out your relationship with God. I thought I could hide forever. I did not know that they eventually push you out and into the public where you are to serve others."

"My God Timothy," I said cupping his wet face in my hands. "You became a priest to punish yourself?" He shook his head and I let go.

"No, it's not like that," he said. "Maybe, in the beginning, that's what it was. But now I know I have a good life and a purpose. It is the life of a priest. Actually, it's not that unusual that I became a priest. After Thomas died I spent many days in the church. I entered the large gothic cathedral in my town any time its door was open. I spent hours praying for forgiveness and asking God for guidance. He led me to the monastery." Father McIntire had gained back his composure.

"Sissy, I know you would never tell, but I must ask." I interrupted his sentence.

"I know a little about confession," I said. "Your story is safe with me."

"Thank you."

144

Father McIntire handed me the walking stick and we walked back down the mountain together.

"Are you going to be okay?" I asked.

"Oh yes Sissy, don't worry about me. Stay focused on your prayers for Rayland and his mother. Rayland needs you."

I left the handsome priest with his muddy boots and watery eyes standing alone in the church parking lot and I cried all the way home.

Flower Pots and a Rabbit's Foot

May 9, 2000 – Dear Diary, death is such a tragic and scary thing. The grim reaper kidnapping our loved ones like a murderer and the living are left in a grief stricken panic. The griever now lives life like a wounded soldier with a hole in his heart and a hundred pound bag of sorrow strapped to his back. The dead transcend into heaven, light as a feather, on spirit wings. Currently, I watch my best friend watch his mother die and it is a painful experience. Yet, I know in my heart that when she goes she will rise into the arms of her husband and true love. She will be free from the world that captured her mind to torment and then captured her body to torture. Still, all of us will mourn her dying and wish that she were still here. The longing we feel for our dead is so intense that it's excruciating having to go on without them.

Timothy McIntire has chosen a life of humbleness and servitude, praying for forgiveness, estranged from his family, hiding in his church. He is not the only one hiding in Grace. I watch Lenore carry her grief and shame like a weighty handbag strapped to her wrist. However, I've come to believe that the dead are still very much near their loved ones and they want us to be happy. Pixie has told me that the spirit around Lenore is a beautiful, peaceful young man drenched in white light. Plus, I saw little Thomas McIntire run happily up and down the playground. Both are proof of eternal life with happiness. It seems ridiculous that death should be so scary. The fact is it happens to all of us. We know that we are born to die. From the very first birth to the very first death, it is how it has been. Still, we cannot wrap our minds around death or accept it. Hazel still struggles with her loyalty to Harry and guilt of having fun if he's not here. I still miss my mom. Yet, if I've learned one thing from this house with its unexplainable sounds, creaks and shadows it is that an afterlife does exist and I believe the people living life on the other side are having much more fun than us.

On Mondays, The Kitchen House does not open until four o'clock. Hazel and I usually spend this day going over our grocery list for the week, ordering supplies and shopping. This Monday, Hazel surprised me. As soon as the boys got on the school bus, Ezra Landis pulled up in front of the house.

"Bye," Hazel said to me as she grabbed her sun hat from off the coat tree.

"I'm going fishing today and the best part is I didn't even have to pack the picnic basket. Ezra did it." Hazel bounced down our steps and up to the waiting car. Ezra was politely holding the passenger door open. After she got in, he skipped around the back of the car with a little dance step of his own. The two reminded me of teenagers and I could not help but laugh. It must have been the dream of Harry in his fishing hat, plus the unfortunate circumstances with Lucinda that permitted Hazel to accept Ezra's invitation. Through Lucinda we have all learned that there are no promises and life is short. The only good part is to know that loved ones will be waiting on the other side.

With a lovely spring day before me, I thought I would do some planting. It would be fun for Sabrina and I to plant some pretty flowers in a pot. Charlie had found several big, blue ceramic pots that someone had put in the trash. Charlie finds the best trash and he's not afraid to pick it up and bring it home. He stacked them in my shed. They need cleaned up, but I believe under all the dirt and mud is a beautiful blue and white oriental flowerpot. I'm aghast that someone would throw them away. It must have been a divorce, death or move. It's those occurrences that make one lighten the load and discard some good stuff.

The day was early and I had plenty of time. I took Sabrina outside and pushed her on the swing set for awhile. I love watching the sunrise over the mountain. I stood in its ray of light and thought about what I needed to do next. When it was time, I took the baby in the house, gave her a sippy cup of milk, and then laid her down for her morning nap. I could hear her talking in her crib, when I called Father McIntire.

"Meet me on Henry's Bridge," is all I said. Soon my chattering toddler had been soothed to sleep by her guardian angels and I was standing on a playset waiting for the priest.

He climbed the play fort looking tired. Although he smiled I could tell he was still sad.

"I have something for you," I said when he reached the bridge. I wanted to give him the rabbit's foot outside on the playset just in case Thomas was watching. After all, I believe Thomas had left it for him. I placed the foot in the palm of his hand and he gently closed his fingers around it and shut his eyes. I think he was praying. When he finished he opened his palm and softly rubbed the worn purple fur. At first, I thought he was fine and that I had done a good thing and then his shoulders began to shake and I knew he was going to lose it.

"Come here," I said pulling the priest into Roman's Tower. Inside the cedar box, the priest allowed his misery to take him. His agony was pitiful. It weakened his knees and sent him to the floor. Curled like a baby on the wooden floorboards, the grown man cried, his large fist clenched around the tiny foot. I sat on the floor next to him hugging my knees and not knowing what to do. I placed my hand on his back, just so he would know that I was still there. I sat in silence and let him cry as long as he needed. When he was done he apologized.

"Thomas is happy," I finally said. "I heard him laughing and he left you a gift. He loves you. It's time to forgive yourself."

"I'm trying," he softly whispered.

"Let's go in and get a coffee," I said getting off the floor and opening the door.

Once inside I could hear Sabrina over the monitor talking again to her ghost friends. I realized we had been outside longer than I thought. I went to get the baby out of her crib while the priest sat quietly drinking his coffee. Sabrina was all snuggles and hugs as I carried her from her room into the café.

"Hey, you want to help me today?" I asked the priest.

"Sure, what do you need?"

"Sabrina and I are going to plant flowers."

"Do you really need help with that?" he asked quizzically.

"I do. Trying to get anything done with a toddler requires a large amount of help and Hazel has gone on a fishing trip with Ezra Landis."

148

"Well, good for Hazel. Sure I'll help."

Father McIntire and I pulled the pots from the shed as Sabrina played in her sand stream. We lined all eight of them up in the grass. The priest began rinsing them off. Sabrina ran over to help and stole the hose. Once we got the pots cleaned they were as pretty as I expected.

"Someone threw these away?"

"Someone did," I said, stepping back and admiring the intricate details crafted on each antique pot. Someone had discarded a nice collection of beautiful porcelain and now it was mine. The pots were stunning on their own and could have been displayed as ceramic pieces, but I felt giddy and excited about filling them with flowers.

"Ready?" I said grabbing car keys from inside the house. "We need to go buy our flowers." I strapped Sabrina into the small back seat of my father's old pickup truck that he keeps parked in my driveway lot and jumped into the driver's seat. Father Tim hesitated a moment before joining us. We drove over to Bloomers Nursery with the windows down and country music blaring. I could tell it felt a little too normal for the priest and made him uncomfortable, but that's exactly what he needed. We parked on the stone drive of the large nursery with its abundance of spring blooms, piled bags of mulch, and odorous soil. We entered the long greenhouse and did not know which way to turn or what to choose. Every blossom radiated appeal and charm and I needed to arrange eight large pots. The thought of it was suddenly overwhelming.

"Okay," I said. "I'm not going to stress. I'll go this way with a cart and pick my favorite shades. You and Sabrina go that way and do the same, we'll meet back here in ten minutes. Go!"

I darted in the direction of yellows and greens while the priest went the other way with my toddler leading the way. There are times when life is best if led by a child. This was one of those times. Children have a way of making everyday, ordinary experiences extraordinary. I gave Sabrina to the priest, not because I like to hand off my child, but because he needs a distraction, his thoughts are too deep. I was hoping that picking flowers with a little girl would help lift his spirits.

I had chosen my flowers hurriedly with gut instinct and was waiting for Father McIntire and Sabrina. When he strolled up, I could tell from his cart that he had chosen all his flowers for Sabrina's liking. It was crammed full with shades of purple and pink with some red impatiens in the front.

"Is your favorite color red?" I asked scanning the contents.

"It is."

We grabbed a couple bags of soil and headed to the checkout. I saw the help wanted sign attached to the register and asked the owner for an application.

"I have a friend looking for a job," I told him. "She's a real smart girl, professional and hard working. I bet she would do well here."

"Send her in," he said. "I'm busy as hell and could use some help."

Once we got back to the house we had the same problem as we had at the nursery. How were we going to arrange these flowers into pots?

"I'll do four pots and you do four pots," I suggested. "We can't go wrong. Flowers are too pretty to ever look bad." The priest and I worked side by side yet independently. I focused on my pot and he focused on his.

Sabrina ran around in-between us with a plastic shovel in her hand and a small pink watering can. I let her sprinkle the flowers with water, which made our job messier, but kept her busy which was more important. Soon Sabrina had left our side and was running up and down the playground. There was no need to be concerned about letting a child of eighteen months run the high playset on her own. My father had done such a marvelous job constructing the gigantic playground. Its high wooden railings were just inches apart all along the ramps, making it perfectly safe for all ages. As Father Tim and I worked on our arrangements, Sabrina ran the playground laughing and rambling to someone. Her vocabulary consists of two word sentences and she used them.

"No wait," she would say running up the ramp as if she was chasing someone. Then pausing, she would yell. "Stop!" after several seconds she would shout, "Go!" and then laughing she would begin to run again. I stopped to watch her and you could tell by her actions, words and movement that she was playing with someone. I just couldn't see them. Father Tim stopped and watched too, but said nothing. After a few minutes he went back to work on his pot. So, I did the same, even though both of us assumed that Sabrina was playing with Thomas.

It took us an hour to plant our pots and the priest was much more meticulous than me. He dug through his dirt methodically and hummed while he worked. He used care while picking his flowers and made sure that their heights and colors would flatter each other. When we were finished, we stepped back and admired our work. The pots contained the vibrant shades of summer and were beautiful. Several of the pots held dark purple wave petunias, light purple verbenas and small pink blossoms that added just a touch of sweetness. There were pink begonias, red impatiens and English ivy in another pot. Two of the four pots I created were done in bright shades of yellow with dwarf sunflowers, snapdragons and marigolds. Each and every pot looked better than I had imagined. It's funny how little things can make you feel so good, but my pots did just that, they exuded happiness.

I pointed to the places along the porch where I wanted the plants to sit. Father Tim carried the heavy containers one by one to their designated spot. We had just finished when Hazel and Ezra pulled up. Hazel looked so happy. The sun had kissed her face that day and her cheeks radiated a soft pink glow.

"Looky how pretty that is?" Hazel said clapping her hands together. I knew she would be happy with the pots. Hazel loves anything with charm.

"Father Tim helped me. Those are the pots he did," I said pointing them out.

"They're all beautiful. You two do good work."

"Well, actually it's we three, cause Brina helped pick out all the shades of pink and purple and just look how they flatter our lilac house." I looked over to my baby girl who was now sitting on a playground platform talking to herself.

"What's she doing?" Hazel said looking over at the baby.

"I guess she's playing with her make-believe friend. Little ones do that all the time."

Father Tim gazed over at Sabrina and then said he needed to go.

"Thank you so much for your help. I couldn't have done all this without you."

"No Sissy, thank you. You're truly amazing," he said giving me a hug.

I blushed at the compliment and embrace when the priest turned to go. Hazel watched our exchange with curiosity, but said nothing. I offered her no explanations and began cleaning up the yard, putting away the gardening tools.

Lenore would be coming soon and I was excited to give her the job application. Shortly after that, the school bus would arrive and a hoard of children needing homework help would come barreling through the door. Jean, the bus driver, has just been delivering all the homework kids to my place and their parents pick them up an hour later. I needed to get Sabrina and myself into the bath and open the café. Hazel and Ezra said their goodbyes while I retrieved the baby. I walked up to the middle ramp where she sat in focused play.

"We have to go in now Thomas," I whispered as I scooped up my toddler. "Thank you for playing with Brina while I planted flowers."

"Bye-bye," Sabrina said waving her hands over my shoulders as I carried her down the playground and into the house.

Losing Mothers

May 19, 2000 – Dear Diary, Lucinda died on Mother's Day, Sunday May 14, 2000, just two weeks after she was told that she had cancer. You hear of such things happening, sudden diagnosis followed by a quick death. It's surreal to watch. The only way I can wrap my head around her dying is to believe that her cancer was merciful and saved her from more years of Alzheimer's disease. In truth, it feels conflicting to consider her cancer and death as an act of compassion, but I don't know how else to get through it.

I feel very thankful that I got to see Lucinda that day before she died. I went up after church with a bouquet of sweet smelling, lavender hyacinths. She grinned when I entered the room. Rayland had been putting a tinted gloss on her thin lips and she looked more like Lucinda. Yet, when her lips curled up to make a smile, I could see the dry, bloody cracks through the shimmer. Her eyes were tired, but her brows were still plucked. I think she was just so worn out from breathing. I gave her a hug and kissed her forehead. She smelled of face cream and sickness. I held her hands and told her she was still beautiful and she smiled again. I knew that's what she wanted to hear. Lucinda's looks were very important to her even in her confused cancerous state. I stayed longer than I usually do, but not to the end. The end was reserved for her children and grandchildren.

Rayland told me it was terrible to watch her die. The very hardest thing one can endure. He said the hospital kept her comfortable and most likely sped up the process. He told me that people came and went all day in Lucinda's room. He believes she was lucid enough to try and tell them all goodbye. Eventually, Rodrick's wife took the kids home, it was just too much for them. Cody went for a nap. After the crowd left and just Rhett, Rodrick and Rayland remained; Lucinda chose to take her last breath. The three grown men watched their mother die on Mother's Day and it brought them to their knees, where they all melted into a puddle of grief around her bed. Lucinda's soul slipped out of her used up body, splashed in their tears, and then drifted away. Rayland came by The Kitchen House Monday morning to deliver the news. His eyelids were puffy and heavy from a sleepless night and endless tears. Hazel tried to feed him. but he couldn't eat. He could only cry, so we all cried with him.

The funeral was Wednesday afternoon and the wake was at The Kitchen House. Hazel and I closed the café for the day and attended the funeral. I sent the boys to school and Lenore stayed with Sabrina and set up for the wake. Rayland had brought over an abundance of food and covered casserole dishes from sympathetic neighbors. Hazel and I added a few simple things, not because they were needed, but rather an attempt to distract our minds.

The funeral was beautiful. Rayland and his brothers did such a fine job representing Lucinda. I could tell from its style and elegance that Rayland had led the way. Each of Lucinda's sons spoke and they all had wonderful, heartfelt things and funny stories to tell about their mother. Their monologues held panache as well as humor. Lucinda did have her own flair and her boys brought it to life. There was a video made from photos and put together with upbeat, feel-good country songs that lifted our spirits. I noticed that in every single picture, Lucinda was gorgeous. It made me wonder, did she ever take a bad photo or did they just not include those. Rodrick's oldest child sang a sweet little song for her Glam-Ma and it brought everyone to tears. Glam-Ma is what all of Rodrick's kids called Lucinda. I believe Rayland came up with the name. He even bedazzled Lucinda a sweatshirt with Glam-Ma written out in rhinestones. Rayland was such a good son.

I was surprised that Rayland had asked Father McIntire to read from Psalms at the service. What didn't surprise me was that it was not Psalms 23, but rather Psalms 139, *for you created my inmost being; you knit me together in my mother's womb.* Baskets of red nail polish were placed at the exit of the funeral home. All guests were told to take one or more bottles in remembrance of Lucinda. Rayland had told me that Lucinda had at least three hundred bottles of red nail polish most of them never used. Lucinda's life with the Alzheimer's consisted of irrational little anecdotes. In this case, it seems that every time Lucinda went to the store she bought a bottle of red nail polish. I took two bottles; one to use during my time of mourning and the other to sit on my dresser as a forever reminder of my classy, stylish, beautiful friend.

On the day of the funeral, it sprinkled warm, soft summer tears from heaven and at the gravesite the most unusual thing occurred. While we all stood crowded under a tent listening to Father McIntire's prayer of goodbye, a large mourning dove flew in and sat on the head of a large tombstone across from Lucinda's burial spot. It was a handsome bird, light gray and muted brown with a soft white chest. It behaved as if it were watching us. It stayed intently focused through the closing of prayer and when we all got up to leave it flew with whistling wings from the tombstone and landed on the hood of the hearse. We all stopped in shock by this peculiar bird that caught our gaze and stared back. Just before it took flight again the bird sang to us in a soft, gentle cry like laments. The last sound heard while leaving Lucinda's gravesite was the cry of the mourning dove.

When we arrived back at The Kitchen House, Lenore had already arranged and organized all of the food. Everything looked beautiful and appealing. The house smelled delicious and looked inviting, which caused everyone to come in and stay for hours. Really, my house is so nice and it's all because of Daddy and Charlie. Guests sat at round tables with plates of food telling stories of Lucinda; and there were are a lot of stories to tell, Lucinda was an innovative lady for these mountains. Her fake boobs were now talked about with humor and not envy or disgust. On the veranda, people sat drinking coffee and tea, watching the children play. Rodrick's kids had a blast in my back yard. After spending weeks sitting in a hospital trying to behave, and then two days at a funeral home they needed to run, breathe fresh air and have some space.

People did not begin leaving until dusk fell, when they realized the day was ending. The leftover food went home with Rodrick and his family. Father McIntire and Pixie Moon-Dust stayed longer to help Rayland, Cody and I clean up and Hazel put the kids to bed. As we washed dishes, swept the floor, threw away trash and picked up toys, we talked about mothers. Rayland was still stunned by the fact that he had lost his mother on

Mother's Day, a holiday he plans to celebrate every year by planting flowers on her grave. Cody spoke of his mother with tears in his eyes. He said they had not really spoken in five years. His parents are born-again Southern Baptist and they do not agree with his lifestyle. They have disowned their middle son for being a gay man and he misses them dearly. Cody believed Lucinda to be the most liberated, swanky, smart and loving mother he had ever met. He adored her. She was his substitute mom. Father McIntire did not pounce on Cody's admission of homosexuality. Instead he admitted that he had not seen his mother either. He described her as a reserved woman who keeps to herself and doesn't reach out much. She works as a realtor in Wisconsin and sells houses on the lake. He believes she likes to be left alone. I was surprised he shared so much. Hazel, who had come back to join the conversation after mothering my children, said her mother died at eighty-six years old. She was a sweet lady who planted flowers, sewed clothes, cooked giant meals and loved her children. Pixie confessed that her mom was a white witch that walked off the mountain when she was a little girl. Since I was to follow up Pixie, I enjoyed her brief and mysterious narrative. Then I told the story of Marie Cooper. It is a story that is known by Rayland and the town of Grace, but news to my new friends.

My mother, like Lucinda, was also a spectacle, just a slightly different show. Whereas Lucinda was a cross between a Barbie Doll and Dolly Parton, Marie Cooper was Elvira and Joan Jett all rolled into one. She had wild, raven, black hair, piercing blue eyes and porcelain skin. She was beautiful, young and fun, an artist and free spirit that used to paint murals on the walls of our home. She gave every room a scenic wall. In our small home she painted a beach, a stone fireplace and a heavenly sky. Charlie's room and mine portrayed a carousel with mythical creatures. To the town's credit, the mural she painted at the library still stands. In fact, Charlie did touch ups on the jungle walls just two years ago. He told me the experience was healing.

"You're gonna think I'm crazy Sis," he said. "But she was there. I could feel her presence. I could smell her as I painted jade green jungle leaves and swirled gray into the monkey's eye. Her musky cologne filled my nostrils."

I didn't think he was crazy at all. I think she was so happy to see him paint. The most vivid memories I have of my mommy are watching her paint. She wore tight, faded jeans and daddy's work shirt, always barefoot, a paintbrush in her hand and her Eagles album spinning on the turntable. She would be singing, *Take It To The Limit*, as she turned a dirty wall into a masterpiece. Just like her favorite song, my mother did take it to the limit. It is how she lived life, and it caused her to die young. Marie Cooper died at the age of twenty-eight, when I was eight years old. She died in a car accident with my biological father. It is always that bit of news that surprises everyone, not the car accident, the father. In truth, Skip Cooper is not my actual father, although he is my daddy and the man who raised me and built me my lovely home.

My mother was just nineteen years old when she became pregnant with me. She had graduated high school and was working as a receptionist for the town doctor. Dr. Johnson was an attractive man with auburn hair and green eyes just like mine. He also had a wife and two young daughters. When my mother became pregnant by Dr. Johnson she probably could have ruined his career and broke up his home, but for some reason she did not. Instead she turned to Skip Cooper, who had always loved her. She told him she was pregnant and needed help. He proposed marriage and raised me as his own child.

You would think that my mother would have stopped working for Dr. Johnson after she married Skip, but that is not the case. She continued on with work and I believe with their secret love affair. Charlie was born two years after me and he is the son of Skip Cooper that is easy to tell. He is his spitting image. I know my mother loved my daddy, Skip. It was evident by the way she giggled and kissed him and Skip worshipped my mother. However, my mother must have also loved Dr. Johnson. For some reason Skip allowed this, or maybe he just didn't know how to stop it.

Skip was taking care of Charlie and me the night my mommy died, I remember we went out to eat that night and had ice cream, because Mommy was working late. When he put us to bed in our mythical room, Mommy still wasn't home. It was the middle of night when the sheriff knocked on the door and woke our sleeping house. He told Skip that Marie had been in a car accident and that she had not survived. In the morning, I learned that Dr. Johnson had also been in the car and that he too was dead. It seems that the doctor had ingested too much wine and was driving his little red convertible mustang too fast on the curvy mountain roads. You think that you know a mountain and that you've learned her switchbacks and corners, but a mountain can surprise you. Dr. Johnson took the hairpin curve at seventy miles an hour with my mother in the passenger seat. She was ejected from his car. His little, red mustang laid a crumbled mess at the bottom of the cliff. My mother laid fifty feet away. Skip Cooper lost the love of his life that night and became a single parent of two.

After my mother and the doctor died, the rumors swirled and eventually landed on me. Everybody noticed how much I looked like the doctor and nothing like Skip Cooper. My straight, auburn hair and green eyes were the talk of the town. When Mrs. Johnson could no longer stand the stories or the resemblance I bear to her children, she took her kids and moved from Grace. Skip however, lived unaffected by gossip. He ignored all the talk and continued to father both Charlie and I and mourn our mother. It was during this time that Rayland became my best friend. After all, the same kids that called him a fag now called my mother a whore and me a bastard, words I knew they learned at home. Adults can be meaner than kids and although they did not say hateful things to my face you could see disgust in their eyes and in the way they scrutinized my face. Lucinda however, was the exception. She was always kind to me and spoke highly of my mother. She would remind me that my mother was a talented artist and that she was beautiful and funny. I think Lucinda really liked my mother and she understood how one woman could love two men. Lucinda also respected my daddy with his silent and steadfast integrity. Skip's love for my mother never faded. His affection and loyalty to me has been unfaltering which makes him my daddy and my hero. Since my mother's death, twenty years ago, Skip has had other girlfriends. He's an attractive guy, a kind gentleman and a hell of a handyman. I've heard it said that if your man leaves you, Skip Cooper can not only fix your plumbing and patch your roof, he can also mend your broken heart and make you feel like a woman again. However, he has never loved any of them like he loved Marie Cooper. She was his one and only.

Once I had finished telling the story of my mother and Skip, I looked around the room at my enlightened friends. I realized there are no mysteries between us. They have told me the secrets that they keep and I have told them of the paradox I call family.

Summer Adjustments

School's out, summer has begun and The Kitchen House looks like a recreational center with the children of Grace dangling from the zip line and playing on the swings. My kids have an abundance of playmates and don't seem to mind sharing their back yard. I admit there are times when I have to referee. I have had to stop fights, console whiny children, and bandage skinned knees. Mr. Baxter, my nosy, next door neighbor, hates the playground almost as much as he hates our coffee shop. In his opinion, The Kitchen House has changed the quiet atmosphere of the town. We have caused more traffic, more noise and now there is ruckus. Personally, I feel The Kitchen House has been good for Mr. Baxter and I would bet his wife agrees. Before, the café, he was still a meddlesome, grumpy old man, but lonely with not enough snooping to do for an actively, inquisitive fellow. The Kitchen House has given him people to watch and material to work with. We have changed his days from boring to curious, he spends so much more time outside interfering and getting involved, especially now that he has a park to watch. I really don't mind his prying. I look at it as having a full-time playground monitor that I don't have to pay. As irritating as Mr. Baxter can be, it's nice to have another set of eyes. The parents of Grace have grown accustomed to letting their kids play at The Kitchen House and they no longer feel an obligation to come down and buy a cup of coffee. Friday and Saturday evenings are the exception, those are the nights the adults come out to play, and they will spend their money freely. In reality, we are the hot spot. Rayland has moved his stage outside. On Saturday nights we begin at six o'clock and end when it's dark. Spectators occupy my porch and yard for hours. The people love the entertainment and every weekend is a hoedown, a party thrown by Rayland.

Rayland still misses his mama very much. It's been a difficult adjustment. In order to get through his sorrow, he has thrown himself into work. For the last few years, Rayland's focus has been solely on the care of his Alzheimer's mother. He put off any innovated work notions that he had for the dance studio, because he didn't have the time to invest. Life has changed drastically for Rayland as it does for any caretaker when their care is no longer needed. He now has time on his hands with too many minutes to bereave Lucinda. In order to get through her death he has begun breathing life back into all the ideas he has shelved over the years. This sort of CPR has resulted into a CDT, competitive dance team. I hear competitive dance is the thing and it suits Rayland. He takes dance to a different level. For Rayland, dance is not just theatrical entertainment; it's a sport and a competition.

Rayland's competition team has begun dancing at The Kitchen House. Before the clog dancers, young girls age eight to eighteen perform. Everybody likes to watch the kids. They're cute and energetic. The young dancers even have Kitchen House costumes worn specifically on Saturday nights. The kids resemble the Fourth of July in their silky blue and white skirts and red sequin half tops and the town eats it up. When the girls perform their routine to the song Independence Day, belted out by Martina McBride, you will hear hoots and hollers that only rednecks can produce. Although I'm tired from long weekend nights, the dancing benefits both Rayland and me on so many levels, the weekly performances help make the girls better dancers, Rayland is advertising himself by showing off his talent and more people are learning about The Kitchen House. I am now a favorite spot for all the dance moms. They happily drive an hour through the mountains to sip a Vanilla Macchiato and watch their little girls perform.

We have also moved Friday nights outside, with country singers taking stage on my veranda. Personally, I love Friday nights when I get to listen to the folksy tunes of John Denver or Cat Stevens. The town loves it too, even Mr. Baxter, regardless of what he says. Everybody brings their own lawn chair and they sit outside until day fades. On Friday nights, my yard is filled with song and the dancing lights of fireflies. Then home my customers go, hand in hand, feeling good. There is nothing better than an outdoor concert to free your spirit and enlighten your soul. It is such a nice way for folks to end the workweek and start the weekend. My daddy loves Friday nights and he brings a cooler of his own beer, since I don't have a liquor license.

Lenore is a big help to Hazel and me on both Friday and Saturday nights. During the day, Lenore has been working at Bloomers Nursery. I am so happy she has found full-time employment, especially since school is out and we no longer have a homework help center. Hopefully, that will resume in the fall. Lenore seems to love her job at the nursery and she is learning all she can. I think learning is Lenore's method to life. She loves to educate herself. When she began working at The Kitchen House, she studied baristas and coffees. Now she studies buds and blossoms. Lenore is probably the most frequent visitor of our town library. She makes weekly trips to the library and then comes into The Kitchen House with her arms full of books and her glasses placed neatly on her head. She sits for hours with her cappuccino and biscuit, flipping through pages of landscaping, flower arranging, botany and the scientific guide to blooms and butterflies. She is a sponge who loves to soak up knowledge and then put it to use. She made me a hanging basket for the porch as a thank you gift. She credits me for getting her the job at the nursery, when in reality I did nothing but pick up an application. Still she's appreciative. The basket she made is a lavish display of brightly colored flowers. It is so unlike the gifts I get from Pixie Moon-Dust, which are also beautiful but stark in comparison. The latest Pixie gift was a glass jar filled with pussy willow branches. Once again Hazel suggested adding white lights to Pixie's creation. Lenore has also been using her new knowledge to beautify her own home. The little yellow house that she rents from my dad is now lovable with its new landscaping and plentiful window boxes. Lenore has dug a small garden patch in the back yard that she is most excited about. Never a gardener before, Lenore's enthusiasm is childlike, full of glee and innocence. She is overjoyed by the miraculous wonder of growth and I get daily chronicles about the flowers and green tufts that have begun to poke through the earth. I know the care she has placed on the home makes my dad happy.

Many times his rental properties have become houses of squalor that inhabit both people and farm animals. Daddy is a live and let live kind of guy, but even he has a hard time when his renter moves the refrigerator onto the porch and lets the mule come inside. He tries to look the other way. After all, he raised Charlie and me in a dirty house. But lived-in and filthy are two different things. When he visits to collect the monthly rent, he gives small lectures and then spends the rest of the day annoyed. I once asked him why he didn't just kick a renter out for being a hoarder. "They're only doing what they know," he said. To survive it, he avoids his renters all that he can and then cleans it up when they move out.

Lenore is different. My daddy runs by there all the time just to look at the pretty changes. He is truly enjoying having Lenore for a renter and she has no idea. She will politely ask him, in her northern accent, if she can make the home more charming.

"Mr. Skip do you mind if I plant some clematis around the base of the mailbox post? I promise to dig it up when I move if you don't like it."

My dad just laughs and shakes his head.

"Absolutely Lenore, you can plant your flowers." My father is not the only male impressed with Lenore. I believe Charlie is in love or rather infatuation. He wants to ask Lenore out, the problem being her intimidating manner. Lenore has built a daunting east coast wall around herself that causes confusion in a mountain man. In fact, I think she is the first woman that actually scares Charlie. Maybe that's why his attraction is so strong. I'm hoping that in time Charlie will either learn how to break through Lenore's wall or climb over it. They would make such a nice couple. Besides, it would be nice if Lenore allowed herself to love again.

Hazel, like Lenore, intimately knows the difficulty in opening yourself up and I'm so proud of her. Hazel and Ezra have become true fishing buddies and friends and they spend nearly every evening beside the stream. Sometimes they take the boys with them to fish and sometimes they don't. I've told the kids that Hazel needs some time with her friend away from everybody so they are not to whine when she doesn't take them. I think they understand, simply because it is an emotion that we all share. Hazel is glowing. She says that she and Ezra are just friends and I believe her. But, I also think she needed a friend, someone more than me who has an abundance of friends and has put her to work. Yes, I gave Hazel a purpose, but Ezra is giving her companionship. Ezra is a sweet, old guy with a kindhearted nature. Not only does he extend his friendship to Hazel, he's considerate of me and my children. In a thoughtful way, he graciously helped me get through the hardest day I've had this year. Father's Day was the anniversary of me being a single parent. It's been a whole year since Beau left. Sunday may not have been the exact date, but it was the actual day. He deserted us on Father's Day 1999. We had spent that entire day celebrating him and after I laid the kids down to sleep, he pulled an already packed suitcase from underneath our bed and told me he no longer loved me. The sting of that moment still causes me to flinch. Thinking about it can produce sadness so heavy that I can hardly get up, which is why we skipped church on Sunday morning. I just couldn't bear the thought of a Father's Day service and happy families huddled together. Instead, I plucked Sabrina from her crib and went into the boys' room, where I laid on the floor while they played with their toys. I listened to them play and then argue and fight, then play some more, jump on the bed and then argue and fight. I think most of the overtures were for my attention, but I just lay comatose on the oval braided rug, barely lifting my head. Eventually, Hazel swung open the bedroom door.

"Get dressed everybody," she says. "We're going on a picnic."

The boys' bickering turned into excited anticipation and they raced around looking for their shoes. I lifted myself up from the hardwood, an exhausted slumber still heavy on my shoulders. I felt a weighted emptiness as if I was wearing a backpack stuffed full of apathy.

"Thank you," I said relieved that someone was willing to walk me through this day. In The Kitchen House, Ezra was waiting with a packed picnic basket, kites and fishing poles. We spent the day at Ezra and Hazel's favorite fishing spot, a valley between two mountain ranges. There the stream flows cold and clear, full of trout and the bank is bursting with colorful wildflowers. Ezra and Hazel placed our blanket and chairs under the shade of a large, red oak tree and we spent the afternoon eating ham on rye, flying kites and watching the fish jump. The scenery was beautiful and everybody was so happy. My children's laughter echoed through the range as they ran through the valley of green grass and flowers. We managed, after many failed attempts, to get our kite high into the deep blue sky. When it was high enough to soar on its own without our manipulation, I held onto its string and we laid on our backs and watched the red kite dip and dance on the wind, just below the white fluffy clouds that floated by. We caught and kept three trout that day. Ezra caught two and Roman caught one. Henry caught a little sunfish and with a whispered apology, he gently released it back into the cool stream. Henry has a love-hate relationship with fishing. It's fun until something is dangling from a pole with a hook in its mouth. Then unlike Roman, who feels like a champion, Henry feels empathetic.

By late afternoon we packed up our picnic, took our three fish and headed back to The Kitchen House. Ezra cleaned up the daily catch with Roman's help, while Hazel pulled more trout from our fridge caught earlier in the week. I started the fire and then called my dad. He loves a good fish fry and I wanted to give him his gift. While the men cooked fish outside, I put together a salad and Hazel made a pot of rice. We ate our scrumptious dinner at the two picnic tables beside the playground. Henry opted for peanut butter and jelly and my father enjoyed the cool refreshing taste of his Father's Day present.

I didn't know what to get my dad this year. He's not a materialistic fellow at all and any tool you think he needs he has. So the last time Pixie was at the house doing a reading, I asked her about her dad's brew.

"It's the best tasting beer in these mountains," she said. I gave Pixie some money and asked if she would put together a gift package with an assortment of several different bottles. What she returned to me was a small wooden crate packed with hay and ten bottles of homemade craft varying in color, from a soft golden blond to a dark reddish bronze. I knew I had done well and my father would love his gift. For me, Pixie brought a jug of elderberry wine.

"Didn't you just have a birthday?" she asked handing over the large bottle of dark purple crushed fruit.

"Last week," I answered. It had come and gone without fanfare and for that I was relieved.

Daddy in fact did love his gift, but his response was surprising.

"Wow, Sissy," he said opening the crate and examining each bottle with the attention of a beer connoisseur. "How do you know Bootleggin Johnny?" he asked.

"I don't know him," I said. "I know his daughter and so do you, Pixie Moon-Dust."

"Well, I'll be damned. Baby Priscilla, now that makes a bit of sense."

I had so many questions for my father, but didn't ask. My dad shared a beer with Ezra while Hazel and I sipped Elderberry wine with our trout dinner. Everything tasted so delicious. Either this was the best meal I've ever eaten or the fruity wine enhanced each flavor. Both Hazel and I could feel the wine's effect from just one glass, so I corked the bottle and savored the taste it left on my tongue and the relaxed feeling it left in my limbs. I watched the day turn to dusk and was enthralled by its beauty. I listened to my children play, running up and down the playground and I felt lucky. My emotions were so vastly different from the morning's dread. As it turned out, the day I had feared, had turned into a day of awesomeness, surrounded by loved ones. That night when I wrote in my diary, my tipsy hand scripted a happy and short paragraph with just enough info to know that I had survived the day.

Father's Day, 2000 - Dear Diary, I woke up this morning feeling sad and alone, a tune of self-pity playing in my head. But after a picnic by a mountain stream and a backyard fish fry my mood changed and so did my song. Somewhere along the day, I began to resemble John Lennon and realized, "I'll get by with a little help from my friends, get high with a little help from my friends, gonna try with a little help from my friends – with a little help from my friends."

Breakfast At Tiffany's & Library Books

June 26, 2000 – Dear Diary, some days move at a snail's pace. The minutes tick by in slow motion and from seven a.m. to seven p.m. I am stuck. I go as far as my yard. You are unable to take off when you have a business. It's like having a baby that keeps you housebound. My favorite days are the ones that move at a comfortable steady pace, with not too much stress and a new friendly face every hour. I especially like meeting new people. I am blessed with travelers who have happened upon my charming café and folks from the city that have heard about The Kitchen House and decided to make the drive. Saturdays are always the hardest, longest and the most memorable day of the week. Other days may blur together like one long extension of the next, but Saturdays are different. They stand out. Saturdays are full of kids, customers, tea parties, fancy coffees, dancing and cleaning until I fall into bed exhausted and sore. Saturdays are good at leaving an imprint on my mind and body and last Saturday I shall never forget.

Destiny Marie, the daughter of Misty Dawn, who is the sister of Beau, had a tea party bridal shower at The Kitchen House on Saturday. Destiny Marie is a spoiled girl, materialistic, young and beautiful. She has pearly white teeth and a stunning smile. She works in the city as a dental hygienist and she is engaged to marry a dentist. Good for her. Destiny Marie was very specific and detailed when Hazel and I met with her about her bridal shower. She behaved so particular and fussy that I called Rayland down for reinforcement. I may not know how to throw a girly-

girly tea party, but Rayland does. Destiny Marie had a theme for her bridal shower tea party, *Breakfast at Tiffany's,* the movie with Audrey Hepburn. Rayland oohed and awed over Destiny Marie's idea, but I had to keep from rolling my eyes. I believe this child forgot that she comes from a coal mining family and not diamond mining. I consider Destiny Marie to be a bit pretentious. However, I woke up early Saturday morning and began working hard to make sure that her bridal shower tea party would be perfect. The dentist was actually paying me well for this party, which both surprised and pleased me. I set up the tea party in the garden area of the yard. It's around the side of the house where the porch stops and you can no longer see the playground. We have planted white flowering bushes up against the house with Lenore's help and made a garden patch that is full of flowers and greenery. Rayland and I carried both picnic tables over to the garden area and covered them with mint green tablecloths, placed vases full of pink and white blooms and set them for tea.

I have begun to collect vintage teacups, teapots and saucers. Charlie picks them up for me at antique stores and flea markets. I have acquired quite an assortment. With my assemblage, it was fun to set a tea party for twelve. Rayland and I had a blast arranging a variety of six flowery gold-rimmed saucers at each table and a mixture of six fancy little teacups. We picked our patterns carefully, making sure that each distinct piece of china complimented the other pieces. The effect is always a hodge-podge of flowery charm. I have little white ceramic pitchers for cream and numerous ornate teapots embellished with floral designs to sit in the center of the table. The tea sandwiches and little cookies that Hazel made were placed on three-tiered silver platters and set on the tables at teatime. The ladies would be served soup in little white bowls. Since this was to be a garden tea party on a hot day in June, Hazel had made Gazpacho, a cold soup full of raw vegetables with a refreshing taste.

During the tea party setup, my kids and Avery Banks ran around being loud and getting into things. I was relieved when Roman and Avery asked if they could go over to the library, which is directly across the street. I thought it was a great idea and I honestly didn't mind when the boys were gone for nearly three hours. It gave us ample time to get everything ready without worrying about two more kids. The boys were still not home when Destiny Marie and her bridesmaids arrived.

I admit now that I was impressed with Destiny Marie's theme and how those girls pulled it off. The young ladies wore black classic dresses, not a hard find. It was the accessories that put them over the edge. They were draped in fake pearls and wearing long black satin gloves that went up to their elbows. Large black sunglasses shielded their eyes and their long hair was neatly piled into ballerina buns. A couple of the girls wore chiffon scarves tied around their head as if they were about to ride off in a convertible with a Hollywood actor. The most ingenious accessory was the long vintage cigarette holder, which was no secret to the ladies as they puffed away. It really was a great scene, a real garden tea party with ladies dressed to the nines. I was greeting each of the girls when Lydia, the librarian, came stomping across the street and up to The Kitchen House.

"Sissy, you need to come with me and see what your boys did to my library."

I felt a little lump in my throat and looked over at Hazel.

"Lydia can you send the boys home and I can come over after this tea party?"

"Oh no! Those boys are not just running off to go play and leaving my library destroyed."

"Destroyed?"

"Go," said Rayland. "I'll call Cody and have him teach my afternoon dance class. I can handle the party and Hazel can handle Sabrina and the café."

I shamefully followed Lydia across the street as the Audrey Hepburns watched, amused and giggling to one another. Just inside the library door, Roman and Avery sat motionless on a wooden bench with pouty faces and downward glances. It was obvious that the frustrated librarian had put the boys in time-out and told them she was going to go get their mother.

"Just go look what they did!" Lydia spit out. "The destruction is around the corner over near non-fiction."

I walked the bending, jungle walls of our small library over to the small nook of non-fiction, praying that the damage was minimal. What I found was incredible. Nearly every single book in the area had been taken from its shelf and used to build a large and elaborate fort and tunnel. The fort was not high and had no standing room. But, it was long and perfect for small scooting bodies. I could tell that Roman had played on the floor at Avery's level, that is, after he had pulled all the books from the top shelves. Really, the long tunneling fort was impressive, like a house of cards. I was awed by the way they had positioned every book. Stacked books had been used to create pillars and walls. Open books were used for the roof. It was a careful and precise procedure to build a structure wide enough and high enough to accommodate both their bodies and not fall over. I felt a little proud and thought about calling my daddy. He would have loved it.

"They did this?" I asked with enthusiasm in my voice.

"Of course they did this!" shouted Lydia. "Who else is here to deface property?"

It was clear that Lydia did not see the artistry in the fort making and she continued with her rambling lecture.

"These are books," she barked. "Not blocks! They are to be read and handled with care. Not tossed around like play things."

I was wishing Lydia would lighten up and stop screaming. The books weren't hurt and nobody reads non-fiction anyway. But she continued on with her emotional rant, close to tears.

"Every single book needs to be put back in its place, its exact place, arranged in order by author's name and library number." She scolded the boys and then looking at me she added, "It's a tedious task that will take hours and since I don't have hours to clean up after your children I assume that you will help them get everything back in its proper place."

Looking up to the walls of empty shelves and then to the mountain of books that lay on the floor, I suddenly understood why Lydia was so overwhelmed. I called the boys over and told them we were going to have to clean up.

"I know," they both said. "We're going to put the books back."

"It's not that simple," I tried to explain. "We can't just put them on the shelf like we do at home. There is an order we must follow." I scanned the floor trying to find the first book. I now grasped why Lydia was on the verge of a nervous breakdown; I too was close to tears.

"O.k. boys, did you pull the books out in order? Because we can just find where you stacked the A's and then the B's and so on and so on."

"Oh Miss Sissy we didn't pull in any ABC order," explained Avery. "We pulled books for their size. If I needed a big book I told Roman to get a big one and sometimes I needed a small book or skinny book or a fat book."

"Alright Avery, I get it."

Lydia seemed amused by my exasperation as if she were enjoying the drama. She stood beside me in perfect librarian pose with folded arms and a crunched up nose, tapping her foot to the beat of the clock.

"Lydia," I finally said. "The boys and I will clean everything up. You can go back to your desk, as I'm sure you have a lot of work to do. I'm sorry that they made a mess. Boys apologize to Miss Lydia so she can go get her work done. Miss Lydia is a busy lady and you need to respect her library and the books."

"Sorry Miss Lydia," came the unison sad response.

"They're sorry," I reiterated. "It was an innocent mistake. It won't happen again."

"You bet it won't!" Lydia snapped and then before she turned to leave she threatened. "I'll be checking your work."

Once Lydia was out of sight, I turned on Roman.

"Roman! I got Destiny Marie's damn bridal shower going on this very minute and instead of being over there helping Hazel I'm having to clean up the library."

"I know," Roman sniffled as the tears began to fall down his face.

"Oh dammit don't cry. Don't you dare. We are not giving Miss Lydia the satisfaction of hearing you cry. You understand me?"

Roman sniffed his tears back and dried his face on the back of his hand.

"Yes Ma'am" he said.

"Now boys, we're going to work together to put back all these books. First, I want you to find all the books where the author's last name starts with A. See this book?" I explained further holding the book out with its spine facing the boys. "This is the book's title," I said, tracing it with my finger. "And this is the author's name. See the first name is James and his last name is Kinney; which starts with K. He should go in a K pile. Now we must find all the last names starting with A and pile them in one spot."

The boys began crawling down the walls of the fort searching for A names and pulling them from their place. This caused the fort to cave in and the books to tumble everywhere leaving no room to pile books, let alone walk. The mess was overwhelming and I was feeling a bubbling rage. I looked to the jungle wall for comfort and peace. I gazed into the tiger's eyes and they stared intently back. I scanned the painted tree upward. A large, thick and glossy snake wrapped around a limb and peered down on us. Higher up, sat the most vibrant and colorful bird ogling us through the tiny green leaves. I stepped around the pile of books and laid both of my hands upon the jungle wall. The boys had grown quiet watching me. I believe I was freaking them out. I stroked the monkey head as if he were real and then without thinking; I kissed a giant pink blossom.

"Your Mommy is kissing the wall," I heard Avery say.

"Mama, give me the strength of your jungle." I whispered into the drywall that smelled of wild musk and then I smiled.

"You ok Mommy?" Roman shyly asked.

"I am," I said composing myself. "Now let's find A names."

As the boys and I piled books, I told them how Roman's grandmother had painted these walls when I was a little girl. She painted the library in the evening after it closed. It took weeks to finish the mural. She would bring Charlie and me to accompany her, because Mama hated being alone. It was fun being in the library at dark after it closed. Mama would plug in her large boom box and put in her Eagles tape interrupting the stillness that lived in the library. Charlie and I would run through the space chasing each other, dancing and being loud. When we grew tired, we went to Mama and lay on our backs and witnessed the jungle walls emerge. It was mesmerizing, watching giant leaves appear and animals come to life. Observing the creation of color is meditative and Mama's brush strokes served as our silent lullaby. Each stroke of hue, hummed us to sleep. Eventually Mama would put away her brushes, wake Charlie and me from the floor and take us home, until the next night when we would find ourselves dancing in the library again.

The boys half-heartedly listened to me talk. Instead, they bickered over the stacking of books and the tearing down of their miraculous fort. We had made slight headway and I had begun to shelf some of the books. However, the progression was time consuming and monotonous and more than two hours into the process I realized I was only up to Anderson. The feeling of strength and calmness I had received from the jungle walls had left me. Now I felt overwhelmed, angry and frustrated.

"This is going to take for-fucking-ever!" I shouted out without thinking.

The boys stopped to watch me cry and Father McIntire walked around the corner.

"Hazel sent me over to check on you," he said.

"Tell her I suck!" I cried. "I can't help her with the damn party and I'm sorry." Father McIntire turned to the boys to get a more positive response.

"That's a pretty impressive pile of books on the floor. What's going on here?"

"We made a tunnel fort," Avery explained. "It was so big and long and went all the way around the corner. But now we got to put all the books away and Miss Sissy is freaking out."

"I'm not freaking out Avery Banks!" I turned to the priest. "Every damn book is off the shelf and somewhere along this tunnel fort. I've got a business across the street that needs me and I have left Hazel with all the work, a party to run, plus two kids to watch. I guess I am freaking out a little." My hands were shaking and I felt the urge to wrap them around the small necks of Roman and Avery.

"Hazel's doing fine," said Father McIntire. "She told me that Henry was a big help and played with his little sister all morning long. Now Sabrina is taking a nap; and the party, well, I wouldn't worry about that either, Rayland is hosting the bridal shower and it looks like he's having more fun than the Audrey Hepburns."

I smiled at the priest who had just comforted me.

"Thanks," I said.

"Don't thank me yet. We have got to get all these books put away. I got an idea that might make things go faster."

The boys began handing books up to Father McIntire and in any sort of order, just whatever was in front of them. He alphabetized them as he went J, R, T, U, Z. The A's weren't too hard to finish, because I had already organized those. The rest began to fall into numerical order as we closed the gaps. Father McIntire and I now worked side by side and had fallen into the same rhythm. I now carried a new energy. I had oomph and my frustration had vanished. In fact, I think we were having fun racing through the pile of books being tossed up to us by the children. It was like an Olympic event, seeing how quickly we could get them shelved. It took us another two hours to work our way through the alphabet, but those two hours went so much quicker than the previous two. Before I knew it, every book was in its place and the boys were spinning on the floor like breakdancers.

"Thank you," I gratefully said to the priest, a smile stretched across my face. "Let's not do that again," I said to the boys.

"The fort was cool though, wasn't it Mama?"

"It was cool Roman," I confirmed.

"But you did kind of freak out didn't you Miss Sissy?" I suppose Avery needed confirmation as well, after all it was the first time I've yelled at him.

"I did freak out Avery."

"Yeah," Avery whispered over to the priest. "She even kissed the wall."

Father McIntire began looking at the jungle wall for maybe the first time, noticing all the detail and color that leaps from the mural and awes your mind.

"Wow!" was all he said. But, that one word was enough. The mural truly is wow. The priest placed his hand in his pocket as his eyes scanned the jungle. I believe he did this to touch the rabbit's foot. Then he smiled at me.

"Let's go," I said.

Both boys exhaled expressions of glee. Then sitting on skateboards with fast working arms they raced out of the library and across the street.

The priest and I stopped at the librarian's desk to let her know the books had been put away. Lydia was knee deep in a Star magazine and eating a chicken salad biscuit from The Kitchen House.

"Did you go across the street?" I asked. I was puzzled; as I had no idea she had even left.

"Well, of course I did," she said. "I do eat lunch. Besides, I wanted to see how Destiny Marie's tea party was going and let Hazel know what was keeping you so long. You should thank me."

"Should I?"

"Yes, because I look out for you, and right now there is a stranger over at your house, a real peculiar kind of guy, just weird lookin if you ask me. Miss Hazel said he's been hanging out there all day. I hear he's waiting on that blue-haired pixie you hang out with."

"Thank you Lydia," I said through clenched teeth.

"Anytime Sissy. Me and the hubby will see you tonight to watch Rayland's cloggers."

"Can't wait." The priest and I headed out the door and into the blaring June sun, the afternoon light causing my eyes to blink.

"Did you notice a stranger at my house?" I asked.

"No, but I guess I wasn't looking for a stranger," the priest suggested.

"Who were you looking for?"

"You," he blushed.

Cole Spencer, Paranormal Investigator & Web Blogger

June 29, 2000 – Dear Diary, it's funny how one event triggers the next. Life is a continual drama with layers upon layers. Beau's leaving caused Hazel to offer me help. Hazel's offer and her coffee initiated the inspiration for a café. The café activated the introductions of so many different people into my life. The different people are the layers of days and experiences piled on top of each other like a tiered cake. Each layer compliments the next with a different taste, knowing that one savory sweet moment could not exist without the flavor before it.

When I returned home from the library fiasco on Saturday, there was indeed a strange man sitting at my coffee bar sipping an espresso. I introduced myself as Sissy, the owner. The man told me his name is Cole Spencer and that he works as a paranormal investigator and blogger. He explained to me that he came across Pixie's website and saw the orb pictures that had been taken on Easter. Those orb photos had caused Cole Spencer to hop in his car and drive from Cleveland, Ohio to Grace, West Virginia to have coffee in my café. I offered to call Pixie, but Cole told me he had already set up a reading with her for Sunday morning. He had come down a day early just to get the feel of the house and snoop around. I knew Pixie had a reading in the morning, but I didn't know the details. Maybe there is a code of psychic – client confidentiality like a lawyer or a doctor, because Pixie never reveals her clients and I never ask.

As much as I hate to admit it, Lydia the librarian was correct when she said Cole was peculiar. He is an odd sort, not ugly, in fact very attractive with an unusual sense of style. He's young, maybe twenty-four, with a cool indie look like an arty kind of fashion. On Saturday, he was wearing a short sleeve, dark blue checkered dress shirt with a thin orange tie and tan pants. His pant legs were rolled up to his shins and on his feet were a pair of brown and tan vintage shoes. Cole Spencer wore thin wire frame glasses around his big brown eyes. His dark hair is cut very short on the sides, almost shaven, and then left long, thick and full on top. His thick hair is brushed back and gelled into place. His most unique characteristic is his thin handlebar mustache that also gets gelled into place. Rayland thinks Cole Spencer is adorable and he flirted with him some, but Rayland flirts with everybody.

Cole ended up spending the entire day at The Kitchen House, not leaving until closing time. During his Saturday visit he walked around the café with an analytical eye, making me nervous. It was as if The Kitchen House was under scrutiny and he was an inspector. He ran his hands down the bookcase and scanned the titles. Then he went to the bathroom and returned with a *Time* magazine. He sat on the burnt orange couch and read. He then put the magazine down, moved to the brown chair and people watched. He ate lunch and dinner at a wooden table, two meals of tuna salad and biscuits. He sipped espresso and peach iced tea at the coffee bar. Then he sat out on the veranda watching the children play, ate his pie and watched the clog dancers from a picnic table in the yard.

When Pixie showed up that evening to watch the cloggers, she immediately recognized Cole Spencer as her morning reading and the two hit it off like peanut butter and jelly. Pixie basically gave him his reading Saturday night. Cole practically did a back flip when Pixie told him that a grandma figure was with him, that she was enjoying the clog dancing and that she loved his mustache. It seems that Cole's Nana had died two years ago and in her dementia state she had told him he should grow a mustache to hide his overbite. After her death, he did.

By nightfall on Saturday, I was completely drained. I had slept restlessly the night before and then had awakened early to make tiny sandwiches and set up a tea party. Then I was interrupted to clean the library, followed by a day of work that moved into the hosting of entertainment and a crowded café. I could barely stand as I loaded the dishwasher and wiped down counters. Hazel was worn out as well and she sat in a chair, an exhausted lump, with not enough strength to help me close up shop. While we were in this state of utter fatigue, Pixie and Cole approached us and asked if Cole could do a paranormal investigation at The Kitchen House in the morning.

"What exactly is a paranormal investigation?" I asked.

"Oh it's really no big deal," said Pixie. "It just requires some equipment. Cole would like to go through the house with an EMF meter in order to detect electromagnetic fields and a thermal scanner to find cold spots."

"Like Ghostbusters?"

"I am actually a ghost hunter, as well as a website blogger," explained Cole. "I would like to receive some verification that there are actually ghosts in this house and then blog about it on my website."

"Well Cole," said Hazel standing up in her Mama Bear position with her chest puffed out and her hands on her hips. "There are definitely ghosts in this house and it doesn't take an EMF thingy or some thermal hoochie-ma-bob to find them. But we don't want our ghosts to get upset or feel put out by some hunter coming in here loaded down with equipment trying to snoop them out."

"Miss Hazel, I would never intentionally upset your ghosts."

"Well, it's not your intentions I'm worried about."

Pixie interrupted the stand off between Cole and Hazel. She assured Hazel that she would be with Cole every step of the way. That she would sanctify and do a healing afterwards and that if she felt any energy become upset or edgy she would stop the investigation immediately. She then told Hazel that ghost hunters were really no big deal, just people who believe in the other realm but have no psychic ability, so they need equipment to prove it to themselves and others. This last statement managed to calm Hazel and offend Cole Spencer. Hazel and I agreed to the ghost hunting. In the morning, Hazel went fishing with Ezra for the day and I took the kids to church. I loaded the car with Sabrina's baby backpack and a sack of food. The kids and I would have a hike and lunch in the mountains after mass. I wanted to make sure I was gone long enough for Cole Spencer to do his thing and then clear out.

I loved the homily that morning. It was actually about the things I had already been pondering, how we are all connected and the funny way people come in and out of your life for reasons that eventually make themselves known. Vainly, I wondered if he was talking about me. After mass, during our hike, we ran into Father McIntire. I wasn't surprised. I know that the priest escapes into the mountains whenever he can and always after his Sunday work, so I had packed an extra sandwich. We hiked up to a large flat spot in the mountains where my children could run off some of their energy. I took Sabrina out of her pack so she could walk through the field of wildflowers and get personal with nature. It was so nice to have the weight of Sabrina off my back. She is not yet two, still little (my smallest baby), but after awhile I feel the heaviness of the pack and it pulls on my shoulders. When she kicks her feet, which is constantly, I spend the hike fighting for my balance. It also didn't help that the day had turned hot. The sun beat on my face and I dripped sweat. By the time we reached the clearing, which is not far, I needed a rest. I lay in the grass and listened to the priest play with my kids. They giggled and ran about chasing each other in circles, playing a game of tag. It was a sweet and relaxing feeling to close my eyes and listen to the voices of my children and the song of the birds. I must have dozed off, because I awoke in a panic. The voices had gone. I sat straight up, my eyes darting across the landscape. Seeing no one I jumped to my feet and began screaming their names.

"Roman! Henry! Tim!" I shouted. "Tim where the hell are you?" I was terrified, moving in circles, close to tears, not sure which way to go when I saw them approaching from the woods. Roman and Henry were in full sprint, having heard their names and Sabrina was on the hip of the priest, a wildflower in her hand. When I think back now, the sight was precious, but at the time I was too panicked to notice.

"What the fuck!" I shouted at Father McIntire. Running to the kids I scooped them into my arms. The boys were stiff against my embrace, their eyes huge, slightly traumatized by my outburst, which included the shouting of fuck to a priest.

"I'm sorry Sissy," he said still holding my baby, unsure of how to react.

"Mama it's fine," said Roman. "We just went into the woods to look at the trees and flowers."

"Yeah," said Henry. "Father Tim was teaching us the names of plants."

I snatched Sabrina from his arms and kissed her head and she held out the long stemmed purple flower to my nose.

"Smell Mama."

I inhaled the plant and then looked to the priest with apologetic eyes.

"We didn't mean to scare you Sissy," he tried to explain. "You fell asleep and I knew you were exhausted, so I took the kids to the edge of the woods and kept them occupied."

"Thank you," I said feeling like a total asshole. "I'm sorry, I was just so scared when I woke and the kids were gone. I think it's my exhaustion. I must have fallen asleep to their laughter and woke up to the sound of nothing and I just freaked out. I'm sorry for the way I acted. I didn't mean to cuss at you."

"You're a good Mama," Father Tim smiled. "I should have known better than to take the cubs too far from the lioness."

"How long did I sleep?"

"About an hour."

"An hour?" I questioned. Could he be right? It seemed that just a few minutes had passed. I felt ashamed by the amount of time I had lain unaware and angry that I could fall asleep while my kids played on a mountaintop, another bad mom move.

"Sissy, you're exhausted," the priest defended. "You wake with the rise of the sun to fill everyone's coffee cup and you don't stop until the moon is high in the sky. It's okay to unwind for a minute and you only relaxed, because you knew the kids were safe and being watched."

He had read my mind and brushed away my insecurities. He had watched my kids for an hour and let me nap in the sun and I had been rude and swore at him. No wonder he's the saint and I'm the sinner.

"Can we go to the gazebo?" Henry asked breaking the tension.

"If it's alright with your mom?" Father McIntire answered.

"Only for a moment. I'm sure Father McIntire has things to do."

I loaded Sabrina into the baby backpack and we walked deeper into the trees. The boys schooled me with their newly obtained knowledge as we hiked and soon the gazebo appeared. We had discovered the gazebo in the winter and it had looked magical, a rustic hideaway sitting on a white sparkling mountain. I had been back in the verdant spring and sat among the flourishes of awakening blooms, each season breathtaking. In the summer the mountain is just as generous with its beauty, lush and green. I now looked forward to seeing the gazebo in autumn. The kids sat on the wooden floor planks and played with the carved figurines shaped by the priest, a bear, fox, wolf, and raccoon. While the kids played, Father

McIntire and I talked like best friends. I told him all about Cole Spencer, paranormal investigator and web blogger, and how he had seen the orb photos I took on Easter which Pixie had posted to her website. I spoke low hoping the boys were too busy with their imaginary play to hear much. I was not worried that the ghost hunting would frighten the boys, but rather they might be jealous to not be part of a paranormal investigation made official by cool phantom gear.

Hazel, as tired as she was last night, made Cole Spencer show her his ghost tools and explain how they work. Cole went out to his car and brought in a black canvas bag that was filled with ghost hunting paraphernalia. He placed each item onto the coffee bar and explained its use. Across my bar lay a flashlight, a camera, a digital recorder with microphone, an EMF meter, thermal scanner, motion detector, and a pad of paper with a pen. The equipment looked ordinary to say the least, not at all scary and nothing to carry on his back that would shoot slime, like in *Ghostbusters*. The flashlight, camera and pen and paper were obvious tools and didn't need explaining. Cole said that the digital recorder would pick up EVP's, which stands for electronic voice phenomena or rather the voices we cannot hear. The EMF meter, that looks like a calculator, is supposed to measure the fluctuations in electromagnetic fields, which means it basically lets the investigator know if any ghosts are walking around. The thermal scanner reminded me of a radar gun used by police to track speed. The scanner is supposed to find cold spots, another indication of ghosts. The motion detector looked just like Sabrina's baby monitor. Pixie was right. This was just a bag of stuff as goofy as spy gear and as simple as a magician's case, not at all impressive or scary. Funny, but as far as communicating with the dead goes, I think I was more impressed with Pixie's homemade broom and bag of salt. I suppose Cole Spencer reminds me of Inspector Gadget while Pixie's herbs and rosewater appeals to my feminine and earthy side. However, Father McIntire seemed truly interested in Cole Spencer. I got the idea that he would have liked to be part of the ghost hunt.

The kids, priest and I sat at the gazebo for a long stretch of time. We were content in our talk and play and unaware of the minutes as they ticked by. Suddenly I noticed the sky had changed. The sun was not so hot and I had grown very hungry. The boys and Sabrina must have made the same discovery, because soon after this, they all started to whine. It suddenly became clear that we had stayed too long. The priest helped me walk the crying kids through the mountains and back to the church parking lot where my car was parked. Hazel was already home when the kids and I returned. She had lit a candle and probably said a prayer. She told me the house felt peaceful and nothing looked out of the ordinary. I believe she had checked every room for signs of disturbance. I could smell the sage in the air and I knew Pixie had done a cleansing when Cole had finished his search. The kids, Hazel and I were all physically drained from the long and busy weekend. We ate leftover meatloaf sandwiches for dinner that night with three-day-old potato salad and a whole bag of chips; each of us feeling starved and tired. After dinner, I made the kids take a bath and they went to their rooms early and without complaint. Once I had everyone settled, I went to Hazel's room to check on her. She was sitting in her chair with a magazine in her lap, no doubt reading some Hollywood gossip.

"You think we're okay?" I asked.

"I hope so," she responded. Both of us were nervous about pissing off an army of ghosts.

"Are we okay?" I shouted up at the ceiling trying to address the other realm. As I turned to walk out of Hazel's room, I was suddenly overwhelmed by the smell of baby powder. The scent was so strong it nearly took my breath away.

"Do you smell that?" I asked Hazel who had suddenly taken her nose out of the magazine and put it in the air.

"Baby powder," she whispered.

"Why baby powder?" I asked, completely taken back and intrigued.

"Maybe they're trying to comfort us. Let us know it's fine."

"So, you think we're being coddled by the spirits?"

"I do," said Hazel. "And I'll take the pampering with a grateful heart".

Fourth of July

I was going to be closed on Tuesday, July Fourth, giving Hazel and I three days off in a row, which I felt we desperately needed, but my daddy talked me into staying open.

"We can turn it into a money making holiday," he said. Hazel agreed. My original plan was to take the kids into the city. Rayland and his cloggers were marching in the Charleston Parade. I thought we could get there early to set up chairs and then after the parade just hang out in the city all day long., then see their huge fireworks display at night. But that means I would miss the Grace festivities and Daddy seemed to think that it would look like a snub on my part.

"The Kitchen House is an integral part of this community," he said. "It is important that you participate in this town's humble attempt at an Independence Day celebration." Because of the guilt he made me feel, we not only stayed open, we participated.

Grace is the biggest of the small towns that make up Spring County. Spring County is a tiny little insignificant patch on a very significant mountain range. Grace holds the Spring County Courthouse as well as the one high school that all of the Spring County children attend, the fire station, police station, a small medical building, the post office, the library and the largest supermarket. It also makes a gracious attempt at holding a parade and a fireworks display. We do all right with fireworks. The firemen shoot them off over at the high school and the bleachers are filled. I can actually watch them from my front porch. The Spring County budget is small and the display is not as spectacular as the big cities, but they are still good enough to excite the hillbillies around here. Once the firemen are done with their show, the rednecks of the town, my father being one of them, shoot explosives into the sky until the wee hours of the night. The parade on the other hand is pretty pathetic. It usually consists of a slew of old veterans holding flags and boy scouts on bikes that are patriotically decorated in red, white and blue streamers. However, this year Skip Cooper, my daddy, got himself involved and told everybody he was going to turn our pathetic parade into a proud Fourth of July 2000 parade. Then he did just that. He went to the monthly community meeting held at the municipal courthouse and encouraged each town to build a float. He talked like a motivational speaker when he asked them to come together as a community to work on a float that represented their little town. He said we were going to start something new in this millennium; we were going to start having a kick ass parade. The people not only got excited, but became inspired and more than a dozen floats were built to run in our little parade.

Each of the five little towns that make up Spring County built a float and one town, Spruceville, built two floats because they couldn't agree on style, symbolism or design. You would think common sense would tell you that their symbol should be a spruce tree, but for some reason half of the town disagreed. So, they split into teams, and two of Spruceville's most aggressive know-it-alls led the groups. The conflict produced a stressful June and start to July, but resulted in two beautiful floats. One float was a Spruce tree, and the other float was a waterfall and stream, where actual water pumped, tumbled and flowed down the back of a flatbed truck. Besides the town floats, businesses and organizations were inspired by my dad's idea and they built floats too. The quilters had a float that was simple but charming with the ladies sitting in rocking chairs and a quilt stretched out between them. Lydia's husband built her a library float by painting shelves of books onto large pieces of plywood and she sat in the float's center dressed as Mother Goose. Lenore rode on the Bloomers Nursery float surrounded in flowers and throwing handfuls of Bazooka bubble gum. Of course, my father made a Kitchen House Float, which was a small replica of my purple house with a big Kitchen House sign on its front fake lawn. Daddy drove the float with Sabrina next to him strapped into the car seat and Hazel rode on it dressed in her red, white and blue best. She held a large coffee pot in one hand and waved to the cheering crowd. Charlie and I walked behind the float throwing Tootsie Pops and Starbursts. My boys opted out of our float and instead they walked, dressed in their uniforms, behind the Boy Scout float. The Boy Scout float was the most impressive. It was a giant white rocket with the year 2000 written down its side. The rocket actually tilted and raised and at every block it would stop and shoot confetti into the air with a loud bang and lots of smoke. The rocket float was the handy work of those crazy pinewood derby men. Working alone, they have the mentality of apes beating their chests at one another. Together, they evolved and the best float was built. Besides the floats there was the high school marching band with their trumpets blaring that got everyone excited. Another crowd pleaser was the marching firemen and policemen. They carried a big boom box and every block they stopped and did a dance off with breakdancing moves that Rayland would have loved. Actually it was quite hysterical. Many of the churches marched in the parade, all wearing matching T-shirts and passing out their Vacation Bible School flyers. St. Mary's was not one of them. The old veterans led the parade and this year they did seem proud with their heads held high and smiles on their faces. It was just what my daddy had imagined. The Proud 2000 Fourth of July Parade is one the veterans will remember as being special.

After the parade the festivities moved to The Kitchen House. Early this spring my daddy had done some renovation work for a guy who owns a party store in the city. As usual, my daddy did some wheeling and dealing and the Party Hardy Outlet provided us with a gigantic bounce house for the day, free of charge. Those things are usually a small fortune to rent. The bounce house was set up at the far back corner of my lot and children invaded my yard. Parents could not pull their screaming kids away from The Kitchen House, which is exactly what my dad wanted to happen. Soon Daddy had the gas grill fired up on the sidewalk and was selling hotdogs for one dollar and burgers for two. Inside The Kitchen House, patrons could purchase their drinks. We also sold sides of macaroni salad and watermelon slices until we ran out.

Rayland had promised he would entertain us from 2:00 pm to 5:00pm with as many dancers as he could get. I kind of thought that most of his dancers would opt out and want to spend the Fourth of July in Charleston cooking out in their own back yard. Surprisingly most all of the girls and cloggers he asked were excited to come. The dancers arrived in truckloads. They took the stage happy and enthusiastic and sparkled like crazy in their red sequin tops and blue shimmering skirts. A white sailor cap completed their outfit with patriotic charm. Being a gay country boy, Rayland has choreographed numbers for every upbeat, nationalistic song I can think of, from Lee Greenwood's, *God Bless The USA*, to *Yankee Doodle Dandy* and everything in-between. For over three hours that afternoon, the girls performed them all, God bless Rayland.

After 5:00pm the dancers left in a hurry, anxious to get back to Charleston in time for fireworks. However, Rayland and Cody stayed at The Kitchen House and said they were going to see Grace's display this year from my front yard. There were others with the same idea. Although many took off to head over to the high school and claim a good seat, others stayed at the café and a few more showed up at The Kitchen House an hour or so before fireworks were to begin.

Christy and Avery Banks decided to stay at my house for fireworks, and Pixie Moon-Dust showed up around 7:30pm. During that time, I was searching the playground taking notice and counting heads. Suddenly my attention was on Avery Banks. The child was sitting on a wooden swing and flying so high. His legs were twisted crudely about him with no pumping action, yet the laughing boy nearly reached the clouds. The scene made no sense and denied the laws of physics. When the swing would go forward Avery's head would fall backwards and giggles would fill the sky. I looked to see where Christy Banks was, if maybe she had just done an underdog that I had missed, but she was on the veranda with Lenore and Charlie clearly in conversation.

"How is that child flying so high?" I said out loud to myself just as Pixie Moon-Dust walked by.

"Easy," she replied. "His father is pushing him." It was at that moment I realized that besides actual living people my yard was filled with spirits.

"How many are here?" I asked Pixie.

"So many," she answered laughing. I chose to take it no further and asked Pixie nothing else. It was probably best that I had no idea how many ghosts were walking around my yard. However, I did silently stop and take my own sort of inventory. I looked over at Rayland and Cody who sat at a picnic table with two heaping plates of macaroni salad and a hamburger and whispered a "Hi," to Lucinda who I was sure must have been sitting beside them. I gazed over to Lenore and visualized the handsome, dark boy drenched in white light that Pixie had once described to me. Through a telepathic introduction I communicated. "Hi Christopher, I'm Sissy, welcome to my home." I saw Hazel and Ezra over by the bounce house watching the kids jump and I made a shout out to Harry, Hazel's deceased husband. I then eyed my daddy and in a hushed tone I spoke out loud, "I hope you're having fun Mama." My eyes were scanning the playground hoping to visually see Thomas. I felt a desire for the young ghost child to show up and wave in my direction. Instead, Father McIntire made an appearance. He too had finally made it to my front yard and was eager to watch the fireworks. Just before the sky went completely dark, I gathered my children together and led them to a blanket I had placed in the yard. Father McIntire joined us. Avery and Christy Banks spread their blanket next to mine. My dad went through the crowd passing out sparklers to all the young kids and I prayed nobody would get their eye poked out. Nobody did. Once again, my daddy was right. It was a good thing to be open on the Fourth of July and even better to participate.

July 4, 2000 – Dear Diary, it seemed like all of Spring County ended up in my yard at one time or another today. I believe I saw every face I have ever met from these parts and many new ones. The entire day was so full, but I didn't have the feeling of being overwhelmed like I usually do when we're busy. Instead, I just kind of glided on invisible skates, talking to people and making coffee. It turned out that socializing was the biggest purpose of the day and business came secondary. Some people didn't even buy anything. They were just here to hang out and let their kids play. Besides that, I had lots of backup. Charlie and Daddy spent all day at The Kitchen House working and so did Lenore. Lenore showed up directly after the parade and she brought me a hanging basket of flowers she took from the Bloomers Nursery float display. Lenore is very kind and I trust she is healing slowly. She's a different person from the frightened and sad lady that landed here six months ago. Grace, West Virginia has been good for her and Charlie is infatuated. I believe she is sweet on Charlie too; another sign she is starting to absolve herself. The two spent the entire day working side by side and then shared a blanket together to watch the fireworks. Speaking of couples, Ezra showed up for the day and helped out Hazel. It was fun to watch those two chase after my toddler and eat hotdogs off the grill. They make for cute companions. I do believe Hazel had a great day, first as queen of The Kitchen House float and then mingling on the lawn until bedtime. In fact, it seemed that everyone had fun, me included.

Moreover, I could feel an abundance of happiness all around me. It was as if the emotion "joy" radiated from one person to the next. The energy at The Kitchen House was pulsating and I consider this to be the composition of my ghosts. I believe I felt the vivacity of spirits. Just as Pixie had once told me, there was definitely the remarkable presence of an unseen jubilee going on. No doubt the high spirits were producing cheeriness and there was merriment felt all around.

Mystic Mayhem

July 8, 2000 – Dear Diary, maybe I am naive to believe in my ghosts and not feel a bit frightened or trust that the earthly world and spirit world can pleasantly coexist. I know my home is haunted and yet I feel it is a warm home full of love. I believe most people fear the supernatural. They find it creepy and they overlook its sublime beauty. Writers and filmmakers are great at making the spirit world a place of demons and evil darkness. I don't understand what inspires this. Why would they want to cause fear of a spirit world, when in fact, it is where each and every soul is heading? It's true that as soon as we're born our days are numbered. The time we have been granted in this realm is limited. I, for one, find it comforting knowing that a parallel universe exists and I call it heaven. Experiencing my ghosts has confirmed my faith in God. It feels reassuring knowing that my mom is watching over me and that her perfume lingers in my walls. I like the fact that my house once held another family that loved this home. Who am I to begrudge them their house? After all, they were here first. This business about chasing ghosts away makes no sense at all, especially when ghosts are much more polite than the living. Spirits tend to be subtle, they take up little space and for the most part they leave you alone. Humans on the other hand are self-centered beings who have somehow formed the notion that they are the only ones with the right to be here.

On Wednesday night, I let Avery Banks spend the night. I had to watch him on Thursday anyway while Christy worked at the hospital. This way he didn't have to be pulled from his bed at the crack of dawn and brought to my place. Also, the boys could sleep in. That evening Hazel, the kids and

I made pizzas from biscuit dough. When the kids were done eating I said they could watch a movie. I had checked out *Chitty Chitty Bang Bang* from the library, an old classic favorite of mine, and everyone was excited to see it. Hazel loves watching movies with the kids. The boys had decided they would camp out on the living room floor. We made a bed out of comforters and quilts on top of the hardwood and I put in the movie. I had just sat down for the first time that day when the phone rang. I thought about ignoring the call, but after five rings I picked it up.

"I would like to make a reservation for an entity," the lady on the other line said.

"A what?" I asked.

"An entity."

"I'm sorry you have the wrong number."

"Is this The Kitchen House, the haunted café in West Virginia?"

"Yes, it is."

"I thought you did teas and I was trying to make a reservation."

"Oh, we do have teas. I'm sorry I misunderstood you."

"Oh that's quite alright. I'm so excited. There will be six of us for an entity. You know, your transcendental tea party."

"My what?"

"Your Transcendental Tea Party. Oh the girls and I are so thrilled to have a high tea party in a haunted house. In fact, this whole vacation should be one awesome adventure after the next."

The woman was now talking a mile a minute and I was still trying to wrap my head around what she had said.

"This trip has been a year in the making. I can't believe it's almost here and now to add one more road stop along the way is super exciting. The girls and I are heading out on Friday morning and I figure we'll be in your vicinity around noon. Who would have thought I would be so happy to leave my husband and kids at home for a week and take off for some fun and sun without them. Does that make me sound like a bad person?"

"I don't think so."

"I don't think so either. However, my kids sorely disagree. They cannot understand why I would want to go to the beach without them. So I can actually enjoy it, I told them. Maybe I shouldn't have said that, but give me a break. My whole life revolves around them. I need some Tina time. I don't think that's too much to ask. Honestly, my girlfriends and I just want to get away from the daily grind of life for seven short days, then home again and back to work. It's just a little respite with best friends. We have rented a condo on Virginia Beach with a pool, wet bar and everything. Can you imagine a pool that looks out onto the ocean? Perfect, simply perfect. I honestly didn't think it could get any better. Then I read about your little place in the mountains. Mapping out the trip, I realized how close we will be, so of course, we must stop and do an entity. I mean really, where will we ever find another place to have a Transcendental Tea Party. It's the coolest thing I've ever heard of. Silly, but I think I'm more eager for the entity party than I am for the beach. We should be passing through Friday around noon, if we leave on time. We may be a little late. We do have to find the place winding through the mountains and all, so let's make the reservation for 1:00 pm. How does that sound?"

"You said you read about The Kitchen House?"

"Oh yes, on a blog, you know, Mystic Mayhem. You see I'm kind of a geek when it comes to the paranormal stuff, although I don't tell anybody. They might think I'm weird. But, I just love to read real live ghost stories. So in secret, I troll the computer in search of supernatural happenings and spiritual occurrences, like angels and stuff. I guess you could say the paranormal websites are my porn. My favorite blogger is Mystic Mayhem. He is so casual about the hauntings and such a descriptive writer. I just loved what he wrote about your haunted café in the mountains with pixies, purple houses, women in long satin black gloves and children running about. Honestly, it sounded like delightful chaos."

"Mystic Mayhem?" I questioned.

"Oh, you haven't read the articles yet. Girl, you must, you must. Wait a minute. Are you Sissy? Oh Sissy, I can't wait to meet you. You sound so very cool. Now you did jot me down for a Transcendental Tea party for six people at one o'clock on Friday? Oh, and make the reservation under the name Tina."

"Yes, I have it. We'll see you on Friday."

As soon as I hung up the phone with Talking Tina, I went to the computer and looked up the site, Mystic Mayhem. There loomed the face of Cole Spencer floating in the night sky. To me the website looked Sci-fi and fake, not at all like the divine encounters I've had from the other side. I read through his home page, which listed his experiences and credentials and I summed up that Cole Spencer is kind of full of himself. I went to his photo page and saw that the last pictures posted were of my place. He had several photos of my charming, purple house with an empty porch; which he must have taken on Sunday while Hazel, the kids and I were away. His camera had captured many orbs. Most of them just looked like water spots; which made me think that Cole Spencer had sprayed his lens. Then I noticed the outline of a figure looking out the upstairs window. The apparition did not remind me of a grown man or a young child. It looked like an adolescent. It was most likely the ghost of twelve-year-old, William Owen Kitchen. He was probably curious about Cole Spencer and quite possibly wanting to be photographed. After all, preadolescent boys like to be shocking. I clicked off the photograph and onto the blog of Cole Spencer. Cole did not just have one blog about his visit to my home. On the contrary, the guy had at least a full week of articles about his two day stay in Grace, West Virginia. There was a whole series of descriptive paragraphs about my home with catchy titles. As I quickly scanned through them, I eventually landed on the blog titled *Hosting an Enti-Tea (aka), A Transcendental Tea Party.*

In the blog Cole Spencer describes Destiny Marie's bridal shower with dramatic tone and highlighting, using play on words and metaphors. I could see why Talking Tina liked him. He called the bridal shower tea party an "Enti-Tea" and he described the young ladies in high fashion. Somehow, Cole Spencer had concluded that the Breakfast at Tiffany's themed tea party was actually an attempt to summon a dead aunt (I suppose one that went around looking like Audrey Hepburn). The article was pure fiction aside from the fact that all of it was true. The girls were having an afternoon garden tea party dressed like a dead woman, but none of it had to do with connecting to the deceased. The reality is that Destiny Marie, the bride, likes diamonds, classic movies and themed parties. I now understood how a reporter could take down all the facts to conclude something that didn't really happen. I found the article absurd and ridiculous, so before reading the rest of the blogs I called Pixie Moon-Dust.

"You wouldn't happen to be on the Mystic Mayhem site?" Pixie asked as she picked up the phone.

"I am. Can you come over and bring a bottle of your daddy's elderberry wine?"

"I'm on my way."

Pixie, Hazel and I sat up late into the night reading the blogs of Cole Spencer. Hazel and Pixie took the articles well and thought they were interesting. Personally, I was a bit offended by Cole Spencer and the influence of the elderberry wine helped loosen my tongue so I could speak my mind. Cole certainly has a way with words and his own confident perspective. In his first blog titled, *The Kitchen House*, he describes my pretty lavender farmhouse as an indigo Victorian where ghosts stare at you from the many gables.

"Indigo!" I said out loud. "My home is nowhere near that deep shade of purple. According to Charlie, and he would know because he painted it, the house is lilac trimmed in wisteria, not indigo."

"I don't know how important the color is?" Pixie quipped.

"Very important," I responded. "Its color is its charm."

"What I mean Sissy is that the story is about the ghosts in the gables and not the color of the house."

"And about that, he said that ghosts, meaning plural, stared out at you from the gables, trying to sound all scary. I saw the photo. It was just one ghost looking out the window. William, a twelve-year-old boy, doing what boys do, making people nervous."

I suppose I was irritated, because I didn't like the light that The Kitchen House was being painted in. I do not want The Kitchen House to be feared, when in fact, it is a sacred home. Words and descriptions such as indigo, gables and ghosts made it sound too haunted. Yes, my home is purple with gables and ghosts, but it's not scary. Why did he have to be so wrong in his rightness? If I was irritated when I read about the house, I was down right angry when I read about myself. Cole Spencer wrote a blog titled, *The Ladies of The Kitchen House*, in which he defined Hazel, Pixie and me. In the blog he describes my kids as blond little rug rats. He estimates my age at twenty-five and Roman's at ten, when in fact, I turned twenty-nine years old at the beginning of June and Roman will be nine in September.

"He's got me cranking out babies at the age of fifteen," I shouted.

"Oh, he just thinks you look young. Take it as a compliment," Hazel said.

"Well, how in the hell do I take this?" I said reading on. In the very next sentence Cole Spencer describes Sissy, the homeowner and barista as beautifully plain. "This makes no damn sense at all. You can't be beautifully plain. You're either beautiful or plain."

"Maybe he meant to write plainly beautiful."

"That's a nice thought Hazel, but I don't think so."

As we read on, I continued to grumble over each inadequacy in the Mystic Mayhem blog as Hazel and Pixie took it all in stride. Cole Spencer saw Hazel as a jolly grandmotherly type with enchanted recipes and a delightful laugh. Pixie was basically described through the eyes of an admirer. He mentioned her slight frame and tiny ballerina feet, the way her blue hair shimmered teal in the golden sun, her large mystifying gray eyes and the aura of the luminous shades that surrounded her. He referred to her as if she were a real pixie that had floated here on translucent wings.

"I think Cole Spencer is a fake," I proudly pronounced after reading his blogs.

"I don't think so," said Pixie. "He's just put you on the map. Think of how many people will read his blog and want to come visit the charmed, purple cafe in the mountains with fairy looking psychics, jolly grandmas and a plainly beautiful barista."

"Beautifully plain," I corrected.

But, regardless of how I felt about Cole Spencer's perspective of the place, he did in fact put Grace, West Virginia and me on the map, a place where we've been missing. Bringing business and attention to Grace will hurt none of us. Actually, this is huge for Pixie as well. Talking Tina and all her friends want a reading and there will be more Enti-Teas to come. It seems the two experiences go hand in hand, a transcendental tea party followed by a psychic reading. Funny, how things evolve. I had thought I would host a few birthday tea parties for young girls. I'm sure that's what Rayland and Cody envisioned when they pitched the idea. I plan on calling the men in the morning to see what they think. I'm a little worried about Rayland's thoughts, remembering the fit he threw over Lucinda's séance. Oh Lucinda, I just bet she'll come to my Enti-Teas. The thought made me smile.

"Maybe we should get to bed," Hazel proposed, looking over at my grinning face. "I think Sissy is a little tipsy."

It's true the blog reading and wine sipping had wiped me out. I'm sure it had wiped out Hazel and Pixie too, so I suggested that Pixie spend the night. When she didn't object, I knew she too was tired. Roman, Henry and Avery were lazily sprawled all over my living room so Pixie laid her blue head down on The Kitchen House couch. And she was peacefully sleeping before I made it up the stairs to my own bed.

Busy, Busy Summer

August 28, 2000 – Dear Diary, it seems so long ago since I last opened your pages to fill you with ink. It's hard to believe the kids head back to school next week. This summer has soared by in a mystical magical sort of way, like a brightly colored kite sailing on the wind of Gladden, here one minute and then gone the next.

It was really Cole Spencer's blog that caused this summer to be so bizarre. Well, the blog in accumulation with many other things. After all, before the blog there were the orb photos taken on Easter and posted to the Pixie Moon-Dust psychic readings web page that brought Cole Spencer to my door. Still, before the orb photos or psychic readings, there was the idea of hosting a high tea at The Kitchen House suggested by Rayland and Cody. However, before the consideration of afternoon tea was the vision of a café as foreseen and created by my daddy and brother. Yet, the idea only transpired, because my husband had left me. Fatefully, before my husband left me there was an old, empty, haunted clapboard house sitting in the center of my beautiful mountainous hometown. It is actually the collection of these specific events that has caused my summer to be so utterly strange and busy.

July and August have been filled with garden tea parties and hosting out of towners. It's been a little over a month since this tea sensation started, but it feels like it's been going on the whole summer. Hazel and I have embraced the titles *Enti-Tea* and *Transcendental Tea Party* and even had Pixie add it to the website. In July we began making reservations for Enti-Teas almost daily. Before we knew it, we were scheduling three or four tea parties a day. As the summer went on, the reservations continued to increase. People came from all over to drink tea with ghosts. Much like Talking Tina and her group of friends, they would be passing through on their way to a vacation destination and make a detour to check out The Kitchen House. My home has become a pit stop. Hazel bought a guest book that sits on the coffee bar and we encourage our out of town patrons to write down their name and state. Some even write down how they heard about The Kitchen House and what brought them here. Their reasons usually include that they like the idea of sipping tea with their dead grandmother or visiting a haunted café.

While talking to our customers, I discovered that for the first few weeks it was Cole Spencer's blog that brought the attention to The Kitchen House. It has grown and expanded from there. Usually, someone reads the blog, gets all excited, and gathers a bunch of friends who are open to the idea of a transcendental tea party. The group makes a reservation for an Enti-Tea and then calls Pixie Moon-Dust to schedule a psychic reading. After the mystical experience, each individual tells their friends and family about their divine tea party and more reservations are made. Some of the visitors go online and leave comments on Cole Spencer's blog. There are actual long conversations about my house on that website. Both Hazel and I enjoy going online and reading about the tea parties. It has become our favorite pastime and it is much more entertaining than television. I'm not sure how many of the stories are factual and how many are conjured up by the imagination of the tea sipper. However, I believe that all of them hold some bit of truth and sacredness and that my house is holy.

Most people write that they can smell the scent of their deceased loved one or feel their presence next to them while in my home. Others write that they felt someone touch their hand or shoulder while sipping tea in my garden. One woman stated that she felt someone playing with her hair and she instantly knew her mother was behind her braiding it. Another commented on the taste of lemons. She wrote that she put the sour citrus piece of fruit in her mouth and it tasted exactly like her grandmother's apple pie, and not like a lemon at all, it even felt warm. Someone else claimed that they felt a cat jump into their lap, curl up and sit down. Another felt the wet nose of his beloved dog. These words and stories have floated out into the universe from cyberspace and have reached other people who desire a supernatural tea party. I find it fascinating how news can spread so quickly and it's amazing how many people want to drink tea with the dead.

Hazel and I have taken numerous calls for reservations and we have heard all types of requests.

"Can the house be completely dark and quiet for the tea party?"

"No."

"Do you make extra sandwiches for the spirits at no cost?"

"No."

"Can we bring our Ouija Board?"

"No!"

Hazel had one strange caller who asked if we would be having a Dumb Supper on Samhain.

"A what on what? Hazel asked the man.

"You do know what a Dumb Supper is?" he questioned in which Hazel responded magnificently.

"I know my suppers aren't dumb."

The man just laughed and explained to Hazel that a Dumb Supper is a feast for the dead eaten in complete silence on Halloween night, also known as Samhain.

"Hell no, we won't be doing that!" Hazel told him.

The Enti-Teas are certainly diverse and bring in a very motley crowd. For the most part I can tell a blog reader when I see one. They're all a bit weird; sort of a ghost hunting geek, with the exception of Talking Tina, she was actually very pretty and nice. The blog readers are usually a bit like Cole Spencer, a little socially backwards who would much rather speak to the dead than the living. Then there are the people of normalcy that think having an Enti-Tea would be fun. These people are lighthearted and adventurous. The kind of person that will drive fifteen miles off course in order to look at the biggest ball of yarn. I like these reservations the best. There are also the ones that dress up for the tea party, women who show up in big floppy hats and white gloves. I believe this to be an inspiration from the blog about Destiny Marie's bridal shower. All of my neighbors get a kick out of these ladies and they come over just to watch them. Honestly, it's so cute that Hazel and I decided to have hats and fur stoles available for anyone who wants to add dress up to their tea party. We hung the hats and stoles from the coat tree and they're a big hit.

Usually any lady that comes not dressed up for tea joyfully puts on a hat and wraps a fur around her neck. However, rumor has it that the hats and stoles belonged to women that are now dead. I suppose that could be true since I bought them from a vintage site on E-Bay. I also bought a shit-ton more of flowered teapots, cups and saucers. I now have quite the collection. The Kitchen House has also hosted three separate tea parties this month in which the dress up was not acceptable by my neighbors or anyone else in Grace, West Virginia for that matter. It even led to a town meeting.

The first faction wouldn't have caused such a ruckus if two equally weird and perverse parties didn't so closely follow. Our first eccentric Enti-Tea was a party of transvestites, three lovely men dressed in drag and eating dainty little sandwiches. Truly it was a riot and I immediately called Rayland and asked him to come over. Rayland made it to The Kitchen House before the transvestites had finished their lemon sponge cake. He said that he flew through the mountains at the chance to see queens in Grace and I think it did him some good. Rayland feels like an outsider in his hometown. The queens made him look almost normal. The transvestites were actually very nice. Rayland and I talked to them for a full hour after their tea party. As it turned out, the queens were friends of Talking Tina, or rather acquaintances. They said that Tina and her girlfriends attended a drag queen show in Virginia. Afterwards they all hung out together drinking. Tina told the queens all about the transcendental tea party and convinced them that they too needed to have such an experience. I'm glad they did.

The second odd tea party we hosted was even stranger than the first. It was a tea for four people, which consisted of two unconventional couples on a double date. They were dressed in costumes, similar to hats and gloves, but really so much more than that. The men wore full handsome suits with jackets and vests. Hanging gold watches dangled from their breast pockets and top hats sat on their heads with goggles fastened around the brim. The women were both dressed in corsets, their boobs spilling out the top in Victorian style cleavage. One woman had on what I can only describe as a petticoat and the other had large feathers in her hair. The ladies also wore dangling gold pocket watches and chunky gold jewelry. It looked like something from out of a movie, and when they left I discovered it was. I looked up the words goggles, pocket watches, corsets and top hats on the computer by just doing random searches and I soon discovered that there is a fashion or rather a cultural sub-genre known as Steampunk. The style is certainly Victorian, but the trend is science fiction or science fantasy. The people who dress in these costumes are smart people, perhaps brilliant, inspired by the works of H.G. Wells and Jules Verne. I'm sure on most days they wear t-shirts and jeans and may go around with their head in a book. But, for certain occasions they put on corsets, long skirts, watches and hats and walk around looking like sexy, Victorian, fashion models.

"Oh my God," I told Hazel. "The Kitchen House has made pop culture."

I had never seen anything like it before. The style was fascinating, intriguing and titillating. If I were not a mountain girl, tied down with three kids and a coffee house, I would run off to New York or L.A. and join this cyberpunk sub culture.

A few weeks later, when I thought I had seen it all, I spoke on the phone to a polite voice that made an Enti-Tea reservation for six. What arrived were four grown men and two adult women dressed like Marvel superheroes. They explained to me that they were comic book fans and had traveled to The Kitchen House on their way home from a Comic Con festival. The sight of the party was bizarre and it rattled my neighbor, Mr. Baxter, who wouldn't leave his porch. The group seemed nice but weird. They asked me to put their loose-leaf tea on ice, which made sense considering that the day was ninety degrees and they were wearing leotards, tights and capes. It was truly surreal to look out in my garden and see a sexy Wonder Woman and an even sexier Supergirl drinking tea and laughing with Superman, Spiderman, The Flash and some character from *Star Wars.* I believe this unusual group of characters would have been seen as harmless if they had not played on the playground after their tea. They chased the kids up and down the ramps in a game of tag that thrilled the children and flipped out the parents. I knew the superheroes were safe adults just having fun and the kids loved it. I kind of enjoyed watching all the excitement and hearing the laughter. Mr. Baxter did not and he about had a coronary at the sight. After a bunch of concerned phone calls, Mr. Baxter managed to secure a town meeting at the Spring County Mayor's Court. There, he proceeded to tell the people that The Kitchen House was holding tea parties for perverts and worse. Mr. Baxter talked terrible about the drag queens. As if men can't wear dresses if they want to, I mean really, what the hell business is it of his? He spoke of the corsets worn by the Victorian ladies and since he doesn't know the fashion, Steampunk, he called them women of the night. He further stated that pedophiles, referring to the superheroes, ran around on my jungle gym chasing little kids. Of course, Hazel and I showed up at the town meeting to defend our business and our morals. Daddy came too and he turned out to be the problem solver and voice of reason, which pleased the mayor and relieved him of any responsibility. Mr. Baxter dramatically stated that he did not want The Kitchen House to shut down. That was not his intention. He only wants its patrons screened more closely.

"After all," he said, "we live in the town of Grace."

Naturally, I responded defensively to Mr. Baxter's allegations.

"How in the hell am I supposed to screen the customers?" I asked. "It's not like I want a house of weirdos. They just sometimes show up. And just because they're weird doesn't mean they're pedophiles. Honestly, Mr. Baxter! Do you really think I'm going to let a bunch of perverts chase my kids?"

After a much heated argument by Mr. Baxter and additional comments by other ignorant neighbors, my dad suggested that Mr. Baxter start up a block watch for our town. He encouraged him to talk to neighbors for interest and make a phone tree list that can be passed through the community. He suggested that volunteers constantly survey the playground and that the neighboring homes be watched as well. My dad clinched his speech by saying the safety of the children living in Grace is the responsibility of the whole town. Mr. Baxter took my dad's words to heart and he now has a new project, and even better, a mission. Hazel has been thinking of sewing Mr. Baxter a cape.

To add to our busy, crazy summer, with each and every tea party reservation there is a psychic reading scheduled. The readings are actually more time consuming than an Enti-Tea. While Hazel and I will have only one tea party for a reservation of six, Pixie will have six individual readings. There are not enough hours in the day and since Pixie was doing the readings after closing, we found there are also not enough hours in the night. Pixie did some creative marketing and pricing modifications and it helped some. Group psychic readings are thirty minutes long and not a full hour. Even that kept her at my house long past midnight and it put travelers back on the mountainous roads in the middle of the night. This is not very responsible on our part and made us all a nervous wreck. Hazel and I began to let Pixie do the readings in the living room, but that was not the best solution. Actually, it was full of many issues. For starters, it just seems so more invasive. We now had strangers all over our house and not just confined to our kitchen and back yard. Second, this is also my children's home. We had stolen the place where they went to get away. Daddy didn't like having people in the house either. As far as he is concerned, at The Kitchen House all are welcome, but our private living space is off limits. Even though he played it cool at the town meeting in defending our patrons, he still doesn't want a group of superheroes hanging out in my living room.

My dad decided the best solution was to build Pixie her own little house in my back yard. He said it would take him a week, so we should try to schedule our tea parties seven days out. However, it only took him a weekend. That's when I knew it was going to be amazing. When Daddy is passionate about a project he flies through it at a much greater speed. It's as if the project itself gives him energy and he does not stop. He chose the garden side of my yard for The Pixie House, which makes sense. It's where we set up the garden tea parties, it's away from the playground and it's the prettiest part of my yard. The Pixie House sits just beyond the large flower garden that Lenore and Hazel frequently tend. It's a tiny house about the size of a shed or a playhouse for a very large child. Really, that's what people think it is, a large playhouse, when actually; it's a pixie house for a real pixie. In reality, it's not a house at all and more like an office space or rather a room. The Pixie House has no running water or bathroom, for that Pixie has a key to my back door. However, it does have electricity and an outlet for a radio or space heater and from the ceiling hangs a large ball light with white ceiling fan. The Pixie House is just one square room furnished with a small round wooden table and four chairs. My dad covered its floor with thick green carpet and he papered the interior walls with pink rose buds. In the far back corner of the room is a ladder that leads up to a narrow loft bed made with a thin camping mattress, pillows and a quilt. This way Pixie can sleep in her office if she's too tired to drive to her real house. The inside of The Pixie House resembles a dollhouse and quite frankly so does the outside. The little house has a high peaked roof with light gray shingles. It has two front windows with attached white flower boxes and a window on each side.

The windows have screens so they can be opened without letting the mosquitoes in. There is a nice cross breeze that flows through the small space. Hazel sewed four sets of lace curtains for The Pixie House and Lenore filled the window boxes with purple petunias. The exterior of the little house is painted wisteria, the same color as The Kitchen House's trim and shutters. The Pixie House has white trim and a bright white door with a brass knocker. Around the base of the house my dad positioned a little white picket fence. The fence is close to the house and does not create a yard, just the illusion of a yard. From the fence Pixie hung a cute little sign bordered in painted flowers and scripted with the words *The Pixie House – Psychic Readings Done Here.*

I love The Pixie House and so do Hazel and the children. The kids want to play in it, but we insist they stay out.

"Let them in once and it will never be the same," I told Pixie. "It's best if it's off limits to children. Besides, they have the playground." I think Pixie was relieved that I shared this view and now she could openly keep the kids away.

At the end of the construction, after the house was painted, the curtains were hung and the flowers were planted, Pixie decided we should bless the house with a sanctifying party. My dad opted out of attending, although he was invited. When Pixie asked my daddy to come to her sanctifying he just laughed.

"I built it kid. I'll leave the blessings up to you."

That Sunday night, The Pixie House sanctifying party was held under a full moon and attended by me, Pixie, Hazel and Lenore. Christy Banks took my kids for the evening, including Sabrina and she was happy to do so. She said she was looking forward to an evening spent playing with a baby. That night, Hazel, Lenore and I met in front of the little house. At 8:00pm, just as instructed, we rapped on the door using the brass knocker. Pixie opened the door in dramatic fashion. She was wearing a flowery, silk robe over top of her skimpy t-shirt and long skirt. Her face was aglow. Pixie had powdered her cheeks with silver glitter. Her blue hair was teased out and wild. She stood in the doorway solemnly holding a ceramic bowl of oil with both hands. Suddenly, she began to pray while the three of us stood before her with big eyes and closed mouths. In a reverent voice, Pixie asked God to bless the little house with light, kindness, love, and protection. She then dipped two fingers into the oil and made a cross on the door. Stepping outside the doorway, she began walking around the house and we followed. She stopped at each window, dipped two fingers into the oil, and then rubbed them around the wooden pane, while speaking a blessing. After she had anointed the windows and door she invited us to come inside. In the house, Pixie lit a pink candle. She told us that pink symbolized love and kindness and that was the only energy invited into the home. Pixie placed the candle in a bowl of water that sat on the table. She explained that Buddhist monks believe that as candle wax melts and drops into water, it washes away evil and sorrow. Pixie had already set the table with plates and food. A large baked loaf of bread sat on a cutting board next to a bottle of olive oil and a jar of salt. Pixie informed us that bread and salt should be the first items to enter a home and that you should never run out, bad news for me because we always run out of bread. Sitting beside the bread, was a large bowl of fruit. Pixie told us that the initial meal in a new house should always include the first fruits of the season. It was tight in the little house with not much moving room, so, we four sat at the table and dined on bread, oil and an assortment of berries. After our meal, Pixie picked up the pink candle and raised it up to her forehead.

"God bless this house. Fill it with the presence of peace. Allow harmony and love to abide here and spirits to feel welcome." Next, she handed the candle to me.

"Your turn," she said.

I was not sure of what to say and I felt a little on the spot, but I raised the candle in the air and spoke.

"Dear God, bless this little house with love, good health, prosperity and kindness."

"Good Job!" Pixie encouraged. "Now pass it to Lenore."

If I felt uncomfortable, I knew Lenore felt twice as uneasy. But then she reminded me with her words and actions that she was a team player and she was brilliant. Lenore held the candle high above her head as if it were an offering. She spoke in hushed tones, but did not lack confidence.

"God, let all who come here receive what they need. Let the answers serve as comfort. We ask that you bless this house with harmony and hope."

Lenore then passed the pink candle to Hazel who finished off the blessing.

"Dear God, open this house to people and spirits who are kindhearted with good intentions. Fill its space with positive energy and shine down your beautiful divine light." Hazel handed the candle back to Pixie.

"Amen," said Pixie before blowing out its light.

"Amen," we three repeated.

After the blessing we went outside. Pixie had a bucket of her daddy's elderberry wine on ice and paper cups, so I lit up a bonfire. The moon above the mountains was full and the wind, Gladden, was behaving as a soft summer breeze. The four of us sat in chairs around the fire laughing and talking. As the deep fruity wine started to loosen my thoughts, I focused on the distinct characteristics of us four women. My brain was taking an inventory and I was making a mental list of our distinctions. We were truly different from each other in every way.

Hazel, the nurturer, will soon be seventy-one years old, although her boundless energy and spunk matches a woman of twenty-five. Hazel is the definition of jolly. She radiates happiness and shines with creativity in the brightly colored muumuus she sews for herself. Hazel is optimistic at every turn; yet, she is practical, stable and loyal.

Lenore is far from jolly. She is serious with a classic look and an uneasy smile. Her beauty is delicate, her mind intelligent. She enjoys sharing her wisdom, but not in a superior way. Lenore is humble and kind. She lives life as a teacher and cannot help but impart knowledge on others. This is her gift.

Pixie cannot easily be explained. She is an enigma, a walking contradiction, completely sane in her craziness. She is a free spirit that is balanced and grounded. She is eccentric and nonconforming with blue hair and a full back tattoo. Yet, she is mild mannered and quite refined. Pixie is perceptive, intuitive, calm, but alarming. She talks to the dead and hangs out with the elderly. She is aesthetically drawn to the beauty and nature of the physical world and the nonphysical. She reads the Bible nightly and always includes God in her pagan rituals. She can be slightly scary and intimidating with her benevolent personality. She truly makes no sense and yet she makes complete sense.

Then there is me. According to Cole Spencer I am the paradox, beautifully plain. I am a single mom trying to raise three kids on a dream. Yet the vision is not even my own, but rather the inspiration and creation of my daddy. I am traveling a course that someone else has mapped for me. I am a passenger on my own journey. I suppose that's the way my life has always been. To be honest, I believe that's the life of everybody. I just happen to realize we're not in the driver's seat on the road through life and this makes me the blessed one. I've learned that once you recognize you're free from the wheel and allow the universe to transport you, life becomes easier. Being a passenger, I don't worry about the drive and can focus on all the beauty I'm passing through on life's journey. Quite frankly, I wouldn't want to miss that.

Oh Henry

September 7, 2000 – Dear Diary, I have been through the death of a parent and growing up poor. I managed teen pregnancy and a move away from home before I was ready. I have lived with a cheating husband who deserted me with three kids in a campground. I've worked hard, long hours and made no money. I have cried, lost, fought, grieved and struggled and none of it prepared me for the last two days.

School had been in session for two days when Henry told me he had a stomachache. I know his second grade teacher, Mrs. Lynch, is a bit intimidating and his class size is large. Spring County has more seven year olds than anything else, so I thought Henry was just having anxiety. Besides, he didn't complain much and still wanted to be outside on the playground. That evening he had diarrhea and I thought it was either nerves or the flu. I put everyone to bed early that night. Henry didn't feel well and the rest of us were tired and worn out from the start of school and change in routine.

It was around eleven o'clock when I woke from a dead sleep. It felt as if I had been shaken awake. I remember jolting up first and then hearing Roman.

"Mommy!" he shouted. I quickly threw off the sheet, flung my legs over the side of the bed. There in front of me stood the ghost of Owen Kitchen, a full apparition blocking my way. He was dressed in dark green, overall fishing waders and a white shirt. He looked as if he had just come from fly-fishing in a mountain stream. I locked eyes with the shadowy figure until I was then pulled from my trance when I heard Roman's anguished shout for the second time.

"Mommy!" I jumped from my bed pushing past the spectral being and ran down the hall and into the boys' room. I stopped dead in the doorway as I took in the sight. For mere seconds I felt frozen with fear, shocked and paralyzed. I had never been so scared in all my life. I could feel the presence of Owen behind me and I saw Emma Kitchen before me. Roman sat straight up on his bed crying and visibly frightened. Henry lay in a comatose sleep, unaware that the ghost of Emma Kitchen was sitting on the floor beside his bed leaning into his tiny body and pressing both of her dim gray hands onto his forehead.

"Get off him!" I screamed at the ghost mother as I ran and scooped my child's weak body out of bed and away from her phantom touch. Henry woke up to the sudden movement and jostling that I had caused. He whimpered in pain, his little hands grasping at his belly. I hugged him close to me, whispering soft hushes into his ear. His cool forehead was pressed up against my cheek and the sensation of its touch caused me to realize that Emma Kitchen had been keeping his fever down. In that moment I fully understood that the ghost of Owen Kitchen had woken me up to check on my kids and that the ghost of Emma Kitchen had been mothering my sick little boy. I looked down to where Emma had just been sitting, but the apparition was no longer there and Owen was no longer in the doorway. The two ghosts had done their job. I was awake, alert, knew Henry was sick and I could take it from here. Sabrina was now crying in her bed and Hazel was at bottom of the stairs frantic and confused.

"Sissy what's wrong?" I heard Hazel's scared voice shouting.

"Roman get your sister," I said, but Roman didn't move. He had seen the ghosts too and was still frightened.

"It's okay Roman," I said. "They were just trying to help us. They woke us up. I think they may have even saved him."

Henry wiggled and cried out in my arms. Holding his stomach he moaned the word Mommy right before he threw up.

"Oh Baby," I said. I laid Henry back down and peeled off his shirt that was covered in vomit. Roman leaped off the bed and ran to his baby sister. I picked Henry back up. I could feel the warmth of his body on his bare back. His fever was starting to rise now that Emma's hands were gone from his forehead.

"I have to get him to the hospital," I said to Hazel as I was coming down the steps. I crossed through the living room carrying my feverish son and into The Kitchen House to head out the back door, the closest route to my car. To my surprise, as I entered the café there stood Pixie Moon- Dust. She had been sleeping in The Pixie House due to a late night appointment and must of woke with psychic intuition. Either that or a ghost got her up too. The cordless phone was already in her hand as if she was anticipating my arrival. As soon the door cracked she dialed 911.

"It will be quicker and safer if he goes by ambulance," she said. Pixie was right, however, waiting for the squad nearly killed me. I simply wanted to put my child in my car and race through the mountains. Instead, I sat down on the couch with my sick little boy in my lap and waited for the sound of sirens. Hazel ran and got Henry a new shirt and one for me as well, since mine was also covered in vomit. I pulled my dirty shirt over my head, while Henry lay across my lap and put on the clean one. Then I dressed Henry as he groaned. Roman appeared in The Kitchen House doorway with Sabrina in his arms and tears on his face.

"Roman," I said. "I am so proud of you. Thank you for waking me. Henry is going to be fine, we just need to get him to the hospital."

Roman didn't really respond, still stunned from it all. He just held his sister on his hip as she dangled down half of his body. He looked like such a strong little man at that moment. Soon the sirens were upon my house and Henry was placed on a gurney. They were taking him to CAMC Women's and Children's Hospital in Charleston. Both Hazel and I went in the ambulance with Henry. Pixie stayed with Roman and Sabrina. I tried to focus only on my child and pray intensely, but I couldn't help thinking about the ghosts. My mind shifted from Henry to Roman. It must have been terrifying for Roman to see the ghost of Emma Kitchen. The way she leaned in and over Henry grasping his small head in her hands was frightening. I don't know how Roman comprehended the chilling site and there had been no time to comfort him. A mother gravitates to the child that needs her most. Roman will be fine once the shock wears off and hopefully Pixie will give him a hug.

As Henry was lifted from the back of the ambulance he cried out my name softly, in tender whimpers, like a scared puppy and I could do nothing. As I followed the gurney in through the hospital lobby, an overwhelming feeling of helplessness flooded my body. Each step felt like a walk through rushing waters. I weakly waded through a river of vulnerability, scared shitless. There in the hospital lobby were Rayland and Cody. It turns out, Pixie had called Rayland after the ambulance left my house and since he lives close to the hospital, he and Cody beat the ambulance there. They were waiting in the emergency room as Hazel and I came through. What a relief it was for Hazel and I to see those two loving men.

"Oh Rayland," I cried falling into his arms.

"He's going to be fine Sissy, just fine."

He comforted me as my little boy was zipped past and through the double doors, where I could not go. Cody took Hazel's hand and led her to the couch. Hazel was as white as a sheet and I could tell this whole ordeal was taking a toll on her. We had not been comforting each other. In fact, the both of us had drawn inward. Cody brought Hazel a cup of coffee, but it tasted like tar and not her house blend, so she couldn't drink it. Instead, she just sat, blankly staring, wringing her hands. Cody sat beside her rubbing her back. Henry was in the back with doctors and we were up front being asked questions about health coverage and finances.

"Yes, I'm the person responsible for the bill. Now what the hell is happening?"

It was the most powerless position I've ever been put in. I wanted to break through the double doors, see my baby boy, and find out what was going on. I answered the questions about insurance and money and soon they figured out I had neither. Just when I thought I couldn't take it any more a doctor in green scrubs approached. He introduced himself as Dr. Schmidt. He told me that Henry had suffered a ruptured appendix and needed emergency surgery. It felt surreal as I listened to the words spoken by Dr. Schmidt - appendectomy, infection, critical, surgery. Rayland stood behind me grasping my shoulders. He was either holding me up or keeping himself from falling. Hazel and Cody leaned into one another with the same intent of holding each other up. We all listened to the doctor's words with a tolerated resilience. However, none of us felt strong. As Henry lay in surgery, there was nothing to do but wait. I called Pixie, to check on the kids. She assured me that Roman and Sabrina were fine. She told me that she was staying with them through the night, but she had arranged for Pops and Ma Jaspers to come in the morning. She then told me to call the Jaspers because they were beyond worried. She had also informed my daddy and I should expect his arrival at any time.

"How's Roman?" I asked.

"He'll be fine," was all she said. Not much comfort for a worried mother. I paced the floors of the hospital lobby. I couldn't sit down although Rayland wanted me to.

"Come sit," he would say patting the seat next to him. I would raise my hand and brush his words out of the air like they were pesky gnats flying around my head. I could not settle my body and I could not settle my mind. I had a deep relentless worry that something was terribly wrong. Pacing helped. It aided my body to move past the screams and shouts that were anxious to come out. It relieved my mind of twisting and turning and kept it focused on an even, fast track of thought. My thoughts were a conversation of persuasion. It was me trying to convince myself that everything was okay, that Henry was in good hands, and that he was receiving the care he needed and appendixes are removed every day. It's basically routine surgery and no big deal. My daddy showed up nearly two hours after surgery had begun and still we had no news. As the time moved on and we were left unaware, everyone's worry took deep root. However, we said nothing.

In a small town, news travels fast. Mr. Baxter, the president of Grace's block watch and my neighbor, heard the sirens as the ambulance pulled up to my house. He witnessed my baby boy come out the back door on a stretcher and be placed into the emergency vehicle. He saw Hazel and I huddled together as we walked down the sidewalk and got into the ambulance. He saw the blue-haired Pixie come out onto the porch with the other two children and remain outside with them until late into the night. He watched Pixie rock the baby in the white rocker that sits on the porch. He saw Roman climb up into the porch swing, lay himself down and let it sway him to sleep. He wanted to go over and talk to Pixie, ask her questions, find out what was going on, but he didn't want to disturb the tired children. Instead, he called the rectory and woke up the priest. He told Father McIntire all that he had witnessed. He knew this man of the cloth that hung out at the café, would run to comfort and pray with us. He would get all the details. Mr. Baxter would later call the priest and find out everything. After waking the priest, Mr. Baxter began calling the rest of the neighbors and told them what he saw. My meddlesome neighbor spent the wee hours of the night waking up our small town. I cannot be upset with Mr. Baxter for spreading the news so quickly, without any concrete information, because I know with each house that he woke up that night, they began to pray for Henry. Prayers for my child flew from the windows in every household in Grace and filled the night sky above where my child lay. It is a thought that comforts me and fills me with faith. I wholeheartedly believe in the power of prayers and I have no doubt that as my child lay in surgery the entire town of Grace prayed.

Six hours after surgery began, Dr. Schmidt entered the hospital lobby with his face drawn and beads of sweat across his forehead. I knew then that my unrelenting worry was justified. He told us that Henry was out of surgery, but instead of sounding reassuring he began to emphasize the severity of Henry's condition. Along with the ruptured appendix Henry had Peritonitis. He explained this as an abscess filled with pus. They had removed the appendix and as much of the poison as they could, but the infection had gone into the bloodstream. Bottom line, Henry was septic. Bacteria was flowing with his blood, circulating throughout his little body. Worry was far from over. The consequences of Septicemia are organ failure leading to death. My child was not in recovery. He was in ICU. Henry had begun a course of IV antibiotics that would hopefully kill the bacteria before he went into full-blown septic shock. I was the only one permitted back into the Pediatrics Intensive Care Unit to check on Henry. The others stayed in the waiting room, huddled together for solace and strength.

I walked alone back to the PICU. It was a walk of anxiety, each step full of fret. I wondered how many other parents had taken this walk back to their child. Hundreds of thousands, possibly a million parents, dropping their prayers as they went, their fallen imprints creating a path of unease. It was a walk on white ceramic tiles bursting with burdens and I stepped lightly. Henry was sleeping in a high bed in an alcove room all by himself. He looked so small and unaware. He was as pale as the white blanket that was pulled up to his small chest. IV bags and wires hung all about the sides of the bed and into my child's bruised arms. There was one hard plastic chair beside Henry's bed, which was good, because my legs had given out. I was immobilized at the sight of Henry. I felt weak, desolate, helpless, powerless and alone. I sat in the chair next to my sick boy and studied his baby face, his small nose with a smattering of freckles, his long blond eyelashes and fluttering lids. I could tell he was dreaming. His new school haircut fanned out across the pillow in strawberry blond wisps. He was adorable and he was pathetic. Staring at him had caused my tears to flow in abundance. I began to shake with gasps of air like a hysterical child. Salty water and snot sat on my lip like a pool and there were not enough tissues. I needed to settle my sobs and be a strong mother, but the crying was uncontainable and overpowering. I rested my head on Henry's bed and began a conversation with God. I would not call it praying; but rather pleading, begging, negotiating. It was as if God was the attacker and Henry and I were his victims. I must have worn myself out. At some time I stopped my weeping and maybe even fell asleep with my head upon Henry's bed. I know this, because I remember waking. I remember opening my eyes and seeing a large orb that hung in the air above Henry's bed. It was similar to an orb in a photograph only much more wondrous, extraordinary, and real. It looked as if someone had blown a huge magical bubble that was floating in the air. The orb resembled a ball of white light, but paler with a transparency and a vague luster of color. Its splash of color reminded me of an oil spill. It was the same purple, pink swirl that swims in the small puddle on the driveway. The orb did not pop or vanish as I continued to look at it, but rather hung over my child like a tiny planet of hope and light. I honestly believe that I was seeing an angel and I suddenly felt the need to seriously pray. I slipped my hand out of Henry's and tiptoed away from my sleeping son. I snuck through the waiting area, unseen by my family. I was not able to speak to others and I needed time to build strength. I went searching for the hospital chapel. Turned out it was not that difficult to find. It's not far from the critical care unit.

Once inside the chapel, I fell on bended knees. Completely humbled I began to pray like I have never prayed before. I spoke softly and the words flowed easy from my lips. Everything I had to say was right there at the tip of my tongue. I did not stumble across thoughts, but rather simply conversed. I was well into prayer when I felt someone beside me, but in my meditative trance, I did not open my eyes. Soon my words were being echoed. A quiet tenor singing my words after they left my mouth. By his voice, I knew that it was Father McIntire kneeling beside me. His soft sound resonated my feelings and faith. His smooth echo sent my prayers through the chapel filling its every space. He laid his hand upon mine and we continued to pray, me in the lead and him following closely behind. Although we spoke in utterances that flowed one after the other, it sounded as if we were talking together, our overlapped sentences blended, merged and mixed. There was something holy about the intermingling of our words. The repetition felt sacred and reverent. Soon I felt a rush of comfort flow through me, a thin stream of contentment that ran down my inner core and I trusted it to be the feeling of answered prayers. This surge of emotion caused me to open my eyes, turn my head, cup the face of Father Timothy McIntire and kiss him fully on the mouth. He must have felt this same surge, because he kissed back. It was a fervent kiss filled with passion and emotion. This fat kiss carried more in it than lust. It was a reaction to sorrow, the release of heartache, the embrace of faith and the feeling of disparity and anguish overcome by a sensation of bliss and hope. It was a kiss of compassion, comfort, torment, agony, desire and love.

Just as Strong as I can be

September 15, 2000 - Dear Diary, we walk through things we could not fathom, conjure up strength from thin air and trek through the impossible. Somehow we are our strongest when we are at our weakest. There is a level of trouble where you have no control. Life forces you to submit to woe. You must surrender any power you think you have to the universe and live on faith. When life breaks you and sends you down on bended knees, you realize your strength. Surprisingly, it is in our loss of power where resilience lives. We are tough when we realize we are fragile.

Henry's hospital stay has been ten days of pure hell and we have successfully lived through its fiery embrace. Henry will be released from the hospital tomorrow morning and I can take my child home and slowly try to get back to some normalcy. That is if things will ever be normal again. The last ten days have been a series of events as I watched my child recover from near death. Ten days does not sound like a significant chunk of time when you think about life's experiences. Nevertheless, these last ten days have felt like an eternity. I have not left the hospital since arriving with Henry. In the beginning I could not bring myself to leave the premises. Henry was so sick. What if something were to happen while I stepped away? In the last few days, when I knew he was better, I figured what's the point. I've been here this long. I can just wait it out beside my boy. So, I've been sitting; sitting on the dock of a sickbay, eyes cast onto a white wall horizon, feet floating on sterile tile, watching time roll in and out like waves. The clock on the wall has a second hand that moves. Minutes turn into hours, mornings turn into afternoons and days turn into nights. Inside these walls, time had ceased. Beyond these walls, I have two other children that need mothering, a business with scheduled tea parties, customers to serve and a Homework Help Center that has just begun. My life is a pulse. It moves at a rhythmic speed, to a beat of its own. Thankfully, in my absence, my loved ones willingly picked up the baton and conducted my life's song.

Roman and Sabrina have been staying with Pops and Mama Jaspers this whole time and Beau is back. He came when he heard Henry was sick. Of course his parents called him, because I did not. He comes up to the hospital daily for a couple of uncomfortable hours and then heads back to his parents. Judy is not with him. It seems they have split. Beau told me that they had been living back in Florida where he had a job as an airboat driver, taxiing tourists through an alligator filled river on a flat bottom jon boat that is propelled forward by an automotive engine. I'm sure it was a job he loved. While Beau spent his days in an alligator swamp, Judy worked as a receptionist for a plastic surgeon. It didn't take long for the newly divorced plastic surgeon and Judy to start up a fling, leaving Beau out cold in his wetland. Beau was sleeping alone in the recreational vehicle and Judy was at the doctor's mansion when his parents called him about Henry. Two days later Beau collected his last paycheck from Ron's Airboat Rides, bought a used motorcycle and headed back home to West Virginia to check on his child. Henry had been in the hospital for five full days before Beau's arrival.

Hazel has been coming back and forth to the hospital every day. In addition to visiting, she brings me a change of clothes. In the morning, she starts the coffee at The Kitchen House and waits for Lenore and Charlie to show up around 9:00 or 10:00. Then she hands over the day's work and responsibilities to them and rides into Charleston with Ezra Landis as her chauffeur. They hang at the hospital for a few hours, and then head off to Pops and Mama Jaspers to check on Roman and Sabrina and then back to The Kitchen House to relieve Lenore and Charlie. Lenore has taken some time off from Bloomers Nursery to help with The Kitchen House and her boss Randy has been very reasonable. He even sent over a basket of flowers. I truly thank God every day for Lenore. She has continued on with the few Enti-teas we had scheduled this week and has been tutoring kids at The Homework Help Center, which is back up and running. She kept our Friday night folk singer booked and Rayland and Cody danced with their cloggers at The Kitchen House on Saturday, despite my absence. I've heard that business has actually been good over the last two weeks. Lenore and Charlie have everything under control and the folks continue to come to The Kitchen House to hear about Henry and offer their prayers and support.

Christy Banks stops by Henry's room during her lunch hour. She has been a valuable advocate and friend to have during this time of need. Not only does she work at the hospital and know the doctors well, she has also experienced sitting in this hospital as a mother, worried about her sickly little boy. Christy is at ease in the hospital setting, when almost everybody else is not. She has brought Henry coloring books, crayons, comic books, soldier men and two hand held video games. She has brought me coffee, soda, chewing gum, mints and granola bars. Like Lenore, she has proven to be a best friend. Christy told me that Avery has been staying with his Grandma Sue, Billy Dean's mama, while she's been working. She said it's actually been good and admitted that she thinks it's finally okay for Avery to have some time with his daddy's family. For so long, she did not trust leaving Avery in the holler without her. The Deans are a crazy bunch. But they are also loving and Avery's family. Christy said Avery is older now, verbal, independent and so self-sufficient she no longer worries about leaving him with this family that puts the fun in dysfunction. She did say Henry and I better get home quick, because Avery's Uncle Lonny has been talking about hooking up a motor to the back of Avery's wheelchair.

"Like I wouldn't get him a motorized chair if that's what he needed," she said. "And, Uncle Lonny is crazy enough to believe that everything needs a motor. He told Avery he could probably get him to roll over 60 mph." I laughed at Lonny's antics and told Christy that we will be home soon.

Father McIntire has shown up at the hospital every evening. He comes late after 8:00 pm visiting hours when everyone else has left and Henry is ready for sleep. I believe he gets away with his nighttime ritual, because he is a priest and they do not shoo him away. We hold hands and talk beside Henry's bed. He tells me about his day and the happenings back in Grace. He keeps me posted on my business, and the neighbors. He talks to me about silly things, like the day the old priest lost his false teeth. He said they looked all over the rectory for nearly two hours, before he found them in his bed covers where they had fallen out during his nap. We spend hours whispering to each other while Henry sleeps, but we have never talked about the kiss. We just go on. I have stopped calling him Father McIntire and just call him Timothy. Each night as he leaves he kisses me again. It is not the same passionate kiss we shared in the chapel, but rather the kiss of friendship, a sweet peck on my forehead or the kiss of sincerity, a soft touch to my cheek. Sometimes he kisses me lightly on the lips like we are an old married couple. I always welcome each kiss and I believe he is just giving me what I need. The kisses are always private, never with anyone else present.

Rayland and Cody have told my daddy that they will bring Henry and I home when Henry is released. Daddy can get Roman and Sabrina from Pops and Mama Jaspers. I'm sure Beau will come by and make it awkward for everyone, but what am I to do? He is my babies' daddy, as much I wish he wasn't. Although it is extremely hard for me to be around Beau, I swallow my heartache, hide my feelings of rejection, and pretend I am not bothered by his presence or absence. I act just as strong as I can be.

Dreamcatchers

September 25, 2000 - Dear Diary, the kids and I have spent the last few weeks adjusting back to normal life. Henry is now well. He's back to his sweet, sensitive and ornery self. It's hard to believe that just a month ago he was near death and although I live with a grateful heart, it doesn't change the fact that we have all been through hell, Roman and Sabrina included. Pops and Mama Jaspers did great taking care of them and still things are stressful. The reality of the situation is that their Mommy was absent, their brother was deathly sick and their deadbeat daddy showed up again out of nowhere. These three things alone would be enough trauma to cause the need for therapy, add the visions of ghosts that woke us up on the night of Henry's ruptured appendix and you have all the ingredients needed to create recurring nightmares.

Both boys have been having restless nights. I believe it's Roman's bad dreams that are also waking Henry. Plus, Sabrina is going through a separation anxiety that keeps her clinging to my legs. We celebrated her second birthday last week with a white cake with pink icing, but instead of her reaching a milestone of independence and terrible twos she has reverted back to being my little monkey. Her arms are constantly around my neck and she does not want to leave my hip. It's not easy running a café with a child hanging from your shoulders. I'm worried about the kids, that somehow the spirits have caused this or rather I've caused this by believing in the spirits and welcoming them into our home. My only wish, my only dream, is to create a life that is best for my children. If I have somehow screwed this up then I am horrible.

I called Pixie to let her know how the kids have been behaving, to see if she could help, and for some reassurance that I am not a terrible mother. Maybe I should have called a child psychologist or even their pediatrician, but I trust in Pixie's heretical devotion over the psychobabble of human growth and development. Pixie came over after dinner last night with her bucket full of tricks, conducting herself as a blue-haired, new age, Mary Poppins. Pixie, Roman and Henry sat at a table for over an hour and in that time Pixie taught them both how to make a dreamcatcher.

From her bucket she pulled several vines of fresh red willow and taught them how to weave them into a circle. Pixie secured the willow wreaths with leather ties. Next, she pulled a ball of hemp cord from her bucket and cut each child a long string of cord. She tied a tight knot at the top of each dreamcatcher and then she guided the boys through the intricate weaving of forming a spider web. For symbolism, she placed a bead on the web that represented the spider. Pixie helped the boys carefully loop and knot the hemp inside and around the red willow. She placed her hands on top of their hands if needed and steered them through the spinning of the web. The three entwined the cord into a delicate pattern. Lastly, they attached feathers to the bottom of the ring. While they worked, crisscrossing strings and tying feathers, Pixie told the legend of the dreamcatcher. She explained that the Native Americans made dreamcatchers. She stressed that Indians are brave and heroic and they get their strength from their faith in the Gods.

"Dreamcatchers are one of the things that give them their courage," she said. Pixie told the boys that the night sky is filled with a zillion dreams, both good and bad. She said we needed to hang the dreamcatchers from the ceiling, above our beds, so they could swing freely. When dreams fly by, they get caught in the web. The good dreams know how to slip through the holes of the dreamcatcher and slide down the feathers onto the sleeper. The bad dreams have not figured this out and they get tangled into the web. When the first ray of morning sunlight hits the bad dreams, they perish in the light.

I don't believe in the power of the dreamcatchers, but my boys do and sometimes all it takes is a little faith in the positive light to stop the nightmares. Pixie secretly told me not to worry. She said I was correct in believing that Owen and Emma Kitchen tried to save Henry. She also told me she had a long talk with Roman and told him that what he saw was a good thing, a blessed thing.

"Only the good are here," she said. Although I am certain this is true, I was still relieved when she told me she did a full house cleansing while we were all away. Pixie said she purified the kids' rooms and circled the space in a protection of white light. Some would say that Pixie's purification is a bunch of white magic nonsense, but just like my children and the dreamcatchers, I believe. As far as Sabrina goes, I think consistency, time and patience is the solution. Eventually, she will trust that I will not disappear again and only then will she stop swinging from my neck.

Changes

Hazel once asked me how it was so easy for my daddy to stick the kids and me in a haunted house.

"Because he doesn't believe in it," I told her.

"He doesn't believe in it?"

"Of course not, you think he would buy a home full of ghosts if he thought they were real?"

My Daddy believes in things that make sense, things that can be seen or heard, explained and understood, and things that have a purpose. My daddy is a skeptic, a cynic and an atheist. He believes in man and all that man is capable of, but he doesn't necessarily believe in God. We are the supernatural beings and science makes the most sense. Daddy pokes fun at our Enti-Tea parties. He believes Cole Spencer is a scamming genius and thinks that Pixie Moon-Dust, although sweet and nice, is crazy like her Mama. Yet, Daddy's opinion has begun to change.

Just a few days ago he brought over the home movie I had made for him. It was the building of the playground. I had recorded the hard working days in short increments of time. I would grab the camcorder any time I had a free moment or if all three kids were outside helping. As I documented the playground construction, I knew my dad would love it. It is a chronicle of his vision, hard work, talent and skill. It's a narrative with Daddy's voice in charge and an account from the beginning, surveying the ground and digging posts, to the end, the completion of the largest backyard swing set I have ever seen. I was able to record and capture the great moments and the frustrating ones. I have video of everyone who helped and lots of footage of my kids. I thought the movie would be entertaining and educational. Daddy showed up at my door Sunday night, just after I had laid the kids down.

"Have you watched this?" he asked.

"No, I just recorded it," I answered honestly. I had never found time to watch the movie before giving it to my daddy.

"You need to look at this," he said popping the tape into my VHS player. The video started out super cute with my daddy and the kids looking over blueprints at The Kitchen House table and then picking a spot in the yard for the playset.

"Keep watching," Daddy said when I looked away for a minute. "See there it is."

"What?"

"There it goes again. That!" he said pointing at the screen. As I continued to watch the home movie I realized what Daddy was pointing to. It was a small bright light that kept floating across the screen. At first I thought it was a moth or bug that flew in front of the lens, but soon it was clear to me that it was neither. In fact, it looked like a penlight, as if someone was pointing a laser penlight to the screen and dancing it around. I followed the light with my eyes as if I were a cat ready to pounce. The light was small and bright. It swirled up and down, zigzagged here and there, floating on and off the screen like a shooting star.

"Keep watching," Daddy said all excited. Soon it looked as if the light split into two. Now there were two lights that raced about chasing each other. The segment ended and then a new day appeared. It didn't take long for the point of light to be back and fly across the screen. As the movie continued and the playground progressed, the balls of light increased. Sometimes in the movie there would be three or four points of light zipping back and forth, landing on Daddy's shoulder or a piece of lumber before taking flight again. In the parts of the video that were taken at nightfall the points of light are abundant. The video showed Daddy and Timothy working by the glow of a large light fastened to a beam while hundreds of pinpoint lights danced around them. Honestly, it looked as if they were building a playground in the Milky Way.

"Did you see those lights when you were taping this?" Daddy asked.

"No sir," I said. "But I believe those are the spirits Pixie Moon-Dust sees."

"The whole damn thing is so absurd," Daddy said. "It just makes you wonder."

I was glad those brilliant points of light left my practical daddy wondering. Wonder is a marvelous thing. Daddy popped out the movie and shook his head.

"I don't know Sissy, all this crazy shit that happens here. Maybe I'll need to spend my next fifty years believing in something."

"I think that would be good," I told him.

The change to Daddy due to the spirits is awesome. The changes in Lenore are phenomenal. In the last nine months, Lenore has changed physically, emotionally and spiritually. Her short bob haircut has grown into a brown shoulder length wave that refuses to stay tucked behind the ears. Her job at Bloomers and the time she spends outside among the flowers and plants has caused her east coast milky white skin to darken to a golden bronze. She just looks healthier. She seems happier too. Still quiet, she is no longer shy. I've learned that her moments of silence are due to her deep thoughts and not social awkwardness. From her expressions and actions, I believe those deep thoughts are no longer from the places of heartache and sorrow, but rather she is finding peace from within. Six months ago Lenore reminded me of an abused child, hiding her emotions behind dark rimmed glasses and teary eyes. Today, I am amazed at her serenity and maybe slightly jealous. I admire watching her work the flowerbed. She hovers over the blooms like Mother Nature, silent and calm, and pulls forth their beauty. She seems content in her work and in her thoughts and honestly, she is beautiful. Working with the kids on homework, she is just as impressive. She brings the same stillness from the garden to the table and sweetly teaches them to think on their own. Lenore seems to do more than recite lessons and help memorize formulas. She opens their minds, cultivates their thoughts, and plants little seeds of knowledge. Just as she pulls forth the beauty of the garden, she does the same with the children. It's a shame that Lenore lost her teaching license. I thank God they could not revoke her love for teaching.

Lenore and I have grown closer these last few weeks. I am grateful to Lenore for all the help she has given me and she knows this. We spend time talking and laughing after homework help ends. On the nights that Lenore works at The Kitchen House, she enjoys socializing after closing, even though she needs to be up early and at Bloomers. I like that Lenore has such a strong work ethic. I like even more that she is loyal to her friends.

Lenore confessed to me that Pixie had given her a psychic reading. She said she didn't ask Pixie for a reading and it came out of the blue while she was running The Kitchen House during Henry's hospital stay. Lenore was alone in The Kitchen House one slow morning when Pixie came in.

"Your angel is beckoning me to talk to you," Pixie said. "Quite frankly he's been bugging the hell out of me to deliver this message. He's pretty insistent and won't leave me alone. So if you could just give me a few minutes and listen with an open mind I'd surely appreciate it."

Lenore said she didn't know how to respond, but it didn't matter, cause Pixie just continued on. She told Lenore that a handsome young man dressed in white with dark black hair followed her. She referred to this spirit as Lenore's angel of love and told her that he was drenched in a silvery white light. She also said that he is responsible for leading Lenore to Grace, West Virginia. Pixie told Lenore that her true love could be found in these mountains and it was this angel's job to guide Lenore to love. Once Lenore finds love, the handsome angel will transcend into the heavens. Lenore said she instantly knew that the angel of love was Christopher and although it sounded like a make-believe fairy tale, Lenore began to cry.

"The task for this angel is not easy," Pixie explained. "Because the love is twofold."

"Twofold?" Lenore questioned.

"Well yes, before you can love another you must learn to love yourself. In other words, your soul mate is right here, but you will not know him until you forgive yourself from whatever it is that is holding you back from self-love."

The entire reading sounded surreal and as if it had been ripped from the pages of a fable. It seemed absurd that an angel of love would lead a rich Connecticut scholar to the Appalachian Mountains to find herself, forgive herself and learn to love herself, so she could be connected to her soul mate. I mean would God really pair Miss Martha Vineyard with an Appalachian Mountain Man? But then again, how did Pixie know all this stuff? I have never spoken to anyone about Christopher (a dark haired, handsome, young man). I have also never revealed the things that Lenore has gone through, the things that have her scarred. I was left dumbfounded. I understand why Pixie told her to listen with an open mind.

Lenore said as bizarre as it was, Pixie's message was the equivalent of a ton of bricks being lifted from her chest. She said she cried to hear that Christopher wants her to find love. She is trying hard to forgive herself, to accept that Christopher is gone without it being her fault and to believe that his soul is happy. She likes the thought of Christopher as an angel in white.

"He is just that beautiful," she said.

As challenging as it has been for Christopher to guide Lenore to love, the task for Lenore is even harder. It must be unbelievably difficult to give yourself a pardon when you feel you have caused a death. Lenore is learning acceptance on a whole different level. Maybe it is this life lesson that brings her closer to enlightenment than the rest of us.

When I think about it, Father Timothy McIntire has been given this same lesson. I should probably not be upset with him, although I am. Since Henry's recovery, Timothy has kept distant. I have no doubt he is hiding in his church and in the hills. He has not stopped by. He has not checked on us. We are now okay, so it should be no big deal. Still, I miss him holding my hand. I miss our long talks and whispered laughter. I miss the sweet kisses that he pressed to my lips and I miss him terribly. I know deep down that I am wrong in this wanting and that it is not acceptable.

Instead of visits from Timothy, I get to see Beau. He's been showing up at The Kitchen House daily and playing with the kids on the playground. He pushes Sabrina on the baby swing and teaches the boys how to throw and catch. I told him to go easy with Henry, not too much activity; but Henry is pretty much back to normal and hard to slow down. Beau bought each of the boys a mitt in an attempt to make up for lost time. I guess he thinks he resembles the song *Cats in the Cradle* and all is forgiven. I do believe the boys are growing accustomed to a father that comes and goes. The only good thing that can come out of this is the next time he leaves, they won't take it so hard.

September 28, 2000 – Dear Diary, I dreamed that God was a game show host. Instead of a white bearded man with his finger pointing through the clouds, I envisioned a sophisticated, debonair, middle-aged, handsome man in a trendy suit. His stylish hair was classic salt and pepper slicked back. His teeth were straight, pearly white and they gleamed a little sparkle when he smiled. In my dream, God had a tan, twinkling blue eyes and a sexy laugh.

My God handed out puzzles. He was referred to as the Puzzle Master and the people were the contestants. Everyone was handed a puzzle as soon as they were born. During life's circumstances and lessons, we found our pieces to our puzzle and put them together. Some puzzles were quicker than others to figure out. Some puzzles could last nearly a century. Sometimes in the game, people could opt out of their puzzle; throw it back to God and die. The next time their turn came around they could enter the world as a new contestant, be given a new puzzle and try to work that one out. Really the game rules are up to you, God just hands out the puzzles and recycles the people.

I noticed in my dream, that although every life and every puzzle was different, the pieces came from the same place. Each soul collected pieces of pain and pieces of joys. When an area of your puzzle was put together, like for instance you found all the pieces to the fish, the contestant received a prize virtue and moved up the moral ladder. The frustrating part of putting together life's puzzle is all the missing pieces that keep you from winning a virtue. The fish would be almost complete, except you could not find his eye, or the trees would be absent of a couple leaf pieces, the blues were always so close in contrast that they were maddening to work with. All in all, the puzzles were difficult.

In the dream, my puzzle was laid out on a large table. As I approached the puzzle, I noticed that the virtues, Resilience and Gratitude, were almost complete, but I had many missing pieces in the virtue section of Acceptance. I picked up a stray puzzle piece and fit it easily into the area of Divine Awareness; I quickly found three more pieces that fit securely into the same virtue. I then took a step back to look at my puzzle in its wholeness. Shockingly, the puzzle expanded in size and I realized there were some virtue sections that had never been touched. For instance, there were only two connecting pieces in the section of Patience and none in the virtue of Trust. I tried to talk to God in a serious manner about this. I was hoping to find out the quickest way to find pieces and obtain virtues. I suggested to him that maybe I should work on the virtue, Faith, and it would lead me to the other pieces I needed. But God responded by calling me, Doll face, and *giving a little laugh.*

"That my dear is the number one mistake contestants make," he said.

God then squirted breath spray into his mouth, pointed at me with his shooter finger and was gone with the twinkling blink of an eye. I was alone with a vast puzzle full of missing pieces when I woke.

A DAY of GOODBYES

October 5, 2000 – Dear Diary, both Beau and Timothy are gone. Each of them told me goodbye in their own way and left Grace. They both went off to go find themselves while I stay home and feel lost.

Beau came early in the morning before the boys had left for school. At first, I was surprised by his visit and then I thought it was nice that he was here to have breakfast with his kids. They all shared a skillet of scrambled eggs and toast. Beau drank about half a pot of house blend that I should have charged him for, but didn't. As the bus pulled up and Jean came in to get her coffee, Beau followed the boys out and gave them hugs and high fives.

"See ya later," he said waving as the bus pulled away. He then came back in the house and told me that he had a job over at Blackwater Falls waiting for him. "I'll be doing maintenance at a campground," he said. "Ski season is just around the corner for Canaan Valley so I'm gonna try to get on at the resort through the winter. If it all works out, I probably won't be able to come home for Christmas. It will just be too damn busy, but it should be good money. I promise to send something your way just as soon as the checks start rollin in."

"Sounds like a decent plan," I said. Canaan Valley is about a four hour drive from Grace. It's also a place in West Virginia where I think Beau would be happy. Not too far and not too close, with beautiful mountains and streams between us.

"Can you tell the boys for me, Sissy? Tell them I'll see them in the spring."

"Yeah, I'll tell them," I said.

"Thanks Sissy, you're the best. And Sissy, I'm sorry. I mean, I'm really sorry. I never meant to hurt you."

"I'm fine Beau." I wasn't about to give him any satisfaction.

"Yeah, I know," he said. "And this Kitchen House, wow, it's just great. I mean really, really great Sissy. You gotta be proud of all this." Beau hesitated for a minute. "I guess what I'm trying to say is that I'm proud of you Sissy. You've done really good without me."

"Thank you Beau," I said and then I wished him luck on his new job. "It'll be fine," I told him. "I'll tell the kids you are leaving and that we'll see ya in the spring."

"You're amazing Sissy," he said, giving me an awkward hug.

"Yes I am," I agreed. Beau wiped the tears from his eyes and kissed Sabrina on her forehead.

"Take good care of um," he shouted over to Hazel who had witnessed the whole scene with fire coming out of her eyes.

"Take good care of yourself!" she shouted back as he walked out the door. Hazel doesn't hide her pissed off very well. It's understandable why she's mad. Beau's plan for himself was well thought out, but his goodbyes never are. When it comes to the kids, Beau pushes his farewell off into my hands. Once again I get to tell my children that their daddy's see ya later meant much later.

Unlike Beau, Timothy put much effort into his goodbye. His speech must have been written, rehearsed, rewritten and then adlibbed. His anticipation must have been days on end waiting for the right time and praying for the strength. He came for lunch and sat awkwardly quiet. This didn't stop me from talking a mile a minute to my best friend who I am secretly in love with. I told him about Beau's pathetic goodbye. I agonized with him how I was going to tell the boys, the best time, how I thought they might react and the fact that feelings of abandonment suck so very much. He listened. He offered encouragement and a positive ideology concerning my kids. He seems to think they don't need Beau as much as I think they do.

"In fact, maybe it's better when he's not around, less confusing, with a happier mommy," he said. "Don't sell yourself short Sissy. You parent with the love and patience of two parents. They don't need anything more than the affection and guidance that you give them. You are their everything and you are enough."

All that he said made me feel good. I wanted to lean over and kiss his lips before he left, but I crammed the feeling down in my gut and picked up Sabrina to cuddle between us. Often when I'm with him I need a distraction or else I feel too good, too comfortable, which is wrong. When I got up to fix Lydia, the librarian, a fancy iced coffee with whipped cream and mint he left, leaving his money on the table and a note under his plate. *Meet me on Henry's Bridge tonight at nine,* it read. I felt like a teenager slipping his secret note into the back pocket of my jeans. That afternoon, just as soon as Homework Help ended and before dinner began I told the boys that their daddy had left. I had thought about waiting until The Kitchen House was closed and the evening was calm. That way, I could have a sweet, sensitive motherly talk full of hugs and embraces while we settled in for the night. Instead, I told them hurriedly before a sink full of dirty dishes and patrons who needed my attention. It was a selfish move on my part and I still feel bad. Honestly, it was because if any fits were to be thrown over this news, tears to be cried, or feelings to comfort, I wanted it done and over in time to meet Timothy on the bridge at nine. I also thought that if I delivered the news in a nonchalant way then their response would be more detached or blasé. After all, this drama is our new norm, Daddy comes and goes, get over it. For the most part, they did get over it or rather accept it and I was only five minutes late out the door to meet Timothy, who was waiting on Henry's Bridge.

To my surprise the first thing he did was grab me and kiss me. Not the sweet pecks at the hospital, but rather the full wet sexy kiss that I had been longing for, the kiss I dreamed about. His kiss nearly bent me over, his face wet with tears, his tangerine lips full, moist and delicious. The kiss on Henry's Bridge was sweet and juicy, romantic and emotional. When Timothy pulled his face back from mine he was crying sweet apologies and sputtering I love you.

"I love you too," I silently said, not realizing just how very much until that moment.

"I'm leaving," he said.

"What?" His words swirled around me. He can't leave I need him. He is my calm; my best friend and now I know he loves me too.

"Sissy, I am leaving the priesthood. I must. I can no longer live this way."

"What way? I thought you were happy? I thought you liked being a priest? You have to stay, I need you."

"Sissy, you silly girl, do you not get it? I am a priest, a priest who has fallen in love with a woman. You are too close and I want you too badly. You sit in the congregation four pews back on the right with two little boys beside you while I stand up front reciting the Apostles' Creed and as those holy words flow off my tongue, I desire you. I go through the motions of mass thinking about your face, your body, and your laugh. It's too much. This church that once felt like my sanctuary is now my prison. Because of my vow I cannot freely profess my love. I am restricted. I chose a life of celibacy, and it never mattered before. Before you, I was content in my loneliness. I filled my days with good deeds and my nights with prayer." Timothy ran his fingers through his hair and looked away and then began again. "Truthfully, it wasn't long after I met you Sissy that I began to feel a temptation and I knew I should stay away. In the beginning, I thought I had it under control. I believed I could keep my attraction at bay by hiding it from others and refuting it from myself. My theory was, if I denied it, it would eventually go away. But it didn't work. Our relationship just kept growing closer and the more it did, the more torturous it was. Honestly Sissy, it's been so hard being your friend and being in love with you. But my other choice was to not be your friend at all. It seems like I have been wrestling with my conscience for so long. I told myself over and over again to push my feelings down to the depth of my gut. I knew I should stop feeding our relationship with compatibility and kindness, but instead starve it, give it nothing and stay far away until it died. That seemed even more painful and I couldn't do it. I then decided the best thing would be a best friend without intimacy. In my sexually stunted mind I thought this was doable. Then at the hospital when you kissed me, I surrendered and my body flooded with love, lust and emotion. It became no longer possible for me not to want you. Sissy, I became a priest, because I was desperately searching for the presence of God and the gift of forgiveness. I didn't find either one until I met you."

As Timothy talked he took short breaks to cry. I cried with him as the swinging bridge swayed beneath our feet, our hands gripped in an embrace. There was so much energy swirling around us. It made my stomach churn with emotion and my head spin in thought. Our talk was a hurricane and I wondered if Mr. Baxter was watching.

"Let's go sit in Roman's Tower," I said leading the priest (who was no longer a priest) from the bridge, up the ramp and into my child's large fort. Once inside he sat down up against a wall and I leaned back against him. It was dark in the fort, but through the small windows streamed a full moon's light and a nice breeze blew in and I could see a constellation of stars.

"Sissy, I have to go," he said again.

"Why?" I asked. "Why can't you just leave the church and come here? Come live with me. Come be with me."

"Would you want that?" he asked surprised.

How can this beautiful man not realize that I love him also? That he is the most stunning man I've ever seen. He is the kindest soul I've ever met. He's compassionate, spiritual, funny and loving. I find him perfect.

"Yes, I want that," I said.

"But, the kids and Hazel."

"They love you too. They don't want you to go. It would be fine with them."

"And you're sure of this?" he said kissing my head. "Sissy, you're very sweet, but it's not that easy. I have given more thought and prayer in leaving the priesthood than I did in deciding to become a priest. I've learned that it takes more faith and courage to leave the church than it does to enter it. Yes, I am choosing to walk away because I have fallen in love with you. I desire you in every way, with every fiber of my being and I can no longer deny it. These are not the feelings a priest should have. So it is no longer acceptable for me to hide within those walls and conceal my emotions by wearing a collar."

"So don't."

"Exactly, I can't. But in leaving, I have lost all security, all means of support. I no longer have a job, a home, or even health insurance. My reputation is questionable, my ministry is gone and I no longer have the respect of my colleagues. I have nothing to offer you, nothing at all but myself and even that is tarnished. And you Sissy, your reputation, your business, it could be ruined as well. Think about it, if I were to walk out of the church and into your bed, what would the town of Grace do? Actually, all of Spring County would erupt in judgment and gossip and the surrounding counties as well. Really Sissy, Grace could not handle a love affair between the priest and the haunted café owner who offers psychic readings. We would certainly be the talk of town and do you know what the people would call you?"

"Let them," I said. "As a child, they referred to me as a bastard. Let them call me a whore."

"And your children will hear it," he said. "Don't you think they have been through enough? Your business will be affected which in turn will affect others, Hazel, Lenore, your dad and brother. Too many people will be hurt by our loving each other and yet I can't stop loving you."

"And I love you, so it's all good."

"I have to go Sissy," he whispered. "I knew from the moment that I decided to leave the church that I would also need to leave Grace. What I didn't know before was your reaction, how you would respond. I didn't know if you would want me too, or if I would creep you out, offend you, or scare you. I only knew that I could no longer live a lie and deny my attraction, or my love. I have been contemplating leaving since winter." This bit of news surprised me and I let out a small gasp. "Do you know how hard it has been for me?" he asked. "Remember the day we built Gladden the snowman? It took everything in me to not playfully grab you, wrestle you to the snow and kiss your face. That's what I did in my mind, but only in my mind. Every encounter after that was the same. Can you imagine the guilt I have, the shame! What kind of priest am I?"

"A human priest," I said flipping around and kissing him. Once again we were crying and kissing, two turbulent seas of emotion crashing together, as our lips pressed together, our hands searched each other's hair, each other's faces, until mine slipped down and began to unbutton my flannel. I pressed his hands to my flesh and I thought he would faint. I'm not sure if it was a look of horror or look of lust that kept him transfixed on my breasts. I slipped my bra off for him.

"Sissy, no." he whispered.

"Timothy, yes. Please, please yes," I said straddling him and pressing my chest into his face, begging for his kisses to continue. I gave him no mercy and eventually he could not hold back. I stood up in the spacious fort to take off my jeans. Timothy laid vertically, his head nearly touching one corner of the wall, his feet nearly touching the other. We made love in Roman's Tower on a hard wooden floorboard with no mattress for comfort or sheet for shyness. We devoured each other in a suffocating wooden box on a hot September night and it was the best I have ever felt. Afterwards, we lay hot and sweaty tangled in each other's arms. Neither one of us spoke. I believe we didn't want to break the spell, disturb the magic that swirled around us in a love filled bubble.

"What now?" I finally asked. He drew in a deep breath before answering.

"Okay, so I go. I go and then come back. How about that? I have already confessed to the bishop that I have fallen in love with a woman and that I must leave the priesthood. I told him just as I was called into the church, I feel like I am being called away and I believe that God has led both callings. The bishop has wished me well and I am free to go. But the people, the town, this is something that they must be eased into or things will not go well for us, for you. Besides that, I have a lot of stuff I need to work out so I can come back as a whole man."

"So, you will come back?' I asked with tears rolling down my face.

"Do you honestly think I can stay away?"

I didn't know how to answer such a question. Yes I do believe people can run away. Some are very capable of running from love, family and friends, running from life. I did not say this though, instead I just cried.

"I go," he said. "I leave the church and the town of Grace with the rumor that Timothy McIntire could no longer be a priest because he had feelings for a woman. We let the town sit with this rumor, get used to it, accept it, grow curious about who she is."

"I think they'll know," I interrupted.

"That's fine, just as long as they realize we were not acting upon our sexual attraction while I was in ministry. That I admired you from afar until I could no longer stand it."

"I don't care what they think."

"I know Sissy, but it's better this way. I'm no good for you right now. I'm too messed up in the head. I need to go off and figure things out, maybe go see my parents and try to make amends. I need to try and figure out how to secure some sort of job or at least discover what I want to be when I grow up, then make a plan to be it. I need to finally come to grips with why Thomas had to die. Once I do, I can come back whole and not be a burden."

"How long will all this take?" I asked sounding a little put off.

"Oh baby," he said kissing the tip of my nose. "Because of you, it shouldn't be long. Because of you, I am almost there."

Town Gossip

October 15, 2000 – Dear Diary, Timothy has been gone over a week and I have not heard from him. I try to believe that he is coming back, but it is hard not to doubt myself. It's easy to assume that he has gone off someplace else to hide. I know I need to not be such a cynic, but my sadness is slowly turning into annoyance. He should at least call. I need to know that he's okay. Mostly I need some reassurance.

I remember my dream where I had no puzzle pieces to obtain the virtue, trust, so I tell myself this is my lesson. I must learn to trust. I fall asleep each night thinking about the love we made in Roman's Tower and I wake in a panic, what if I'm pregnant?

Yes, the town of Grace is swirling with talk about Father Timothy McIntire. Somehow he did leave the rumor (and truth) that he has officially left the priesthood, because he fell in love with a woman that he admired from afar. He must have confessed this secret to someone he knew would spread it around, or maybe, he told the old priest to circulate it. Anyhow, the town is exploding with the juicy gossip. I believe most of the town thinks it's me. They have begun to take inventory of how much time Father Timothy McIntire spent at The Kitchen House. Mr. Baxter recalls the amount of work the priest spent on the playground. He also claims to have witnessed the priest at my house in the late evening hanging out in the play area with me. Others talk about the priest showing up every Friday and Saturday night for The Kitchen House entertainment and they believe it out of character that a priest should want to be entertained. There is gossip about the day the priest planted spring flowers with me. They also gossip about his long walks in the woods. I heard one old coot, sitting at my coffee bar, whispering to his friend.

"I happen to know that Sissy goes for frequent walks in the woods, right behind the church?" he muttered.

Lydia, the librarian, talks about the book fiasco, telling the town how Roman and Avery destroyed her library and how the priest came over and helped me put it all back together. She claims we laughed and carried on like school friends putting the books away.

Then there is the opposing side. The ones that believe the priest is in love with Christy Banks. They talk of all the favors Timothy did for Christy, worked on her house whenever she needed it, and helped Avery with his pinewood derby car. I heard the chitchat of two mothers, talking while they watched their children play in my back yard.

"He did take such a liking to that little crippled boy," one mumbled.

"Oh, you can bet that sexy priest was Christy Banks own private little handyman, if you know what I mean?" the other snickered.

The rumors make me feel angry and it's hard not to react. The same people that believe Timothy loves Christy think that I am still crushed by Beau Jaspers. Their whispered chatter floats around The Kitchen House and lands in my ears.

"Ya know, Beau and that hussy just broke up and he was in town playing catch with them little boys and Sissy acted just fine."

I swear people love to talk and for the most part they talk out their ass. Regardless, the talk has been good for coffee sales. They come in snooping around trying to catch me crying. With snarky voices, they ask Avery Banks how his Mama is feeling lately. Why people get off on another's misery is beyond me. Christy knows that Timothy is in love with me and not her. They were great friends and she called on him often, because he was always willing to help without judgment or pay. But, there was nothing romantic involved. She told me in her subtle way that she knew it was me he loved.

"It'll be fine," she said. "He's gonna come back to you." I shrugged my shoulders and shook my head.

"I hope," I responded in a barely audible tone. Christy Banks just smiled.

"Sure he will. You just wait and see." So I wait, but I am absent of

Christy's enthusiasm and filled with a feeling more like hopeful anticipation.

"Sorry, the town is talking about you," I told Christy.

"Oh hell that ain't your fault. They've been talking about me for years. I figure it gives them something to do." Christy's right. There is harmlessness in their small town gossip, just a bunch of bored folks with inquiring minds.

I think my daddy knows Timothy left because of me and Charlie knows too, but they don't say anything. Both of those men hate drama and believe that your personal life is to be kept private. Neither man would attempt a conversation with me about Timothy for fear I may cry or be too honest. I grew up in a home where we stifled our emotions. Daddy wasn't really a strict parent. On the contrary, he only had three rules; no whining, don't be a baby and brush it off. You could say Daddy is a natural consequence kind of parent. We learned how to recover from our own mistakes and the only prescribed discipline was to not talk about it. Since I cannot talk to them, I talk to Hazel. Hazel is a great comfort. She lets me fall apart. Just last night I laid in Hazel's bed crying as she rubbed my back and smoothed my hair.

"Go ahead and cry," she told me. "Let it all out." And with her permission I did. I bawled and blubbered and in-between sobs, I wiped my snotty nose and told Hazel everything. Well, mostly everything. I told her about the kiss at the hospital, I talked about our walks together in the woods. I told her about our talks in the gazebo and how he made me my own chair. I told her about the night he burned the kids' names into the wooden playground and how I couldn't stop holding his hand. Then I told her about Thomas, the little ghost boy, and the rabbit's foot. I spoke of Timothy's confession. How his little brother fell through the ice and died and how Timothy has spent the last eighteen years blaming himself. I told her the death of Thomas guided Timothy to the priesthood, so he could live a life of humility begging for forgiveness.

"Lord have mercy," Hazel said. "That poor child." Then Hazel cried right along with me, big sobs that shook her whole body. I know I should feel terrible, but it was so nice to have company through misery. Part of me does feel guilty about telling Hazel. I gave Timothy my word of secrecy and then I reneged. Another part of me breathes a little easier with Hazel knowing. Just like Lenore with her undisclosed love affair and loss, some secrets are too heavy to handle alone. I did not tell Hazel that Timothy and I made love in Roman's Tower, but I did tell Rayland.

"O.M.G.!" he gasped in the most dramatic way.

"Girl, you tellin me you had sex with a priest in your child's play fort?"

"Good God Rayland, when you put it like that you make me sound like a jezebel."

"Oh baby I know, and that's why at this moment I love you more than I've ever loved you before." Rayland begged for every detail. Since I have been reliving it in my mind every second of the day, I held nothing back, I told him every facet, from Timothy's scared "no" to my pleading and forceful "yes".

"Oh my God Sissy, you're a seductress, a Goddamn seductress."

"Shut up," I said.

"No really, I knew you were amazing, but this, this is your Helen Reddy, *I Am Woman*, moment. This is your roar." And then instead of singing the song he just quoted, Rayland went into a full ballad of, *You Make Me Feel Like A Natural Woman*. He sang in a baritone whisper as he shimmied in a circle like a stripper and since a dancer is what he is, a pole dancer is what he resembled. I nearly reached into my tip jar for a dollar. After finishing his sexy circular shimmy, he bowed to me three times and called me Queen Sheba, which I did not get, but he found incredibly witty.

"Oh my God, grow up," I said throwing a dishtowel at his face.

"Never darling, don't you know I suffer from Peter Pan syndrome and you my dear bring out my middle school boy."

"Well cram him back inside, he's irritating."

"Spoken just like Daddy."

As Rayland and I poked fun at each other, I realized it had been months, literally months, since I had laughed. Once again, Rayland was there to do what only Rayland can do, pull joy from my pain, and extract laughter from my tears. Everybody needs a friend like Rayland, because sometimes life is just too damn severe and mountain people can be harsh.

The gossip in this small community does not just swirl around the priest and I. Yes, we make up the forefront, but there are a few others that follow closely behind. Lenore, in fact, is a much talked about individual. I'm not sure the town knows what to make of Lenore. She's an enigma. She confuses this Appalachian County and leaves them stumped. There are really no outward traits to make the people dislike her. Quite frankly it would be easier if there were. Then the gossip wouldn't be so random, with no subject matter or irritating characteristics. Lenore has always been polite, kind and mannerly. Lately her polite has turned almost perky, her kindness has meshed with a generosity and her manners now hold personal touches. Funny, but all these changes have been credited to my brother, Charlie, a man often accused of being a male whore. Charlie is seen as a true womanizer with a streak of likable orneriness. He is often accused of using his good looks and handyman talents to lure women into his bed. Daddy has this same reputation. The two are notorious horn-dogs. Fortunately for them, this opinion does not keep them from contracts and work. They are constantly busy from one project to the next. It does however, make the men of Spring County keep a close eye on their daughters and wives when my daddy and Charlie are around.

Lately Charlie has been spending all his free time with Lenore. It's easy to see that during this interval, they have both been altered. Charlie for the first time seems committed and Lenore finally looks happy. The town says that Charlie has transformed Lenore, but I know that is not the reality of it. Yes, Lenore has changed, but Charlie did not influence her revision. Lenore's improvements are a result of her own hard work. Because of Lenore, Charlie is also a changed man. He has fallen in love with her. And it's so nice to see Charlie behave loyally. He has spent his entire adult life playing the field and sowing wild oats. Although he was having fun, I don't know if he was truly happy. Now there is a new spark in Charlie's dark brown eyes and a Cheshire grin is etched across his face. As his big sister, I like his new look. He is a man finally in love and he wears his devotion well. Because sexism is still alive and prospering in the town of Grace, the chitchat focuses more on the appearance of Lenore and less on Charlie. The small talk of small minds, remembers Lenore's short tucked haircut, stiff clothes, tight smile and perched glasses. Their memories are of an uptight hoity-toity, which isn't exactly accurate. Lenore was never an edgy snob, just quietly reserved. I personally like to think of Lenore as a butterfly. She arrived in Grace, woven into a cocoon of protection. Her walls were needed, because behind them she was slowly growing. I imagine it takes a lot of time, endurance and inner strength to shed a heavy skin of sadness, guilt and shame. Then there is the slow gradual process of growing wings of freedom from nubs of pain. I assume the wings start out teeny tiny, the size of a thought or dream. Eventually, if the thought or dream is not spontaneously aborted, it catches hold and begins to develop. I believe the womb of a dream must be the soul. During gestation the wings need to develop their color and grow in size, large enough to lift the dreamer. Lenore's wings are painted in shades of acceptance, forgiveness and faith. They are the wings of self-love and Lenore is beautiful in flight. Charlie is equally stunning beside her.

Truly, Lenore has come a long way. She has finally given herself clemency and has found some things that make her happy; helping the children with their studies, playing with flowers, growing a garden, and Charlie. Pixie was right. Once Lenore accepted Christopher as her angel in white and stopped torturing herself with fault and blame; she opened herself up for love. As it turns out the handsome prince destined to be her soul mate is Charlie Cooper, my mountain man brother. No wonder Christopher, her angel of love, dropped her off on my front porch; fate is a force beyond reckoning.

Pixie however, knows a thing or two about fate. Pixie has the gift of seeing the purpose laid out in the lives of others. For each person she has a little rolled up treasure map inside of her head. Somehow she knows the path of their destiny and has been given an insightful glimpse into the routes that need to be taken. Pixie knows where they can find the hidden trails already made. In regards to Pixie's own life, she cuts out her own trail. Pixie creates detours around carnivals and paths taken just for fun. God may have given Pixie her map, but she creates the adventures along the way. In all honesty, I'm jealous of Pixie's spark and in awe of her spunk.

Hearsay of Pixie Moon-Dust and Cole Spencer has turned into tabloid gossip, juicy, titillating and sinfully delightful. It makes me wonder if Pixie orchestrated the rumor to take the heat away from the priest and me.

Three days ago, Pixie informed me that Cole Spencer was coming to town. She told me that she was giving him a lesson in paranormal interpretation (that's not all she taught him). Pixie said Cole was going to sit in on a couple of scheduled readings at The Pixie House and since the appointment would run late, her and Cole would probably just spend the night. I admit I was a little confused at first, wondering how the two would share her little bed and then I thought of me and Timothy pressed up against each other in Roman's Tower and realized it was possible. I told Pixie that would be fine even though she wasn't asking my permission, but rather being courteous by informing me. That night I heard Pixie and Cole outside after midnight, I smelled their bonfire and took notice of their voices and then I rolled over and went back to sleep.

In the morning, I saw Cole as Hazel and I opened up The Kitchen House. He was our first customer. I don't think the man had slept all night and he looked a hot mess. His stiff handlebar mustache stood out erect from his face as if it had nearly been sucked off his lip. His pompadour hairstyle had been smashed and rubbed with enough friction to turn it into a bird's nest. Hazel couldn't take her eyes off of Cole as he absently stirred his coffee while gazing up to the ceiling.

"Oh my God," she whispered to me. "She put a spell on him."

Mr. Baxter also heard voices that night, which caused him to rise from his bed, grab his glasses from the nightstand, slip his feet into his house shoes and take the phone with him out onto the porch in case he needed to call 911. What he witnessed took ten years off his life and glued his eyes to my back yard. Mr. Baxter claimed in a voice laced with excitement and masked by a false rage, that Pixie and Cole were dancing naked around the fire, trying to conjure up God knows what. Although Mr. Baxter shakes a furious fist when he speaks of Pixie and Cole, you can tell that he was slightly turned on by the sight. It's easy to hear the stimulation and thrill in his voice and he feels the constant need to talk about the incident with everybody. Pixie has defended herself by saying they were not completely naked. She told me privately that Cole was wearing boxers. She also reminds everybody that there is a gigantic playground that blocks the view from Mr. Baxter's back porch to The Pixie House and the dance was not to conjure up spirits, they were simply having fun.

"Gosh, you guys," she says. "Haven't you ever been on a date before?" Everybody listens to Mr. Baxter's story, because it's exciting to hear and we're usually such a boring little town. But even with such a controversial occurrence, Pixie is given the benefit of a doubt. In truth, everybody likes Pixie. She has given good accurate advice on their love lives and relationships. She has conveyed sweet messages of peace from their deceased loved ones. She has taken care of their elderly, spent the time and ran the errands that no one else wanted to and she has delivered her daddy's wares to their homes in secrecy and concealment. She is respected and she is loved. I read Cole Spencer's latest blog titled *Dancing Spirits and Moonlight* and it's obvious that Pixie is the object of his affection and he is indeed spellbound.

The rumors of love affairs have never before been so abundant. The various chitchats buzz up and down the streets. All the ladies of Spring County have turned into cackling hens, merrily pecking at gossip here and there. It makes me wonder if the spirits of The Kitchen House are responsible for creating such a love fest. I think about Pixie wiping down my walls with rose water. "Roses are the flowers of love," she said while spraying her potion all over my home. And surely in my home, love is abundant. I myself have paid witness to a prophecy of love, the divine prediction of a forlorn girl being guided to her soul mate by an angel in white. It's completely amazing and unbelievable, leading me to more questions without answers.

Was it the spices Pixie sprinkled in my carpet that caused Ezra and Hazel to strike up a conversation that turned from friendship into a sweet companionship that soothes them both? Did the spirits afflict the priest with feelings for me? Was it Thomas' doing? Or perhaps, it was written in the stars long before we were born and long before Thomas died. All this gifted insight confuses me more. In fact, the only thing I do know for certain is that my love for Timothy comes from a place somewhere in my center, a deep place, untouched by another, in spite of having been married before.

The universe astounds me with the stories it writes. Our beginning, our middles and our end, each phase a paradox, connecting periods of time into the labyrinth of life. We go from one chapter to the next as the mystery of our existence slowly unfolds. Truly, one's lifespan is the best book ever written.

Keep Moving

November 2, 2000 – Dear Diary, I went to mass last Sunday. I left the kids with Hazel and Ezra and went by myself. I thought it might help. I've never been more wrong. The church no longer feels the same and I feel like a sinner. I listened to the old priest and longed to hear the deep whispered tone of Timothy McIntire saying, "Peace be with you." I wanted so badly to hear his poetically charged Nicene Creed. I wanted to taste the bread that he placed on my tongue and have the wine that he pressed to my lips. My wanting is perverse. I took communion from the old priest and then knelt on bended knee and prayed that my period would start.

After church I walked the woods up to the gazebo. The autumn foliage was bursting with shades of red, burgundy, orange and yellow that danced and waved upon a bright blue sky. Gladden, the wind, was blowing a gentle breeze and the branches swayed in a tapestry of color. The leaves crunched beneath my feet in a playful way and air filled my lungs, but could not clear my mind. In the gazebo I sat on my handmade chair. I played with the carved wooden animal figures that had been abandoned by their creator. When I left, I stuck several of the figurines in my pocket and that night I lined them up on my bedroom windowsill. I have a bear, a deer, a rabbit and a fox. At night, I rub them as if they are worry stones and pray on them like a rosary. To me these wooden carvings are figurines of hope and I softly whisper into the rabbit's ear, "Call him back to Grace."

It was helpful that October was such a crazy, busy month and gave me no time to come undone. I honestly thought that we would slow down after the summer had gone, but I forgot how much people love to wander

244

through the mountains during the fall. Who could blame them? A drive through the autumn mountains is breathtaking. My patrons made tea reservations on Saturdays and Sundays and filled my month with weekends of parties and events. Pixie was twice as busy as me. Every last one of them wanted a reading and the closer it got to Halloween the more reservations we had. Pixie must be plumb worn out from all the dead people she has had to talk to this month. I guess most people thought they were being original and were excited about making their holiday plans.

"Hey, I know, instead of going to a fake haunted house this year let's go to a real haunted house, drink tea and talk to dead family members."

"I'm in."

"I'm in."

"I'm in."

It really is such a good idea and many shared the thought, which means I have been swamped. Thank God Lenore's hours have been cut at the nursery due to the season, because my work tripled this October. The busiest day of the month was Halloween, Tuesday October 31. On Tuesday, we had nine reservations for our transcendental tea parties and each individual Enti-tea consisted of four or more guests. The reality of nine tea reservations is that Hazel and I had to prepare tiny sandwiches and bake enough tea cookies for forty-two people. It's hard for me to even believe that forty-two people have time to drink tea on a Tuesday afternoon. We scheduled the Enti-teas thirty minutes apart. We started our first tea at eleven o'clock and ended our last Enti-tea at four thirty. We worked like servants all day, serving delicate pieces of food on china plates, while our patrons talked of dead loved ones and told ghost stories. I missed the kids' school party and was taught a painful lesson on sacrifice and owning your own business. But I shouldn't complain, because nobody was busier than Pixie Moon-Dust. Faced with the impossibility of forty-two individual psychic readings, Pixie did group readings. Each Enti-tea party spent over an hour with Pixie in front of her little house as she read each guest with fifteen to twenty minutes of divine insight. Still, she did not finish her readings until after 9:00 pm. Pixie literally spent all of Halloween talking to the dead and I believe it nearly wiped her out. Pixie stated that the dead were so much more active that day. Their conversations and antics bounced about her and she responded as an overwhelmed mother. At the end of the night I reacted to a frenzied looking Pixie.

"Good Lord," I said "You look like you've seen a ghost."

"Try about two hundred ghosts," she said chugging down water and rubbing sage on her chest.

While our Enti-teas waited for their psychic readings that had piled up throughout the day, I sent them on a walk of our sweet little town. They poked in and out of our little city, buying antiques, homemade jam and apple butter. I sent them to Bloomers Nursery for pumpkins, gourds and flowers and for fun I told them if they wanted to take a haunted walk they could take the trail up behind the large Catholic Church just beside the graveyard. Many of the out of town patrons were still at The Kitchen House for Beggar's Night, which was a hoot.

Hazel sewed costumes this year for her, Ezra and the kids and they went out as a family. A family of Hillbillies is what she called it, which is politically incorrect if you're gonna trick or treat in a Appalachian Mountain range, but Hazel doesn't care. She found her costumes to be hysterical. When she had everyone dressed, my bunch looked like the Beverly Hillbillies, which caused joy to swell in the hearts of our tea guests. The boys had on handmade bib overalls with one strap fastened, no shirts and patches on their knees. They had potato sacks to hold their candy. Hazel blacked out their front teeth and penciled in some extra dark freckles on top of the freckles they already have. She made the same costume for Avery Banks. He went with them pulled in a wagon that had been transformed into an apple cart. Ezra, who is such a good sport, strapped on a long white beard, chewed on a corncob pipe and pulled the wagon. Sabrina was dressed like a puppy and taken along on a leash, which was actually a safety feature that matched her costume. When she tired of running she sat in the apple cart with Avery. Hazel's costume was hysterical. She had sewn large pockets into the chest of an ugly dress and filled them with small sacks of flour creating the illusion of boobs that hung down to her knees. She added a dirty apron, a wooden spoon and a pouch in her front lip that looked like chewing tobacco. I nearly peed my pants laughing, that is until she handed me my costume, which I reluctantly put on for family pictures.

While Hazel, Ezra and the kids went out begging, I stayed back at the house dressed like Daisy May in a bandanna shirt tied just beneath my breasts and a pair of cut off shorts that entered the crack of my ass. I stuck my hair in pigtails and self-consciously talked to my guests while passing out treats. Although I hated my costume, the out of towners loved it and they had me pose for several pictures in front of my Kitchen House sign. I saw yesterday that several of those photos had already made it to Cole Spencer's blog. There I stood dressed like a hillbilly floozy in a field of orbs, it's fairly unsettling. Halloween actually turned out to be a good day. I admit I was a little worried about the waking spirits. The energy was high and my home a vortex with a rotating door for swirling souls. The spirits circled about dropping emotions and scents with enough power to cause wonder and not produce fear. They're really quite extraordinary.

Now October has left us and I worry about slowing down, not just from a business standpoint, but also from a personal one. I think about Timothy constantly and the only way I get through my days without breaking down is to keep moving. My mind would like to stop on sadness and sit there for awhile, then move two steps left to worry, where I fret about my menstrual cycle, but I don't allow it. In order to prevent sadness and worry, I keep moving. Like Rayland, in my grief, I have thrown myself into marketing my business and it seems to be working.

Not only has there been lots of Enti-teas, more people have begun to use The Kitchen House for their gatherings, and clubs. One morning I got a call from Mrs. Baxter who said that the electricity was out at the Methodist church and she asked if the quilters, who meet there every week at 10:00am, could use The Kitchen House instead.

"Sure," I said. "You're more than welcome."

The quilters showed up in a group of twelve, two round tables of six ladies, working on two very different quilts. Hazel and I made tea, lemonade and lots of coffee and the ladies stayed all morning talking and gossiping, so we ended up making sandwiches for lunch too. Each lady drank enough fluid to float a boat and then ate tuna salad, chips, a pickle and brownies for dessert. I charged each one of them ten dollars. The following week they came back with fifteen members.

"Mrs. Baxter is the electricity out at the church again?" I asked.

"Oh no dear," she said patting my hand. "We just like it better here."

They liked my round tables and Hazel's house brew, but I think they mostly liked that they no longer had to have a potluck lunch. They realized the quilters club could exist without a trip to the grocery store, trying to please everyone and of course, the actual work of having to prepare the shared dish. This way, they could all just give me ten dollars and I could do it all. I suppose since I charged ten dollars a piece the first time, I can't up it and really it is a lot of work. On the bright side, it keeps me moving and not thinking about Timothy. The ladies are sweet to my Sabrina as she sits under the quilting table with her sippy cup and baby doll. As for Hazel, she joined the group. She pulled up a chair right beside Mrs. Baxter and is helping to create a patriotic quilt that will be displayed in next year's county fair.

It is not just the quilters who have taken a time slot of residency at The Kitchen House. Lydia's book club meets here the first Tuesday of every month instead of at the library, simply because of coffee. Also, Lenore hosted a workshop on how to make an autumn flower arrangement. It was really fun. Lenore charged a small fee and I sold beverages and desserts. The ladies made pots from pumpkins and planted purple mums. Lenore says she's going to do another around Thanksgiving and craft a centerpiece for a dining room table. In December, she's planning to teach how to make a Christmas wreath.

It is because of all these activities, and my desire to keep occupied, that I have begun a weekly newsletter that has turned more into a newspaper. At first the newsletter was a way to help me organize my own schedule and market The Kitchen House. I fill the newsletter with small articles about what is happening at The Kitchen House and draw cartoon like sketches to go with my articles. I include details about The Homework Help Center and statements by the children who have brought up failing grades because of Lenore's help. I list a calendar of our events. Tuesday - Story Time, Wednesday - The Quilters Club, and Saturday night - Clogging with Rayland. I write a small synopsis about our Friday night folk singer or band. I even include ghost sightings and strange happenings reported by our patrons. The customers either tell these stories or I find them on Cole Spencer's blog. I have nearly a year of newsletter hauntings from Halloween alone. I enjoy writing the newsletter, it is one more thing that keeps me moving and the citizens of Grace love it. It appeals to their nosy character and curious disposition. Many people have asked if I would include their scheduled event in my newsletter just as a reminder, so I do. I have added scout meetings, Avon and Mary Kay parties and the high school football schedule, which will soon turn to basketball. Since I'm doing all that, I figured I might as well have a page for anniversaries, weddings and new babies. My four page newsletter grew to ten pages this month and I have no doubt December's will be larger. Most exciting for me, is how far my newsletter has traveled. It has been received all over Spring County, carried down to Charleston and has even left the state. Our traveling patrons take a copy of *The Kitchen House News* to serve as a memento. They place it in photo albums and scrapbooks along with captured orb photos and notes from their psychic reading. When I think about it, my newsletter is a souvenir and my home is a relic.

I live in a place with a past and it is holy, a dwelling for lost souls. There are the manifestations of the unearthly beings that have taken up residence and walk around and then there are the people, the ones dumped in Grace by circumstance, and they wander through my front door. So many of them are lost souls, having been misplaced by sorrow and grief. They live in search of something, not knowing what. The spirits hold the questions and the answers and we must figure them out. I believe a curtain divides the people and the spirits. We are split by thin ivory lace, a veil of transparency where connecting souls exist on both sides. Every day that I live in this house I see illustrations that support my theory.

Christy and Avery Banks are perfect examples. Their hardships have been chosen for them. Their humbleness is apparent. Their being is a lesson in compassion. The roles they have been cast in impart empathy. All one has to do is watch and goodwill is inspired. Every day against a backdrop of humility, they play their part and at the end of the day when the curtain closes the one applauding the loudest is Billy Dean. Pixie Moon-Dust, another case in point, a clairvoyant with popularity and status among the supernatural. Pixie's social calendar is that of a mystic cheerleader, messages ring in like cellular calls, blue strands of dialogue crackle like lightning as she converses between two worlds. Pixie embraces her gift, with all its anxieties and responsibility, in the hope that it will lead her to Mama.

Lenore walked through my door, a lost soul who was dropped here by an angel in white, and Father Timothy McIntire is my favorite martyr. He came to Grace seeking clemency within the church walls and pleading for a pardon from his wooded gazebo. All the while, young Thomas flicks marbles into the center circle of mercy, plays hopscotch with pity, crisscrosses understanding, leapfrogs over tolerance and spins circles of forgiveness all around the priest's legs. But like an unaware parent, Timothy is not watching. Instead, he is on his knees in prayer, a perfect position for a little empathetic angel boy to jump on his back begging to play.

Then there is Hazel and I, the ladies who run this lost souls café. This business adventure was an act of desperation. Hazel was living as a new widow. A shade had just been pulled down between her and Harry, her beloved. Hazel stood on one side of the screen frozen, seeking a purpose that would propel her forward. Harry stood on the other side blowing kisses. At the same time my cheating husband abandoned me in a campground with our three kids. Suddenly my task was survival. My goal was primal, make enough money to shelter and feed my kids. Just then the spirits handed the ball off to my daddy who executed a long Hail Mary pass that landed firmly in my hands. I grabbed Hazel by the arm and I ran pulling her with me. I had to, as nobody else was passing out chances.

Thanksgiving

I have never seen anyone happier to prepare a Thanksgiving meal than Hazel. Hazel's excitement started three weeks before the holiday and her enthusiasm matched a child at Christmas. Hazel worked with two lists, scribbling and adding as she went. One list was the menu. It was full of dishes, both savory and sweet. The other list was our guests. Hazel delighted in both lists. She told me she had always dreamed of a full house on Thanksgiving Day. She wanted a gathering of friends and a kitchen warmed with bodies and laughter. Hazel's life with Harry was childless and their circle of family was small. After years of miscarriages and grieving the loss of three premature infants, Hazel accepted the fact that her house would never be full. It was a hard pill to swallow based on the fact that Hazel had always wanted to be a mommy. She would have had ten kids if she could. Sometimes the universe has a different plan for us and eventually we have to come to terms with what is, is. Hazel and Harry learned to be content and fulfilled. Thanksgivings at home were quiet and special with delicious Cornish game hens glazed in port sauce with rosemary roasted red skin potatoes. Hazel treasures those memories with Harry, watching the Macy's Day Parade and football. However, the dream of a full house on Thanksgiving Day never went away, it just slept in her center and kept quiet. This year it was stirred awake and after a long slumber it is ready to party.

Hazel's Thanksgiving was over the top. She went to the grocery every day leading up to Thanksgiving. There was always something she needed for her extensive menu. She made invites with a Thanksgiving Day poem on the inside and her menu scripted on the back. She not only sent out invites, she also called everybody to see if they had been received. She taught the boys how to make a handprint turkey on pieces of big white paper and they created placemats for everyone. She participated in Lenore's flower arrangement class and made the most elaborate centerpiece. Hazel's gusto was contagious and everyone she invited said they would come. Hazel encouraged each person to bring a signature dish. She challenged them to be creative.

"Fix something that represents you," she told them. "It doesn't have to be a lot just enough for everyone to have a small taste."

I thought Hazel was asking a bit much. After all she was making plenty of food for everybody.

"It's my theme," she said when I questioned her. "Besides, it's fun and I have to work with a theme."

Since nobody else seemed to mind, I let it go. Hazel's list of invites included twelve people, who all obliged her request for signature dishes. Hazel's happiness had become contagious. She behaved joyous and giddy and very soon everyone seemed eager for a holiday feast. That is everyone but me. I could not get excited. In fact, I had become solemn and lost in my own thoughts. While my friends looked through family recipes and skimmed cookbooks, I spent my free time slowly writing my December newsletter and fretting about my period.

I had become obsessed with the thought of being pregnant. It was a fear that kept me nearly frozen most days. I tried to tell myself not to worry, that the last three months had been a series of stressful events and often stress disrupts my cycle. I wanted to think rationally, but the fantasy of an unwanted pregnancy took residence in my frontal lobe and nothing else could get in. I was blocked with one thought that propelled around and around causing me to go half mad. I lost my appetite or rather the focus to eat. I simply forgot to feed myself as one might forget to feed a pet fish. I stopped sleeping too. I was restless and agitated. It took me half the night to settle down, only to wake a few hours later. My days were long and I plodded through them. My nights were even longer with small intervals of catnaps. For me, the month of November was like walking through quicksand, strenuous and heavy. I felt weighted as if I were being pulled down. I was wallowing in self-pity, stuck inside a dark haze and Hazel was floating around on cloud nine. Oddly enough opposite moods wasn't our only difference.

During this time, both Hazel and I had begun to find money, coins to be exact, a stray dime in the far corner of the restaurant or an abandoned penny on the coffee counter. More unusual than randomly finding lost change all over the place was that Hazel found pennies and I was being left dimes. The first dime I found was in the bottom of a coffee cup. Every morning I grab the first mug on the left in the line of ceramics placed on a shelf. I enjoy sipping the first cup of Hazel's House Blend while I open up the cafe. That morning in the bottom of the black cup was a new shiny silver dime. I plucked the coin from the cup and stuck it in my pocket. Not more than an hour later I found another dime near a stack of tea saucers. Later that same day, Hazel told me that Harry had been leaving her pennies from heaven. She said in the morning when she woke, there was a penny on her nightstand. It was placed heads up on top of the book she had been reading the night before. Later in the day, she found another penny inside a muffin tin. The next day, I found three more dimes and Hazel found two pennies. We continued to find pennies and dimes up to Thanksgiving Day. It was strange to me that I never came across one of Hazel's pennies nor she my dimes. Not only that, the kids were not finding coins. It awed me that the money was going unnoticed by my treasure hunting, scavenging children, and that although Hazel and I cross paths every day, the pennies and dimes were found by their rightful recipient. One day, I found a dime in the bathroom soap dish and not ten minutes later Hazel found a penny on the back of the toilet.

"How did I miss that?" I said. "I was just in there."

"I guess it wasn't for you," Hazel laughed.

I began taking notes on all the places we found coins. Hazel found a penny in her slippers one night and a penny in her shoe the next morning. Twice I found a dime within the pages of my journal. Hazel called her small pile of copper coins, pennies from heaven, and she was positive Harry was leaving them.

"Harry often surprises me with gifts," she told me. "Usually he leaves them on my dresser and I keep them in my jewelry box." From the box Hazel showed me a small pretty stone, a silver cross pendant, a button, a crystal bead, an acorn, a nail, and an old thimble.

"You found all these on your dresser?" I asked.

"Yes," she said. "At different times of course. Isn't it amazing?" It was indeed amazing and I felt chills go up my spine as I touched the sacred objects.

"But why pennies?" I asked. "And scattered all about the place at the same time I'm finding dimes?"

"I'm not sure," Hazel said. "I don't like to question the spirits. I just accept the gifts."

"It's just strange," I said.

"Well I agree with that, but then again we live in a strange house."

I decided to ask Pixie the significance of pennies and dimes. She told me it had to do with the number. Pennies represent one, as in one body one spirit. In principle the human body and human spirit are the same. Pennies also mean unity. If pennies are being placed in your path, it may mean that there is oneness between you and the spirit who is visiting you and that you and your spirit are in unity. Of course, Hazel is right. Her pennies must be gifts from Harry. But who was leaving me dimes? Pixie said dimes were symbolic of the number ten.

"Ten is the number of completion. It is a one, which symbolizes unity next to a zero, the circle of eternity. In essence, it is the mixture of being and nonbeing. The completing and continuation of all things."

"And what the fuck does that mean?" I asked in my foul mood.

"I suppose that's up to you to figure that out," Pixie said. "But regardless of whether you do or don't, stop worrying. It's quite obvious you're being watched over by an angel and everything is gonna be just fine."

I tried to heed Pixie's advice and quit worrying. I wanted so badly to come out of my depressed state and feel good again. But, the reality of the situation was that my period was three weeks late and Timothy had not called.

Then miraculously, the night before Thanksgiving, I woke to a hot, sticky wetness between my legs and the urge to pee. Pulling back the sheets I let out a long exhale and a sigh of relief. The large spot of red made me drunk with happiness. It was the rose colored icing on the top of my cake, the crushed strawberries in my daiquiri of life. Never have I felt so lucky to wash sheets. I made my way into the bathroom to clean myself up. When I opened the linen closet to fetch a washcloth, there on the shelf stood a tall stack of dimes. Ten dimes in all, stacked as if they had been counted out to make a dollar. I had been left ten of ten to make one hundred. My mind swirled with questions. I was told the number one was symbolic of unity and zero meant infinity, so what did one, zero, zero mean? I was going crazy trying to solve the puzzle before me and then I remembered what Hazel had said. "Don't question the spirits, just accept the gifts."

I thanked God and my angel spirit. I thanked the heavens and the sky, the sun and the moon and all universal creations. Then I decided I needed to pull myself together and get over Timothy. I lined my new collection of dimes along my windowsill beside the carved, wooden animals. That morning I watched a red orange day rise out of a frosted mountain and I was determined to be happy and content.

Thanksgiving Day, November 23, 2000 – Dear Diary, I have so much to be thankful for. Not too long ago I sat in a hospital room beside my deathly ill boy. That same child is now healthy, ornery, lively, funny and energetic. I am now feeling incredibly guilty in regards to my self-pity. I have just spent a month feeling sorry for myself, when the truth is my home is filled with warmth and good things to eat, my friends are loyal and loving, my children are healthy, my daddy and brother are supportive and my life is good. If I am meant to be with Timothy, he'll come back. Suddenly the meaning of 10 is clear. I represent the one, a unique individual. The zero is the symbol of my life complete, a circle of bonds, which cannot be broken. My life is whole and holy and whatever shall be, shall be.

At two o'clock Thanksgiving afternoon, our guests began to arrive and they came in pairs. Christy and Avery Banks were first to show and I was glad. The boys had been waiting eagerly for Avery all day. As soon as he came in the door they raced off to play. Christy's signature dish was a large serving bowl of cold pea salad made with English peas and onion. Christy said it was her grandma's recipe. She made it because Avery likes to help. He calls it cold PEE! salad or Pee-Pee salad. Although she's grown tired of his silly joke, it gets him to eat his peas. Ezra and two of his sons came in right after Christy. The men had made a giant pan of pocket dressing, an Appalachian stuffing famous with the quail hunters. Pocket dressing is a small patty of stuffing the size of a biscuit. The weekend hunters wrap the dressing in wax paper and stick it in their pockets to snack on while traipsing in the woods. I believe they stick a turkey sandwich in their other pocket. The dressing is good and it started me thinking about packing it in my kids' lunch boxes. Next to arrive was my daddy. He came through the door just minutes before Rayland and Cody. Daddy was carrying a bowl of cracklings he had fried himself.

"This bowl of pig skins is a representation of me," he told Hazel, placing the bowl on the counter.

"Hush Skip, you're no pig?' responded Hazel.

"No, but I'm about to eat like one."

"Well, if Skip is pig rinds, we're a sweet piece of pie," Rayland said as he and Cody put down their pies on either side of the cracklings.

"Shoofly pie," said Rayland. "Made with dark molasses. Lucinda baked one every Thanksgiving."

"I brought dessert too," said Pixie. "And I brought my daddy. Here's the paw-paw pudding and here's my Pa."

I was delighted to see that Pixie had collected the paw paws that grew around her home and made the sweet pudding that makes my heart swell. I was even more thrilled to meet her daddy who brought a jar of corn whiskey.

"Hey, Johnny," boomed my daddy as he shook his hand with one hand and patted his back with the other, "Long time no see. How ya been?"

"I'm good," said Johnny. "Real good"

Before introductions could be made, the two men went off to talk and Ezra and his sons joined them. I believe they all knew each other from a business and friendly standpoint. As the men stood off to the side joking and laughing, Hazel and I scanned the dishes of our Thanksgiving potluck. There was PEE! salad, pork rinds, paw paw pudding, pocket dressing and shoofly pie.

"Good Lord," I said. "It sure does look like a hillbilly picnic."

Just then Charlie came walking through the door with Lenore by his side. Lenore was carrying a long, white, rectangular serving plate bordered in squares of black, gray and silver. She placed her contemporary styled plate alongside the Tupperware and revealed its contents. Hazel, Rayland, Cody, Pixie, Christy and I crowded around oohing and aahing. We acted as if she had just pulled a sheet off a canvas to reveal a masterpiece. Lenore had certainly classed up the place and added culture to the counter with her signature dish. She said it was quince with cipollini onions and bacon sprinkled with nutmeg. The presentation was beautiful, but not over the top. Lenore had brought the same charm to the table that she brings to our little town. Her dish looked not only tasty, but also tasteful and classic, a bit like Lenore herself.

As folks mingled, I helped Hazel arrange one table with all the good things she had made; turkey, mashed potatoes, yams, cranberries, green beans with ham and a corn soufflé. The boys had set the other tables with handmade placemats, plates, silverware and napkins. Before eating Hazel requested that we join hands and call out our blessings one by one.

"Just share what makes you thankful," she said. "It's easy to do. I'll go first." Then she called out each of our names individually. It was very sweet and it set a tone. Nearly every single person claimed they were most grateful for the friends around them and I believe they were all being honest. As I looked around the room it occurred to me that we are a family, not all blood related, but certainly a tribe. We are a clan of misfits and we spend our days saving each other.

As my turn approached I prepared myself to call out "Health, healthy kids, healthy friends and healthy me." I had a new appreciation for health and was ready to shout it out loud, but before I could, there was a soft knock on the door and it slowly creaked open.

"Timothy," I shouted instead, as he stood sheepishly grinning inside the front entrance way.

"Mac and cheese with cheese from Wisconsin," he said holding forth a casserole dish.

A Lost Souls Café

December 17, 2000 – Dear Diary, today is the anniversary of The Kitchen House's grand opening. It's hard to believe that another year has flown by and in that time so much has changed. Just twelve months ago, we launched this business with a prayer onto the wings of an angel. Today, I believe our angel is sitting in the café with her feet up having a well deserved and needed rest. After all, she has spent the year carrying our heavy dream on her back, flying from here to there and all around whispering the name Kitchen House into the ears of so many interesting people. What amazes me most is how The Kitchen House evolved from what it started out to be to what it has become. Cole Spencer's fascinating website and blog have certainly been a blessing and the presence, essence, and magical charm of Pixie Moon-Dust is beyond measure. I met Timothy and Pixie the same week, when they came out to bless my house. Little did I know that they would both equally bless my life. It's funny how things work out.

Timothy and I are happily dating. We have decided to take it slow, not because either one of us is unsure, but because I have children who have to slowly grow into the thought that Father Tim is now just Tim and he's Mommy's boyfriend. Timothy is renting a small house in Charleston, not in the best area, but affordable and close to his job. He managed to get hired at the same hospital where we shared our first kiss. His title is Spiritual Care Coordinator and it is a position that is so specifically designed for him that I believe God created this occupation immediately after he created Timothy. The work entails much of what he did as a priest, only now he does it as a layperson and gets paid for it. Mostly what

Timothy does is provide spiritual support to families who are dealing with a death or terminal illness, much like grief counseling. I suppose there is no one more understanding of grief than Timothy. His saga resembles the horrific drug addict who becomes sober and starts working to help rehabilitate other drug addicts. It is a circle of completion and it makes him whole.

When Timothy left West Virginia, he went to Wisconsin to visit both his mom and dad, who live separately. They suffered a sad divorce after they had suffered an even sadder death of their son. It seems no one in Tim's family knew how to deal with Thomas' death. They grieved alone and instead of coming together they fell apart. Tim's first stop was his father's house. Mr. McIntire now lives in southern Wisconsin with a new wife and two different sons, having replaced his broken family for a whole one. Timothy said the visit was awkward at first, but turned nice. He stayed three days at his father's house getting to know a family he had been a stranger to. Timothy said his father seemed relieved that he had left the priesthood and happy that he had found a love. Timothy's father had run away from melancholy, he had eluded misery and fought off woe. He just didn't take his family with him. Maybe he couldn't. I suppose you can't force another to escape with you and I'm sure dragging them along would only hold you down. In the end, Timothy's father was excited that his son had searched him out and happy to know that he too had finally escaped despair. He gave him some fatherly advice.

"You've been out on that ice too long boy, shouting into that black hole. It's time you come in from the cold and join the living. Luckily for you, your Sissy sounds like a piece of sunshine." I cried at Mr. McIntire's honest words and decided I liked him even though he divorced his wife. Who am I to judge?

Timothy said the visit to his mother was much harder. Timothy's mother is still very much living out on the ice. She resides in northern Wisconsin, just two miles from the home where Thomas died. As a realtor, she often sells houses around the lake that swallowed her son, a constant reminder of her baby boy. It is the same water that caused his father to run that makes her stay. It is here she feels close to Thomas.

After three days with his dad, Timothy went to his mom's and stayed with her until his return to Grace and because she is socially listless, she gave him a room and left him alone. It was behind this closed door that he was able to formulate a plan, decide on a future, prepare a resume, make phone calls and set life into motion.

Timothy confessed to me that he spent every evening at the lake. He sat on the pristine and private property of someone and watched the sun set in a pink and purple sky. Nobody ever bothered him. On his last evening at home, he asked his mother to come with him and for some unknown reason she obliged. Together they walked the three mile perimeter around the lake hand in hand. It was the most they had touched since Thomas' death and for much of the walk they were silent. Occasionally Timothy talked, revealing to her the plans he had made. He also told her about the kids, The Kitchen House and me. Timothy said although there was no moment of wisdom spoken or pinpoint of clarity, he felt it was healing for the both of them. The next day, as Timothy loaded his suitcase into the trunk of his car, his mother apologized. It was the first time she admitted that she blamed him for Thomas' death and she cried.

"I'm sorry I hurt you," she said. "It was wrong for me to blame you. It was an accident and you were only a boy too. I know I added pain to the pain you were feeling. It was a horrible thing for a mother to do. I just didn't know how to react. I still don't. I've just been stuck for a really long time. Can you forgive me?"

"It's alright mom," he said. "We're doing okay. You and me are going to be fine. I love you."

Last week he called and invited her to Christmas at The Kitchen House and I believe she's coming. My hope is that Kitty McIntire, Timothy's mom, will visit Grace as often as she can and that The Kitchen House will mend her broken heart and recover her lost soul. All she needs is some healing love and there is no better place to receive it than here, The Kitchen House, a lost souls café. I am blessed to have a house that is a home to the being and nonbeing. It is a place where spirits and people collectively walk about, not only existing in the same sacred space, but also enriching each other's lives. It is truly heaven on earth and by God I own it.

View other Black Rose Writing titles at www.blackrosewriting.com/books and use promo code **PRINT** to receive a **20% discount** when purchasing.

BLACK ROSE writing™

CPSIA information can be obtained
at www.ICGtesting.com
Printed in the USA
FFOW02n1201210318
45784960-46652FF